The Praise for  5 Worlds Is Out of This World!

A New York Public Library Top Te...                          ...on

A Publishers Weekly B...

An NPR Great Re...

A Junior Library Guild Selection

"A bang-zoom start to a series that promises to be epic
in both the classical and internet senses of the word."
—*The New York Times Book Review*

"For kids who love fantasy and other-world adventures,
and for any fans of graphic novels, this book is a must-read."
—R. J. Palacio, #1 *New York Times* bestselling author of *Wonder*

★ "Sensitive writing, gorgeous artwork, and riveting plot,
this is a series to keep an eye on."
—*Booklist*, Starred Review

★ "A dazzling interplanetary fantasy . . . that will easily appeal
to fans of *Naruto* or *Avatar: The Last Airbender*."
—*Publishers Weekly*, Starred Review

"Plenty of adventure as truths are uncovered . . .
Give to fans of Judd Winick's Hilo or Kazu Kibuishi's Amulet series."
—*School Library Journal*

"Epic action, adventure, and mystery will draw you in, but the heartfelt characters
and their seemingly impossible journey will keep you turning the pages."
—Lisa Yee, author of the DC Super Hero Girls™ series

"This stellar team has created a gorgeous and entrancing world like no other!"
—Noelle Stevenson,
*New York Times* bestselling author of *Nimona*

"The beautiful illustrations will have young readers flying through the pages."
—*Deseret News*

"The adventure continues, growing grander of scale
and if possible even more lavish in visual detail."
—*Kirkus Reviews*

"Ends triumphantly and tantalizingly."
—*The Horn Book Magazine*

"Distinctly unique . . . it oozes with imagination and creativity."
—*Bam! Smack! Pow!*

"An intriguing beginning to what is sure to be a fascinating series."
—*BookRiot*

"I dare you not to get immediately caught up in Oona's epic tale!"
—*MuggleNet*

"Beautiful, with a vast array of characters and creatures from the various worlds."
—*GeekDad*

"A magical adventure full of wisdom, humor, and enough girl power
to make you root for Oona in her quest to light the beacon."
—Abigail, age 10

"This book is great! I usually don't like graphic novels,
but this book changed my mind."
—Lucius, age 9

# 5 Worlds

WITHDRAWN

BOOK 3

## THE RED MAZE

Mark
SIEGEL

Alexis
SIEGEL

Xanthe
BOUMA

Boya
SUN

Matt
ROCKEFELLER

Rand

"Many deaths, and many births,
Windows in and windows out."

—Ancient Felid carving, translation uncertain

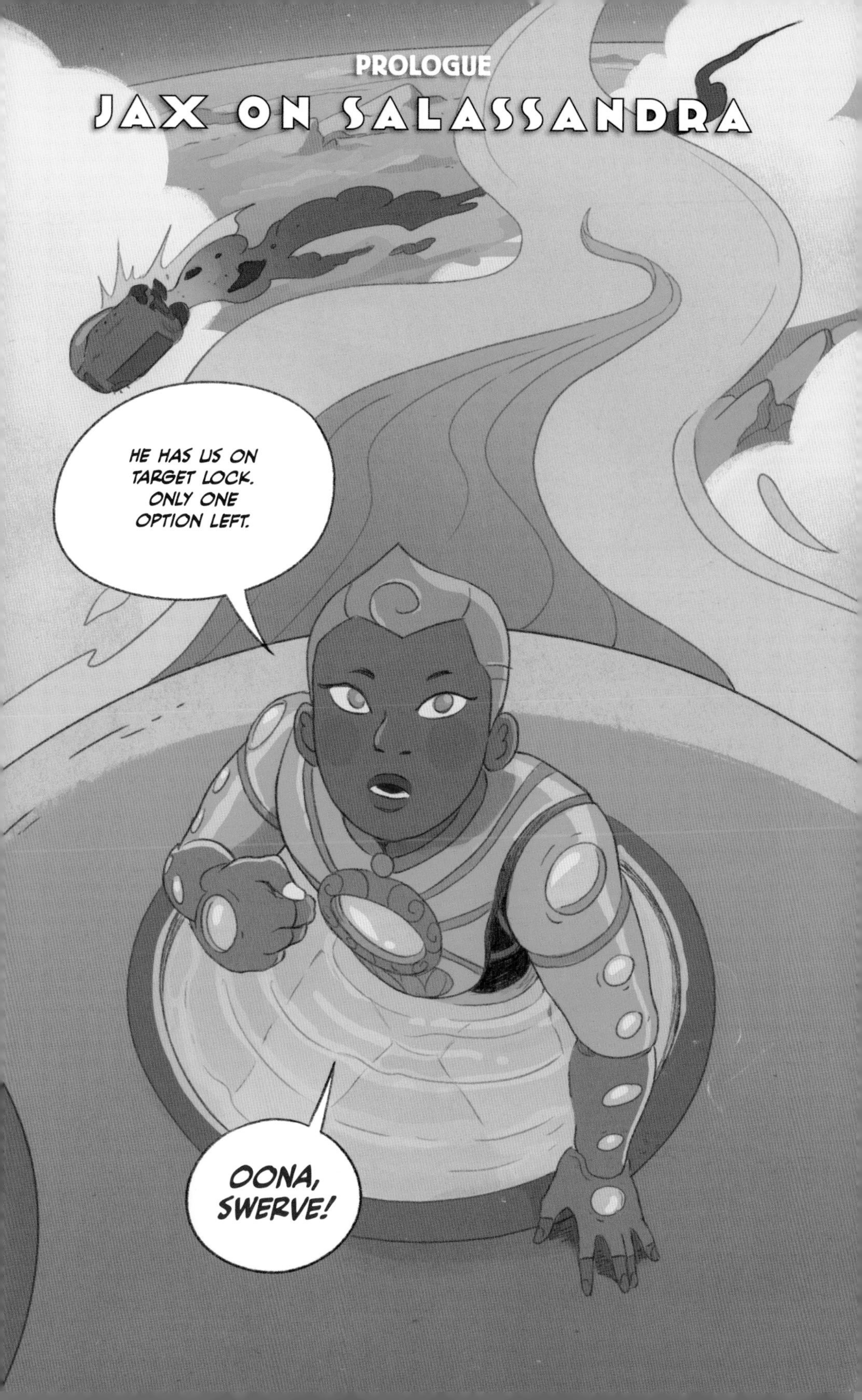
PROLOGUE
JAX ON SALASSANDRA
HE HAS US ON TARGET LOCK. ONLY ONE OPTION LEFT.
OONA, SWERVE!

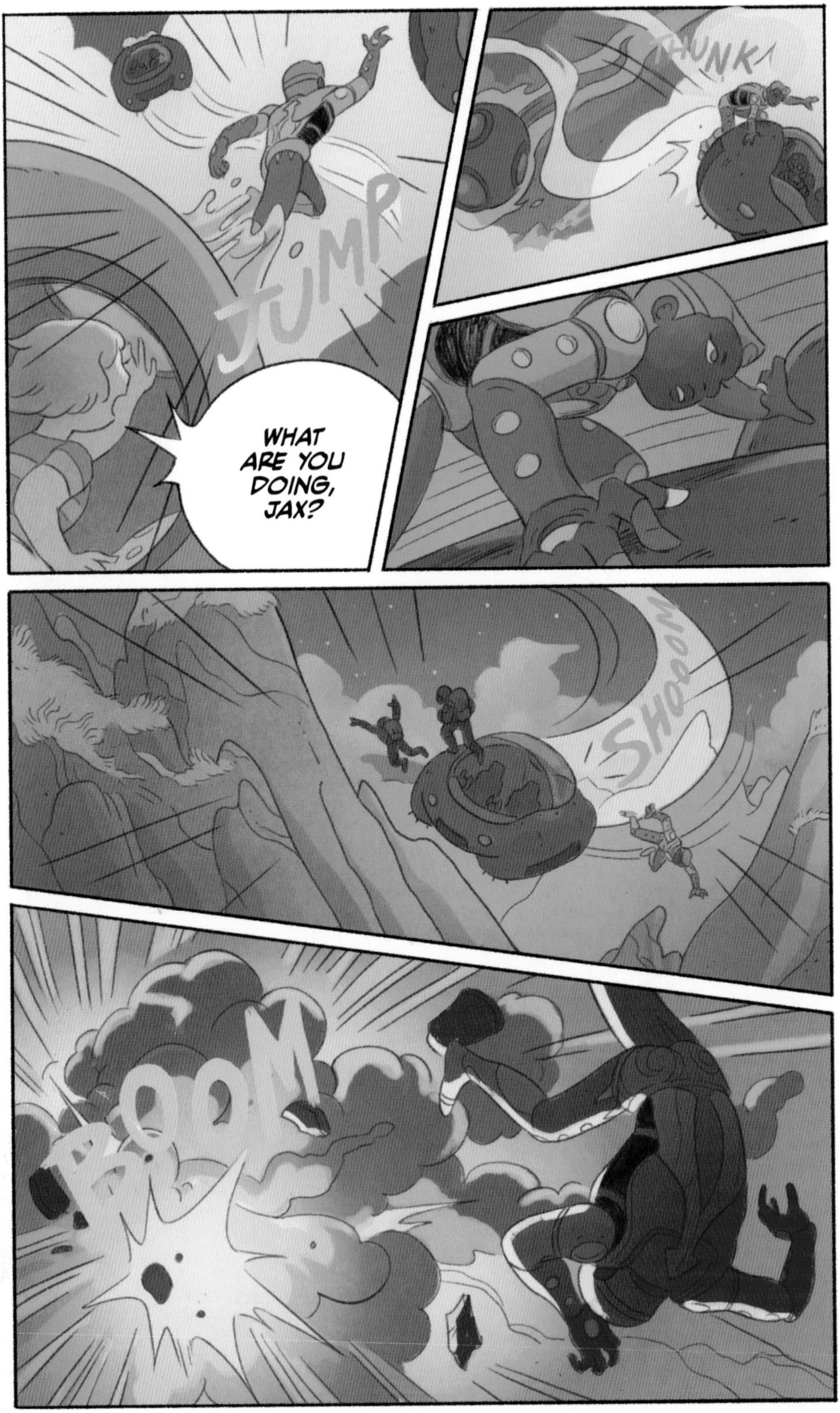
JUMP
WHAT ARE YOU DOING, JAX?
THUNK
SHOOOM
BOOM

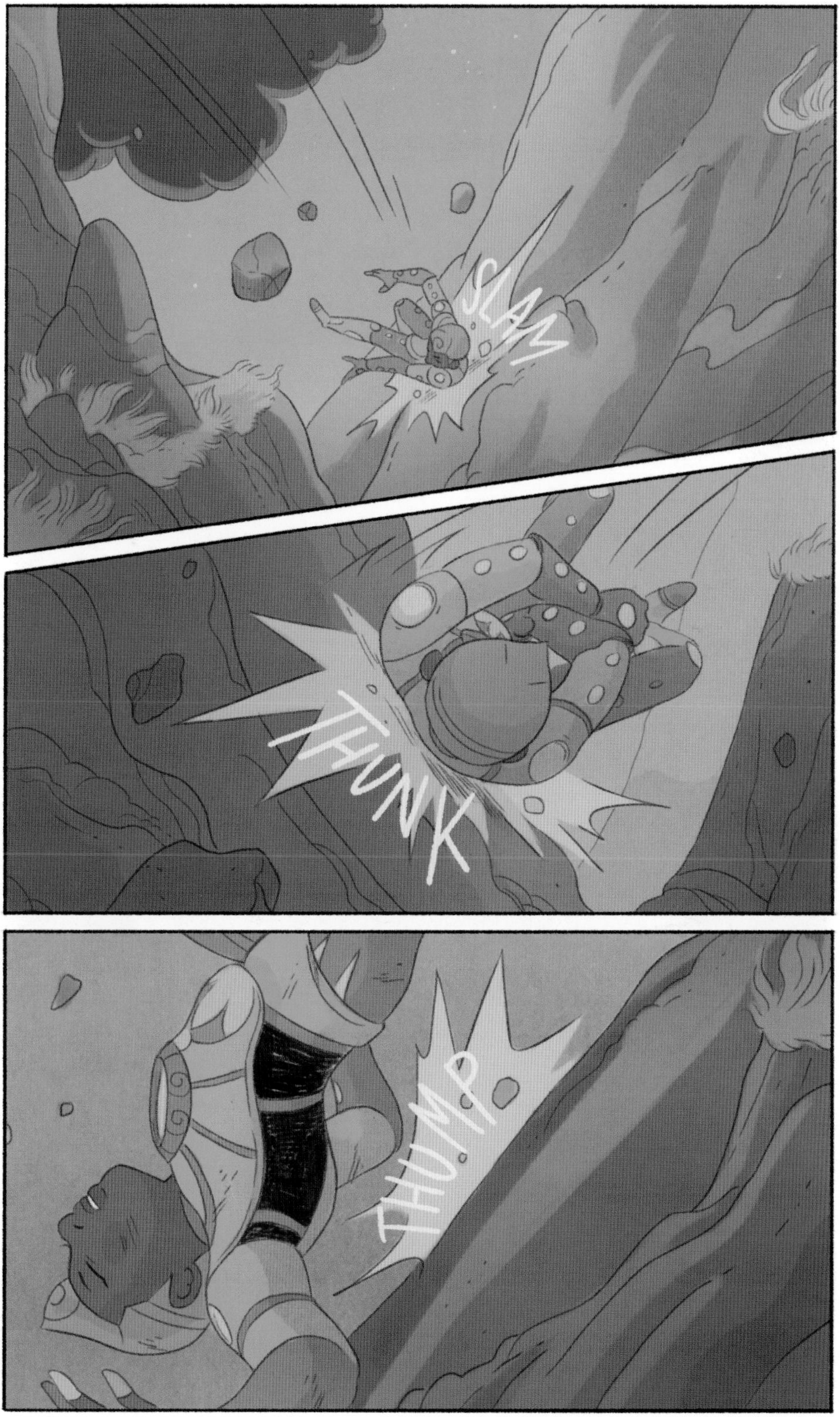
SLAM
THUNK
THUMP

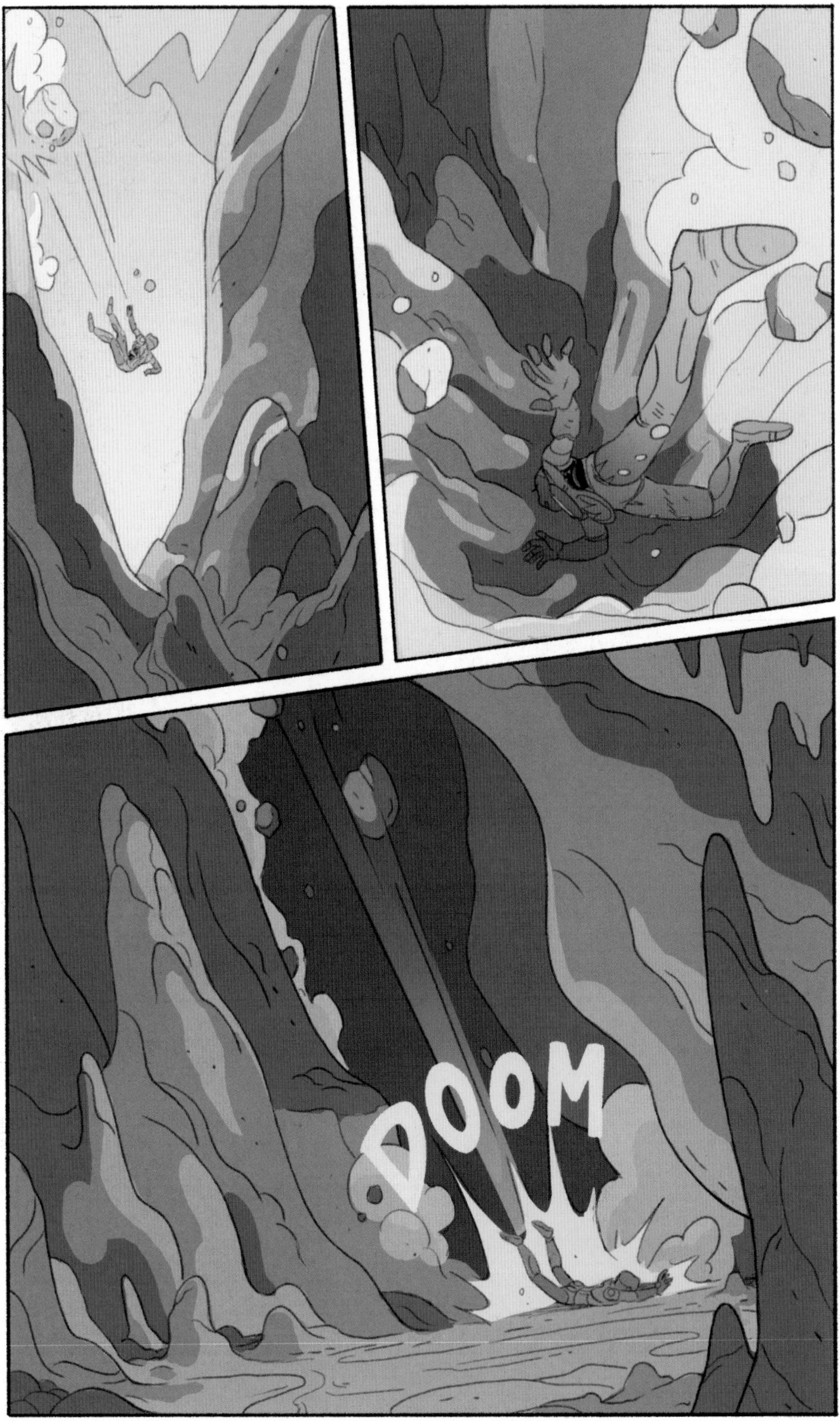
DOOM

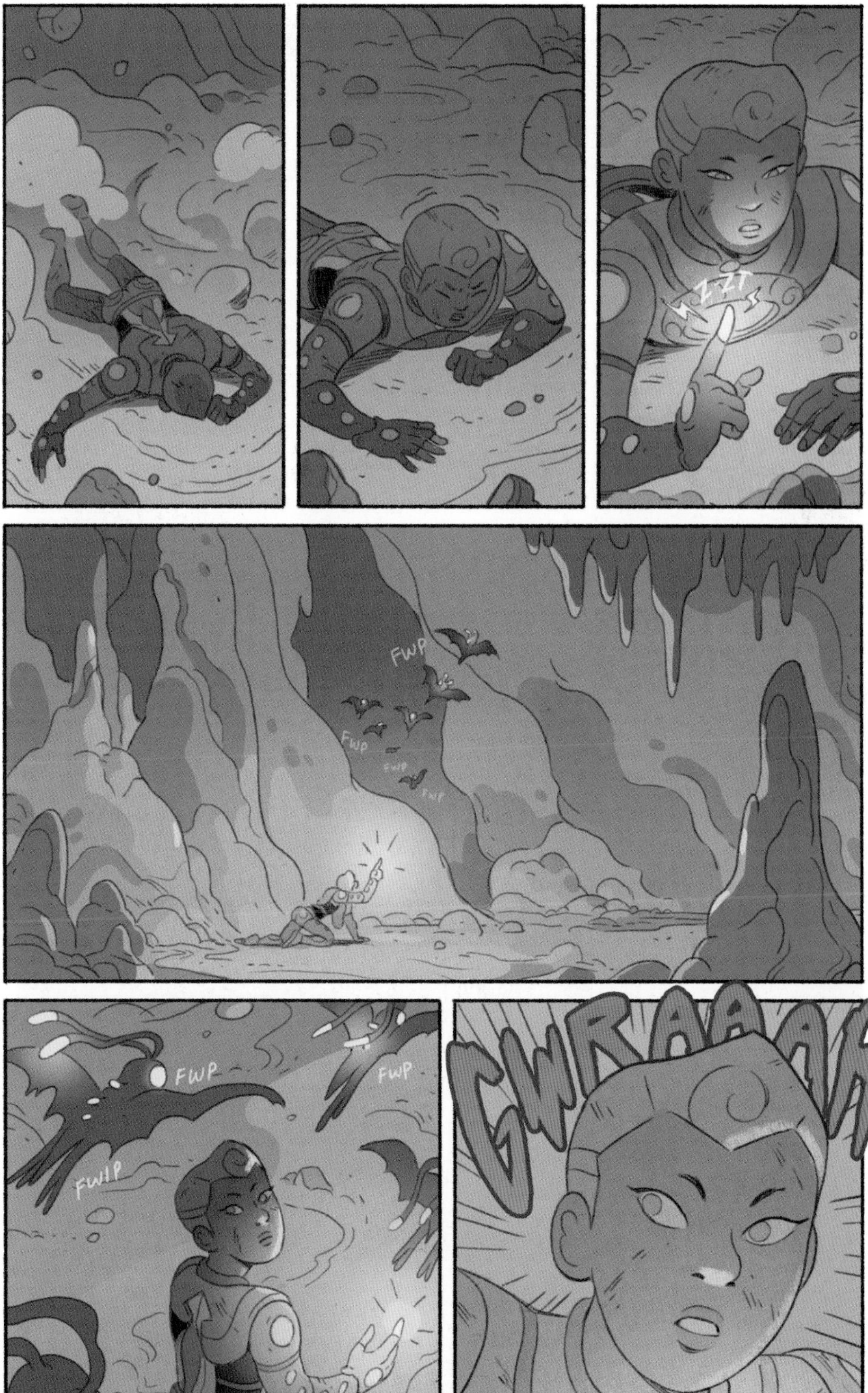
ZZZT
FWP
FWP
FWP
FWP
FWP
FWP
FWP
FWIP
GWRAAAH

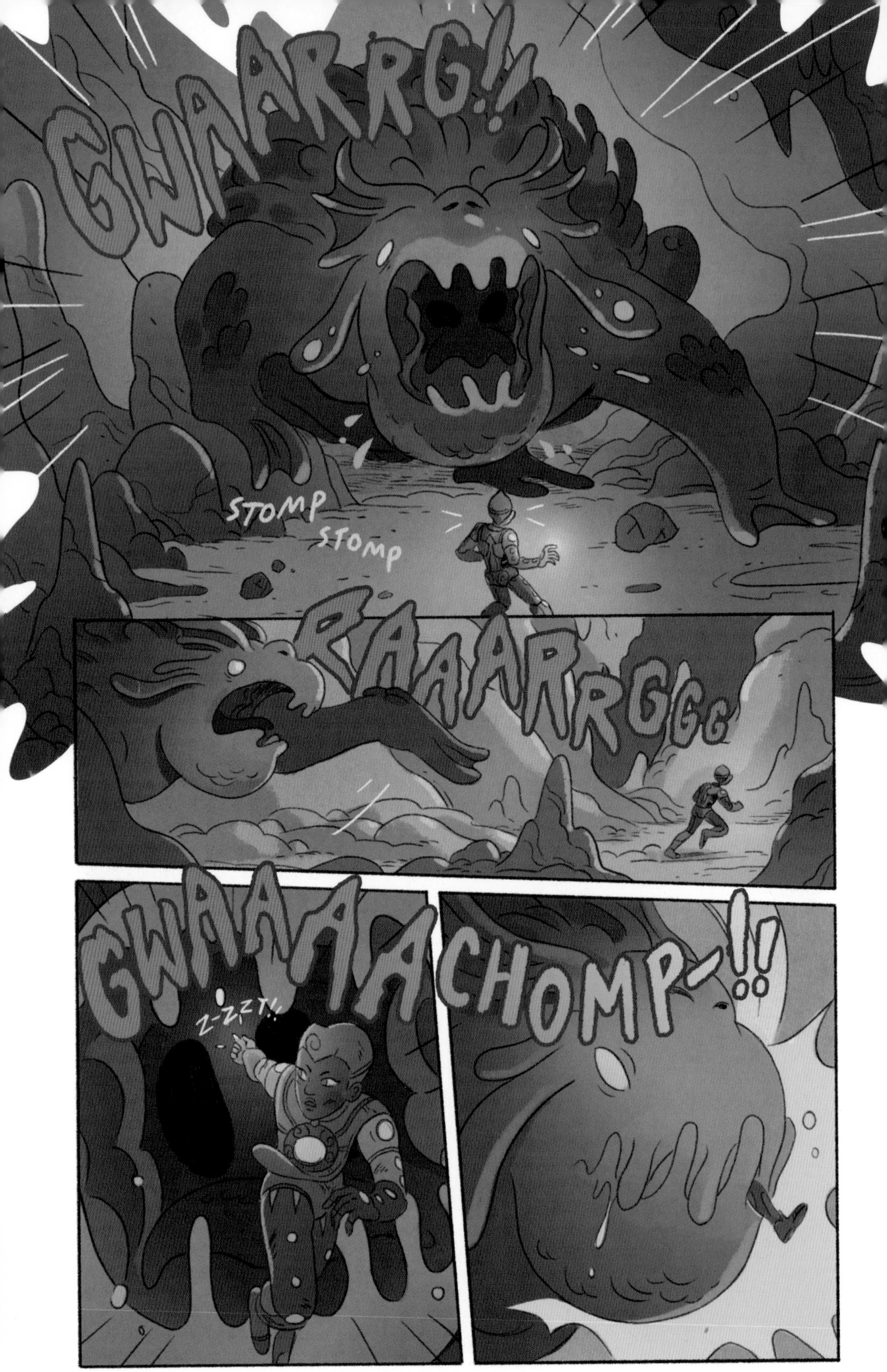
GWARRG!!
STOMP
STOMP
RAAARRGGG
GWAAAA
Z-Z-ZT!
CHOMP-!!

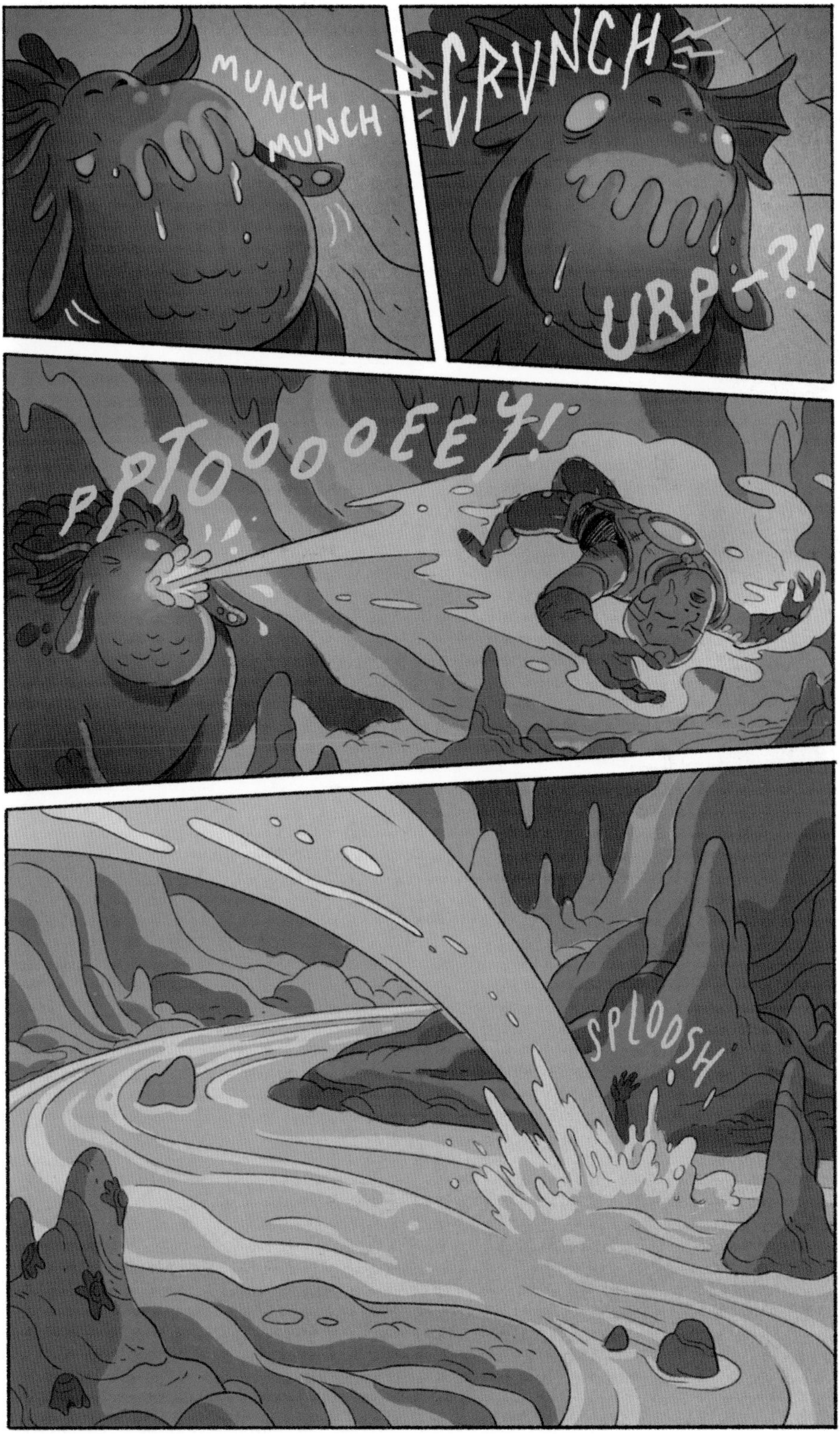
MUNCH
MUNCH
CRUNCH
URP—?!
PPTOOOOEEY!
SPLOOSH

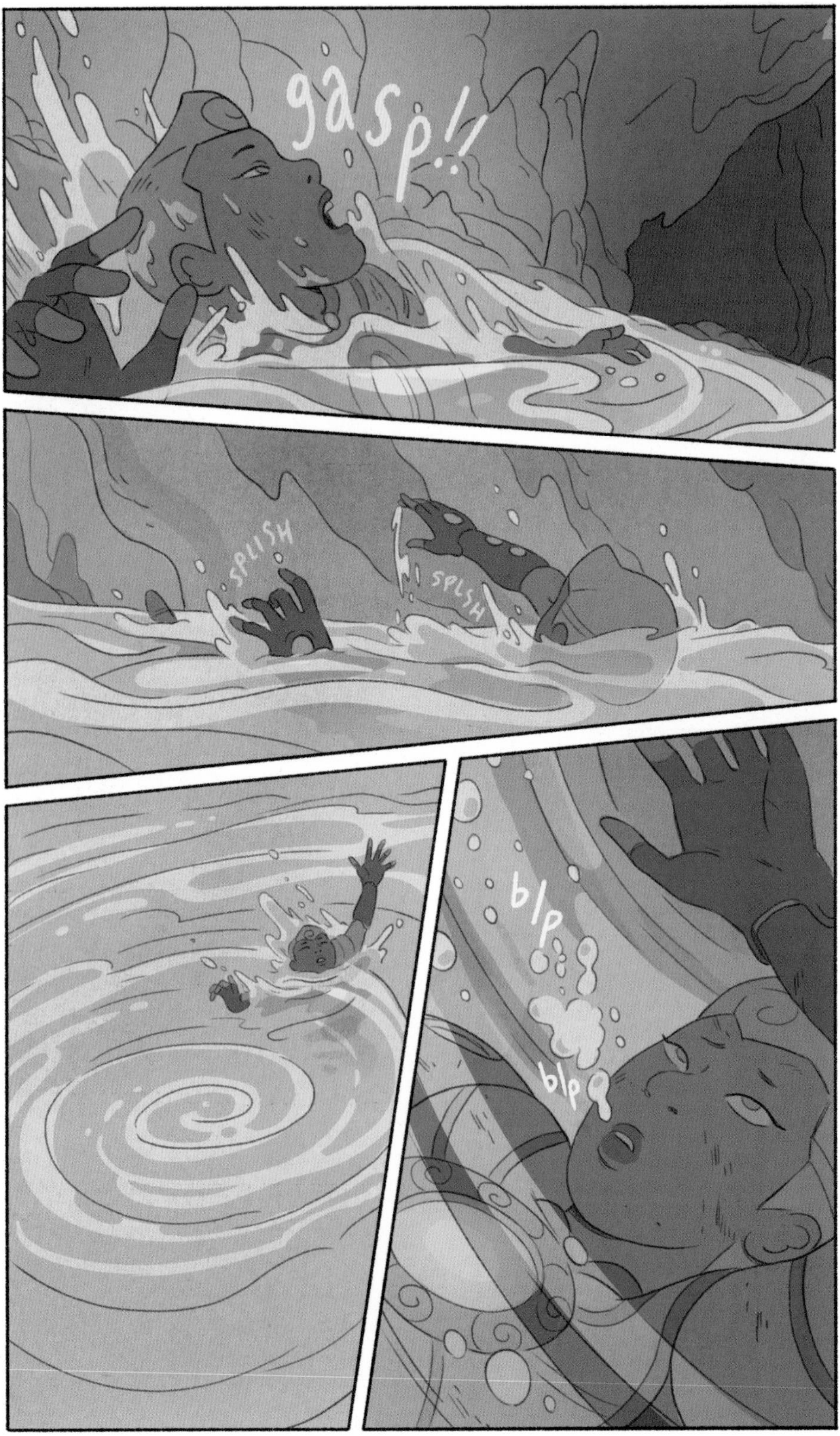
gasp!!
SPLISH
SPLSH
blp
blp

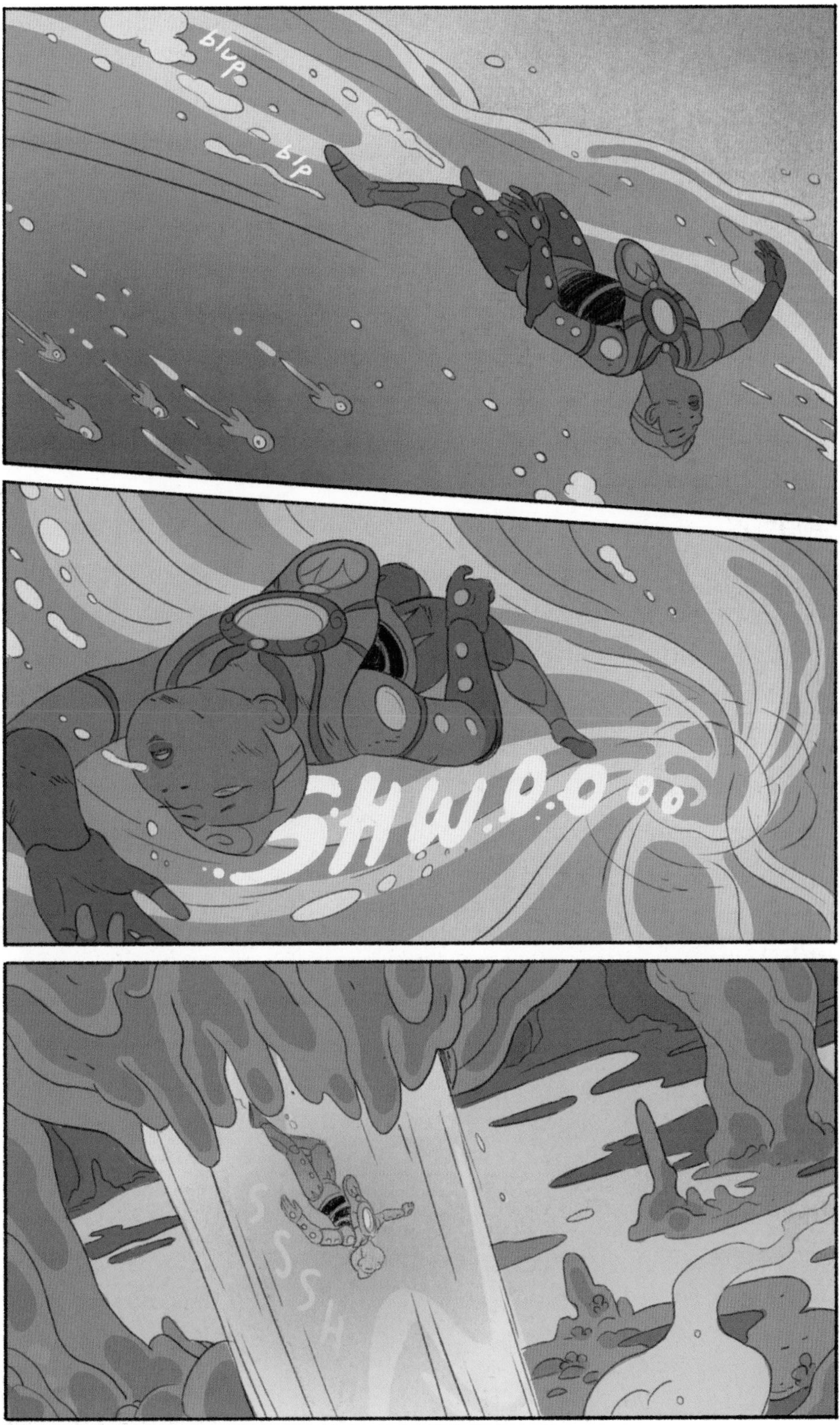
blup
blp
SHWOOoo
SSSSH

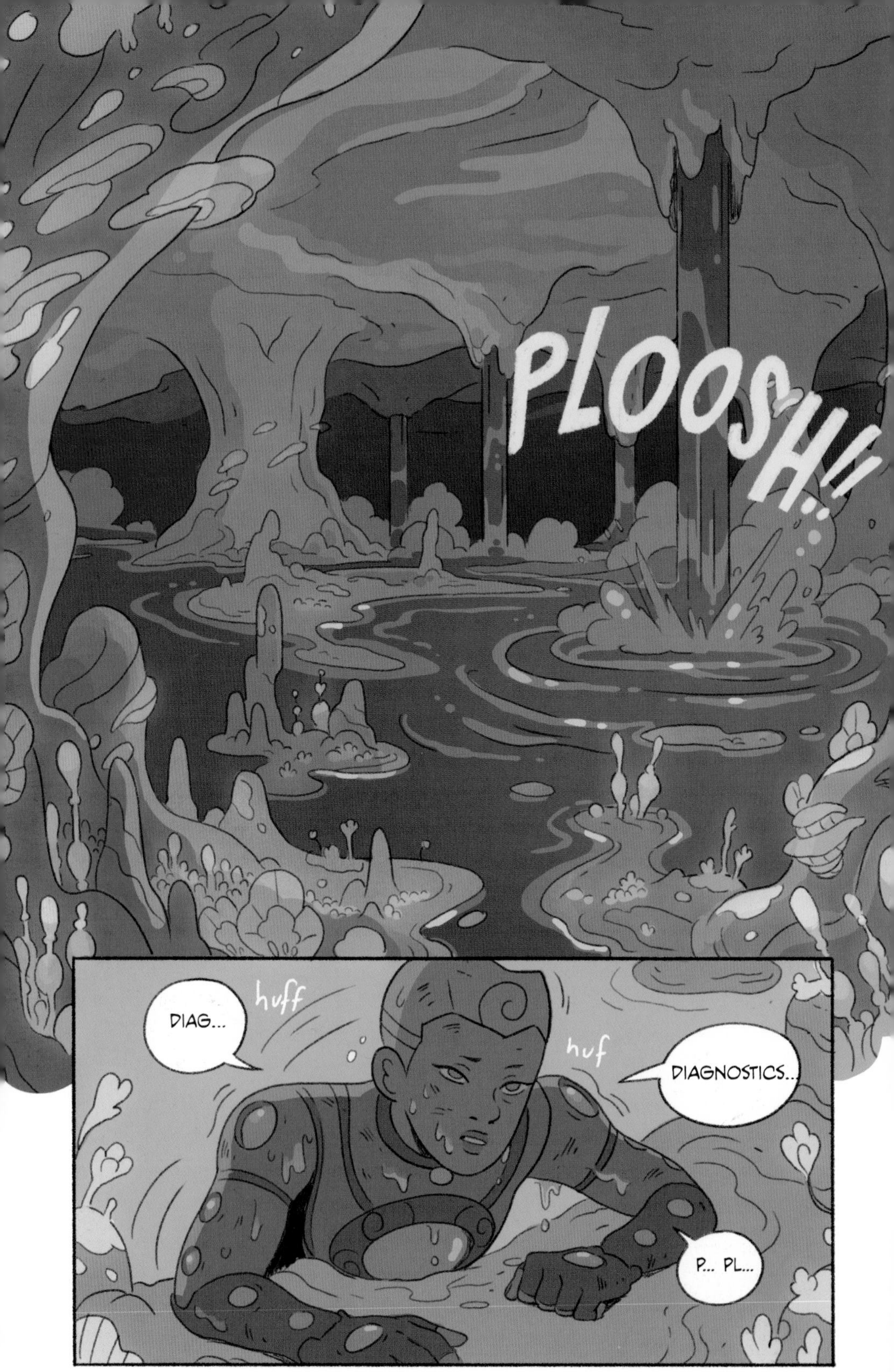
PLOOSH!!
DIAG...
huff
huf
DIAGNOSTICS...
P... PL...

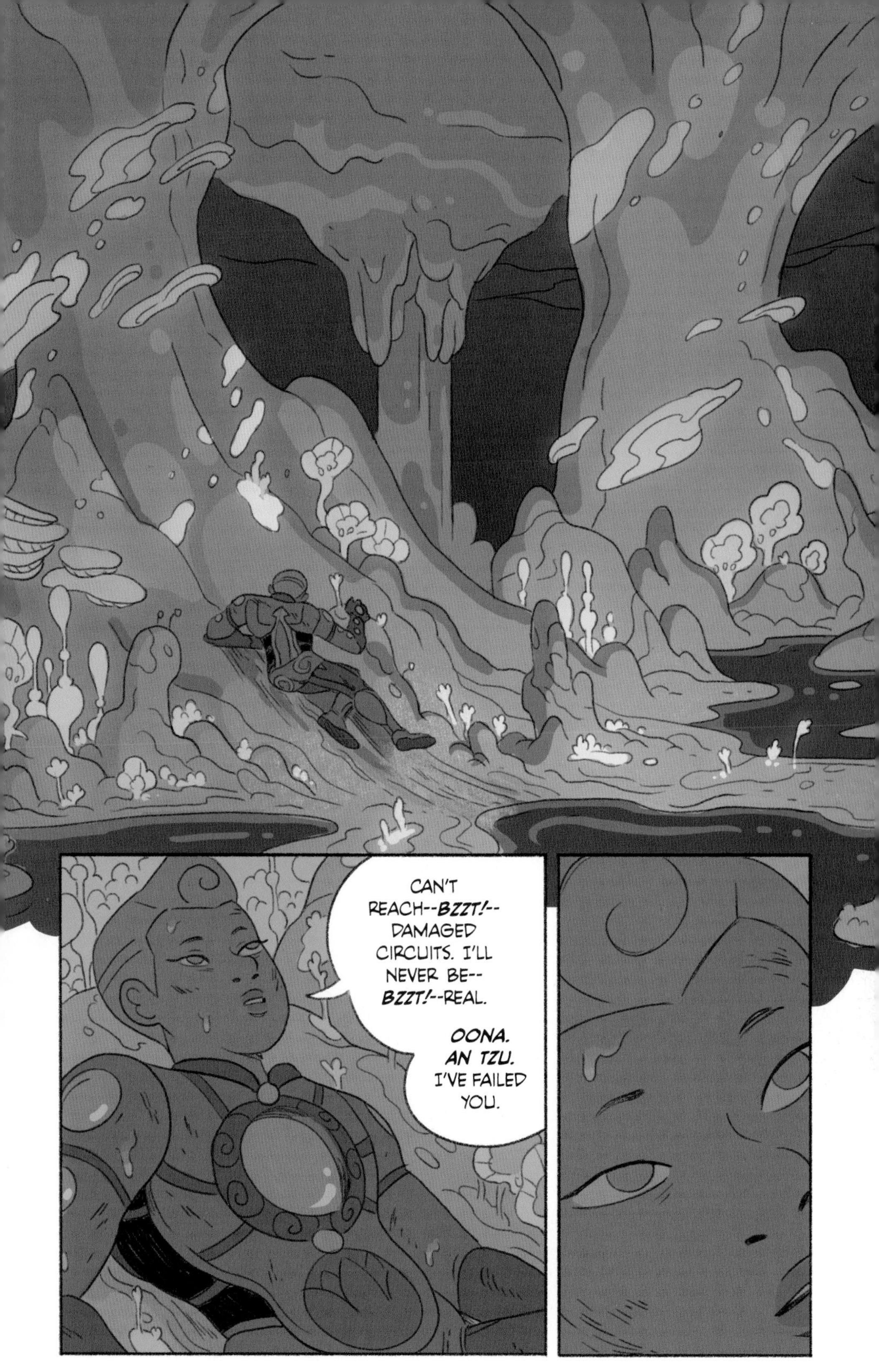
CAN'T REACH--BZZT!--DAMAGED CIRCUITS. I'LL NEVER BE--BZZT!--REAL.
OONA. AN TZU. I'VE FAILED YOU.

# THE SALASSI DEVOTI

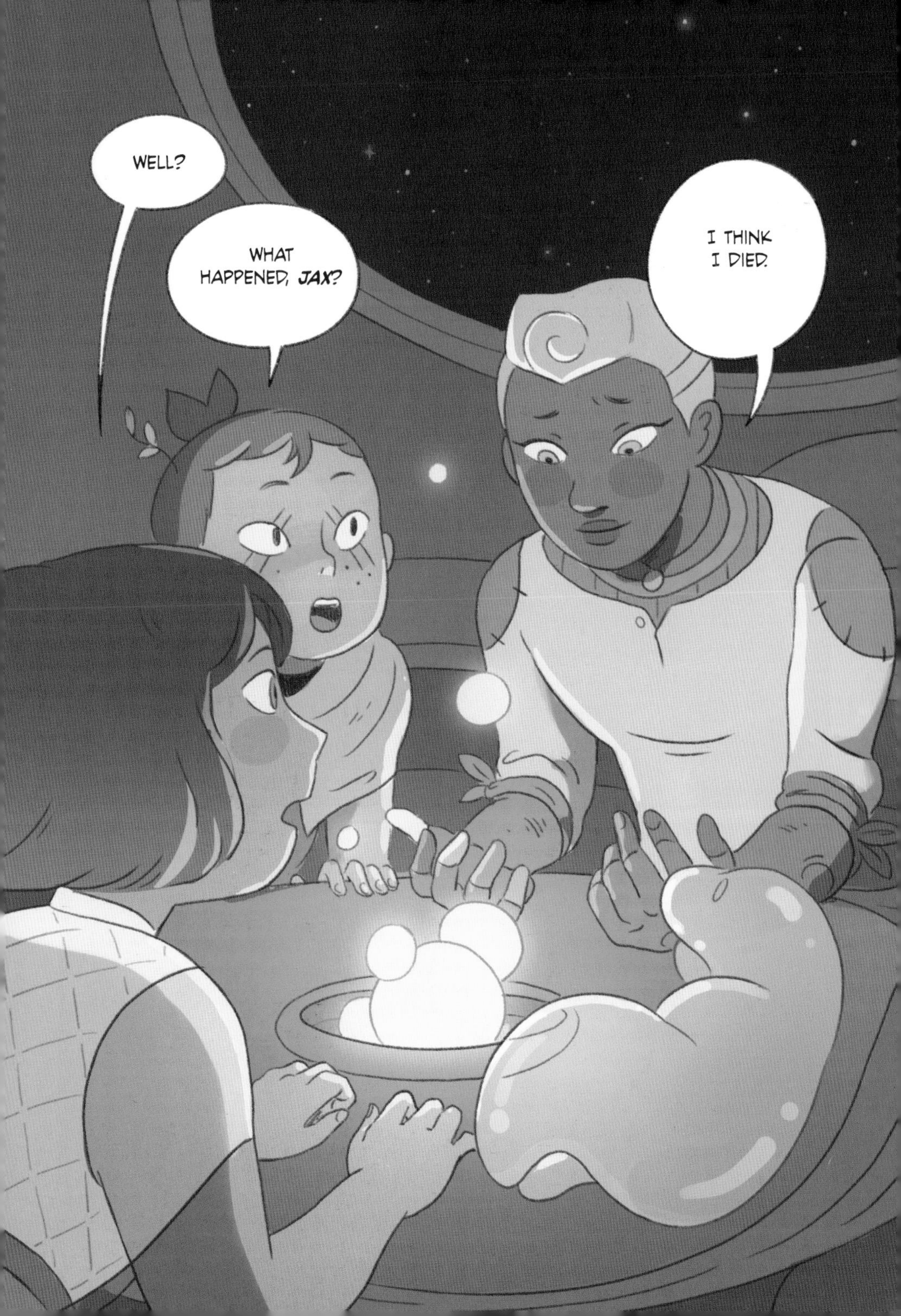
WELL?
WHAT HAPPENED, JAX?
I THINK I DIED.

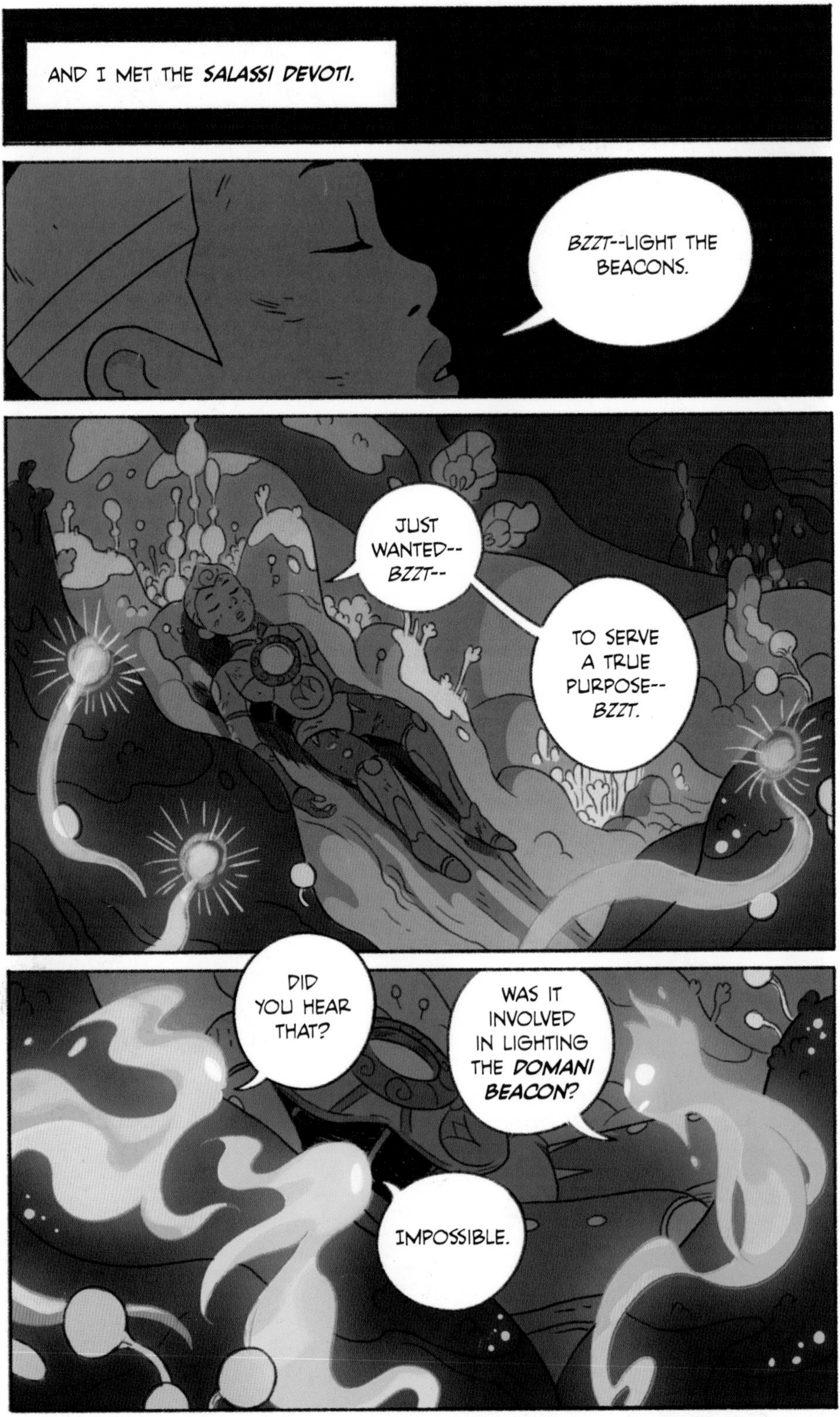
AND I MET THE *SALASSI DEVOTI.*
*BZZT*--LIGHT THE BEACONS.
JUST WANTED-- *BZZT*--
TO SERVE A TRUE PURPOSE-- *BZZT.*
DID YOU HEAR THAT?
WAS IT INVOLVED IN LIGHTING THE ***DOMANI BEACON?***
IMPOSSIBLE.

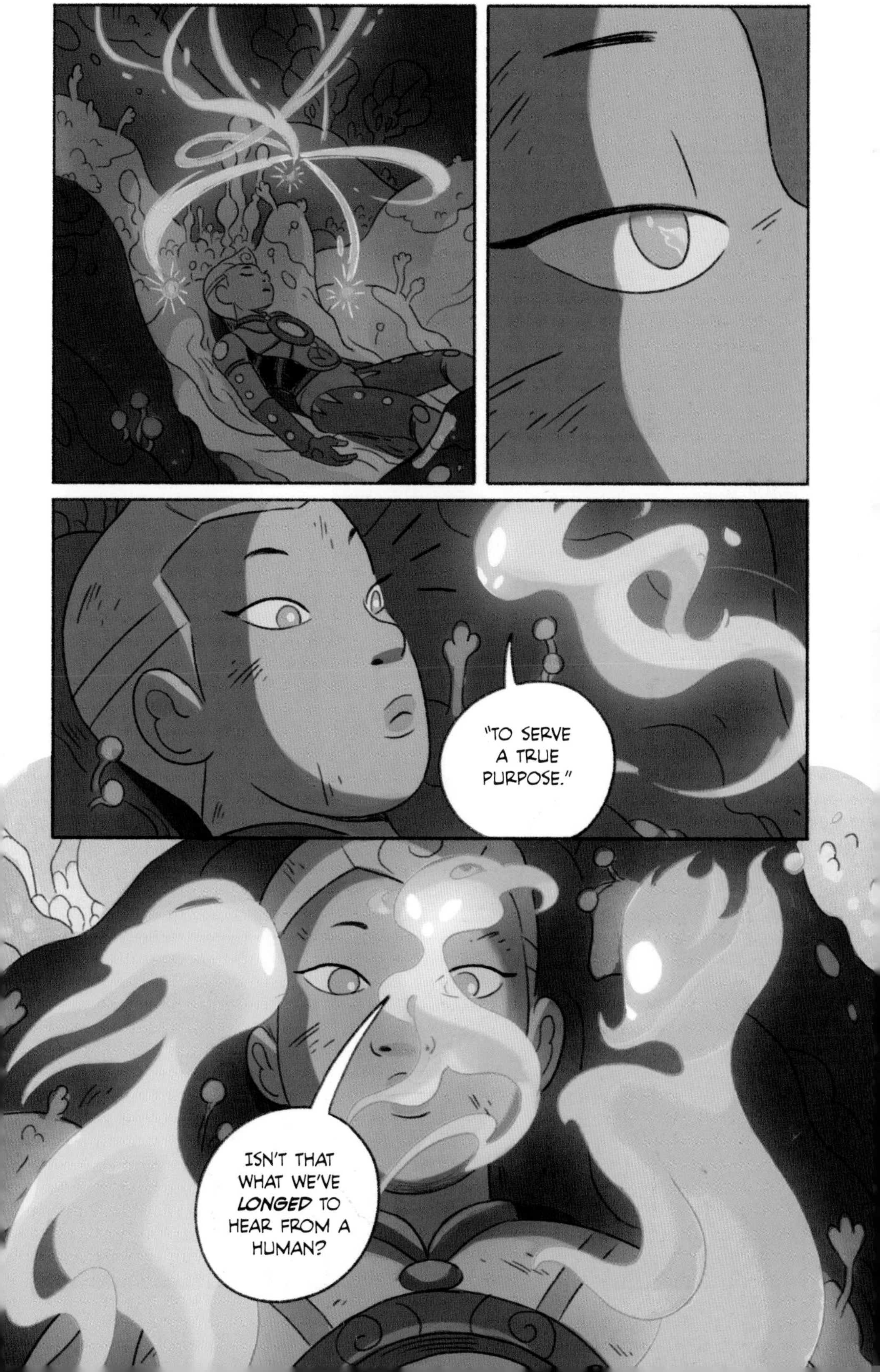
"TO SERVE A TRUE PURPOSE."
ISN'T THAT WHAT WE'VE *LONGED* TO HEAR FROM A HUMAN?

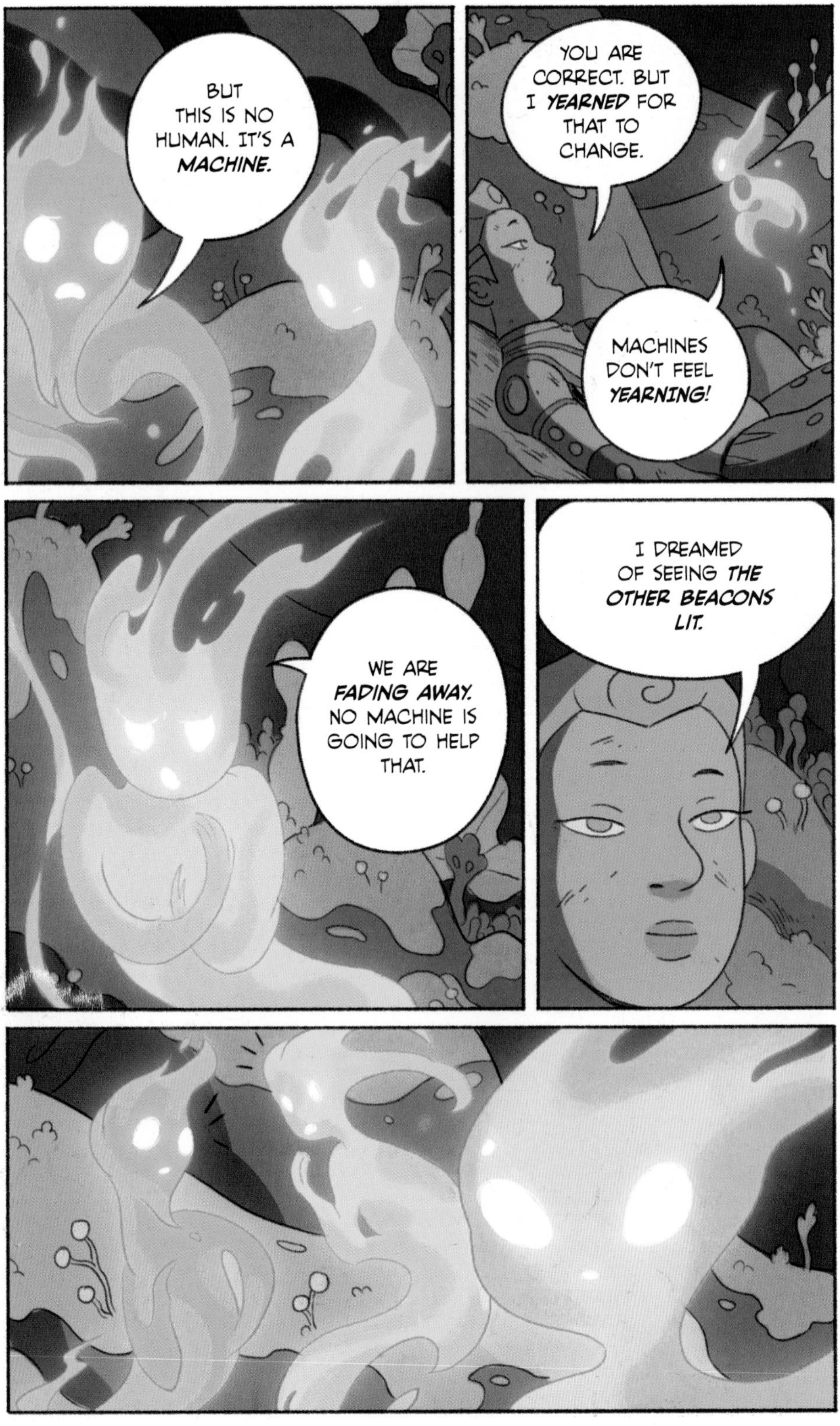
BUT THIS IS NO HUMAN. IT'S A *MACHINE.*
YOU ARE CORRECT. BUT I *YEARNED* FOR THAT TO CHANGE.
MACHINES DON'T FEEL *YEARNING!*
WE ARE *FADING AWAY.* NO MACHINE IS GOING TO HELP THAT.
I DREAMED OF SEEING *THE OTHER BEACONS LIT.*

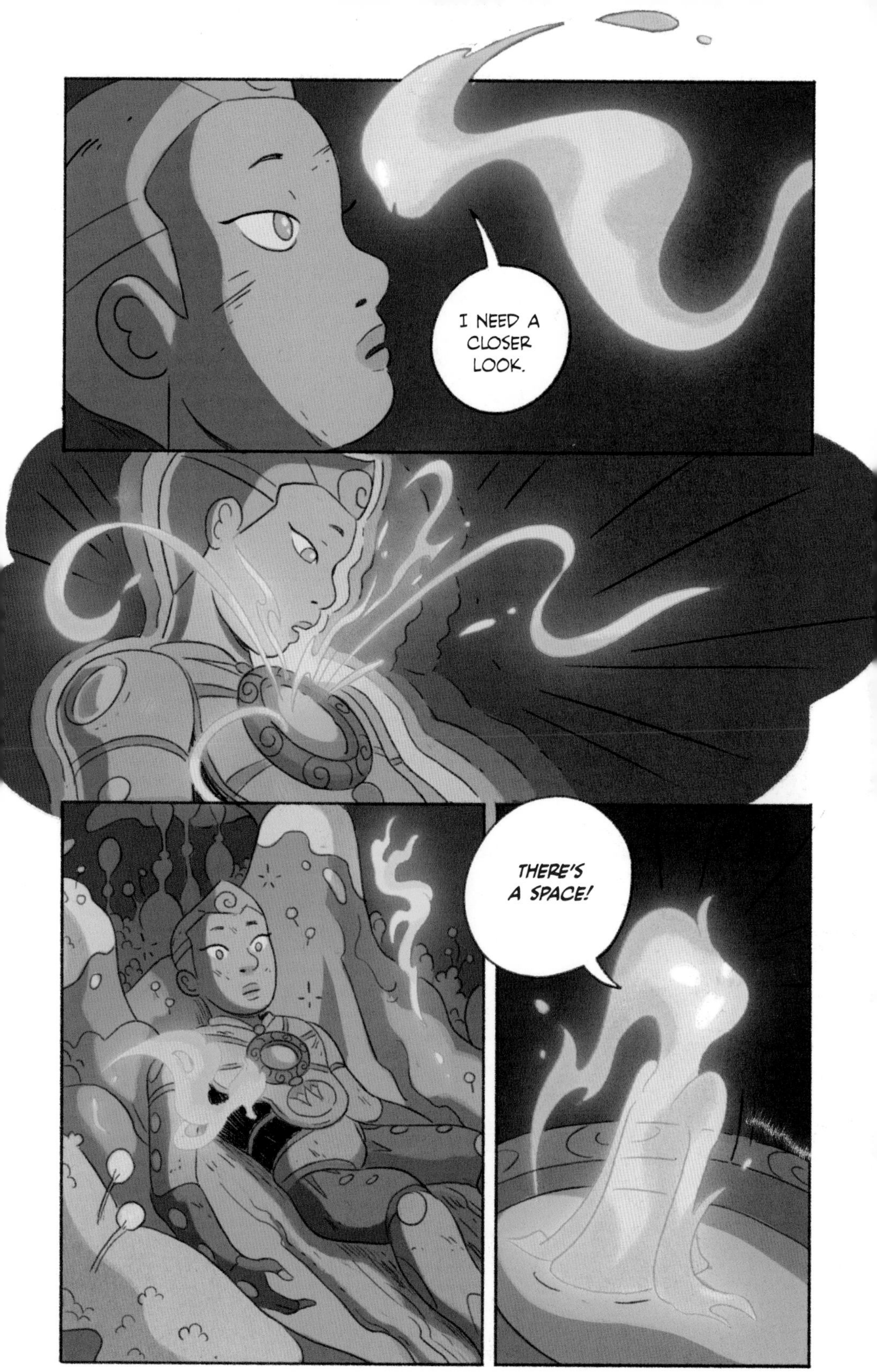
I NEED A CLOSER LOOK.
THERE'S A SPACE!

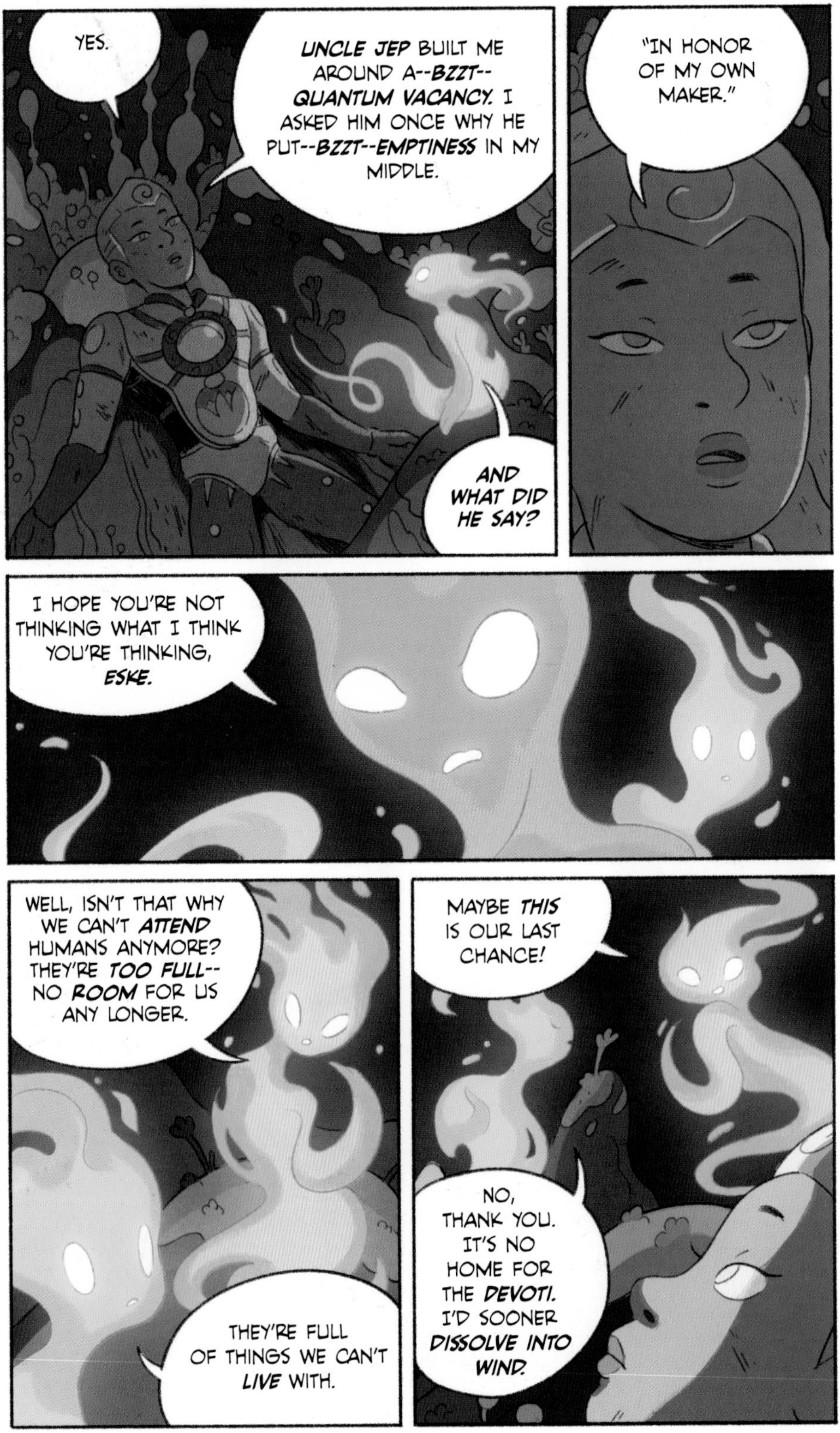
YES.
UNCLE JEP BUILT ME AROUND A--BZZT--QUANTUM VACANCY. I ASKED HIM ONCE WHY HE PUT--BZZT--EMPTINESS IN MY MIDDLE.
AND WHAT DID HE SAY?
"IN HONOR OF MY OWN MAKER."
I HOPE YOU'RE NOT THINKING WHAT I THINK YOU'RE THINKING, ESKE.
WELL, ISN'T THAT WHY WE CAN'T ATTEND HUMANS ANYMORE? THEY'RE TOO FULL--NO ROOM FOR US ANY LONGER.
THEY'RE FULL OF THINGS WE CAN'T LIVE WITH.
MAYBE THIS IS OUR LAST CHANCE!
NO, THANK YOU. IT'S NO HOME FOR THE DEVOTI. I'D SOONER DISSOLVE INTO WIND.

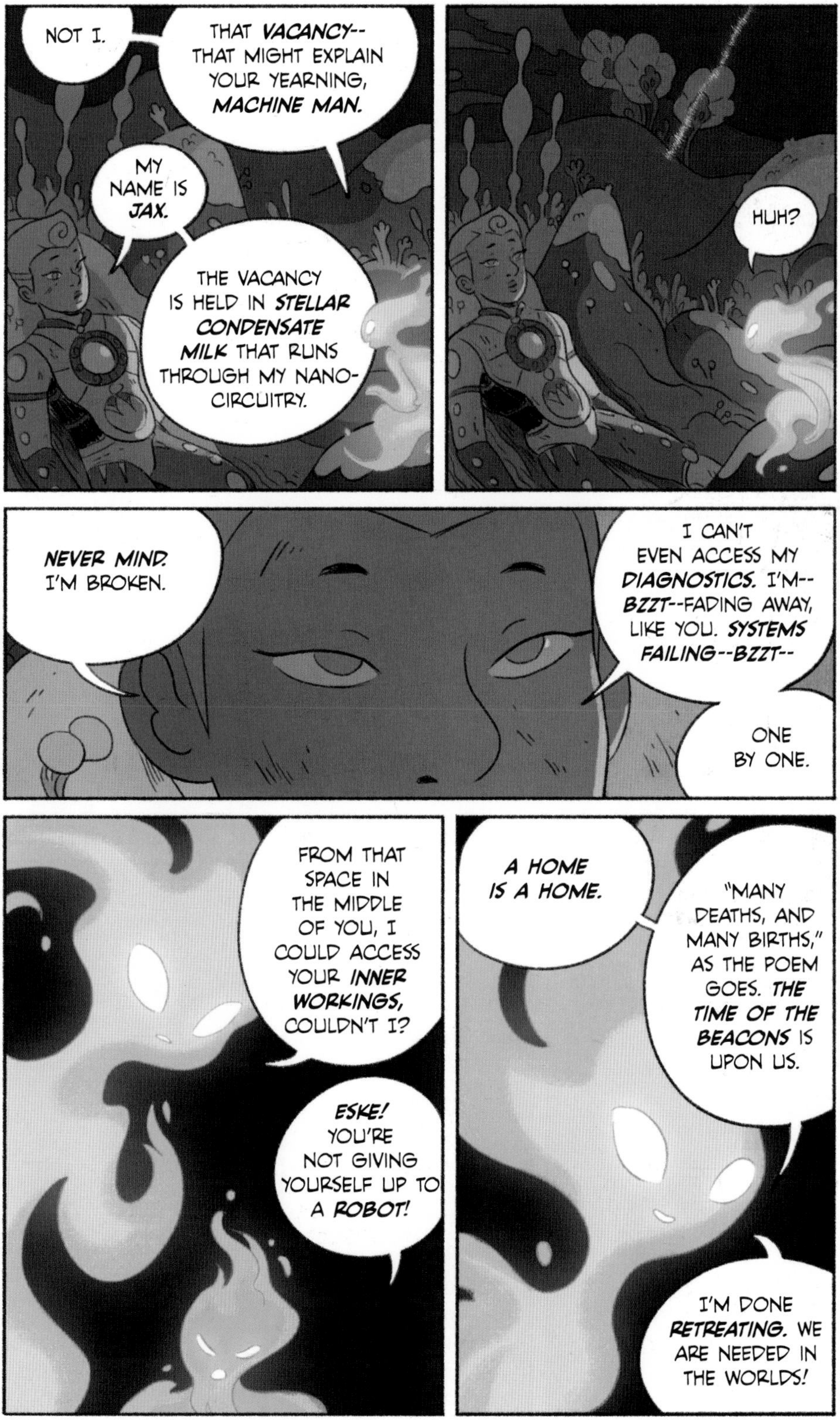
NOT I.
THAT VACANCY-- THAT MIGHT EXPLAIN YOUR YEARNING, MACHINE MAN.
MY NAME IS JAX.
THE VACANCY IS HELD IN STELLAR CONDENSATE MILK THAT RUNS THROUGH MY NANO-CIRCUITRY.
HUH?
NEVER MIND. I'M BROKEN.
I CAN'T EVEN ACCESS MY DIAGNOSTICS. I'M-- BZZT--FADING AWAY, LIKE YOU. SYSTEMS FAILING--BZZT--
ONE BY ONE.
FROM THAT SPACE IN THE MIDDLE OF YOU, I COULD ACCESS YOUR INNER WORKINGS, COULDN'T I?
ESKE! YOU'RE NOT GIVING YOURSELF UP TO A ROBOT!
A HOME IS A HOME.
"MANY DEATHS, AND MANY BIRTHS," AS THE POEM GOES. THE TIME OF THE BEACONS IS UPON US.
I'M DONE RETREATING. WE ARE NEEDED IN THE WORLDS!

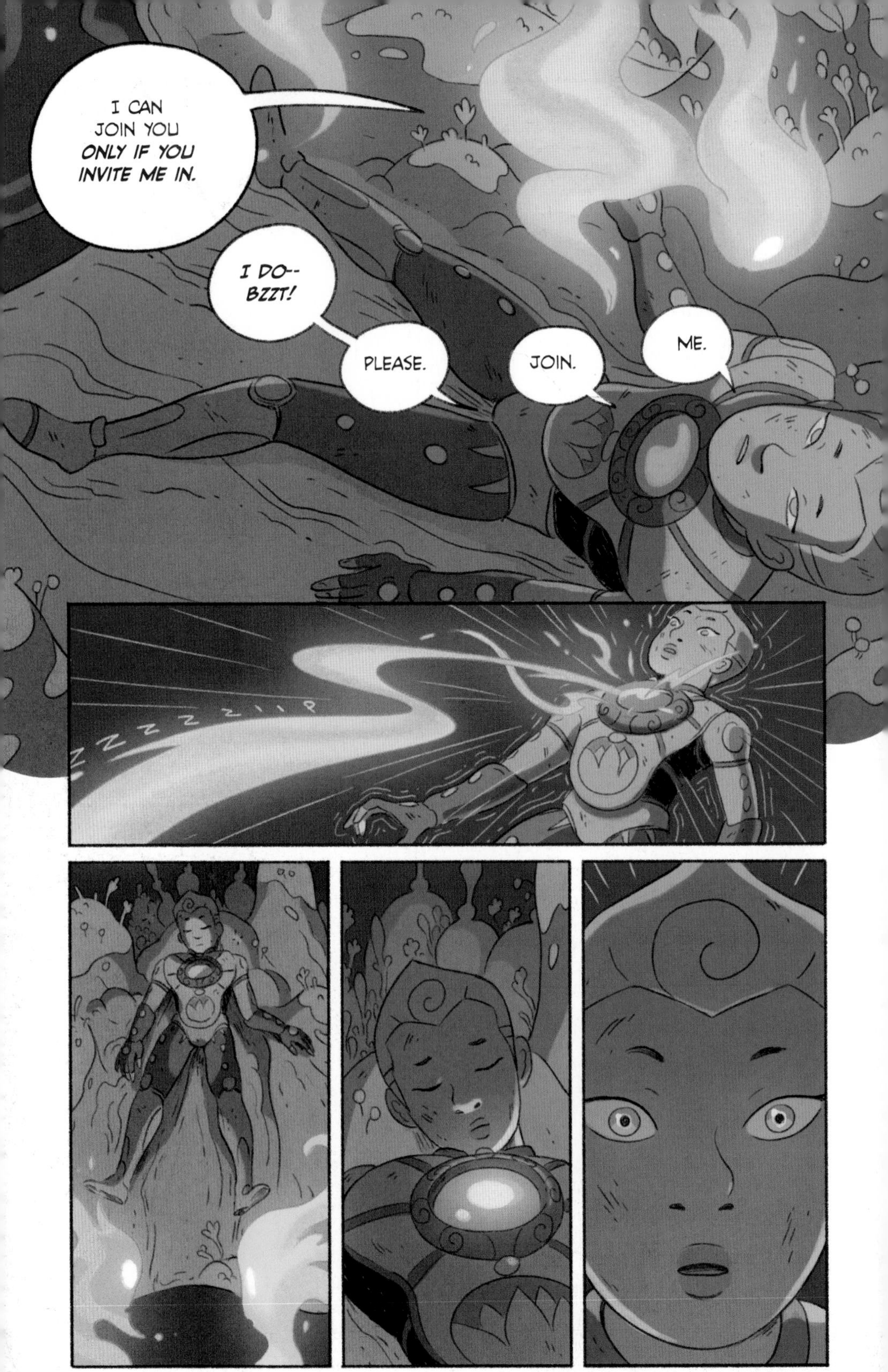
I CAN
JOIN YOU
ONLY IF YOU
INVITE ME IN.
I DO--
BZZT!
PLEASE.
JOIN.
ME.
ZZZZZZZIIP

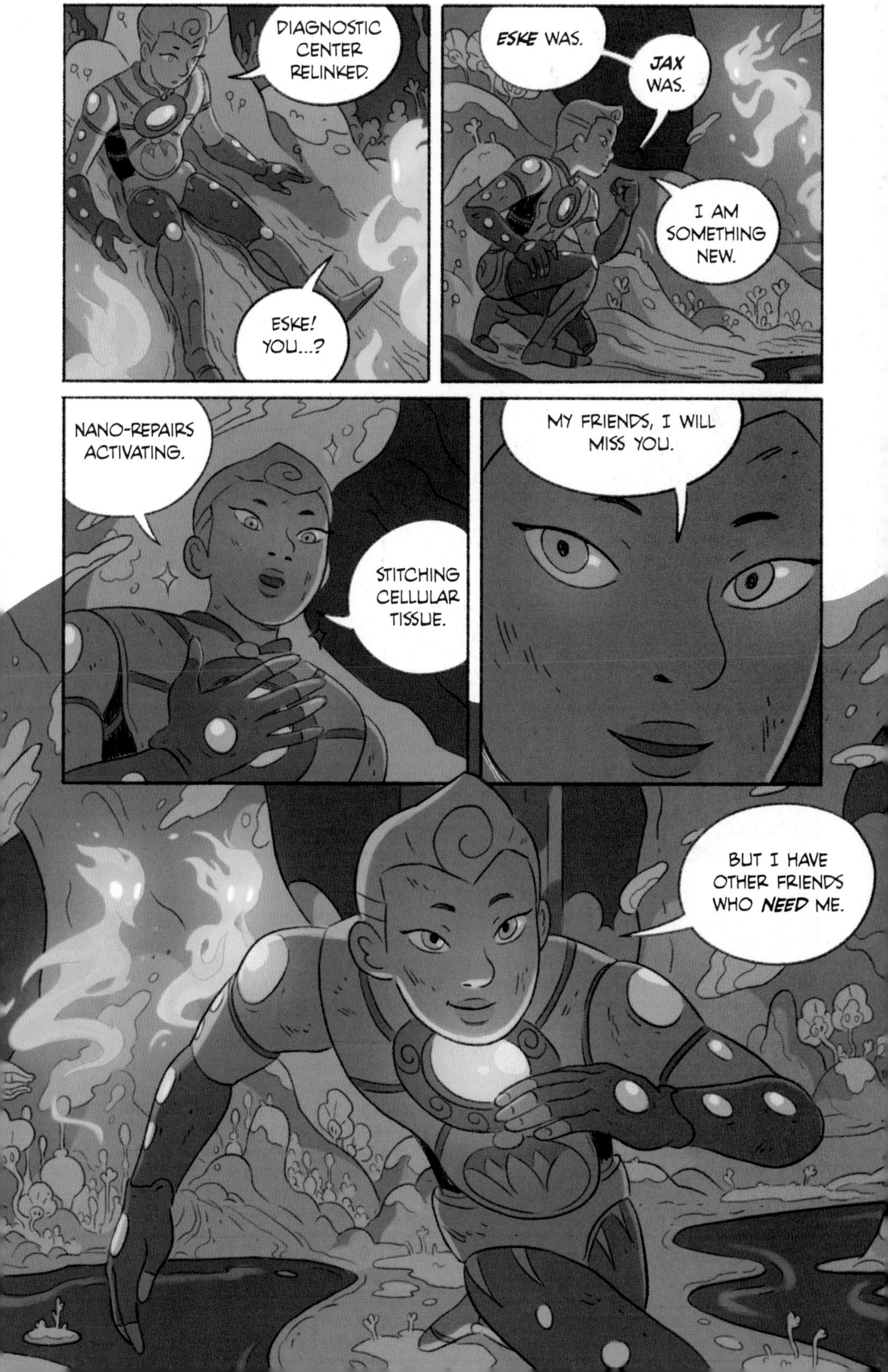
DIAGNOSTIC CENTER RELINKED.
ESKE! YOU...?
ESKE WAS.
JAX WAS.
I AM SOMETHING NEW.
NANO-REPAIRS ACTIVATING.
STITCHING CELLULAR TISSUE.
MY FRIENDS, I WILL MISS YOU.
BUT I HAVE OTHER FRIENDS WHO NEED ME.

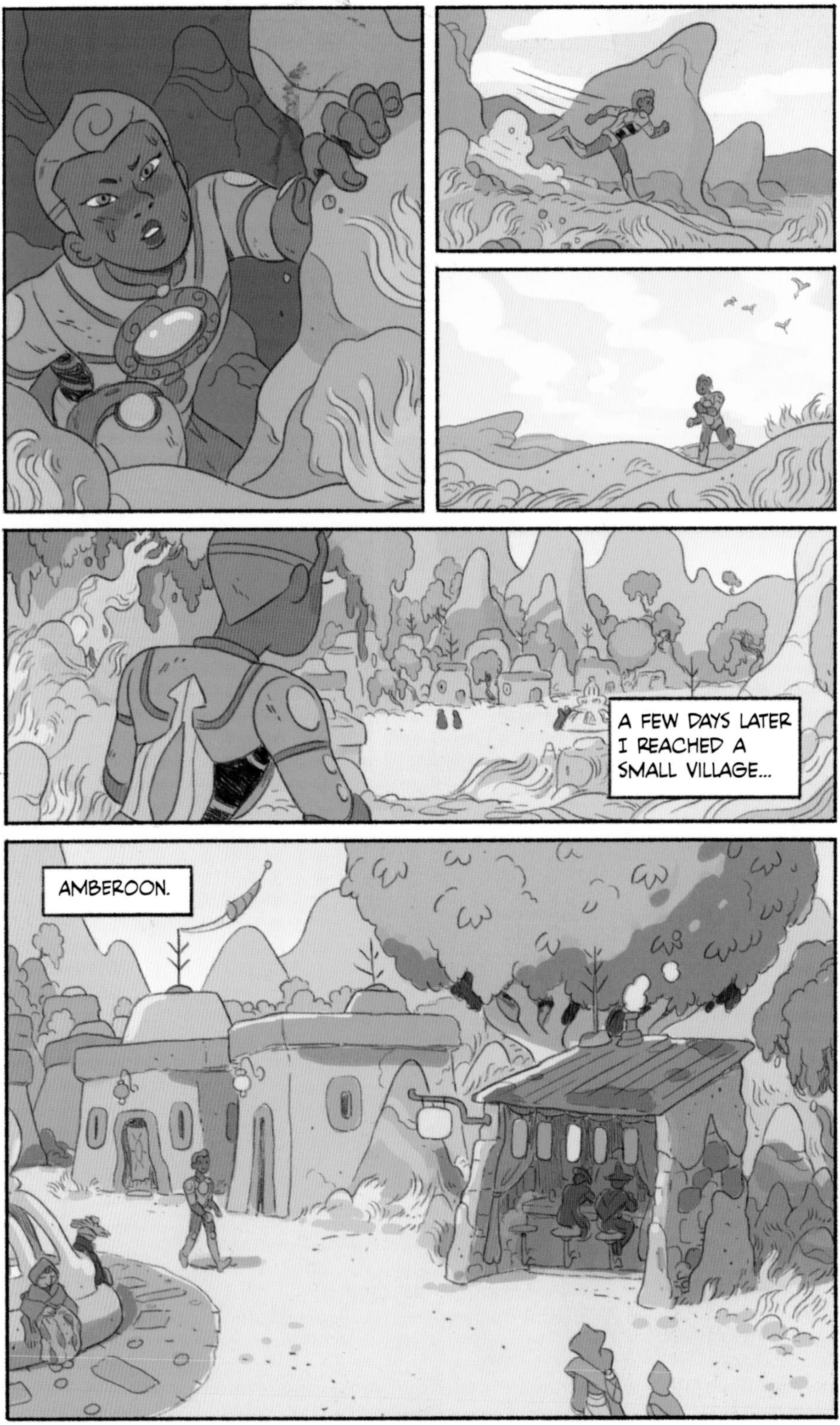
A FEW DAYS LATER I REACHED A SMALL VILLAGE...
AMBEROON.

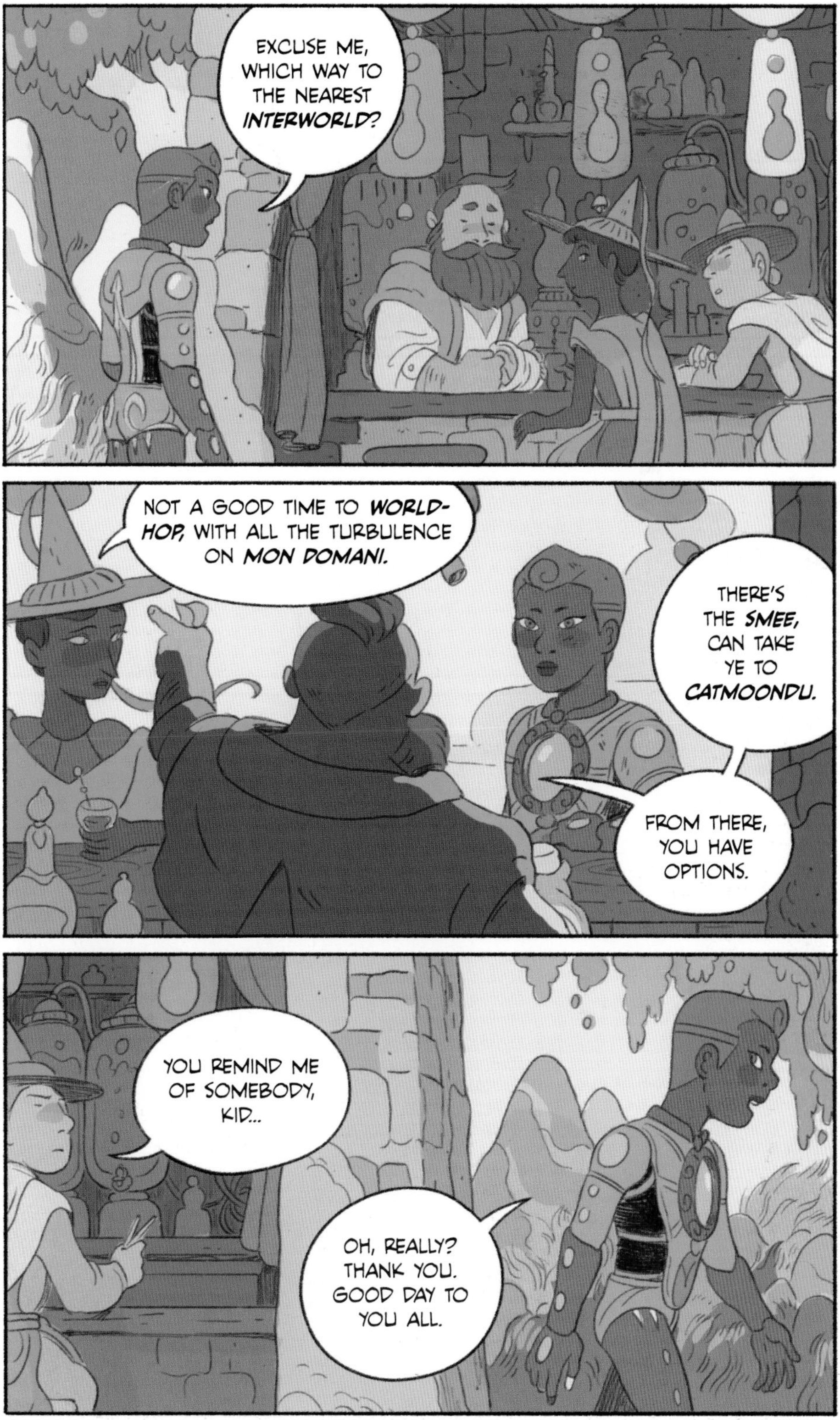
EXCUSE ME, WHICH WAY TO THE NEAREST INTERWORLD?
NOT A GOOD TIME TO WORLD-HOP, WITH ALL THE TURBULENCE ON MON DOMANI.
THERE'S THE SMEE, CAN TAKE YE TO CATMOONDU.
FROM THERE, YOU HAVE OPTIONS.
YOU REMIND ME OF SOMEBODY, KID...
OH, REALLY? THANK YOU. GOOD DAY TO YOU ALL.

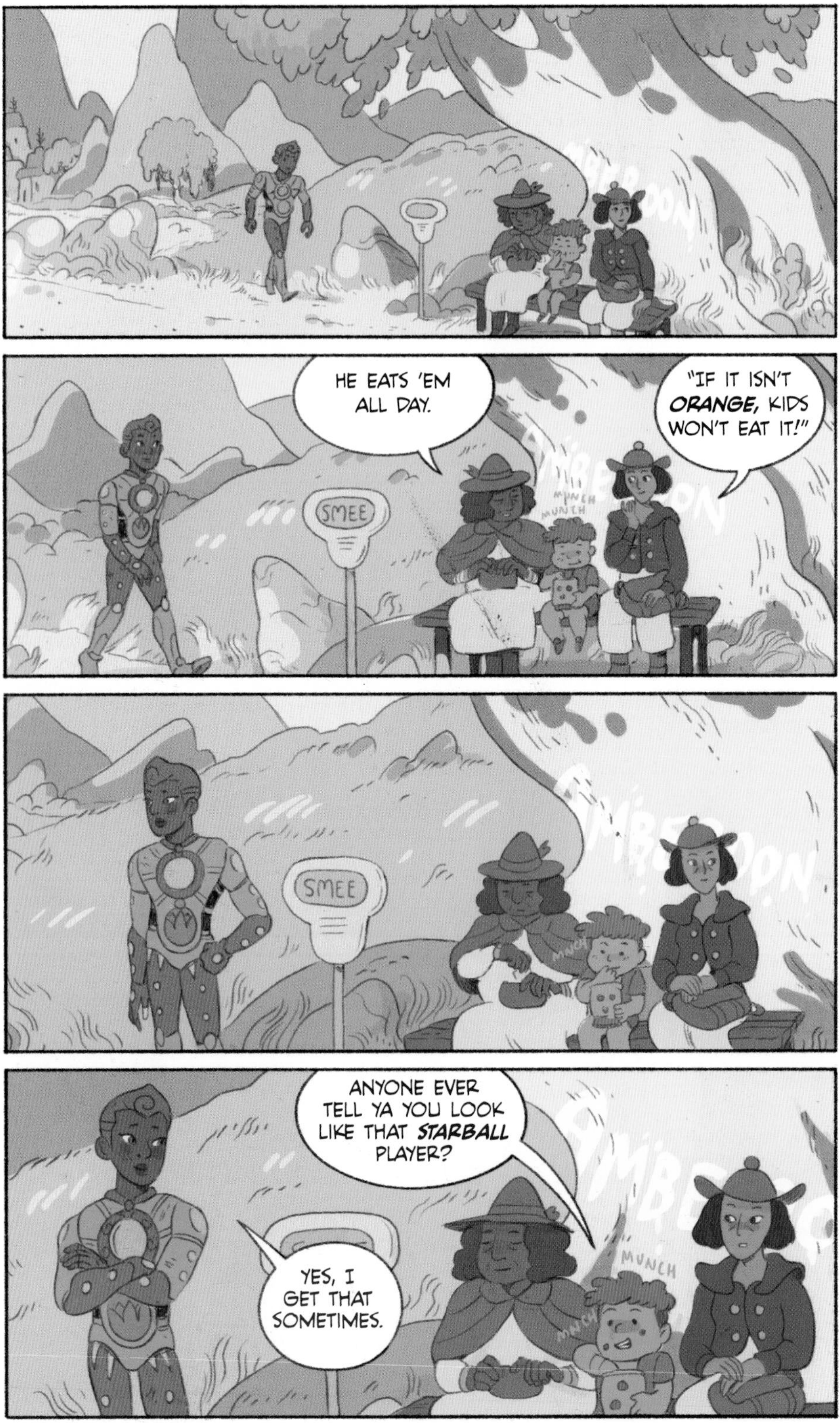
HE EATS 'EM ALL DAY.
"IF IT ISN'T ***ORANGE,*** KIDS WON'T EAT IT!"
MUNCH MUNCH
SMEE
SMEE
ANYONE EVER TELL YA YOU LOOK LIKE THAT ***STARBALL*** PLAYER?
YES, I GET THAT SOMETIMES.
MUNCH

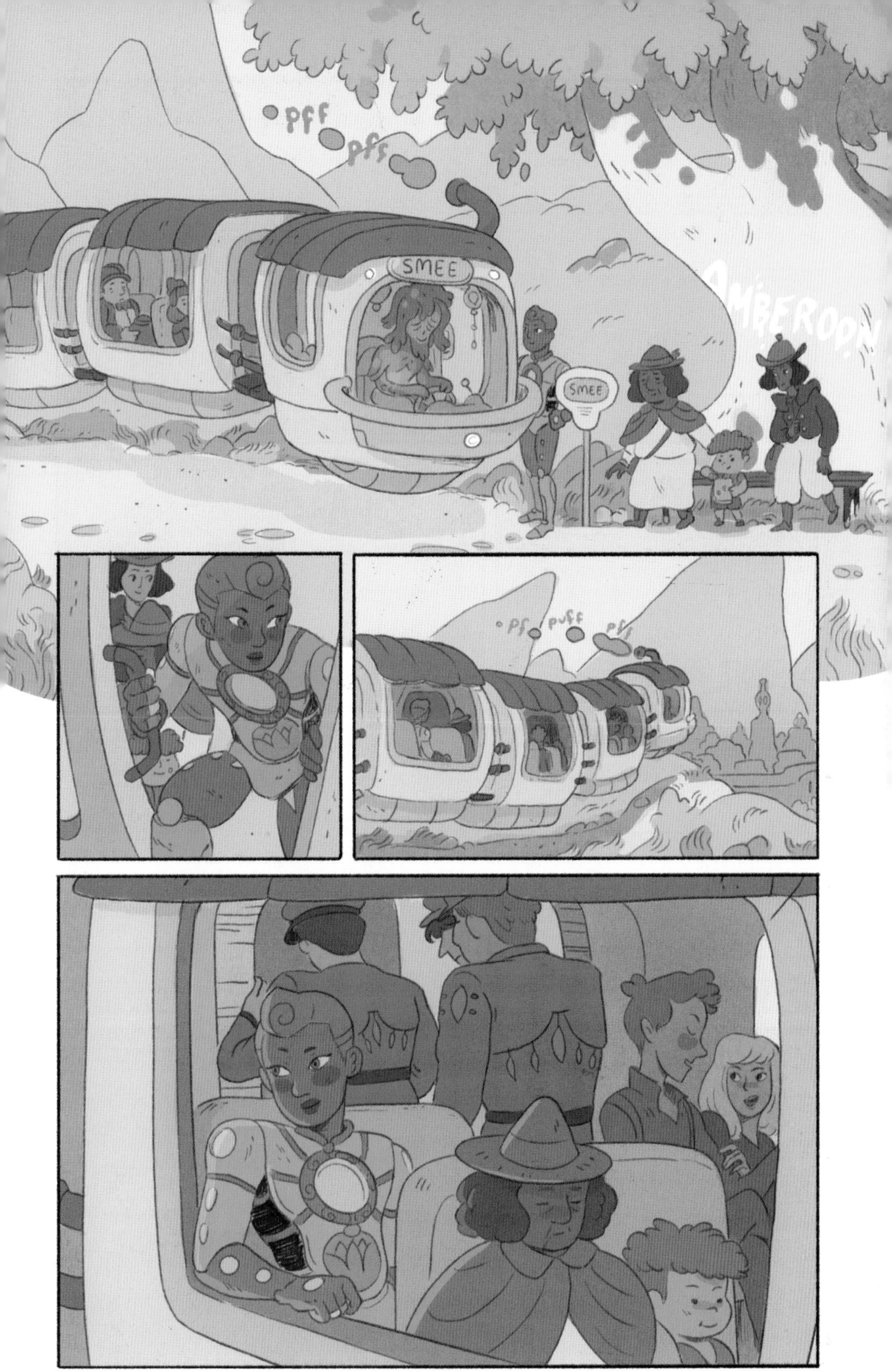
PFF
pff
SMEE
SMEE
AMBEROON
pf
puff
pff

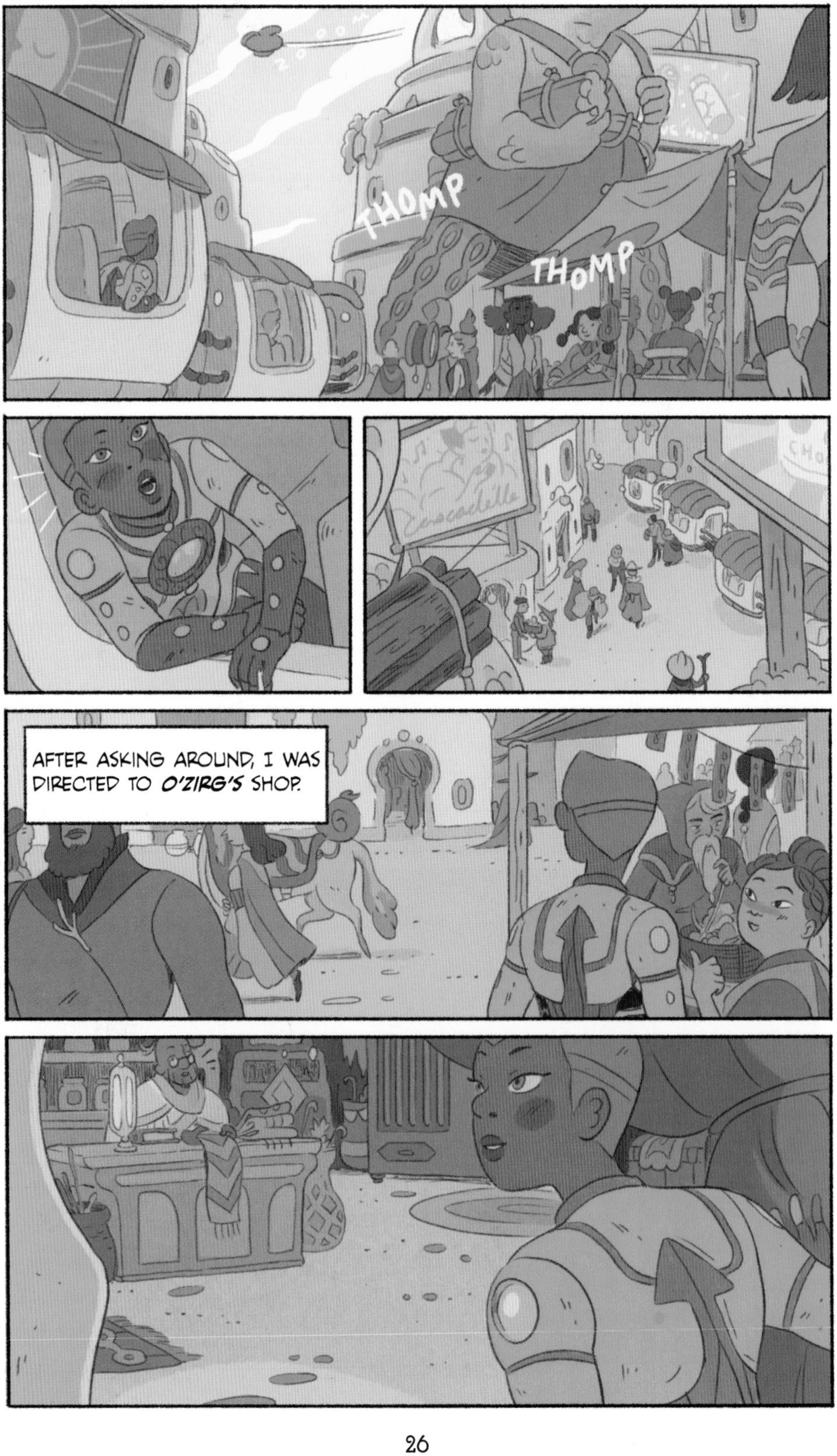
THOMP
THOMP
AFTER ASKING AROUND, I WAS DIRECTED TO O'ZIRG'S SHOP.

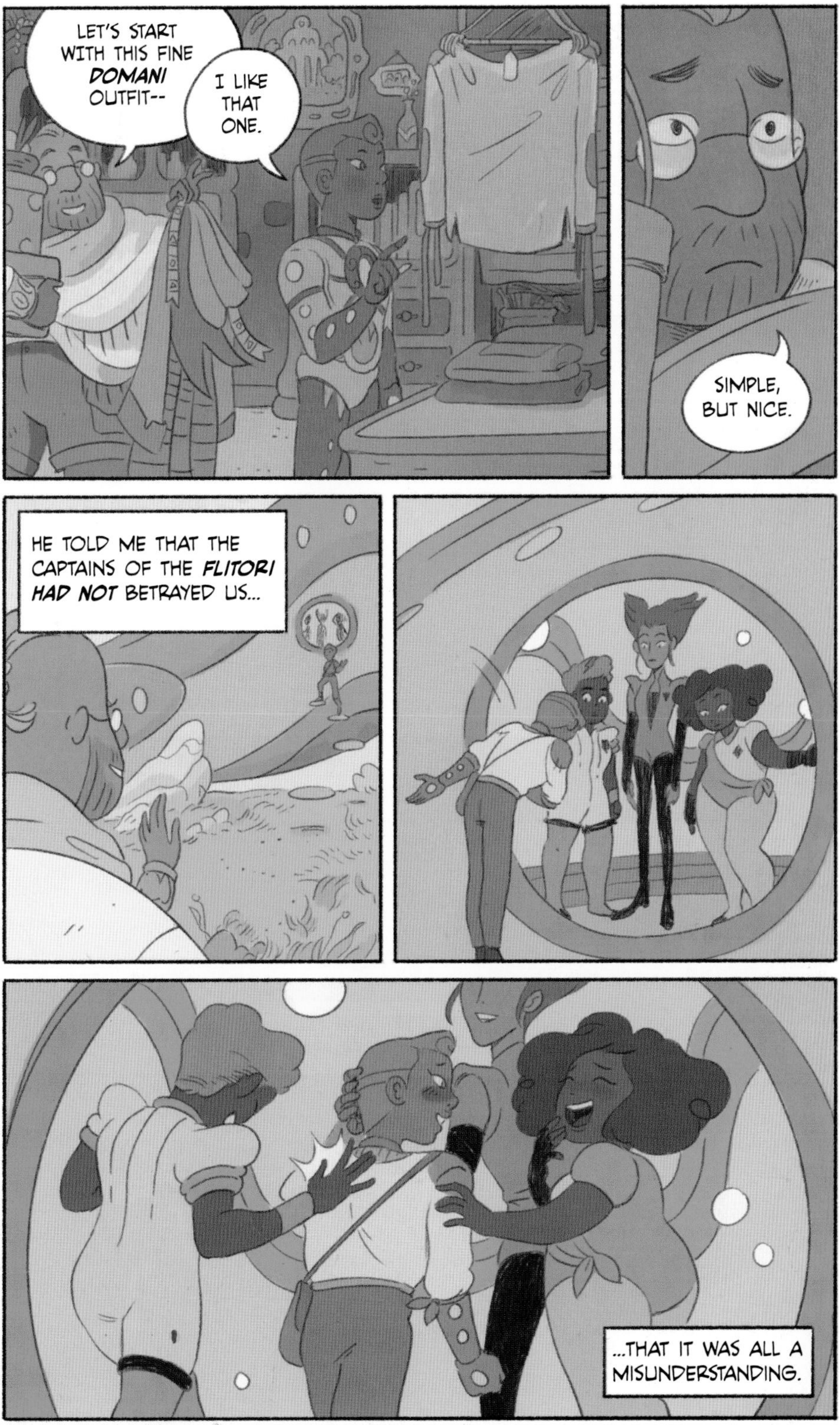
LET'S START WITH THIS FINE *DOMANI* OUTFIT--
I LIKE THAT ONE.
SIMPLE, BUT NICE.
HE TOLD ME THAT THE CAPTAINS OF THE *FLITORI* *HAD NOT* BETRAYED US...
...THAT IT WAS ALL A MISUNDERSTANDING.

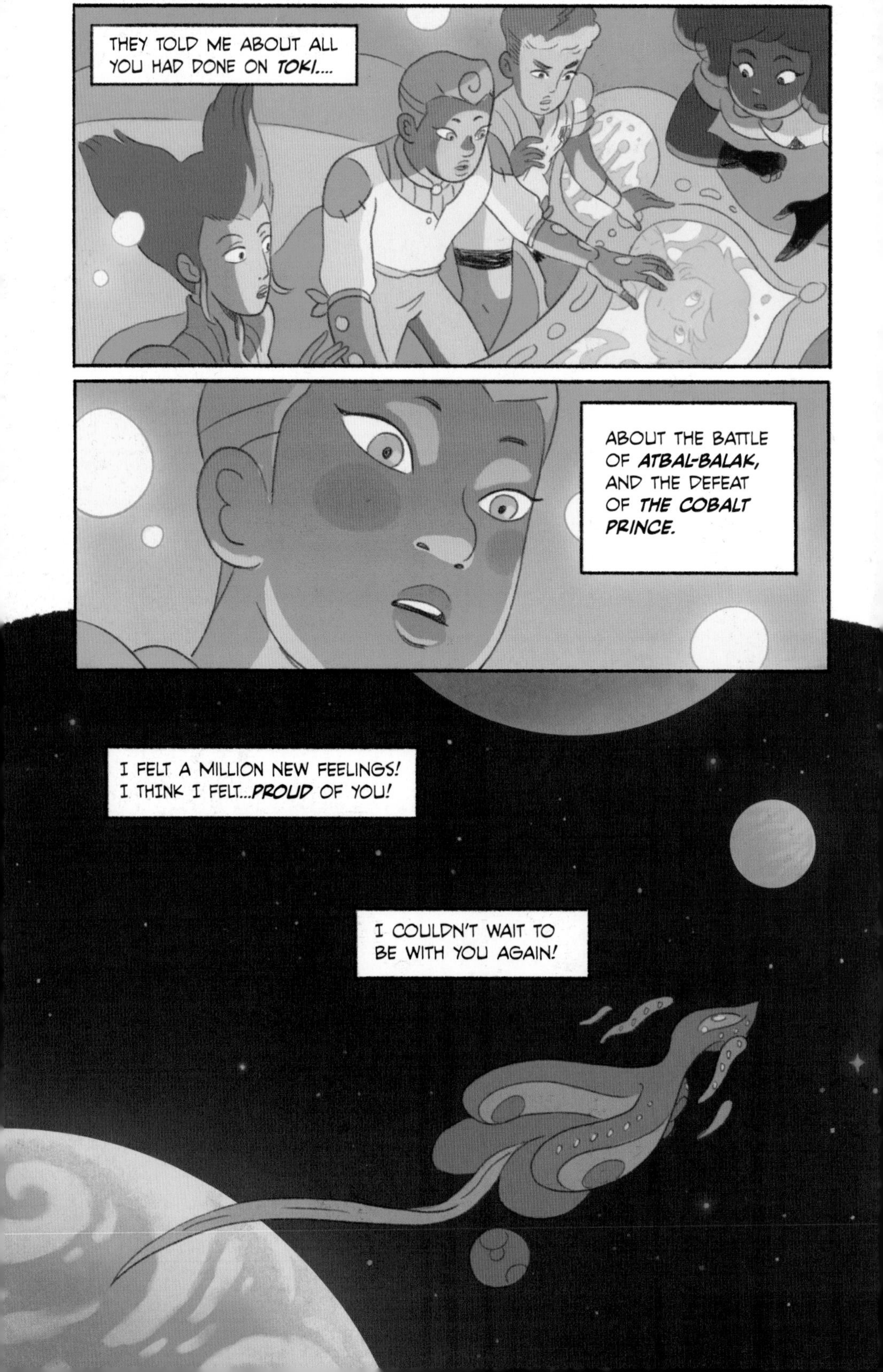
THEY TOLD ME ABOUT ALL YOU HAD DONE ON TOKI....
ABOUT THE BATTLE OF ATBAL-BALAK, AND THE DEFEAT OF THE COBALT PRINCE.
I FELT A MILLION NEW FEELINGS! I THINK I FELT...PROUD OF YOU!
I COULDN'T WAIT TO BE WITH YOU AGAIN!

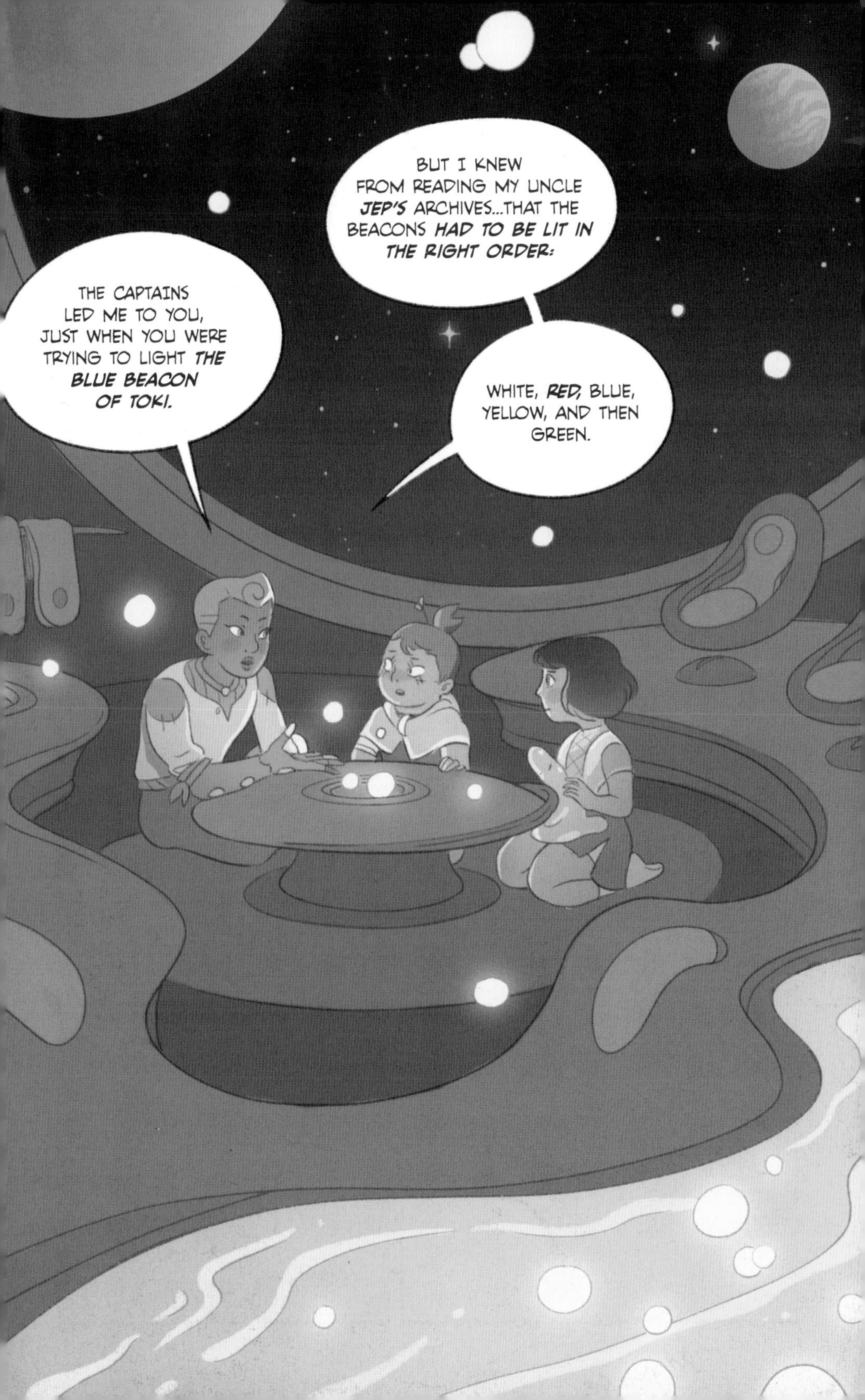
THE CAPTAINS LED ME TO YOU, JUST WHEN YOU WERE TRYING TO LIGHT *THE BLUE BEACON OF TOKI.*
BUT I KNEW FROM READING MY UNCLE *JEP'S* ARCHIVES...THAT THE BEACONS *HAD TO BE LIT IN THE RIGHT ORDER:*
WHITE, *RED,* BLUE, YELLOW, AND THEN GREEN.

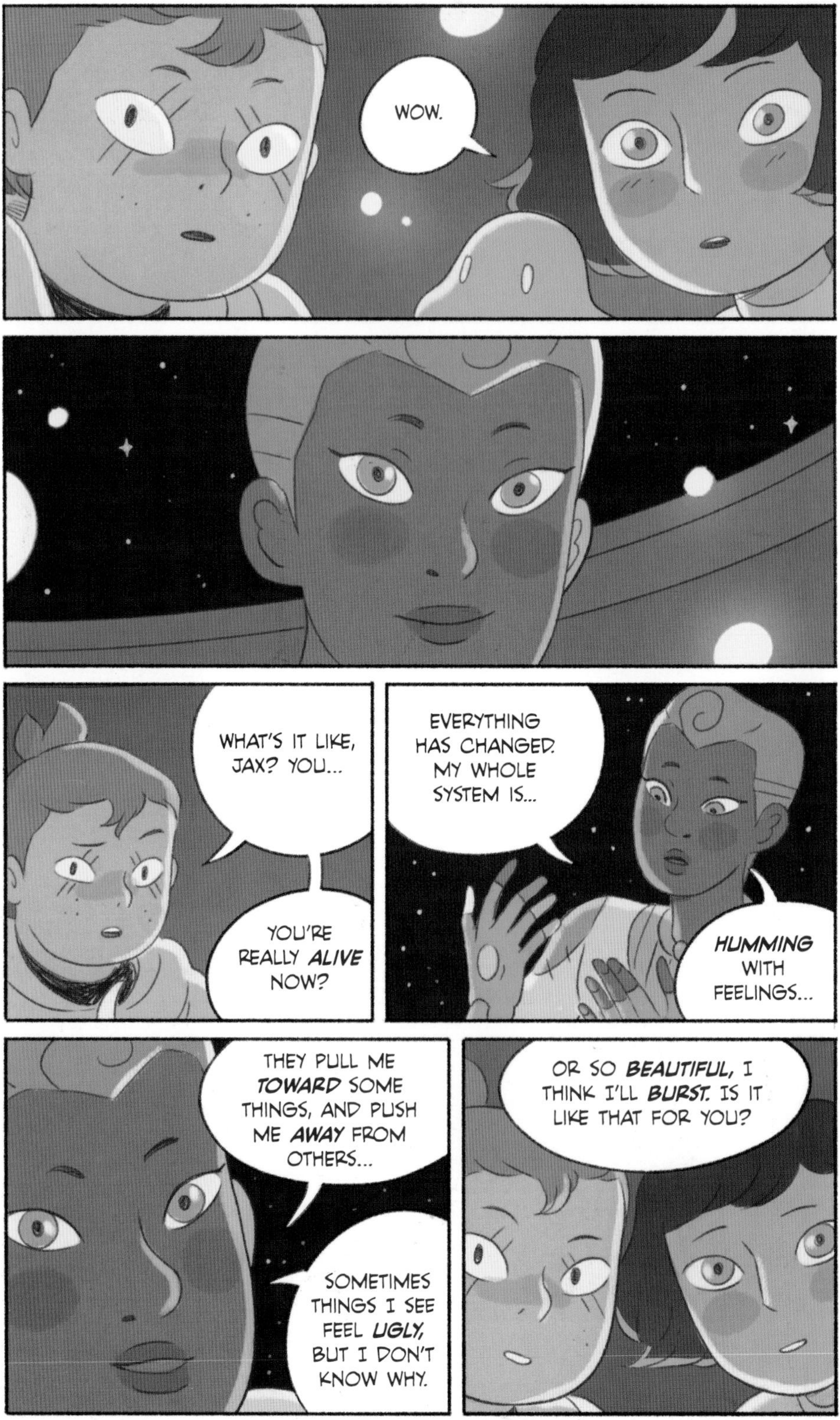
WOW.
WHAT'S IT LIKE, JAX? YOU...
YOU'RE REALLY ALIVE NOW?
EVERYTHING HAS CHANGED. MY WHOLE SYSTEM IS...
HUMMING WITH FEELINGS...
THEY PULL ME TOWARD SOME THINGS, AND PUSH ME AWAY FROM OTHERS...
SOMETIMES THINGS I SEE FEEL UGLY, BUT I DON'T KNOW WHY.
OR SO BEAUTIFUL, I THINK I'LL BURST. IS IT LIKE THAT FOR YOU?

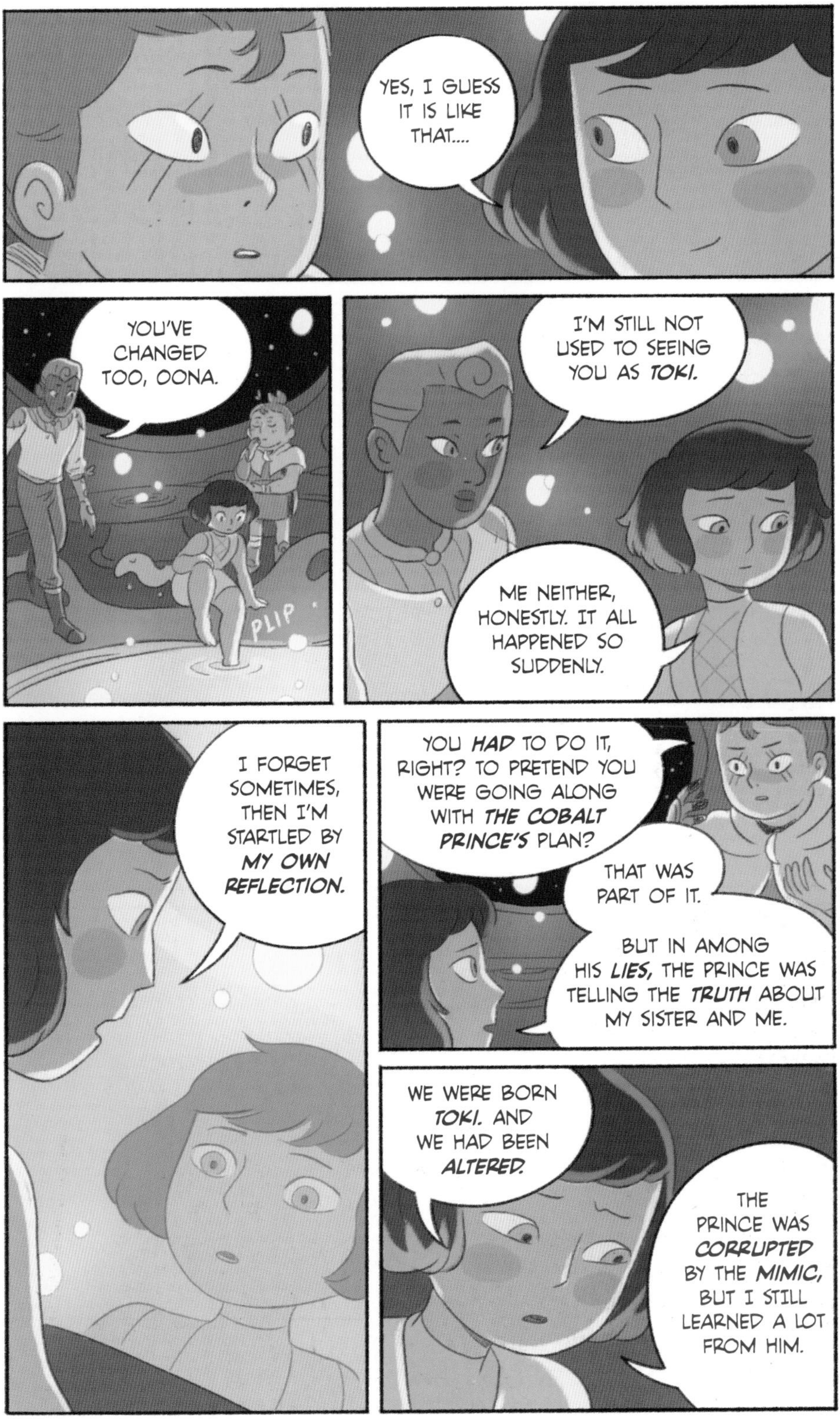

YES, I GUESS IT IS LIKE THAT....
YOU'VE CHANGED TOO, OONA.
PLIP
I'M STILL NOT USED TO SEEING YOU AS TOKI.
ME NEITHER, HONESTLY. IT ALL HAPPENED SO SUDDENLY.
I FORGET SOMETIMES, THEN I'M STARTLED BY MY OWN REFLECTION.
YOU HAD TO DO IT, RIGHT? TO PRETEND YOU WERE GOING ALONG WITH THE COBALT PRINCE'S PLAN?
THAT WAS PART OF IT.
BUT IN AMONG HIS LIES, THE PRINCE WAS TELLING THE TRUTH ABOUT MY SISTER AND ME.
WE WERE BORN TOKI. AND WE HAD BEEN ALTERED.
THE PRINCE WAS CORRUPTED BY THE MIMIC, BUT I STILL LEARNED A LOT FROM HIM.

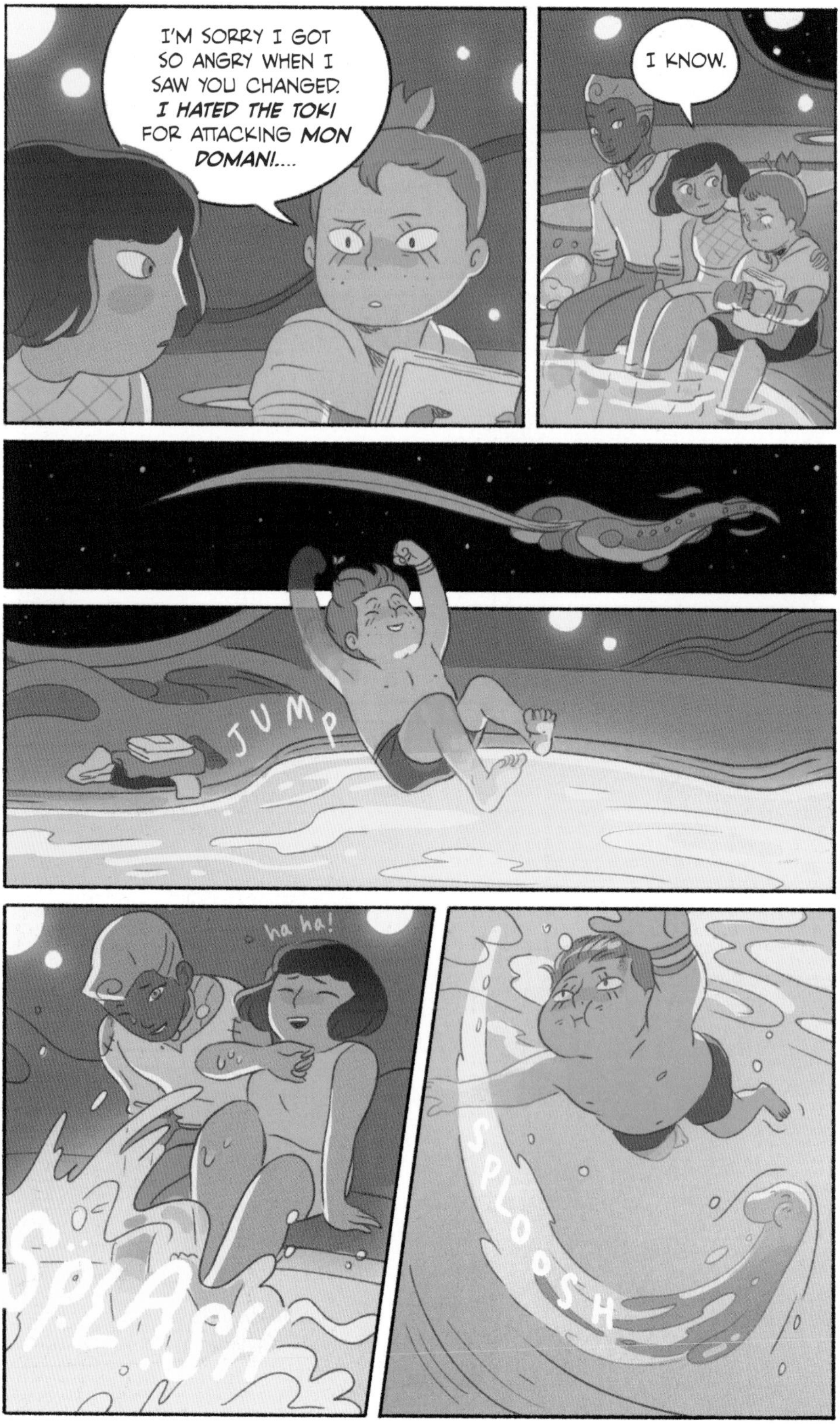
I'M SORRY I GOT SO ANGRY WHEN I SAW YOU CHANGED. I HATED THE TOKI FOR ATTACKING MON DOMANI....
I KNOW.
JUMP
ha ha!
SPLASH
SPLOOSH

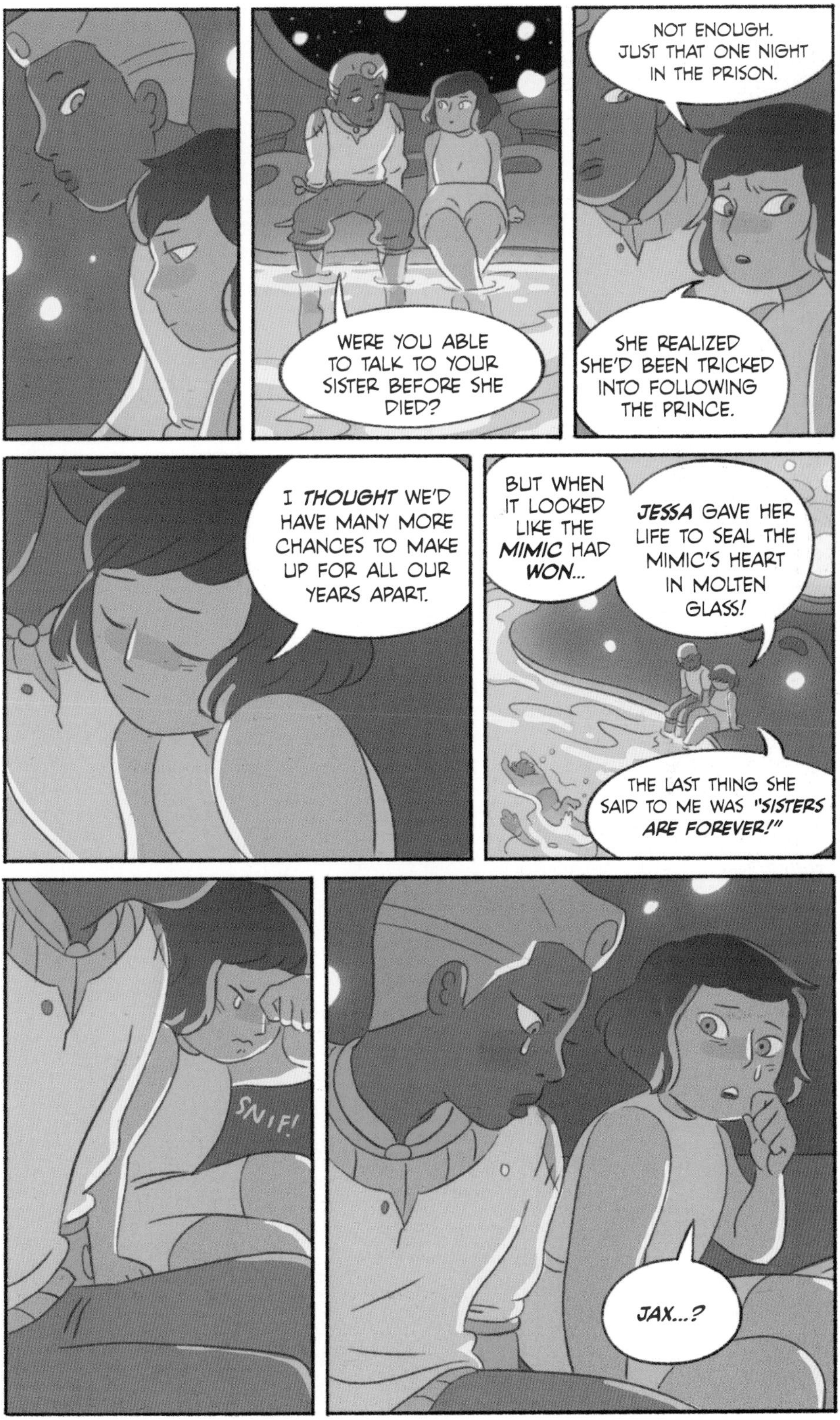
WERE YOU ABLE TO TALK TO YOUR SISTER BEFORE SHE DIED?
NOT ENOUGH. JUST THAT ONE NIGHT IN THE PRISON.
SHE REALIZED SHE'D BEEN TRICKED INTO FOLLOWING THE PRINCE.
I *THOUGHT* WE'D HAVE MANY MORE CHANCES TO MAKE UP FOR ALL OUR YEARS APART.
BUT WHEN IT LOOKED LIKE THE *MIMIC* HAD *WON*...
*JESSA* GAVE HER LIFE TO SEAL THE MIMIC'S HEART IN MOLTEN GLASS!
THE LAST THING SHE SAID TO ME WAS *"SISTERS ARE FOREVER!"*
SNIF!
*JAX...?*

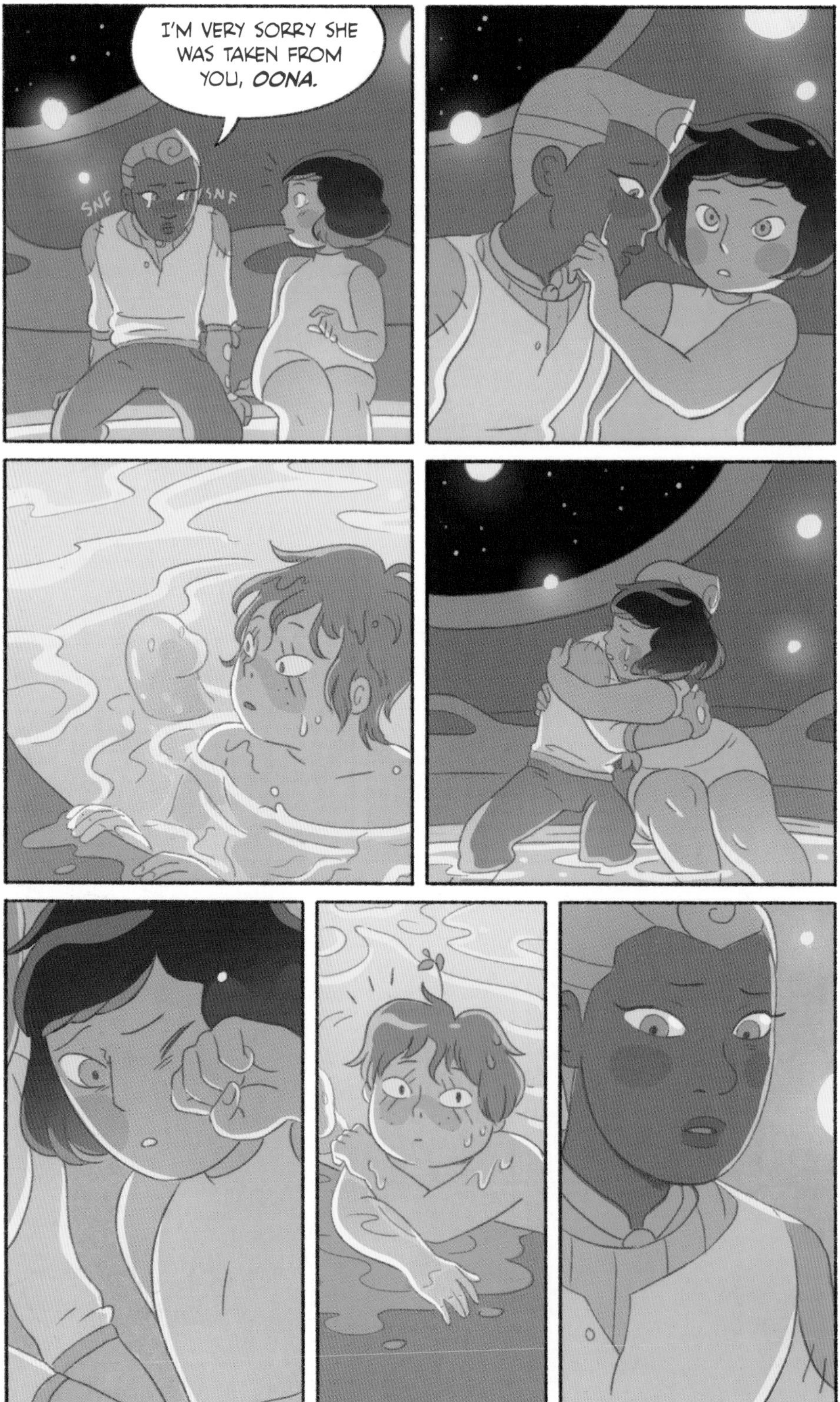
I'M VERY SORRY SHE WAS TAKEN FROM YOU, OONA.
SNF
SNF

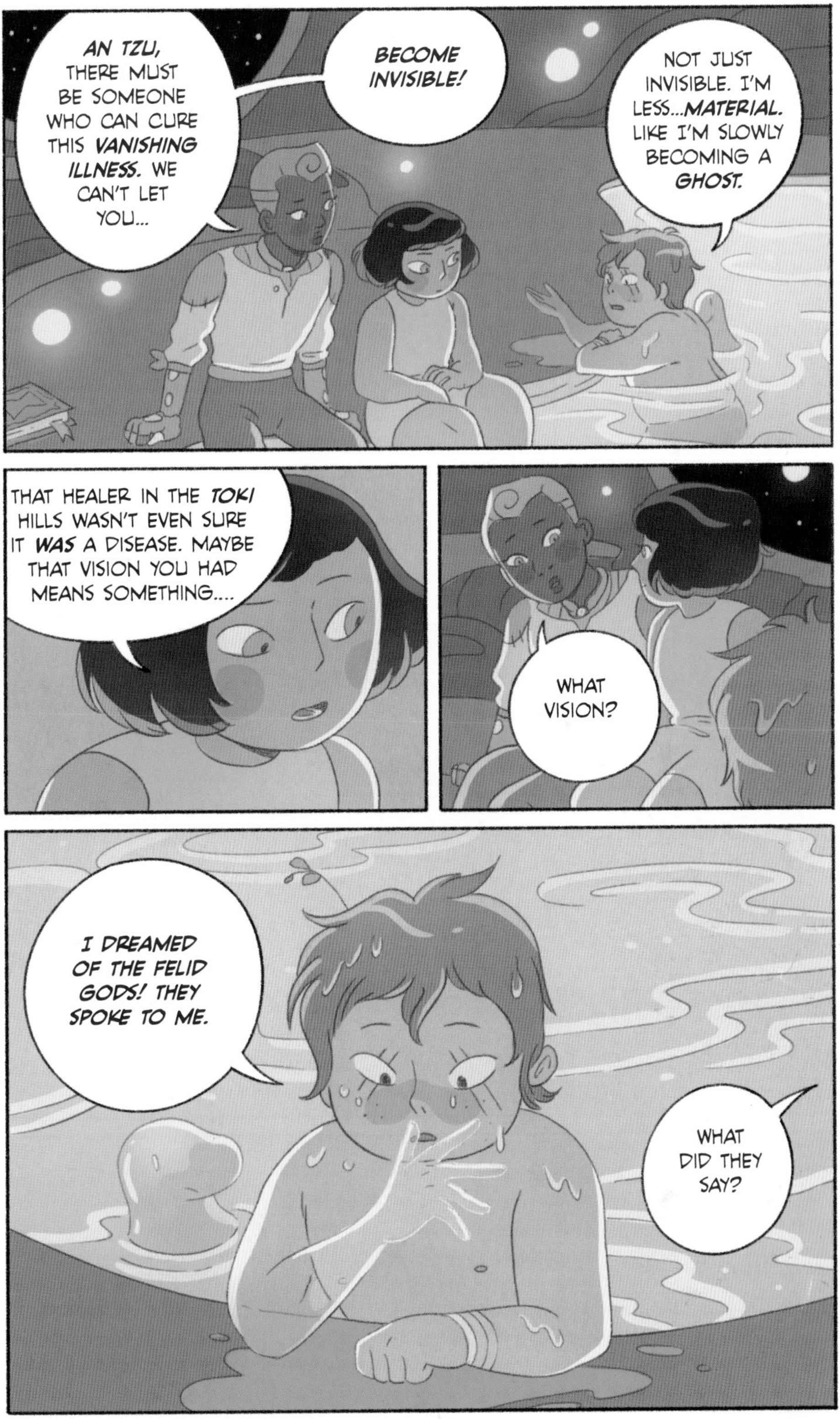
AN TZU, THERE MUST BE SOMEONE WHO CAN CURE THIS VANISHING ILLNESS. WE CAN'T LET YOU...
BECOME INVISIBLE!
NOT JUST INVISIBLE. I'M LESS...MATERIAL. LIKE I'M SLOWLY BECOMING A GHOST.
THAT HEALER IN THE TOKI HILLS WASN'T EVEN SURE IT WAS A DISEASE. MAYBE THAT VISION YOU HAD MEANS SOMETHING....
WHAT VISION?
I DREAMED OF THE FELID GODS! THEY SPOKE TO ME.
WHAT DID THEY SAY?

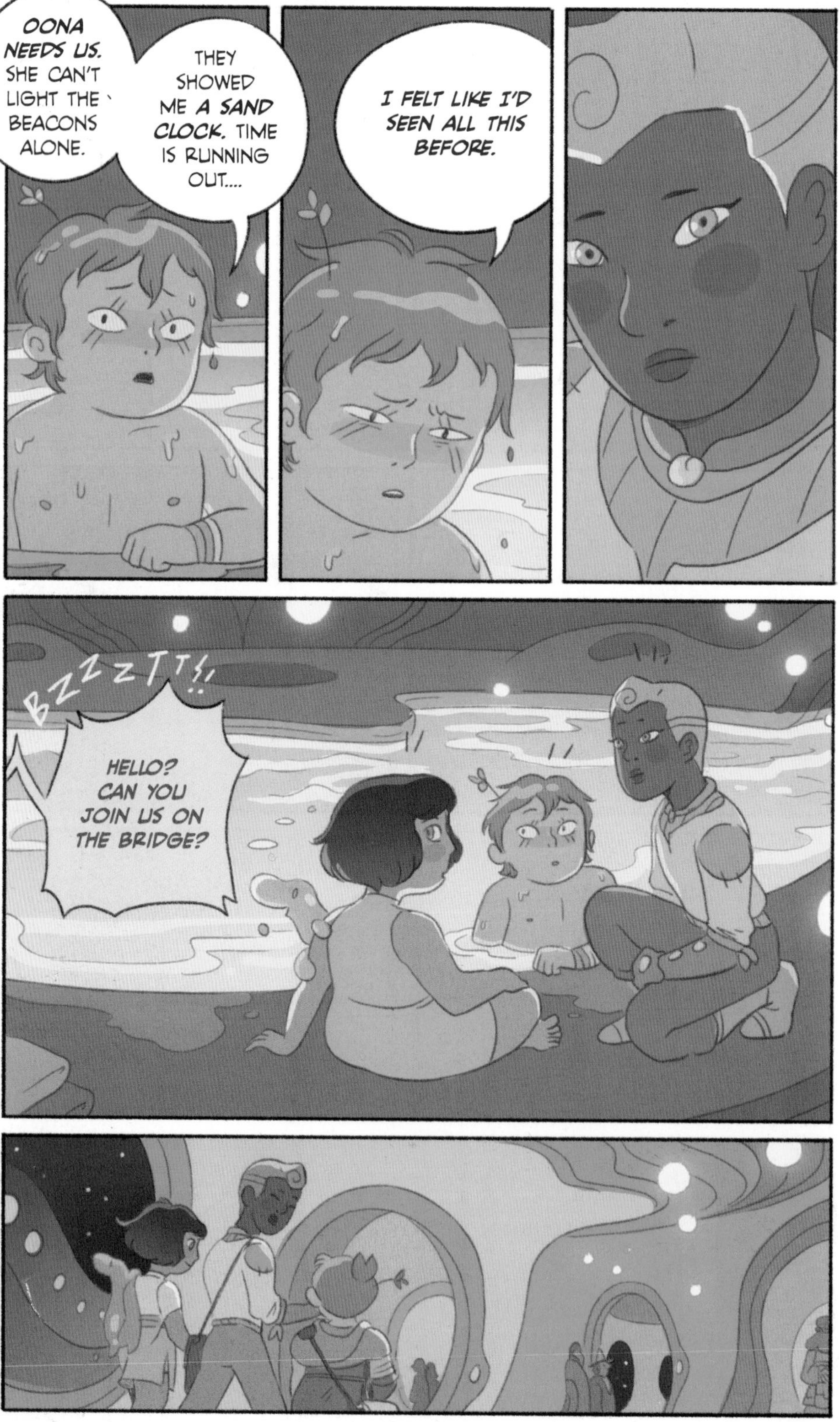
OONA NEEDS US. SHE CAN'T LIGHT THE BEACONS ALONE.
THEY SHOWED ME A SAND CLOCK. TIME IS RUNNING OUT....
I FELT LIKE I'D SEEN ALL THIS BEFORE.
BZZZZTTT!!
HELLO? CAN YOU JOIN US ON THE BRIDGE?

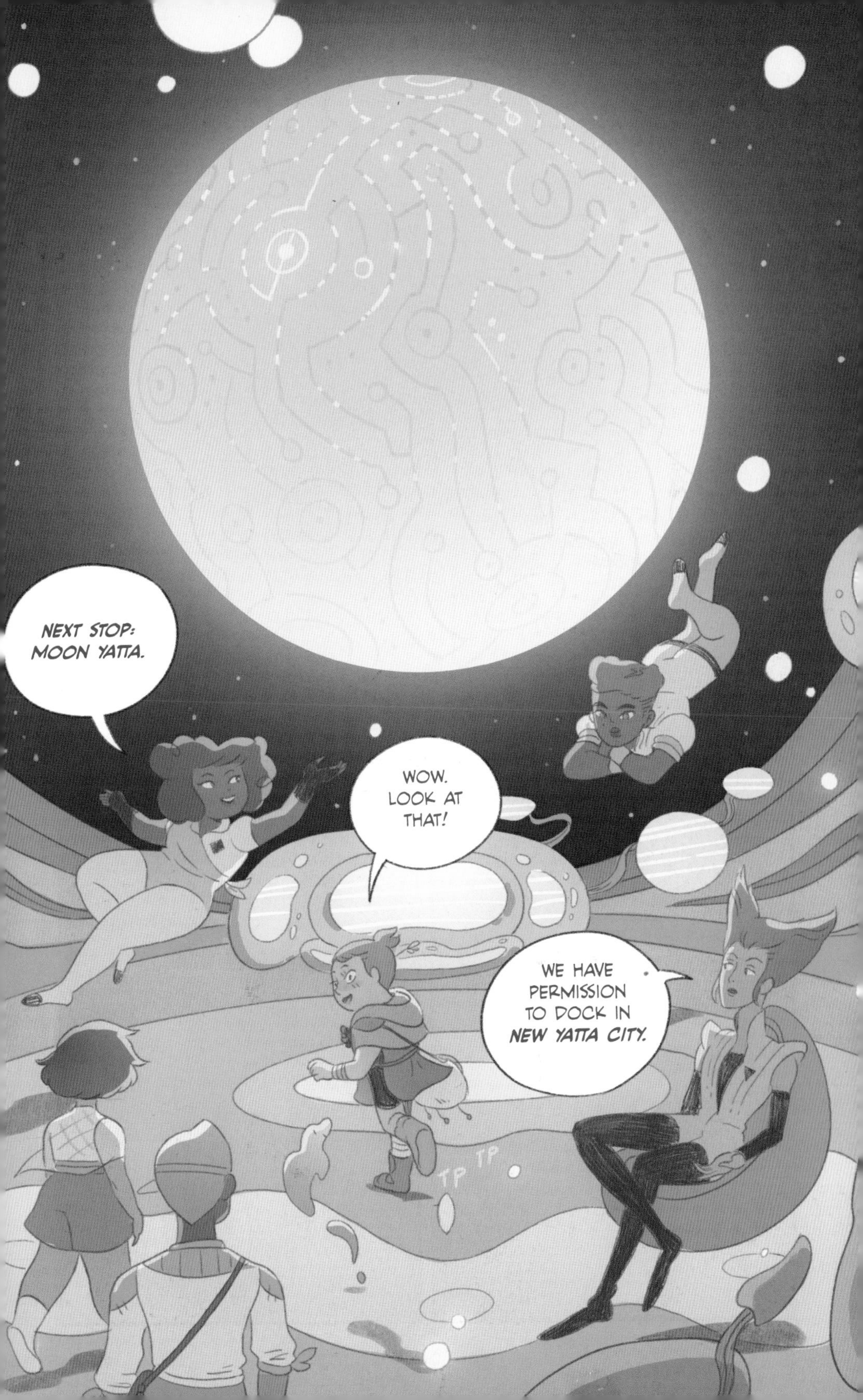
NEXT STOP: MOON YATTA.
WOW. LOOK AT THAT!
WE HAVE PERMISSION TO DOCK IN NEW YATTA CITY.
TP TP

OONA IS ALL OVER THE *CITIZEN FEEDS.*

BLUE BEACON RESISTS

RED BEACON: LIGHT

THE OONA

$44!

PLUCKY

OH WAIT! ANOTHER MESSAGE. GOVERNMENT CHANNEL...

"OONA LEE, JAX AMBOY, AND THEIR ENTOURAGE ARE INVITED TO LAND...

BEER!

...AT *THE GARNET PALACE!*"

BEEP BEEP

OONA, YOU'RE FAMOUS!

HOW ABOUT A MORE *DISCREET* ENTRANCE? LANDING IN THE SOUTHERN DESERT?

TIME IS RUNNING OUT. I NEED TO GO STRAIGHT TO THE *RED BEACON!*

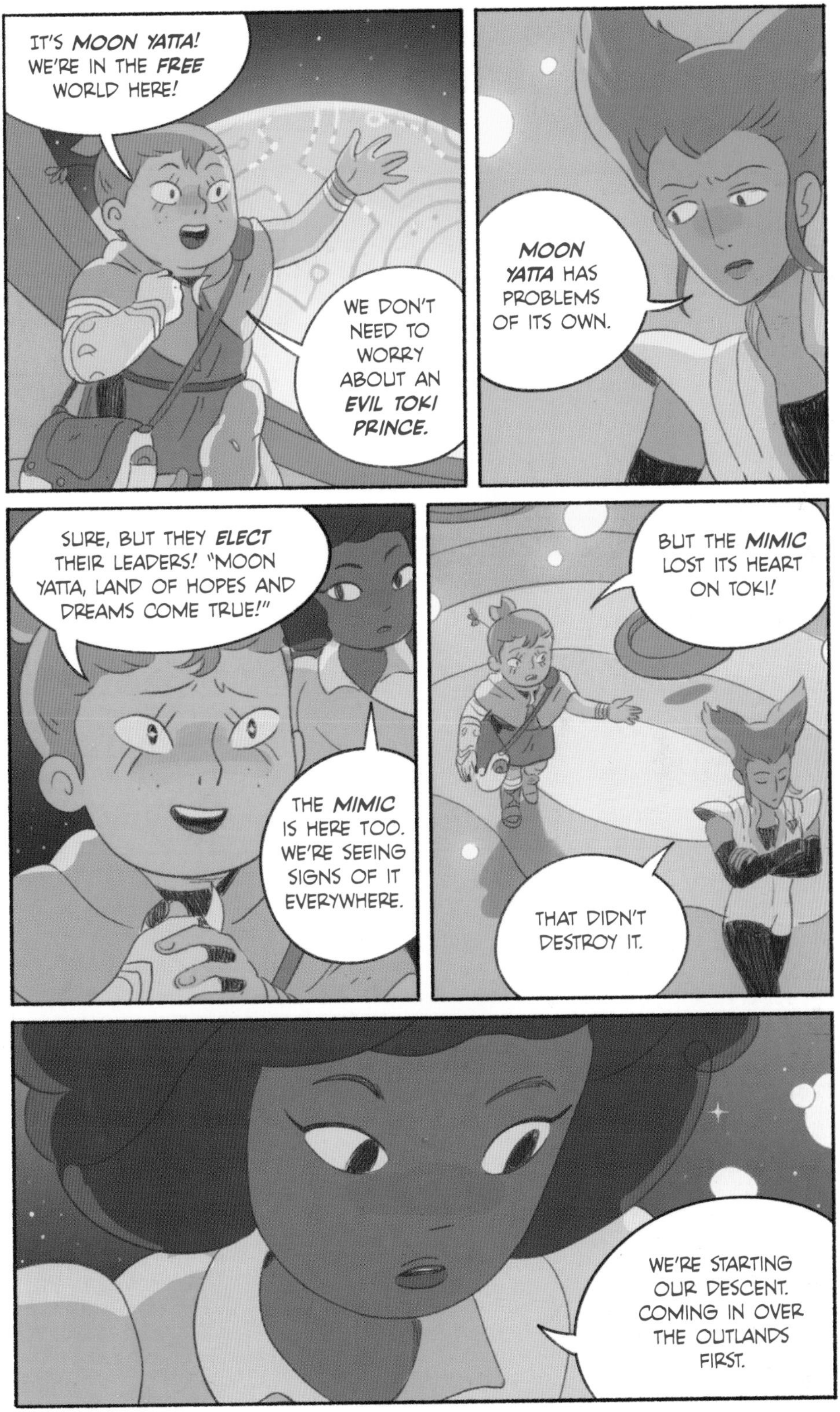
IT'S MOON YATTA! WE'RE IN THE FREE WORLD HERE!
MOON YATTA HAS PROBLEMS OF ITS OWN.
WE DON'T NEED TO WORRY ABOUT AN EVIL TOKI PRINCE.
SURE, BUT THEY ELECT THEIR LEADERS! "MOON YATTA, LAND OF HOPES AND DREAMS COME TRUE!"
THE MIMIC IS HERE TOO. WE'RE SEEING SIGNS OF IT EVERYWHERE.
BUT THE MIMIC LOST ITS HEART ON TOKI!
THAT DIDN'T DESTROY IT.
WE'RE STARTING OUR DESCENT. COMING IN OVER THE OUTLANDS FIRST.

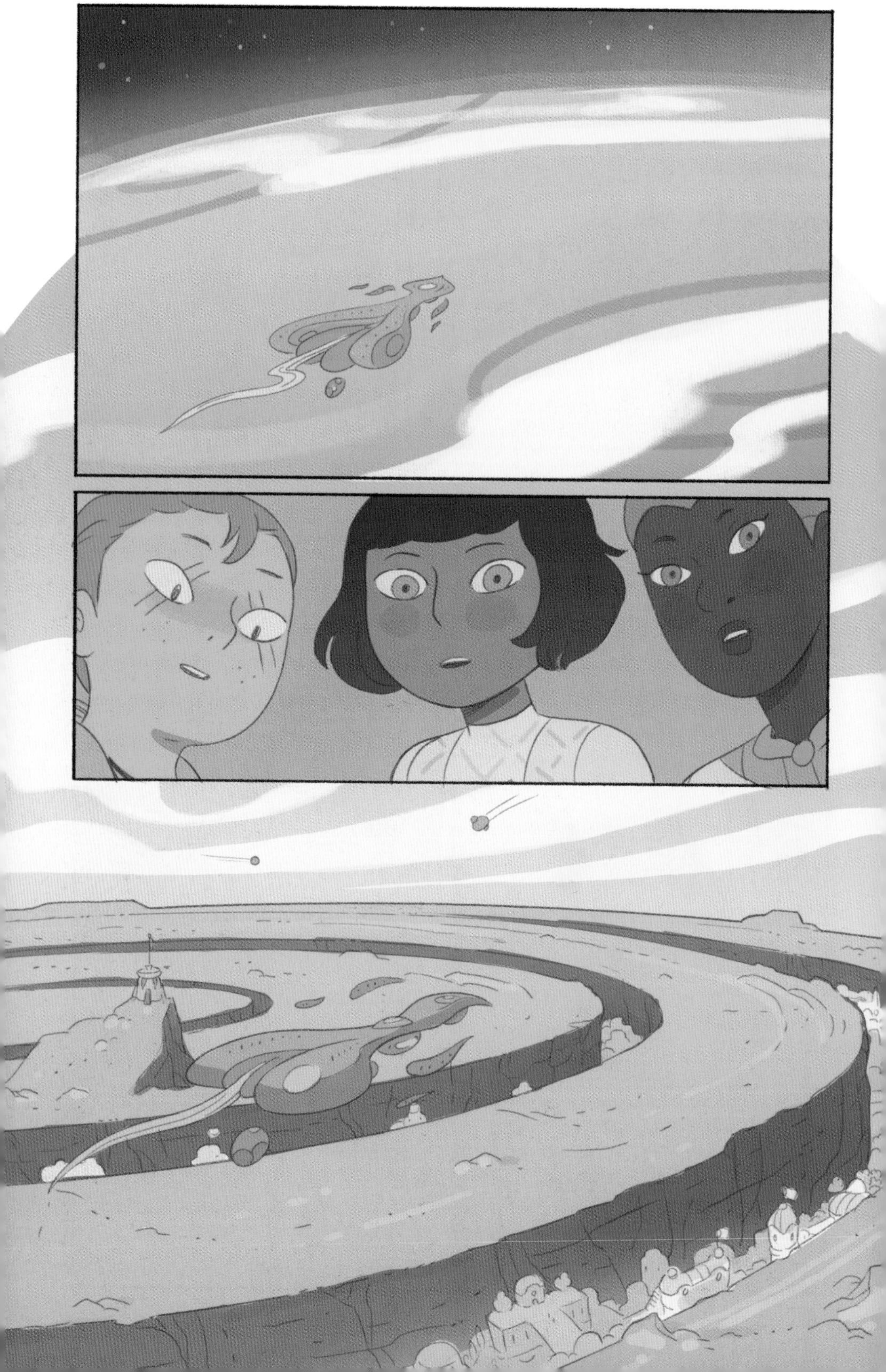

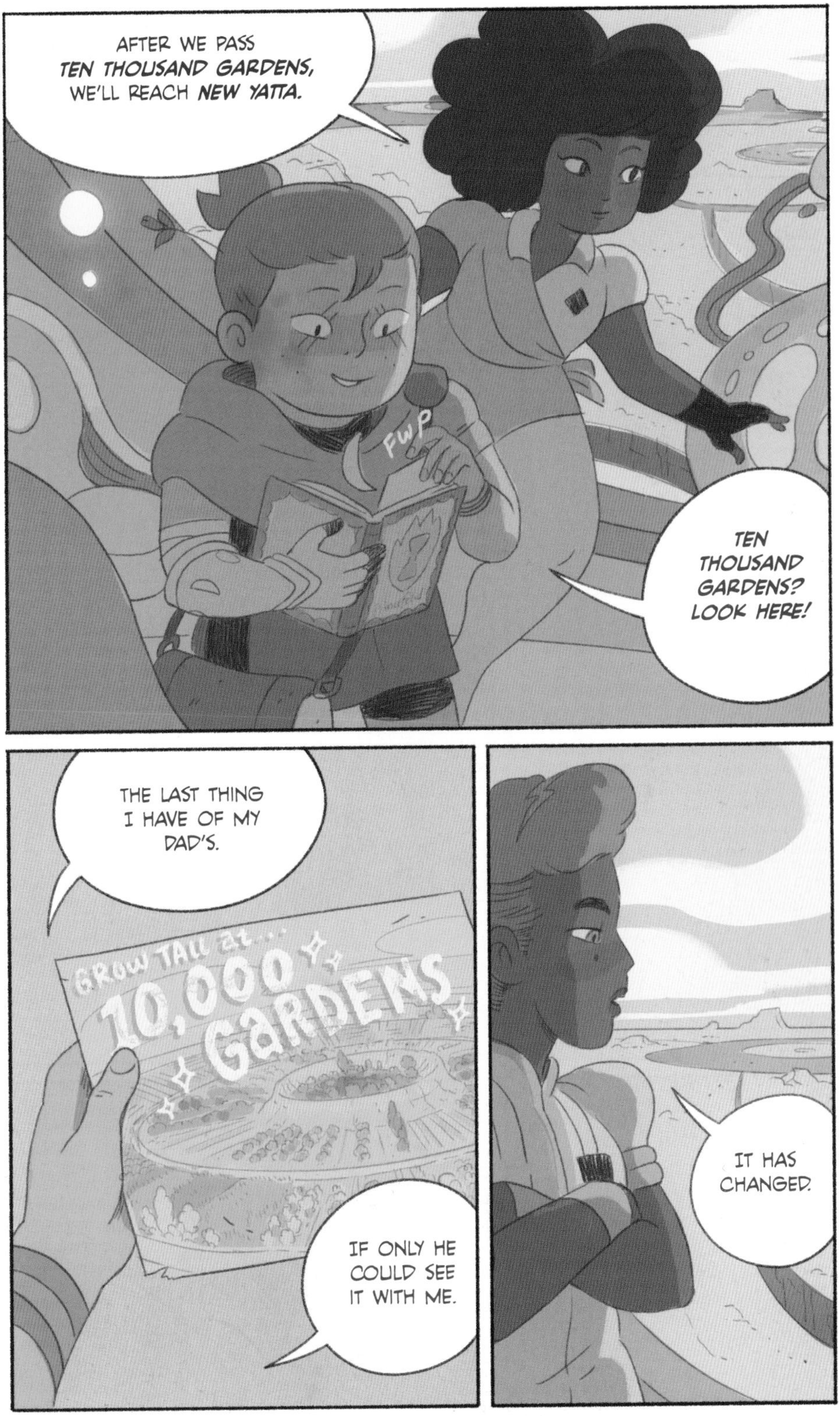
AFTER WE PASS TEN THOUSAND GARDENS, WE'LL REACH NEW YATTA.
FWP
TEN THOUSAND GARDENS? LOOK HERE!
THE LAST THING I HAVE OF MY DAD'S.
GROW TALL at... 10,000 GARDENS
IF ONLY HE COULD SEE IT WITH ME.
IT HAS CHANGED.

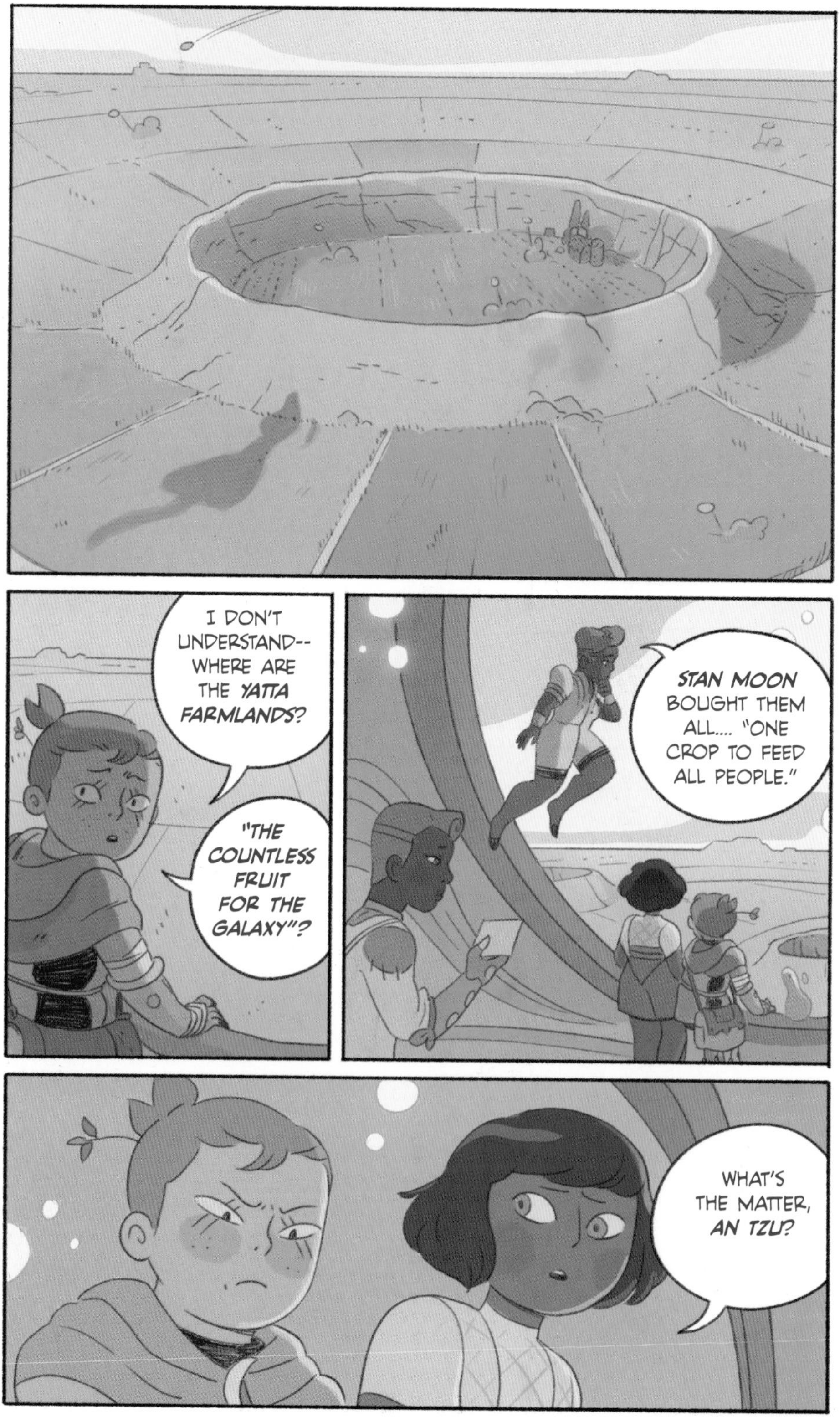

I DON'T UNDERSTAND-- WHERE ARE THE YATTA FARMLANDS?
"THE COUNTLESS FRUIT FOR THE GALAXY"?
STAN MOON BOUGHT THEM ALL.... "ONE CROP TO FEED ALL PEOPLE."
WHAT'S THE MATTER, AN TZU?

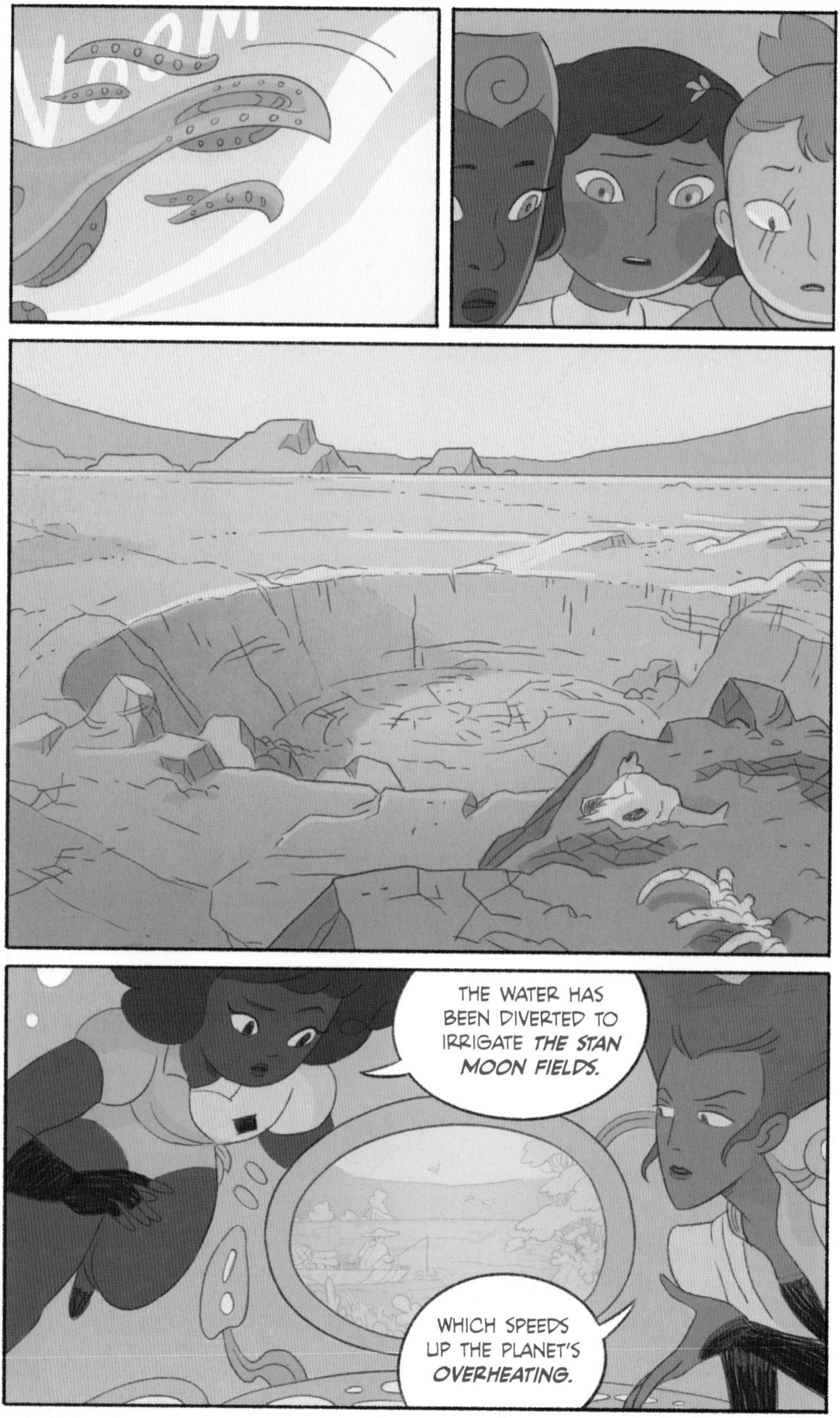
VOOM
THE WATER HAS BEEN DIVERTED TO IRRIGATE *THE STAN MOON FIELDS.*
WHICH SPEEDS UP THE PLANET'S *OVERHEATING.*

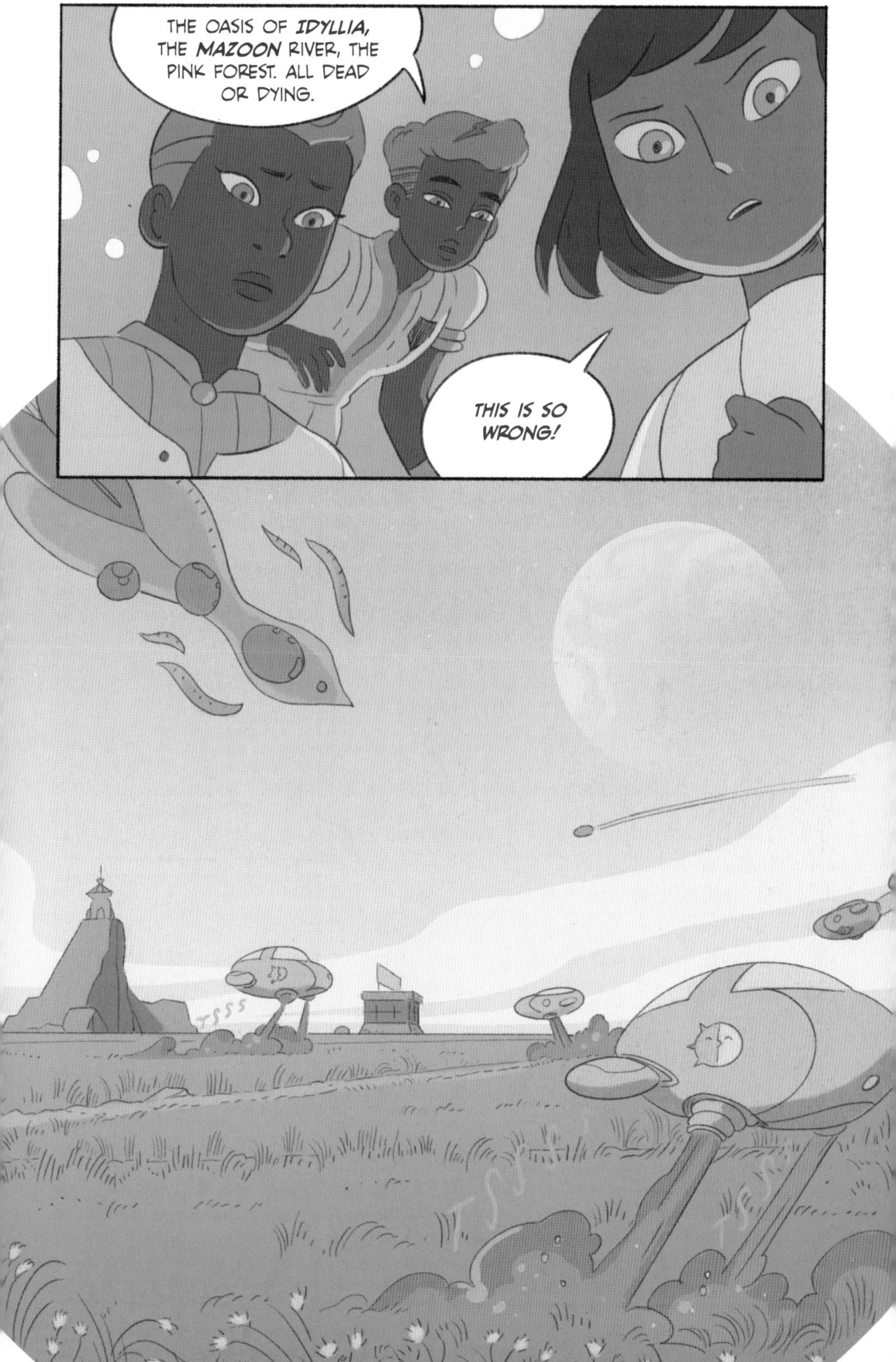
THE OASIS OF IDYLLIA, THE MAZOON RIVER, THE PINK FOREST. ALL DEAD OR DYING.
THIS IS SO WRONG!
TSSS

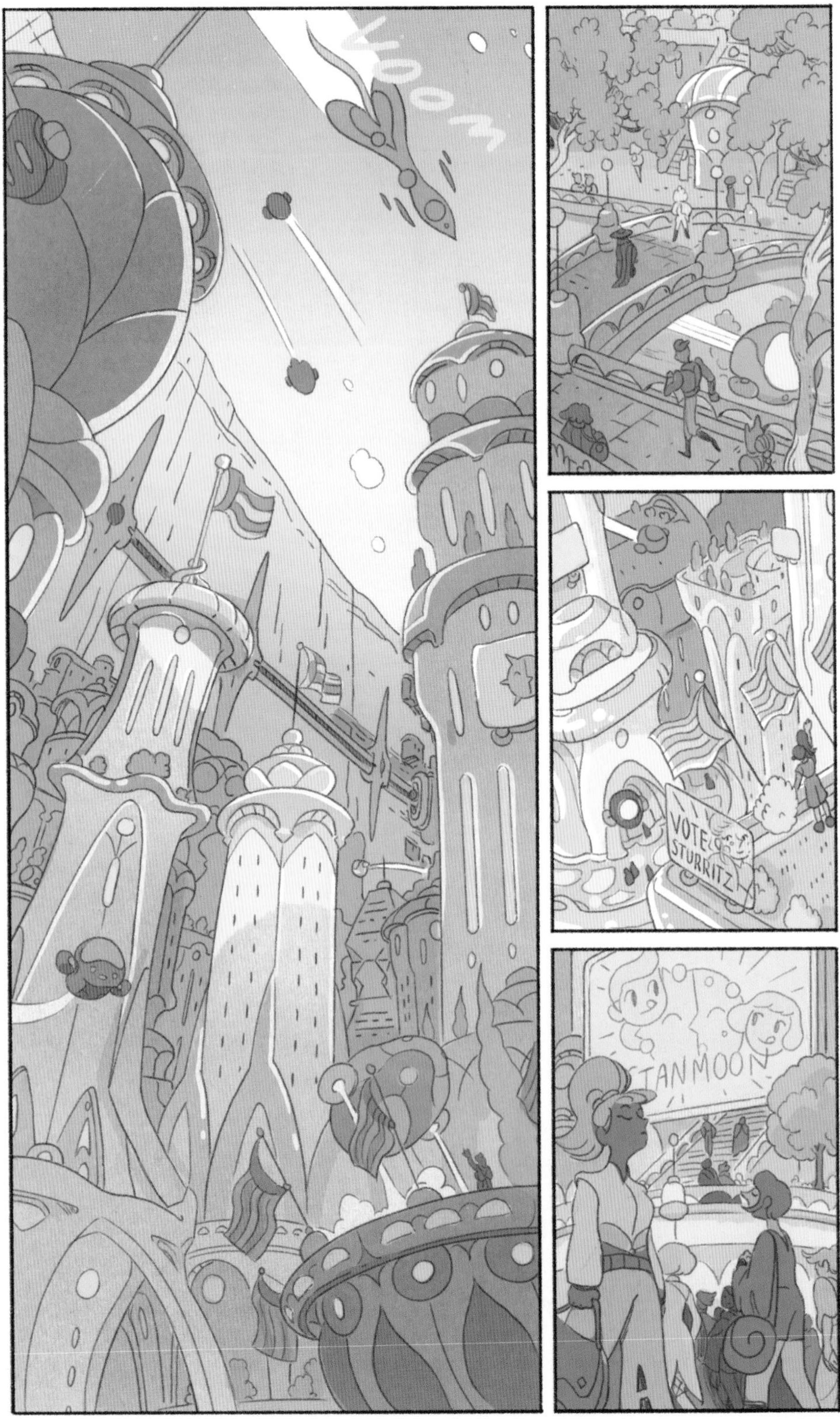
VOOM
VOTE STURRITZ
TANMOON

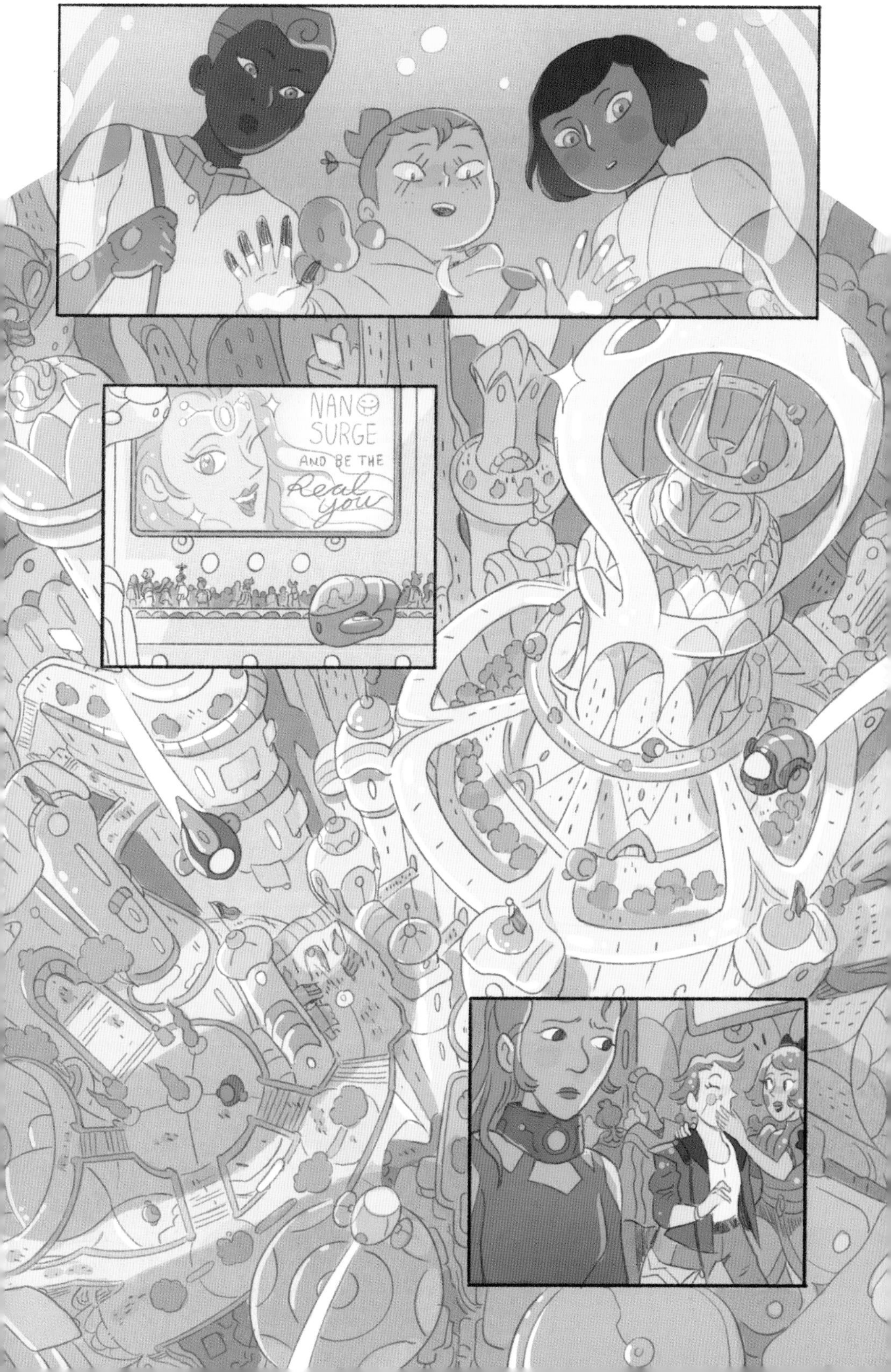
NANO SURGE
AND BE THE
Real you

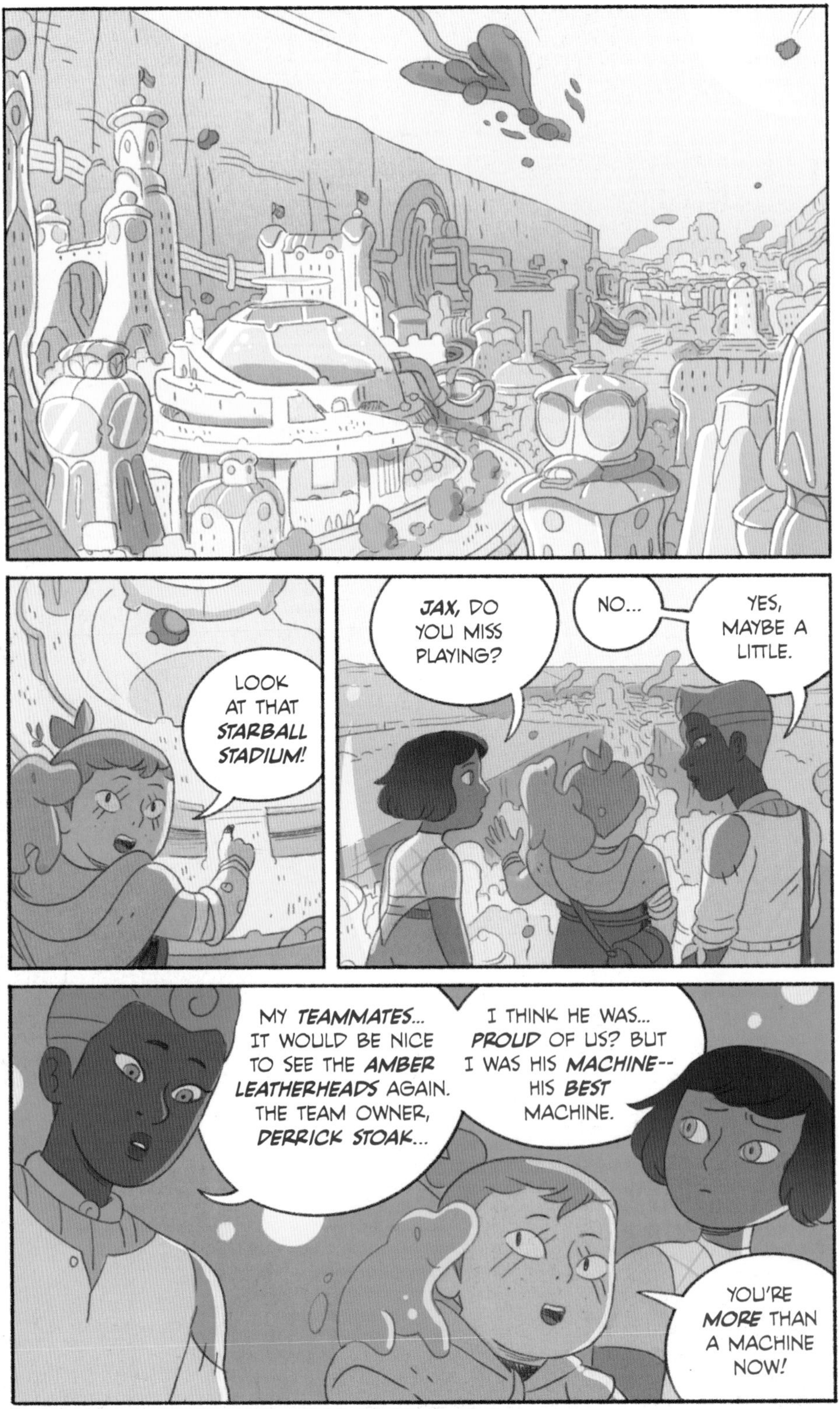
LOOK AT THAT STARBALL STADIUM!
JAX, DO YOU MISS PLAYING?
NO...
YES, MAYBE A LITTLE.
MY TEAMMATES... IT WOULD BE NICE TO SEE THE AMBER LEATHERHEADS AGAIN. THE TEAM OWNER, DERRICK STOAK...
I THINK HE WAS... PROUD OF US? BUT I WAS HIS MACHINE-- HIS BEST MACHINE.
YOU'RE MORE THAN A MACHINE NOW!

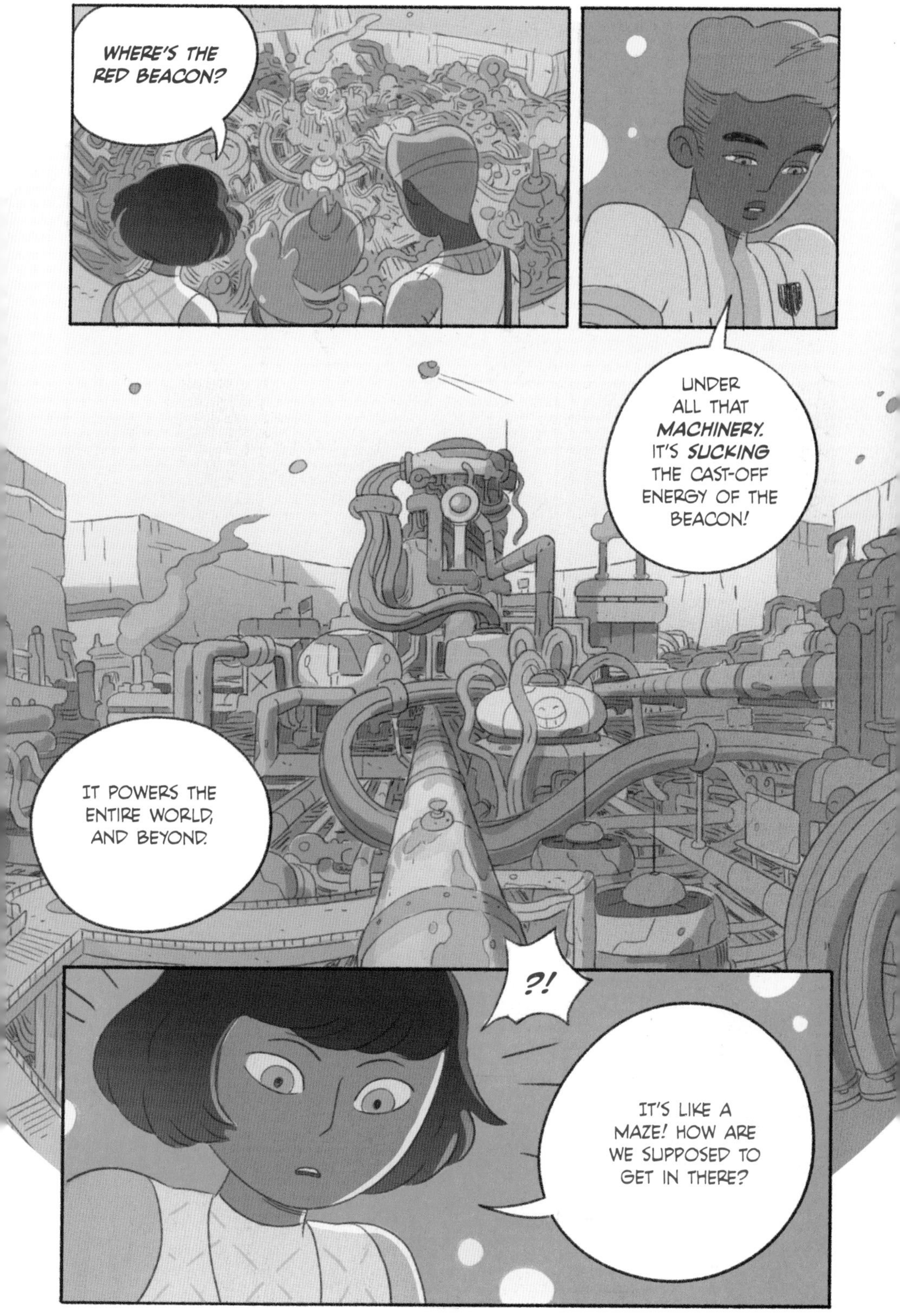
WHERE'S THE RED BEACON?
UNDER ALL THAT MACHINERY. IT'S SUCKING THE CAST-OFF ENERGY OF THE BEACON!
IT POWERS THE ENTIRE WORLD, AND BEYOND.
?!
IT'S LIKE A MAZE! HOW ARE WE SUPPOSED TO GET IN THERE?

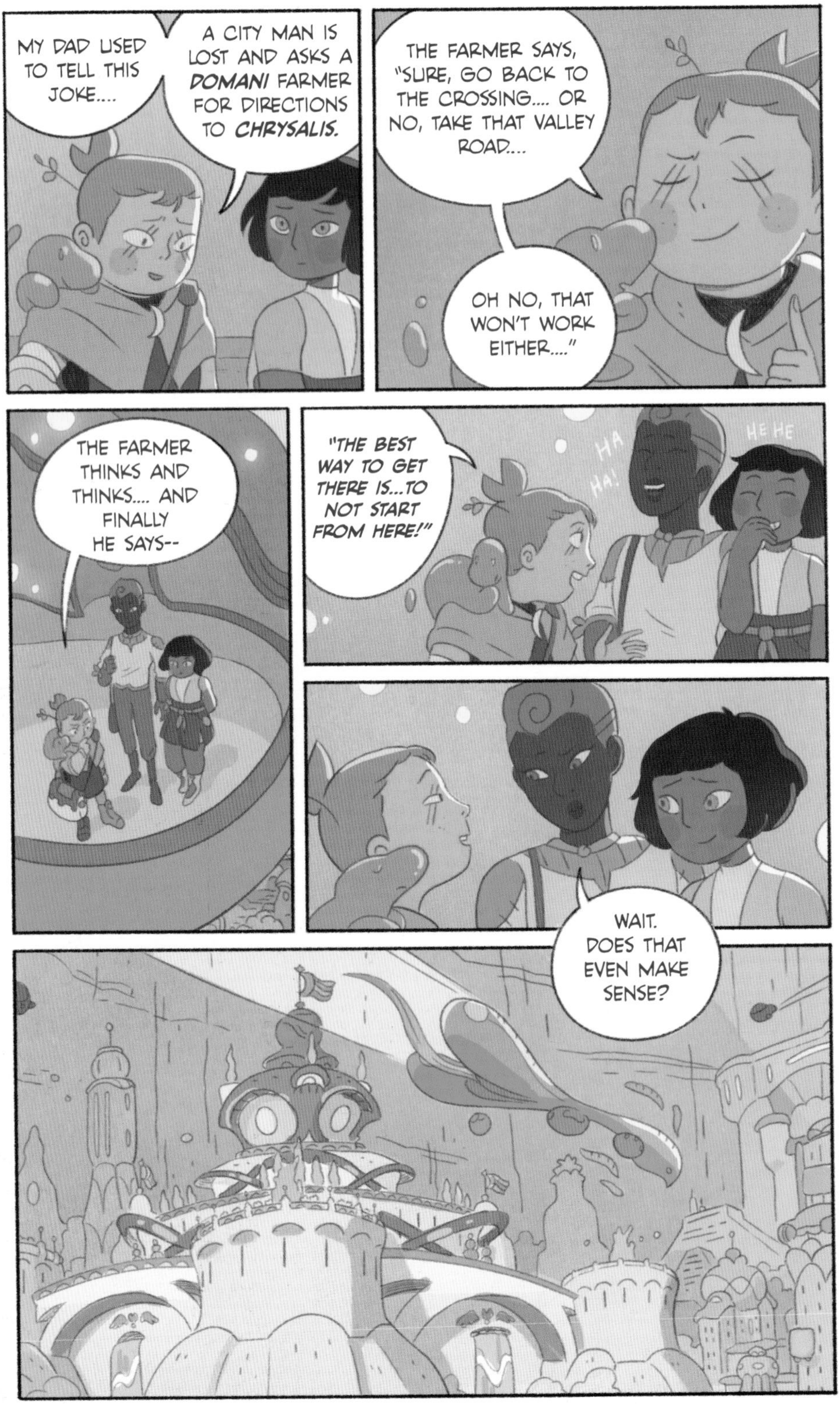
MY DAD USED TO TELL THIS JOKE....
A CITY MAN IS LOST AND ASKS A *DOMANI* FARMER FOR DIRECTIONS TO *CHRYSALIS.*
THE FARMER SAYS, "SURE, GO BACK TO THE CROSSING.... OR NO, TAKE THAT VALLEY ROAD....
OH NO, THAT WON'T WORK EITHER...."
THE FARMER THINKS AND THINKS.... AND FINALLY HE SAYS--
*"THE BEST WAY TO GET THERE IS...TO NOT START FROM HERE!"*
HA HA!
HE HE
WAIT. DOES THAT EVEN MAKE SENSE?

## Chapter 2

# THE GARNET PALACE

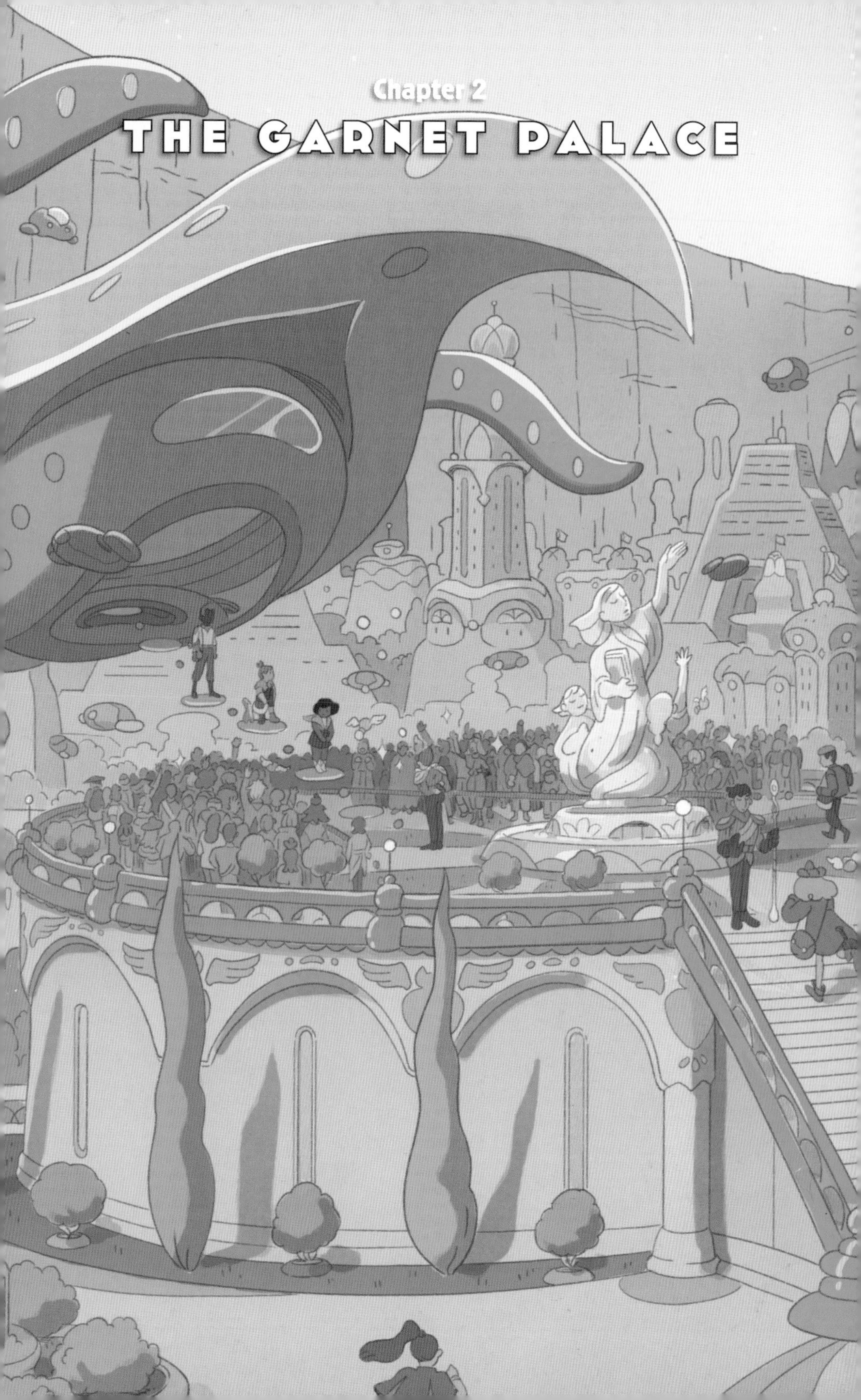

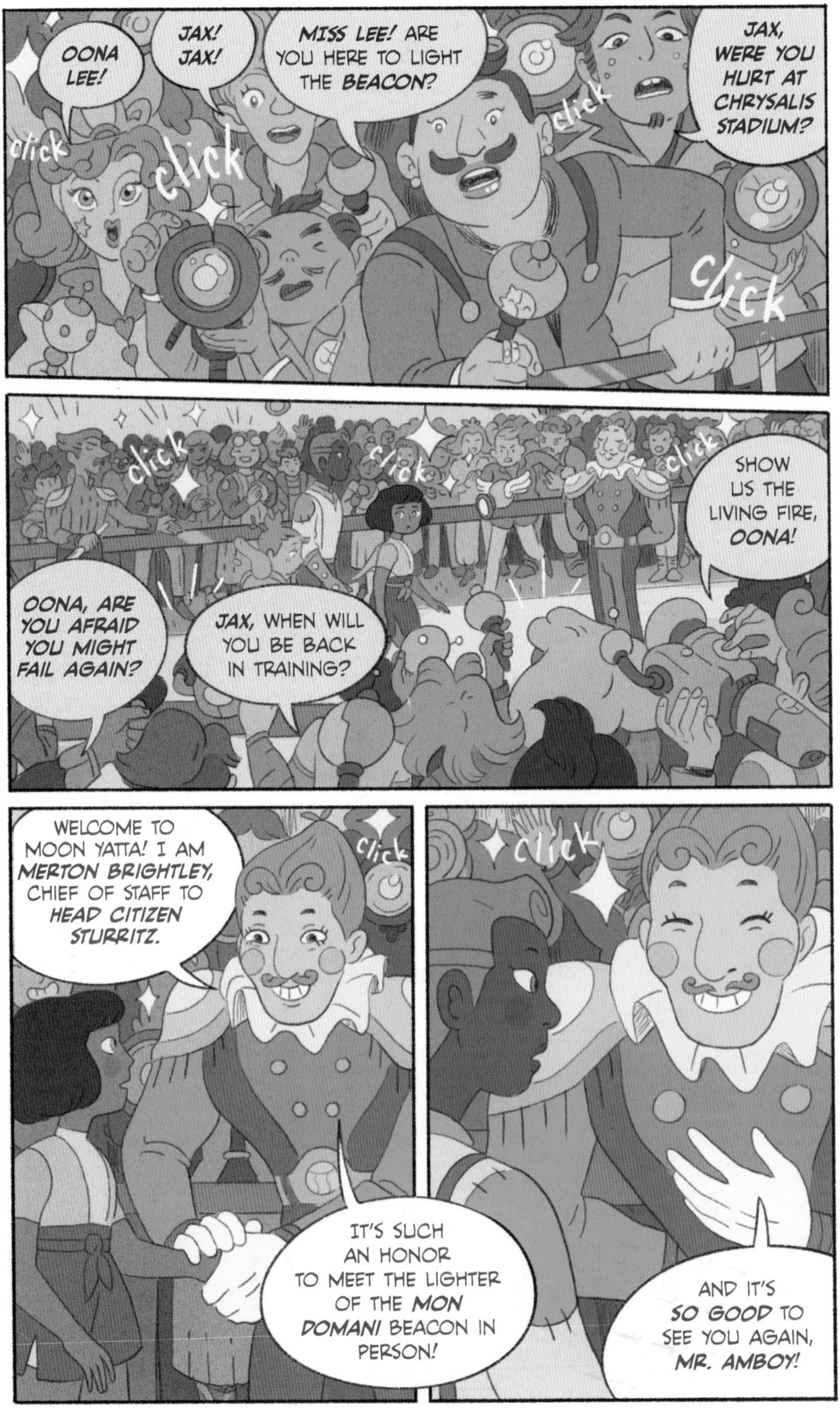
OONA LEE!
JAX! JAX!
MISS LEE! ARE YOU HERE TO LIGHT THE BEACON?
JAX, WERE YOU HURT AT CHRYSALIS STADIUM?
click
click
click
click
click
click
click
SHOW US THE LIVING FIRE, OONA!
OONA, ARE YOU AFRAID YOU MIGHT FAIL AGAIN?
JAX, WHEN WILL YOU BE BACK IN TRAINING?
WELCOME TO MOON YATTA! I AM MERTON BRIGHTLEY, CHIEF OF STAFF TO HEAD CITIZEN STURRITZ.
click
IT'S SUCH AN HONOR TO MEET THE LIGHTER OF THE MON DOMANI BEACON IN PERSON!
click
AND IT'S SO GOOD TO SEE YOU AGAIN, MR. AMBOY!

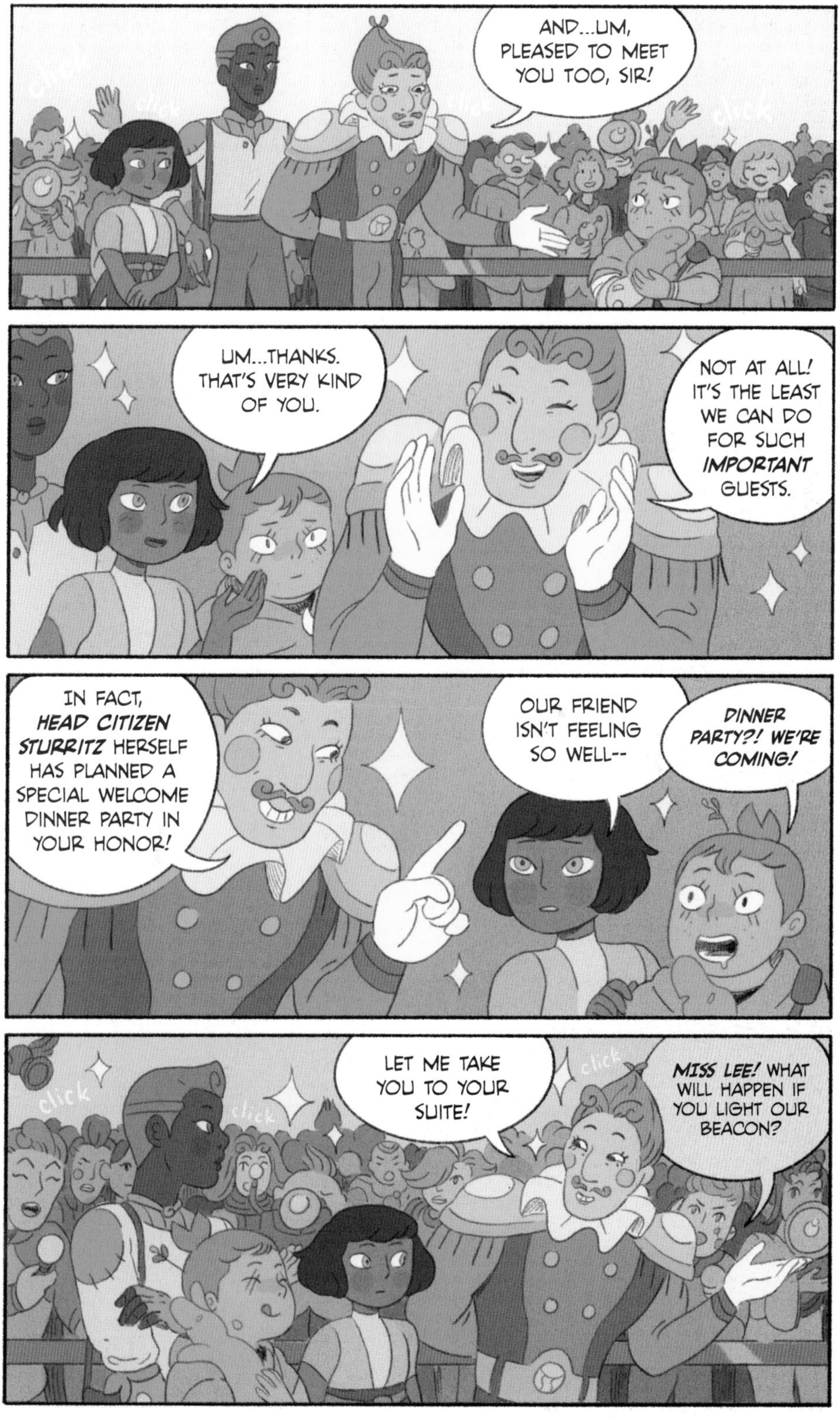
AND...UM, PLEASED TO MEET YOU TOO, SIR!
UM...THANKS. THAT'S VERY KIND OF YOU.
NOT AT ALL! IT'S THE LEAST WE CAN DO FOR SUCH *IMPORTANT* GUESTS.
IN FACT, ***HEAD CITIZEN STURRITZ*** HERSELF HAS PLANNED A SPECIAL WELCOME DINNER PARTY IN YOUR HONOR!
OUR FRIEND ISN'T FEELING SO WELL--
*DINNER PARTY?! WE'RE COMING!*
LET ME TAKE YOU TO YOUR SUITE!
***MISS LEE!*** WHAT WILL HAPPEN IF YOU LIGHT OUR BEACON?

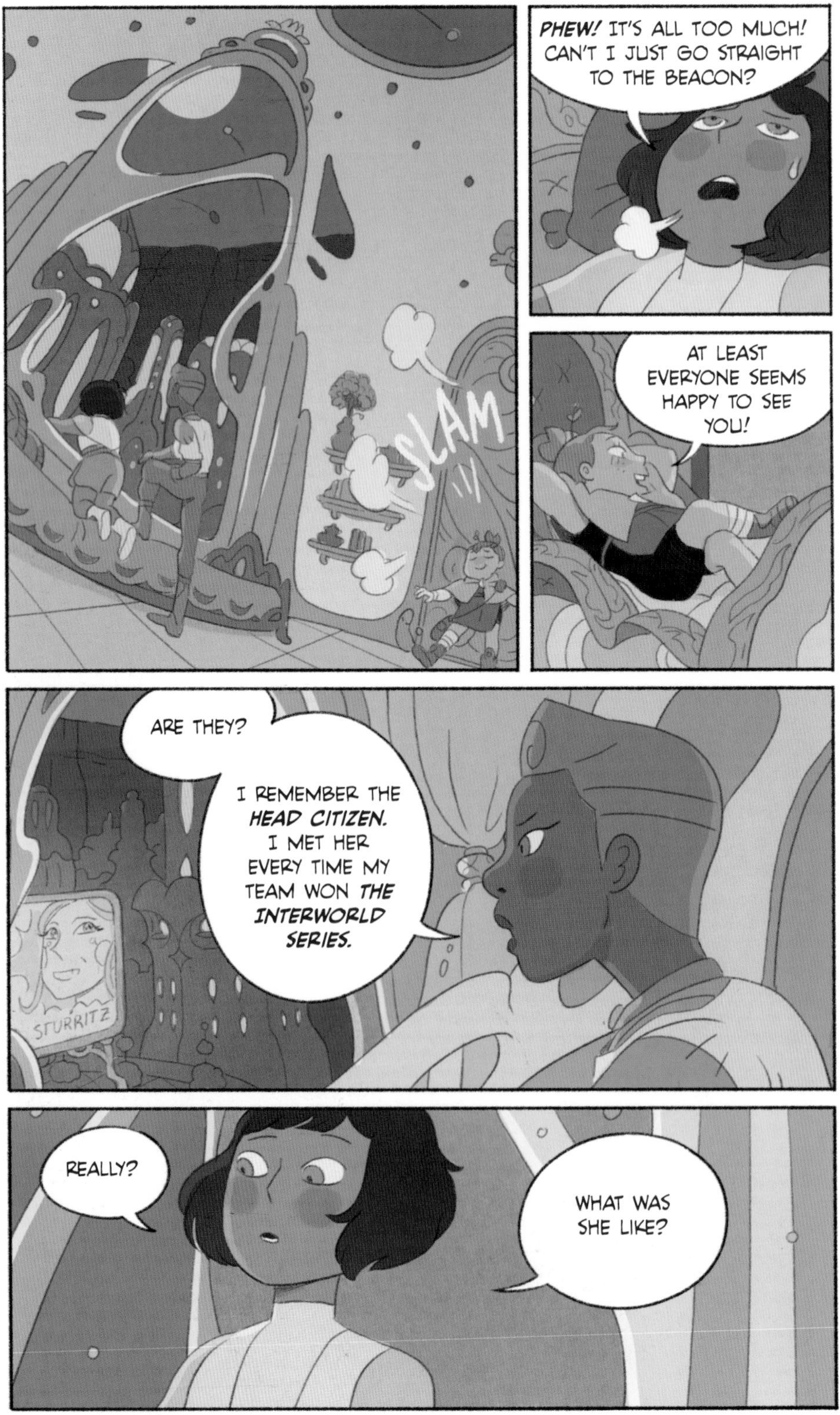
SLAM
PHEW! IT'S ALL TOO MUCH! CAN'T I JUST GO STRAIGHT TO THE BEACON?
AT LEAST EVERYONE SEEMS HAPPY TO SEE YOU!
ARE THEY?
I REMEMBER THE HEAD CITIZEN. I MET HER EVERY TIME MY TEAM WON THE INTERWORLD SERIES.
STURRITZ
REALLY?
WHAT WAS SHE LIKE?

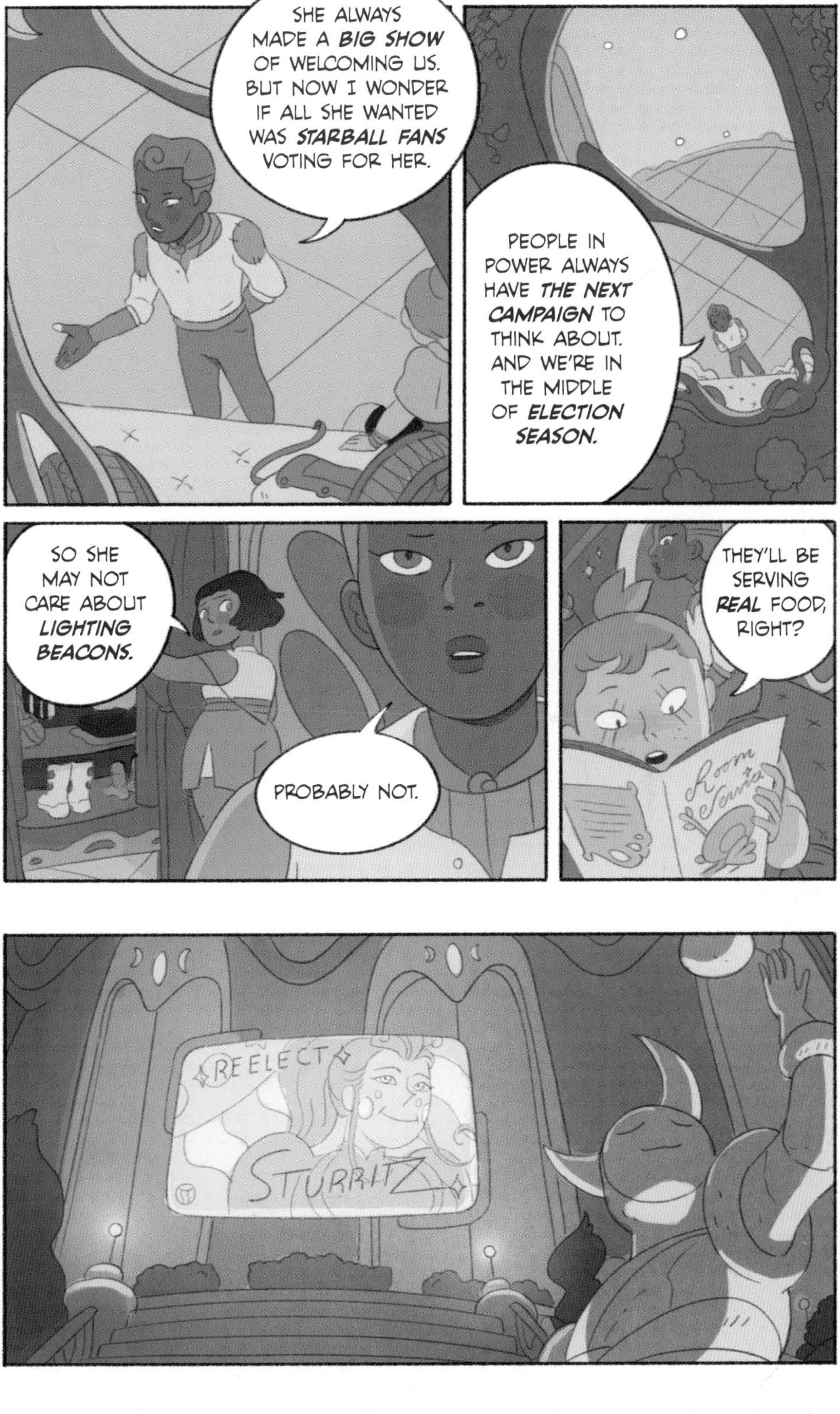
SHE ALWAYS MADE A **BIG SHOW** OF WELCOMING US. BUT NOW I WONDER IF ALL SHE WANTED WAS **STARBALL FANS** VOTING FOR HER.
PEOPLE IN POWER ALWAYS HAVE **THE NEXT CAMPAIGN** TO THINK ABOUT. AND WE'RE IN THE MIDDLE OF **ELECTION SEASON.**
SO SHE MAY NOT CARE ABOUT **LIGHTING BEACONS.**
PROBABLY NOT.
THEY'LL BE SERVING **REAL** FOOD, RIGHT?
Room Service
REELECT
STURRITZ

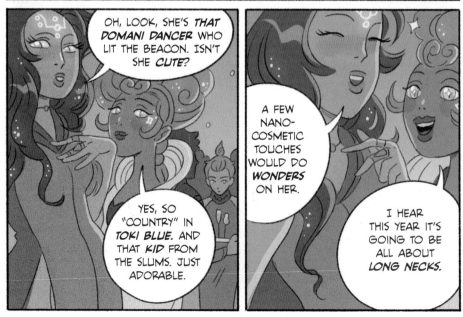

OH, LOOK, SHE'S *THAT DOMANI DANCER* WHO LIT THE BEACON. ISN'T SHE *CUTE?*

YES, SO "COUNTRY" IN *TOKI BLUE.* AND THAT *KID* FROM THE SLUMS. JUST ADORABLE.

A FEW NANO-COSMETIC TOUCHES WOULD DO *WONDERS* ON HER.

I HEAR THIS YEAR IT'S GOING TO BE ALL ABOUT *LONG NECKS.*

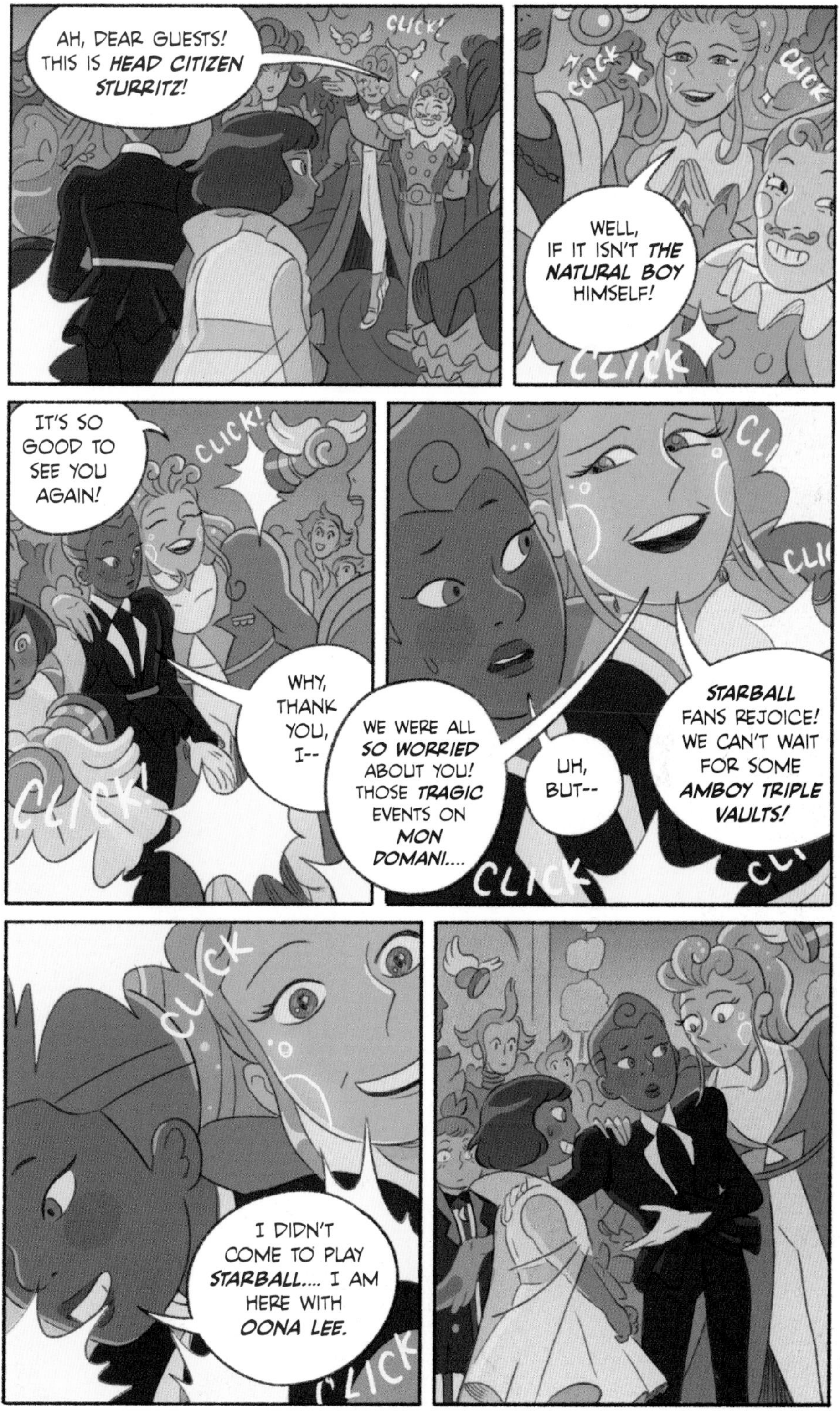
AH, DEAR GUESTS! THIS IS HEAD CITIZEN STURRITZ!
CLICK!
CLICK
CLICK
WELL, IF IT ISN'T THE NATURAL BOY HIMSELF!
CLICK
IT'S SO GOOD TO SEE YOU AGAIN!
CLICK!
WHY, THANK YOU, I--
CLICK!
WE WERE ALL SO WORRIED ABOUT YOU! THOSE TRAGIC EVENTS ON MON DOMANI....
UH, BUT--
STARBALL FANS REJOICE! WE CAN'T WAIT FOR SOME AMBOY TRIPLE VAULTS!
CLICK
CLICK
I DIDN'T COME TO PLAY STARBALL.... I AM HERE WITH OONA LEE.
CLICK

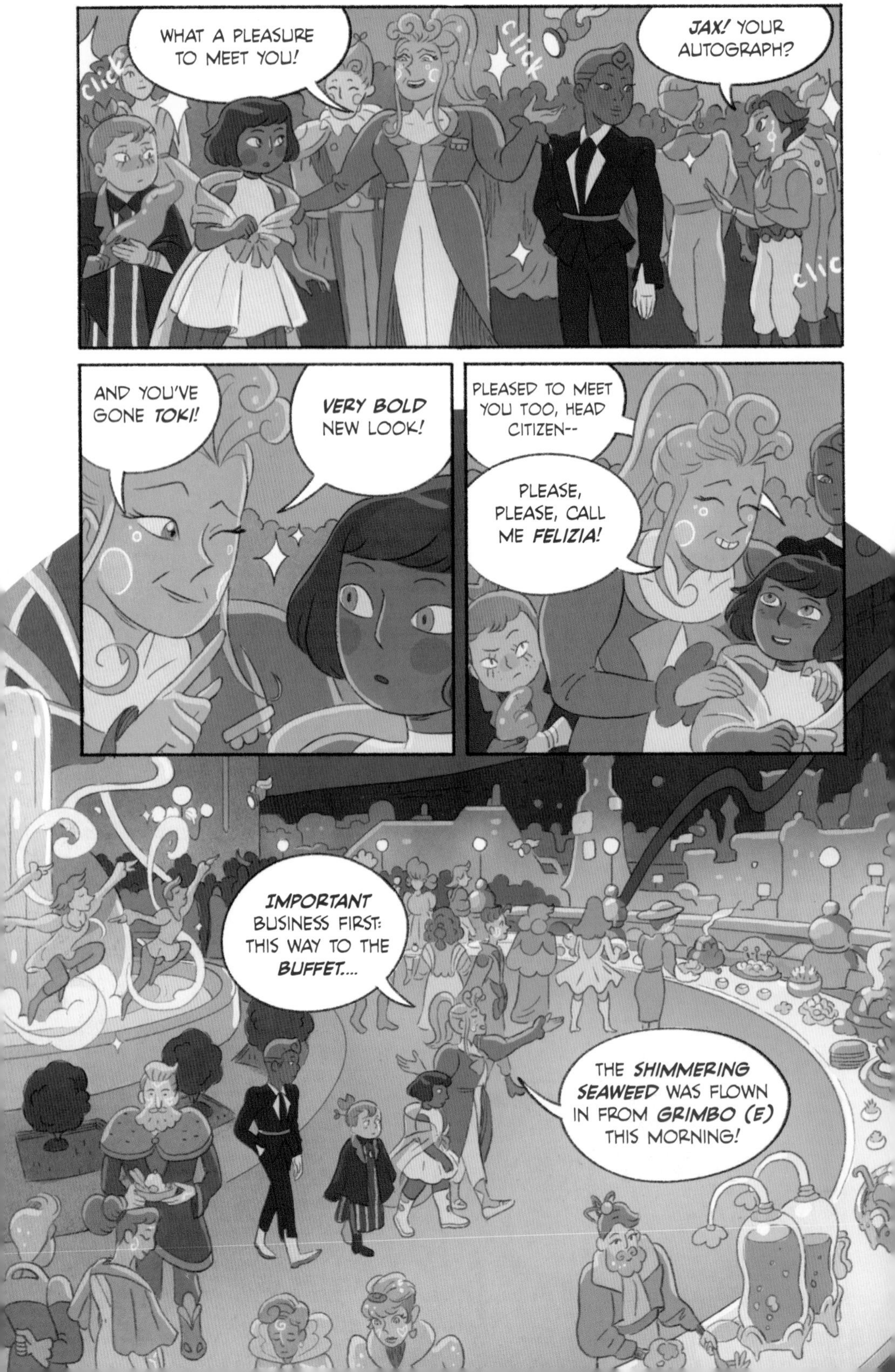
click
WHAT A PLEASURE TO MEET YOU!
click
JAX! YOUR AUTOGRAPH?
AND YOU'VE GONE TOKI!
VERY BOLD NEW LOOK!
PLEASED TO MEET YOU TOO, HEAD CITIZEN--
PLEASE, PLEASE, CALL ME FELIZIA!
IMPORTANT BUSINESS FIRST: THIS WAY TO THE BUFFET....
THE SHIMMERING SEAWEED WAS FLOWN IN FROM GRIMBO (E) THIS MORNING!

SO WHERE ARE THESE *SHAPESHIFTERS* NOW?

IT CELEBRATES *THE BATTLE OF THE RED BEACON.*

THAT'S WHEN THE FIRST YATTANS SURRENDERED THE BEACON.... AFTER THAT, *TRANSFORMING DANCES* BECAME ILLEGAL. PEOPLE WERE AFRAID, YOU SEE.

*LONG STORY.*

MOSTLY STILL HERE, BUT THEY HAVE TO WEAR *FORM-LOCK COLLARS.*

THE ONES WHO REFUSE HIDE IN *THE RUBY DESERT.* THEY FACE *ARREST* IF THEY ENTER ANY POPULATED AREA.

*ARREST?* FOR BEING SHAPESHIFTERS? ON *MOON YATTA,* LAND OF FREEDOM AND DREAMS?

HAVE OUR GUESTS BEEN ENJOYING THEMSELVES, *BRIGHTLEY?*

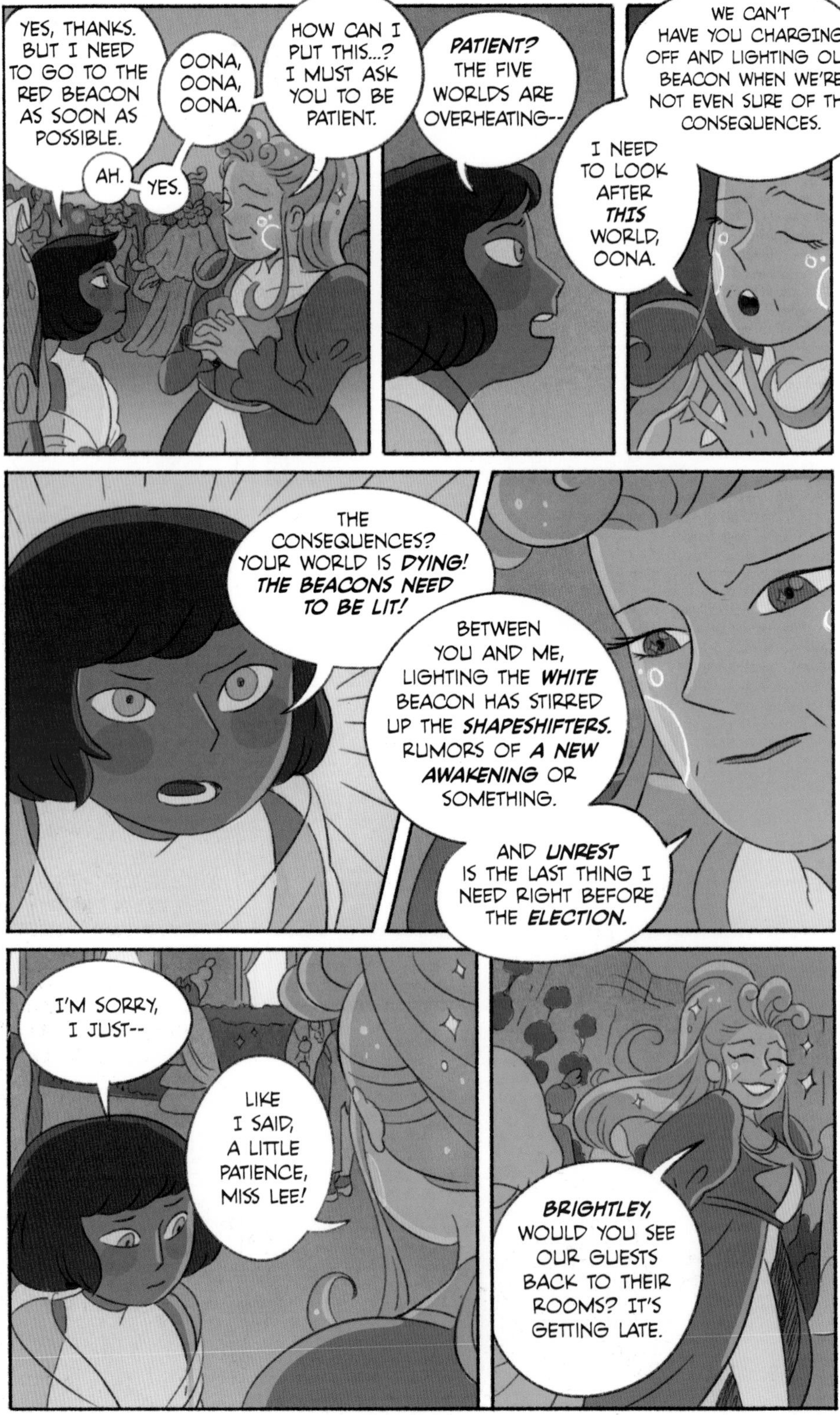
YES, THANKS. BUT I NEED TO GO TO THE RED BEACON AS SOON AS POSSIBLE.
AH.
OONA, OONA, OONA.
YES.
HOW CAN I PUT THIS...? I MUST ASK YOU TO BE PATIENT.
*PATIENT?* THE FIVE WORLDS ARE OVERHEATING--
WE CAN'T HAVE YOU CHARGING OFF AND LIGHTING OUR BEACON WHEN WE'RE NOT EVEN SURE OF THE CONSEQUENCES.
I NEED TO LOOK AFTER *THIS* WORLD, OONA.
THE CONSEQUENCES? YOUR WORLD IS *DYING!* *THE BEACONS NEED TO BE LIT!*
BETWEEN YOU AND ME, LIGHTING THE *WHITE* BEACON HAS STIRRED UP THE *SHAPESHIFTERS.* RUMORS OF *A NEW AWAKENING* OR SOMETHING.
AND *UNREST* IS THE LAST THING I NEED RIGHT BEFORE THE *ELECTION.*
I'M SORRY, I JUST--
LIKE I SAID, A LITTLE PATIENCE, MISS LEE!
*BRIGHTLEY,* WOULD YOU SEE OUR GUESTS BACK TO THEIR ROOMS? IT'S GETTING LATE.

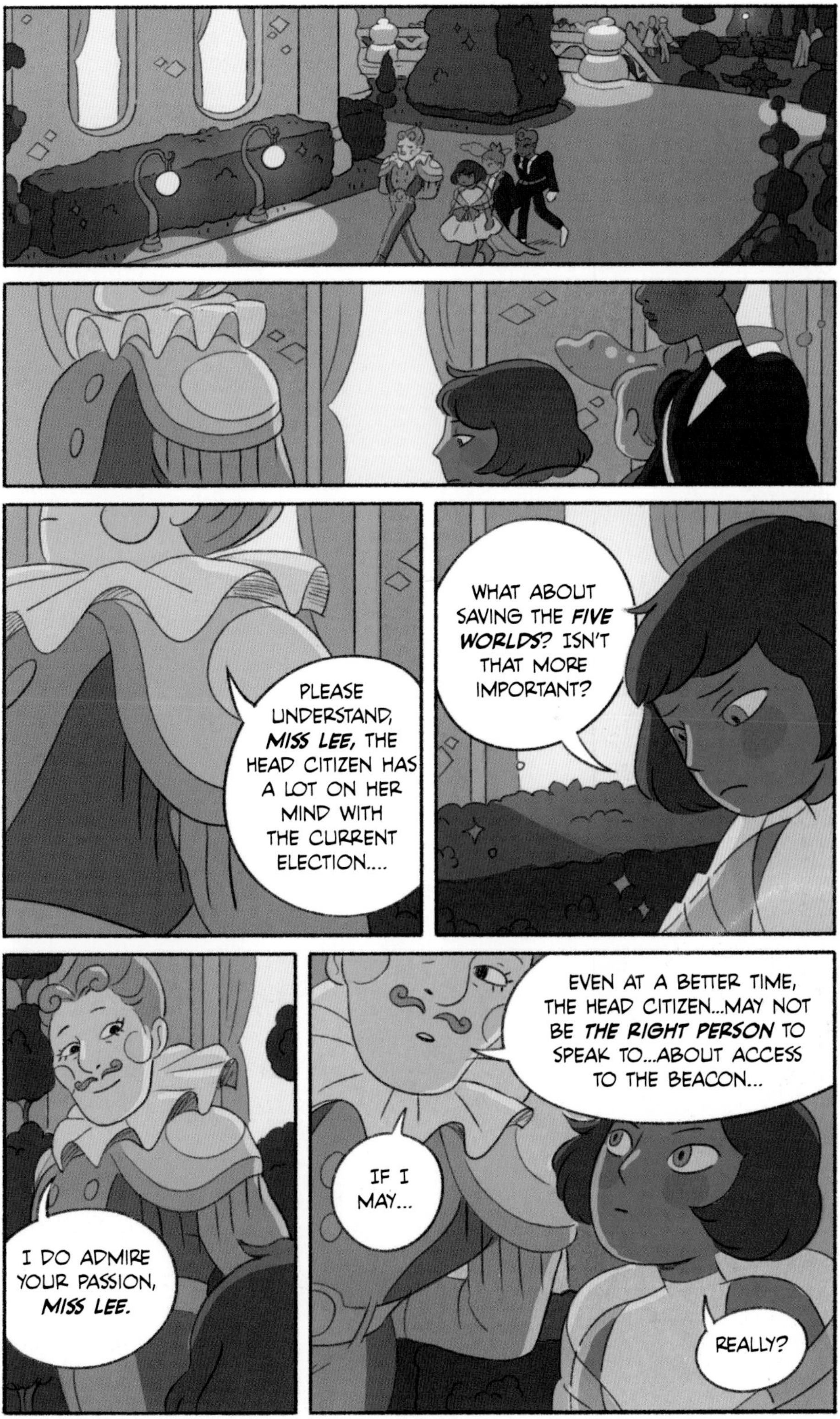
PLEASE UNDERSTAND, MISS LEE, THE HEAD CITIZEN HAS A LOT ON HER MIND WITH THE CURRENT ELECTION....
WHAT ABOUT SAVING THE FIVE WORLDS? ISN'T THAT MORE IMPORTANT?
I DO ADMIRE YOUR PASSION, MISS LEE.
IF I MAY...
EVEN AT A BETTER TIME, THE HEAD CITIZEN...MAY NOT BE THE RIGHT PERSON TO SPEAK TO...ABOUT ACCESS TO THE BEACON...
REALLY?

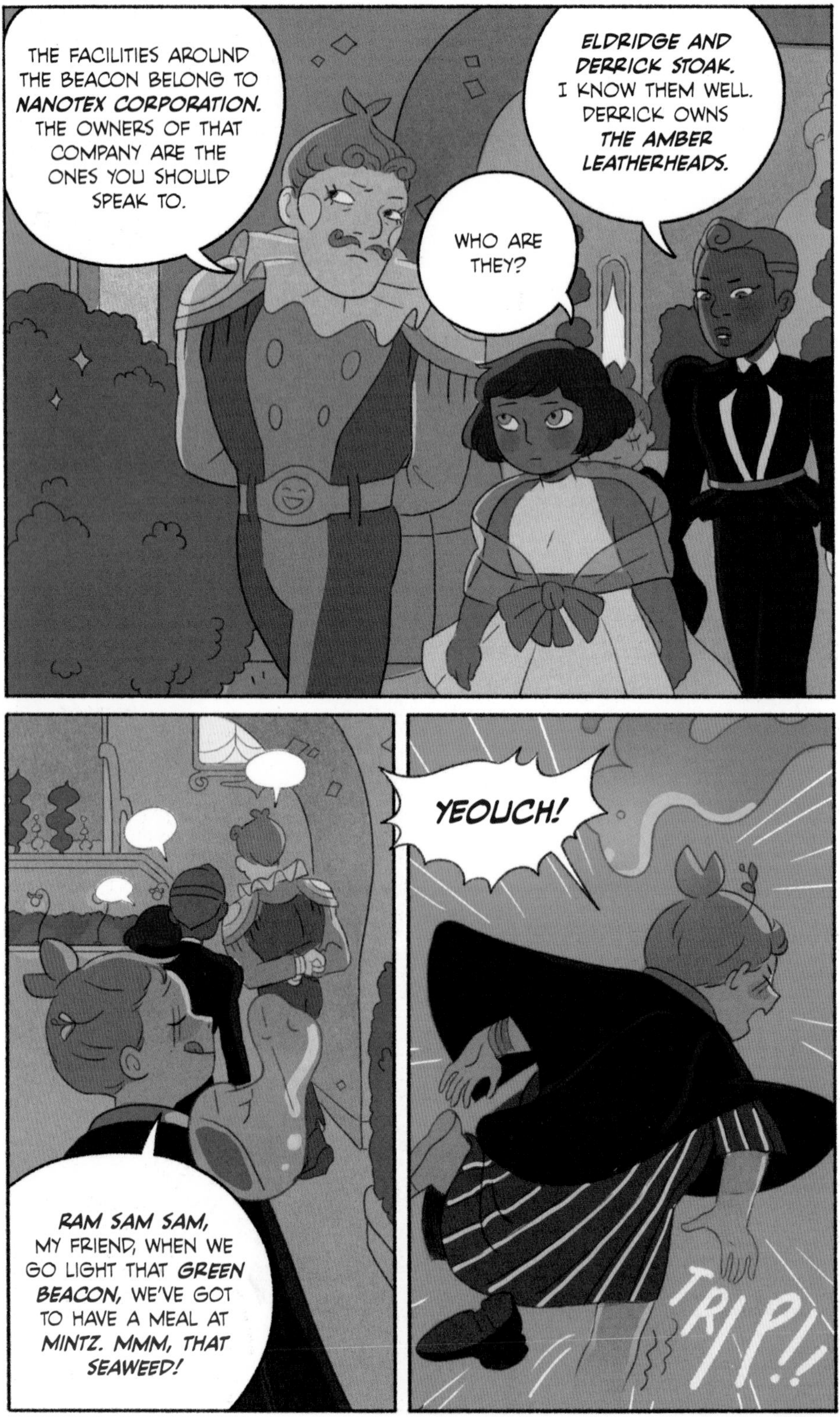
THE FACILITIES AROUND THE BEACON BELONG TO NANOTEX CORPORATION. THE OWNERS OF THAT COMPANY ARE THE ONES YOU SHOULD SPEAK TO.
WHO ARE THEY?
ELDRIDGE AND DERRICK STOAK. I KNOW THEM WELL. DERRICK OWNS THE AMBER LEATHERHEADS.
RAM SAM SAM, MY FRIEND, WHEN WE GO LIGHT THAT GREEN BEACON, WE'VE GOT TO HAVE A MEAL AT MINTZ. MMM, THAT SEAWEED!
YEOUCH!
TRIP!!

Chapter 3

# NOT THE MOON YATTA OF HIS DREAMS

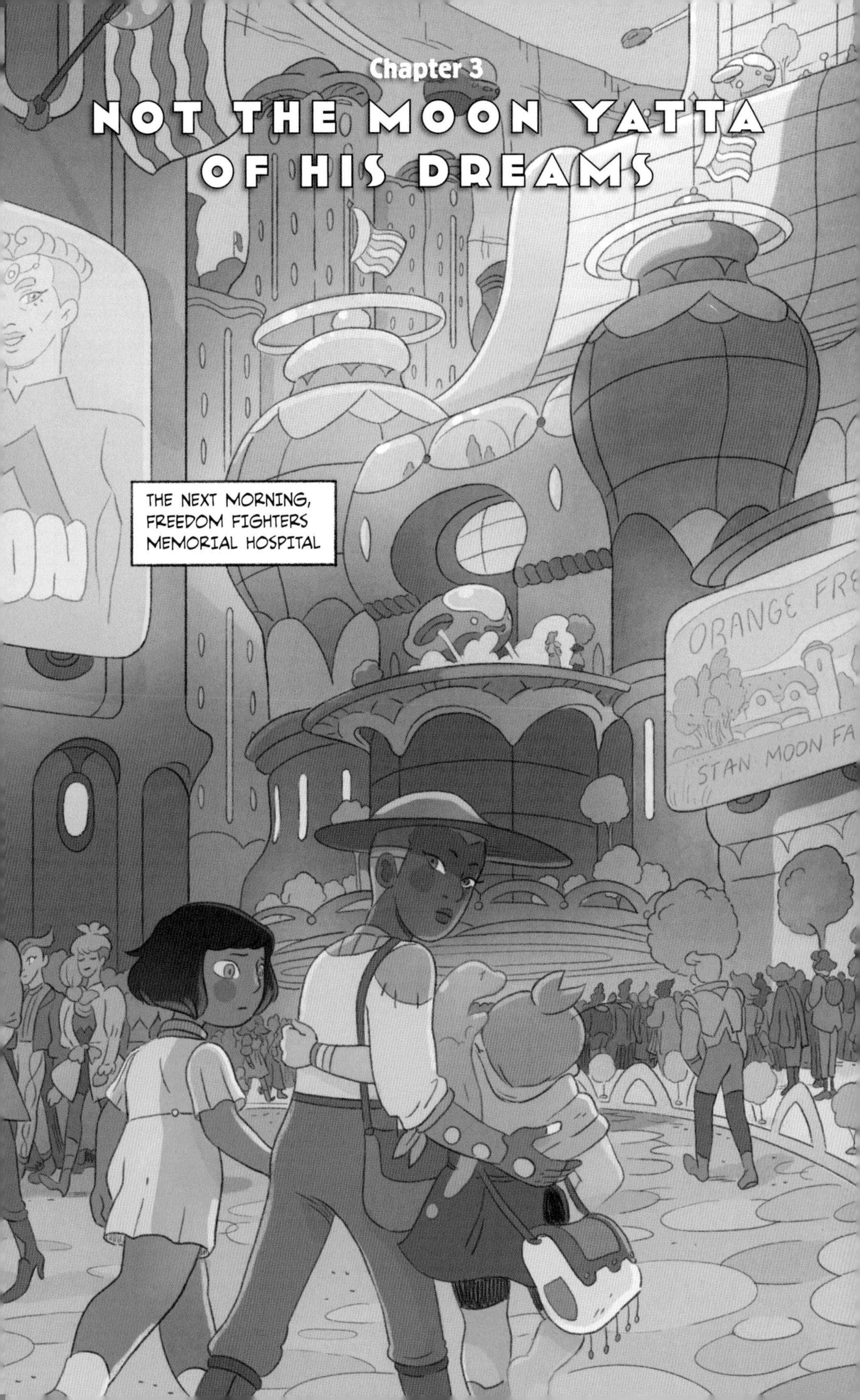
THE NEXT MORNING, FREEDOM FIGHTERS MEMORIAL HOSPITAL

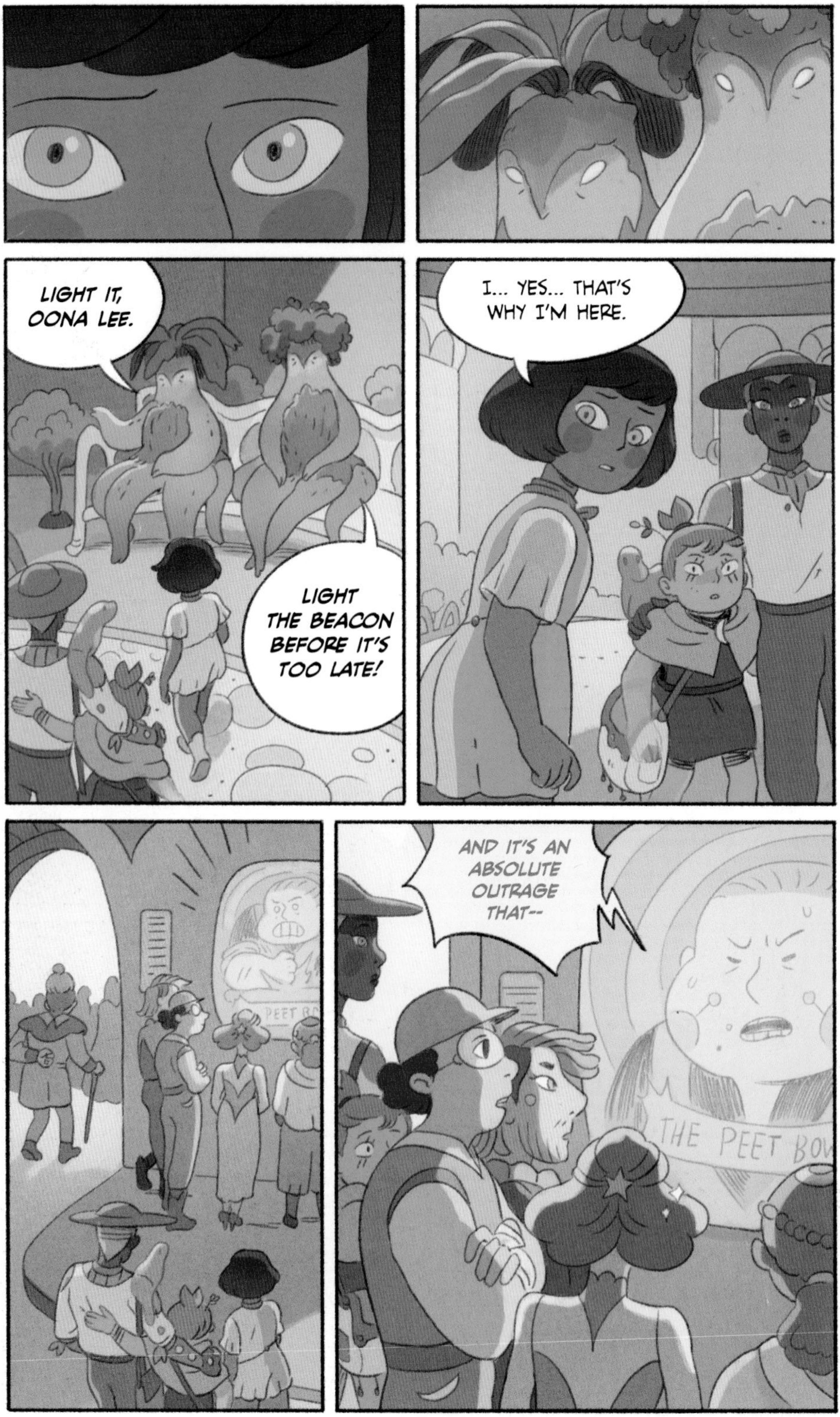
LIGHT IT, OONA LEE.
LIGHT THE BEACON BEFORE IT'S TOO LATE!
I... YES... THAT'S WHY I'M HERE.
PEET BO
AND IT'S AN ABSOLUTE OUTRAGE THAT--
THE PEET BOV

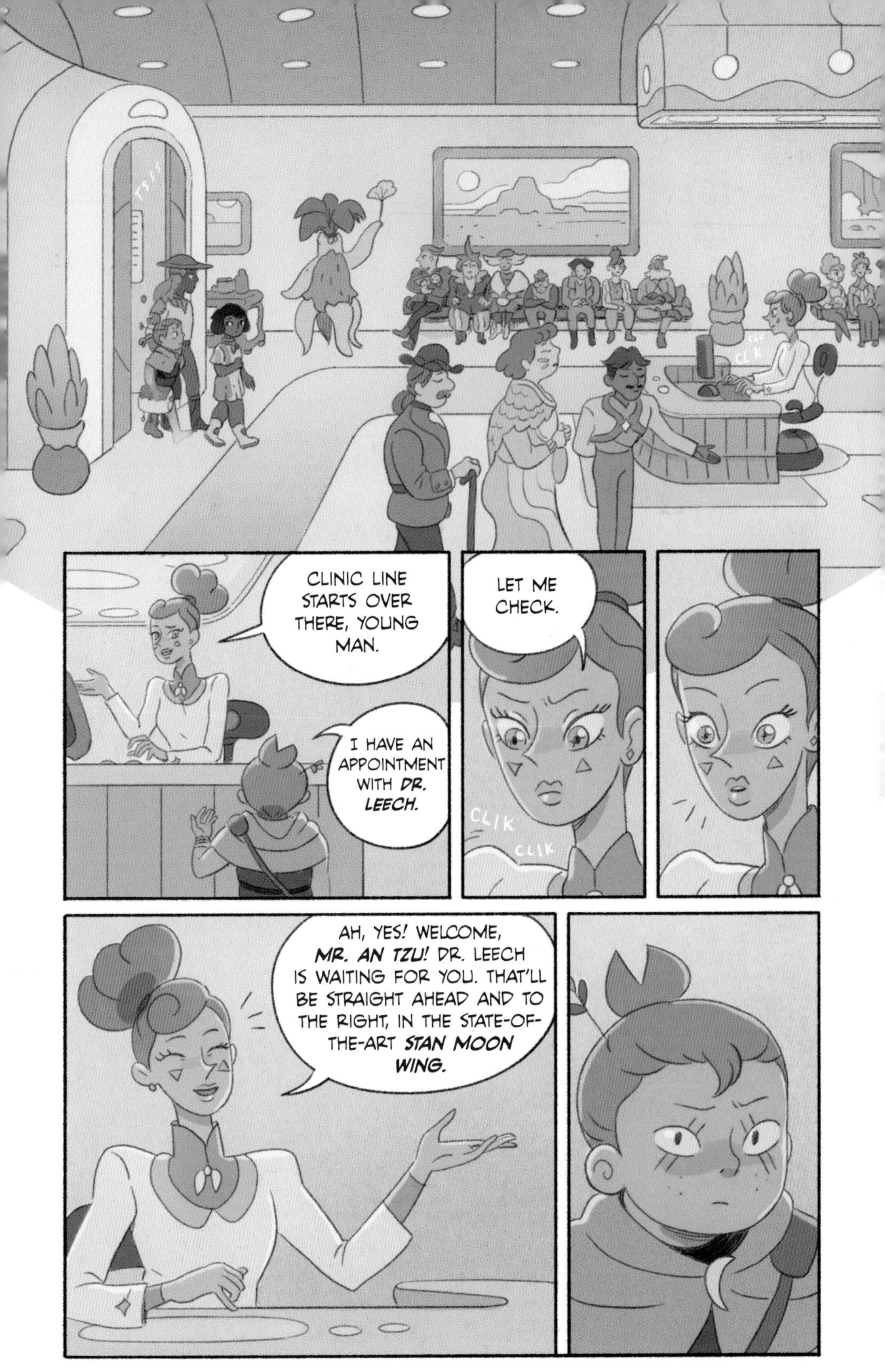
CLINIC LINE STARTS OVER THERE, YOUNG MAN.
I HAVE AN APPOINTMENT WITH *DR. LEECH.*
LET ME CHECK.
CLIK
CLIK
AH, YES! WELCOME, *MR. AN TZU!* DR. LEECH IS WAITING FOR YOU. THAT'LL BE STRAIGHT AHEAD AND TO THE RIGHT, IN THE STATE-OF-THE-ART *STAN MOON WING.*

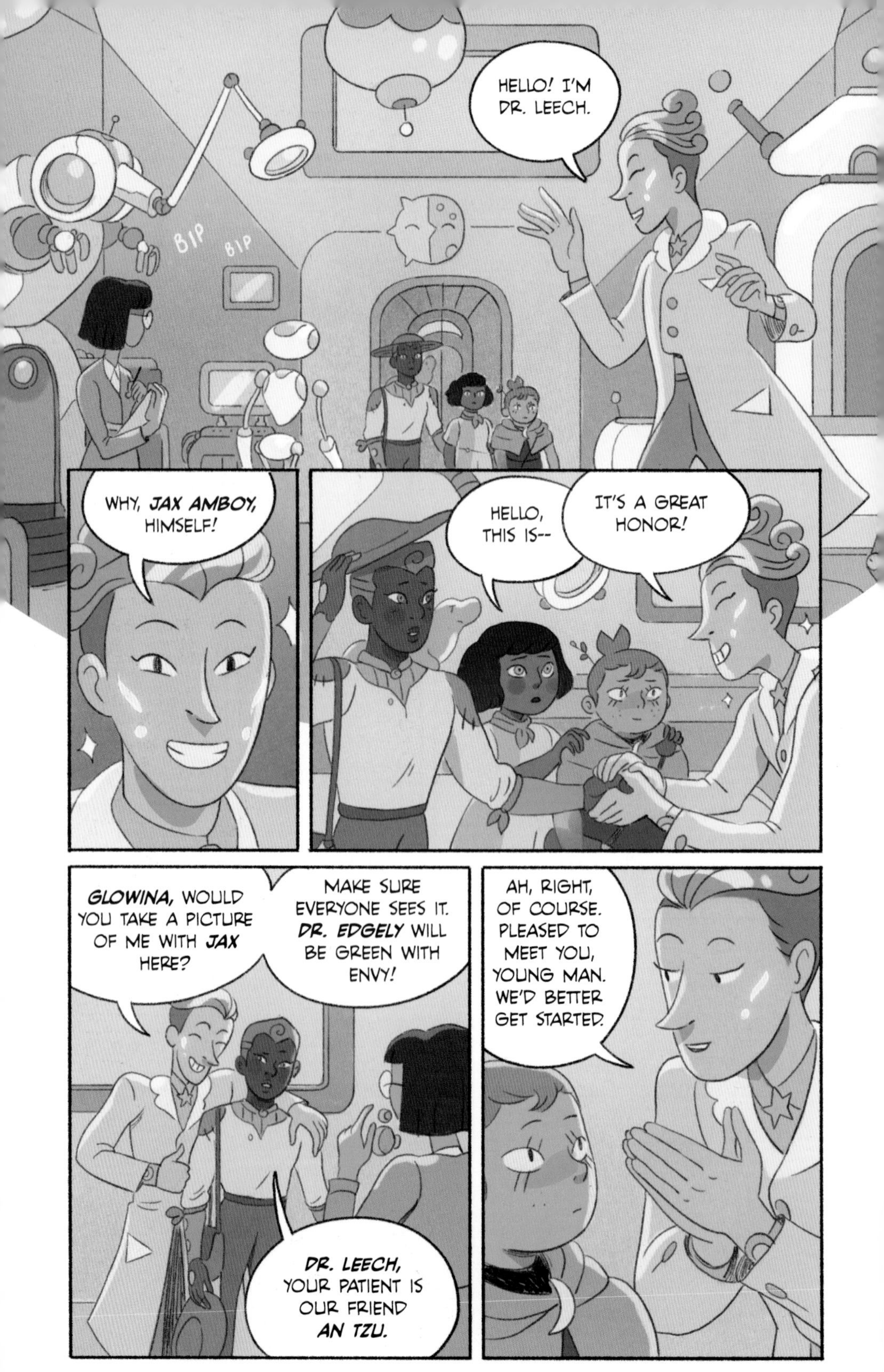
BIP BIP
HELLO! I'M DR. LEECH.
WHY, JAX AMBOY, HIMSELF!
HELLO, THIS IS--
IT'S A GREAT HONOR!
GLOWINA, WOULD YOU TAKE A PICTURE OF ME WITH JAX HERE?
MAKE SURE EVERYONE SEES IT. DR. EDGELY WILL BE GREEN WITH ENVY!
DR. LEECH, YOUR PATIENT IS OUR FRIEND AN TZU.
AH, RIGHT, OF COURSE. PLEASED TO MEET YOU, YOUNG MAN. WE'D BETTER GET STARTED.

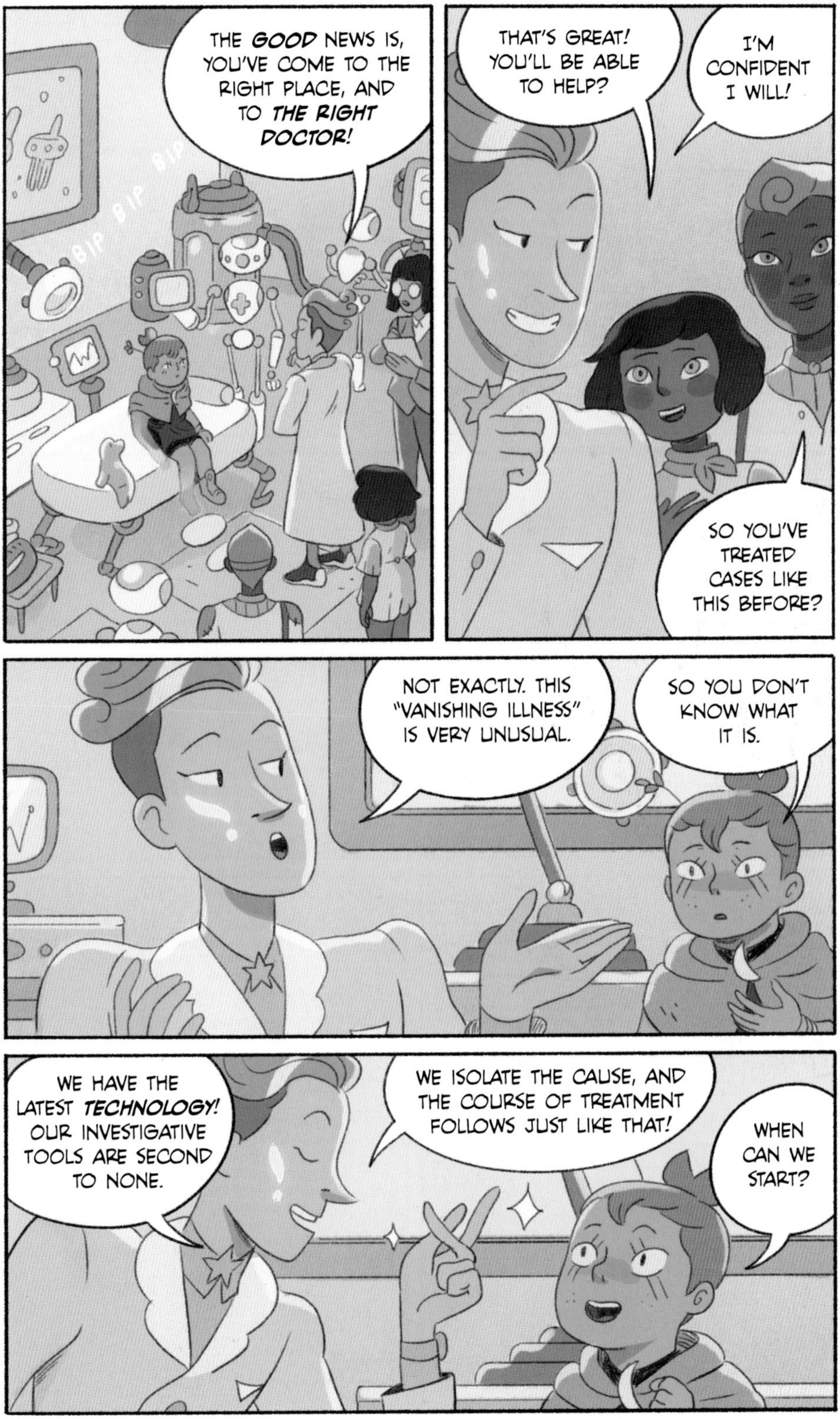
THE GOOD NEWS IS, YOU'VE COME TO THE RIGHT PLACE, AND TO THE RIGHT DOCTOR!
BIP BIP BIP
THAT'S GREAT! YOU'LL BE ABLE TO HELP?
I'M CONFIDENT I WILL!
SO YOU'VE TREATED CASES LIKE THIS BEFORE?
NOT EXACTLY. THIS "VANISHING ILLNESS" IS VERY UNUSUAL.
SO YOU DON'T KNOW WHAT IT IS.
WE HAVE THE LATEST TECHNOLOGY! OUR INVESTIGATIVE TOOLS ARE SECOND TO NONE.
WE ISOLATE THE CAUSE, AND THE COURSE OF TREATMENT FOLLOWS JUST LIKE THAT!
WHEN CAN WE START?

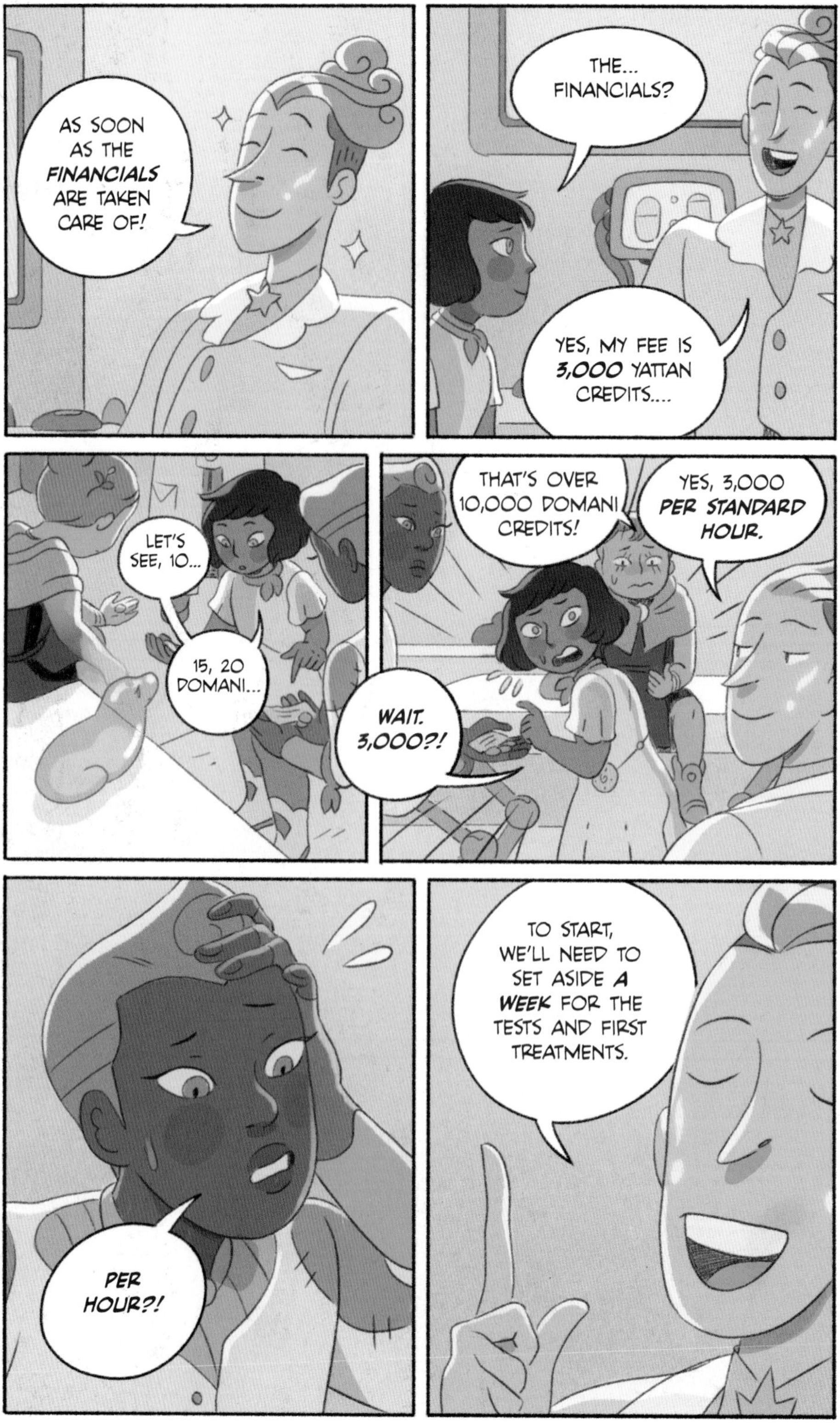
AS SOON AS THE *FINANCIALS* ARE TAKEN CARE OF!
THE... FINANCIALS?
YES, MY FEE IS *3,000* YATTAN CREDITS....
LET'S SEE, 10...
15, 20 DOMANI...
THAT'S OVER 10,000 DOMANI CREDITS!
YES, 3,000 *PER STANDARD HOUR.*
*WAIT. 3,000?!*
*PER HOUR?!*
TO START, WE'LL NEED TO SET ASIDE *A WEEK* FOR THE TESTS AND FIRST TREATMENTS.

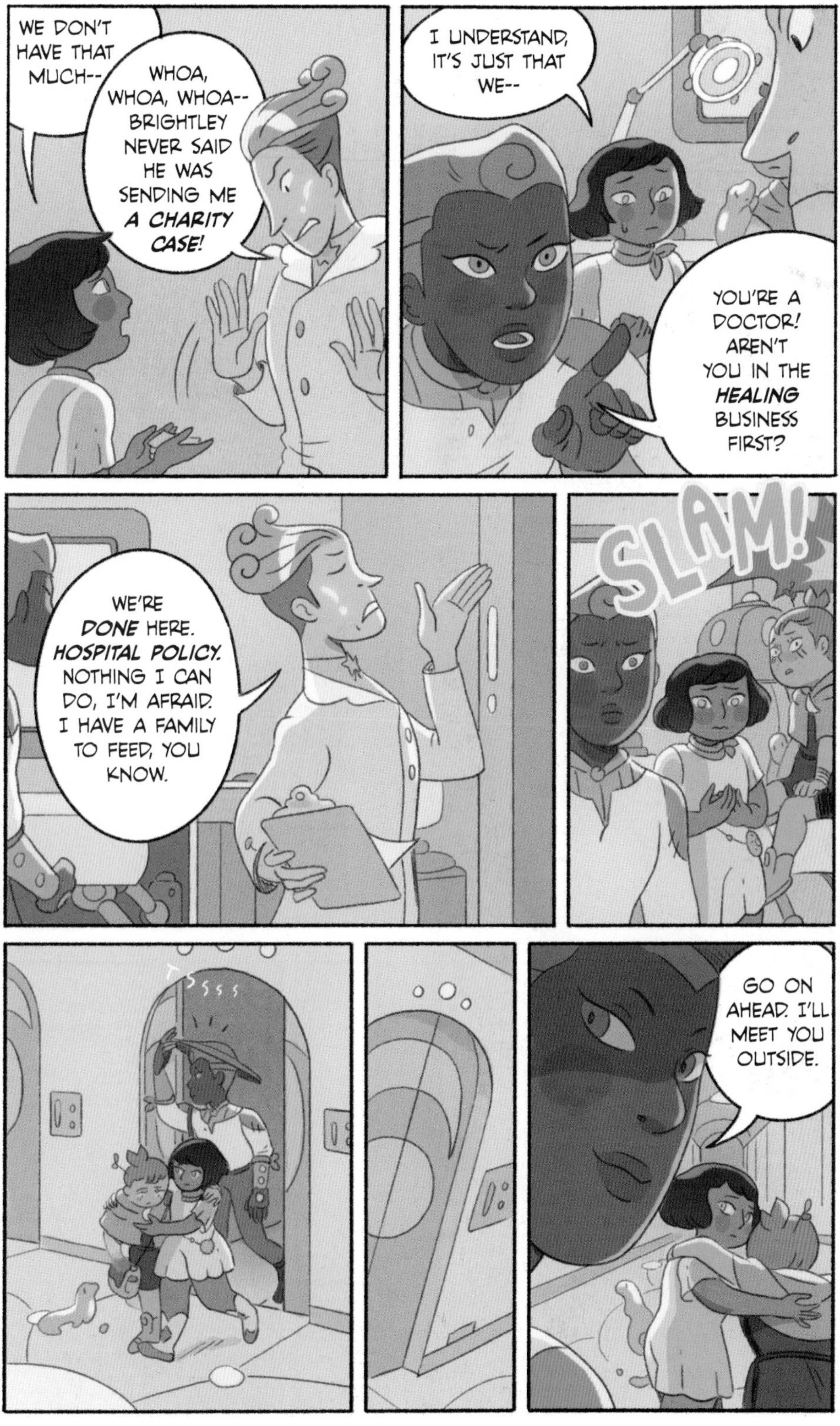
WE DON'T HAVE THAT MUCH--
WHOA, WHOA, WHOA-- BRIGHTLEY NEVER SAID HE WAS SENDING ME *A CHARITY CASE!*
I UNDERSTAND, IT'S JUST THAT WE--
YOU'RE A DOCTOR! AREN'T YOU IN THE *HEALING* BUSINESS FIRST?
WE'RE *DONE* HERE. *HOSPITAL POLICY.* NOTHING I CAN DO, I'M AFRAID. I HAVE A FAMILY TO FEED, YOU KNOW.
SLAM!
TSSSS
GO ON AHEAD. I'LL MEET YOU OUTSIDE.

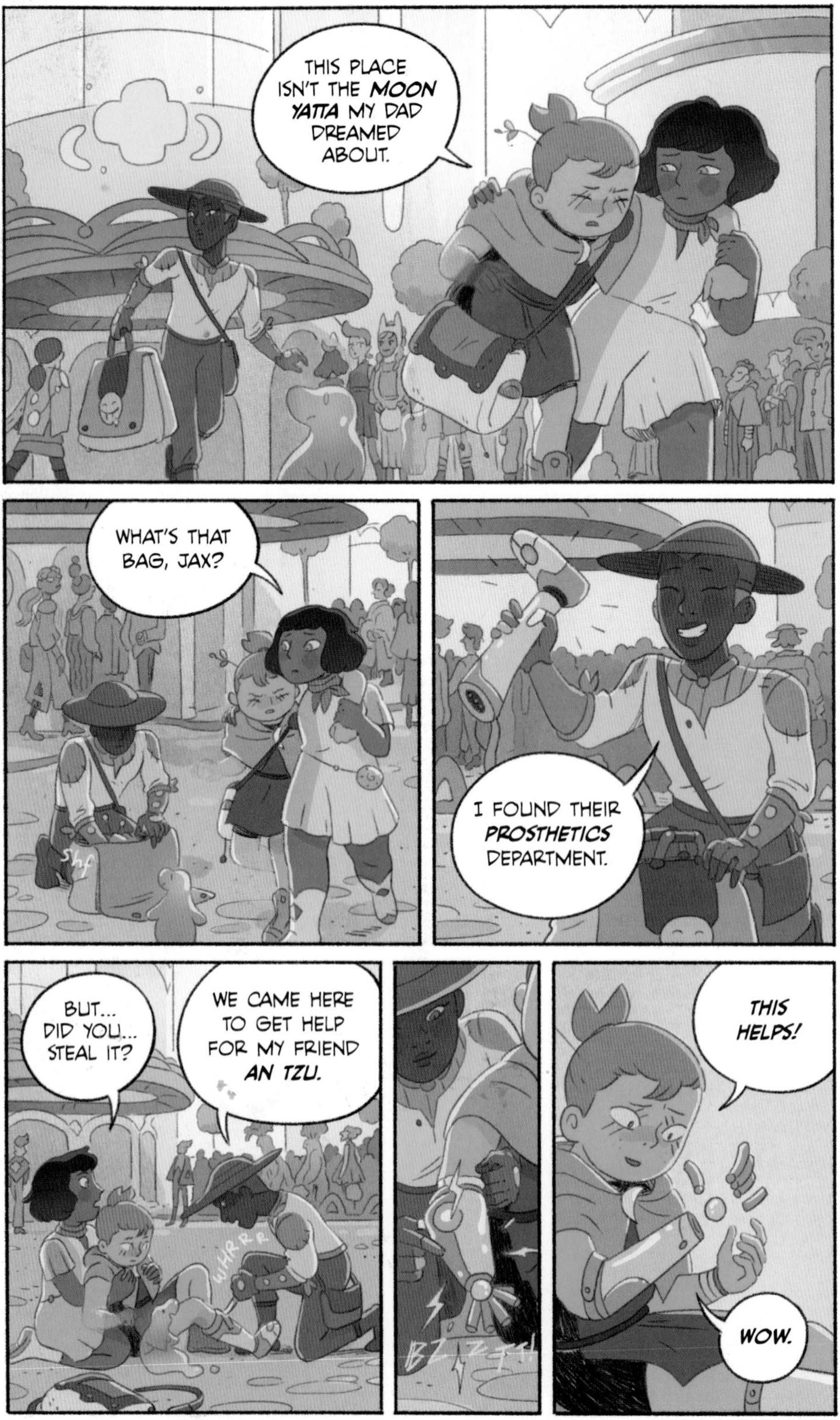

THIS PLACE ISN'T THE MOON YATTA MY DAD DREAMED ABOUT.
WHAT'S THAT BAG, JAX?
shf
I FOUND THEIR PROSTHETICS DEPARTMENT.
BUT... DID YOU... STEAL IT?
WE CAME HERE TO GET HELP FOR MY FRIEND AN TZU.
WHRRR
THIS HELPS!
WOW.

## Chapter 4

# THE STOAK BROTHER

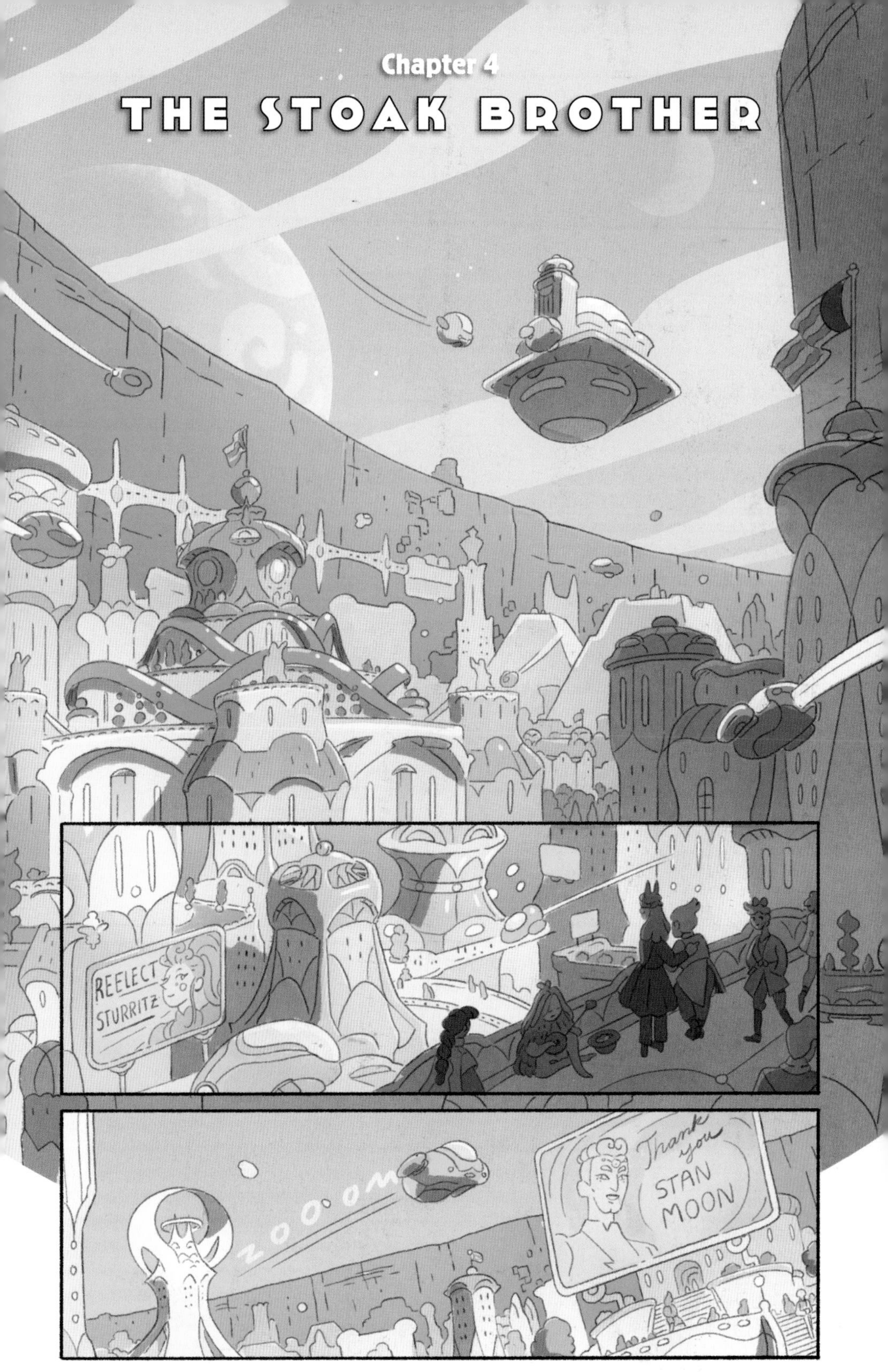
REELECT STURRITZ
ZOOOM
Thank you STAN MOON

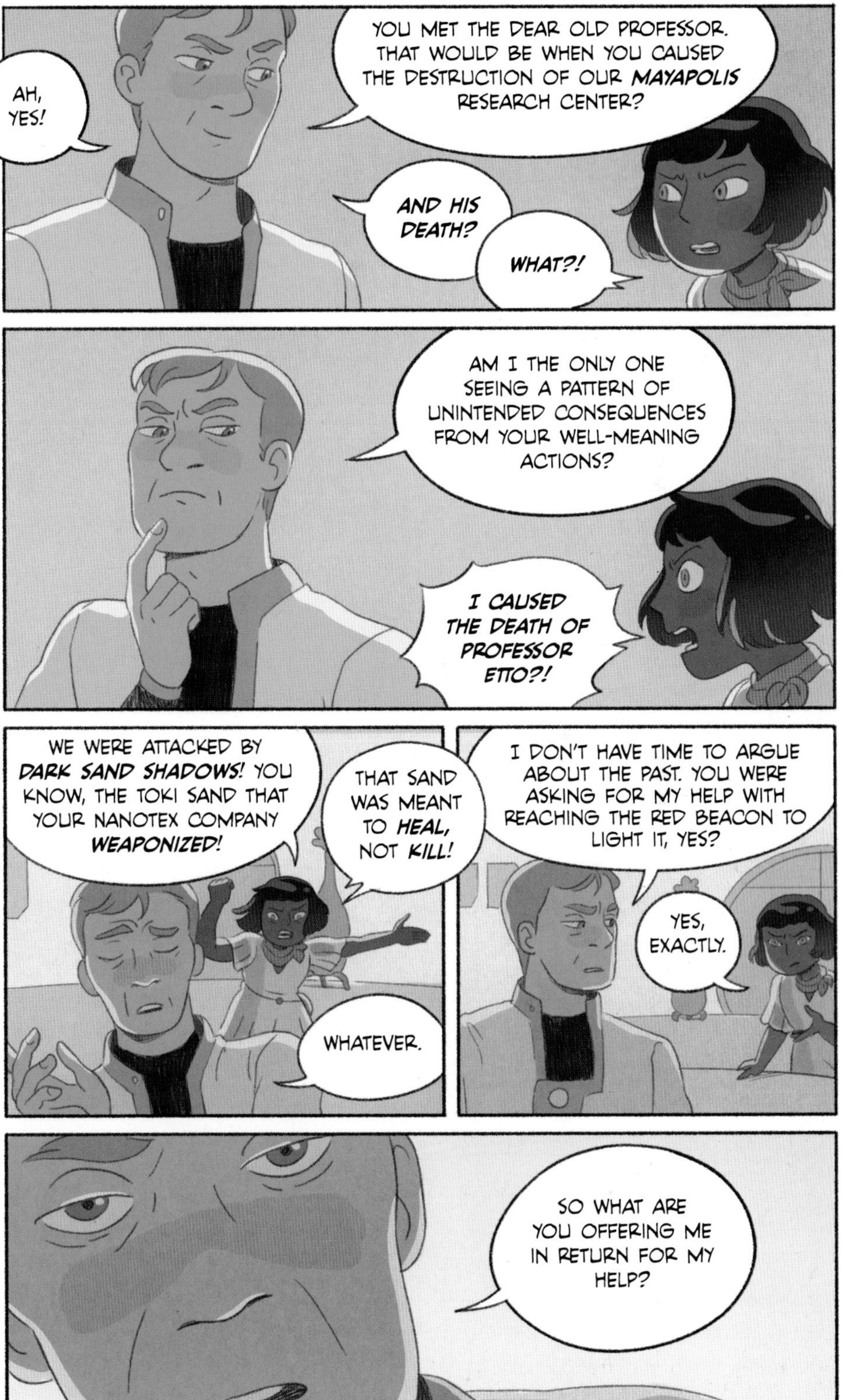
AH, YES!
YOU MET THE DEAR OLD PROFESSOR. THAT WOULD BE WHEN YOU CAUSED THE DESTRUCTION OF OUR MAYAPOLIS RESEARCH CENTER?
AND HIS DEATH?
WHAT?!
AM I THE ONLY ONE SEEING A PATTERN OF UNINTENDED CONSEQUENCES FROM YOUR WELL-MEANING ACTIONS?
I CAUSED THE DEATH OF PROFESSOR ETTO?!
WE WERE ATTACKED BY DARK SAND SHADOWS! YOU KNOW, THE TOKI SAND THAT YOUR NANOTEX COMPANY WEAPONIZED!
THAT SAND WAS MEANT TO HEAL, NOT KILL!
WHATEVER.
I DON'T HAVE TIME TO ARGUE ABOUT THE PAST. YOU WERE ASKING FOR MY HELP WITH REACHING THE RED BEACON TO LIGHT IT, YES?
YES, EXACTLY.
SO WHAT ARE YOU OFFERING ME IN RETURN FOR MY HELP?

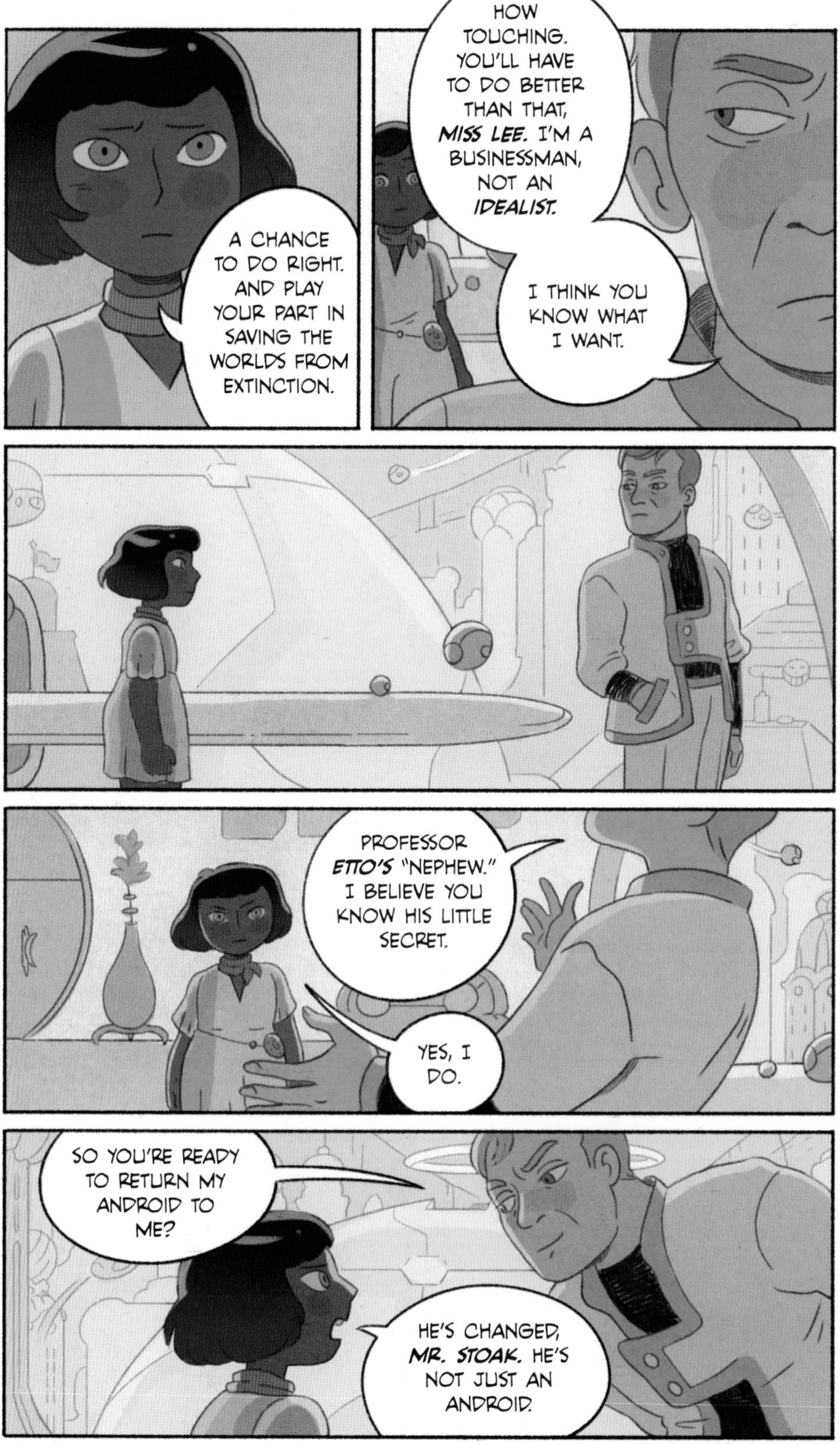
A CHANCE TO DO RIGHT. AND PLAY YOUR PART IN SAVING THE WORLDS FROM EXTINCTION.
HOW TOUCHING. YOU'LL HAVE TO DO BETTER THAN THAT, MISS LEE. I'M A BUSINESSMAN, NOT AN IDEALIST.
I THINK YOU KNOW WHAT I WANT.
PROFESSOR ETTO'S "NEPHEW." I BELIEVE YOU KNOW HIS LITTLE SECRET.
YES, I DO.
SO YOU'RE READY TO RETURN MY ANDROID TO ME?
HE'S CHANGED, MR. STOAK. HE'S NOT JUST AN ANDROID.

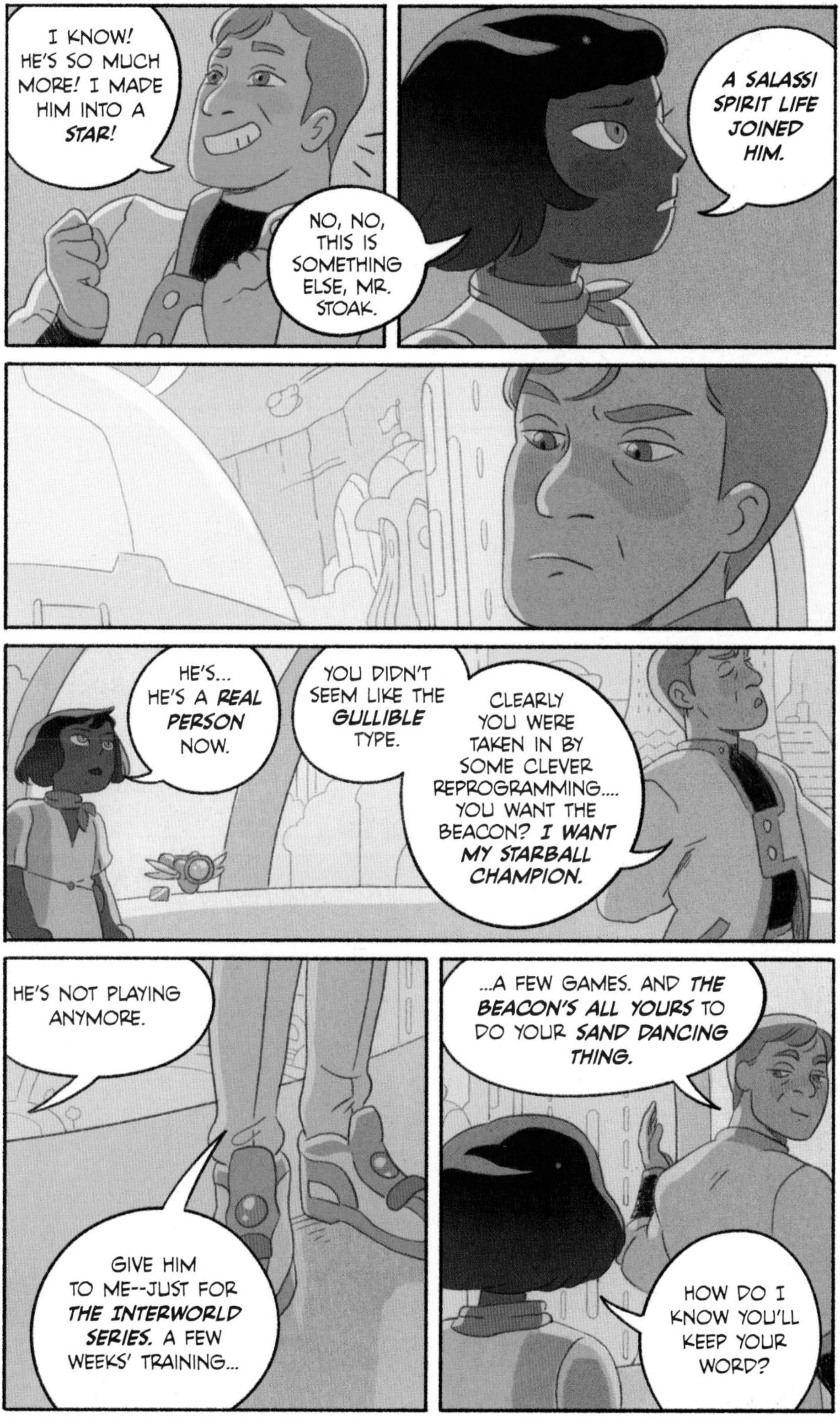
I KNOW! HE'S SO MUCH MORE! I MADE HIM INTO A *STAR!*
NO, NO, THIS IS SOMETHING ELSE, MR. STOAK.
*A SALASSI SPIRIT LIFE JOINED HIM.*
HE'S... HE'S A *REAL PERSON* NOW.
YOU DIDN'T SEEM LIKE THE *GULLIBLE* TYPE.
CLEARLY YOU WERE TAKEN IN BY SOME CLEVER REPROGRAMMING.... YOU WANT THE BEACON? *I WANT MY STARBALL CHAMPION.*
HE'S NOT PLAYING ANYMORE.
GIVE HIM TO ME--JUST FOR *THE INTERWORLD SERIES.* A FEW WEEKS' TRAINING...
...A FEW GAMES. AND *THE BEACON'S ALL YOURS* TO DO YOUR *SAND DANCING THING.*
HOW DO I KNOW YOU'LL KEEP YOUR WORD?

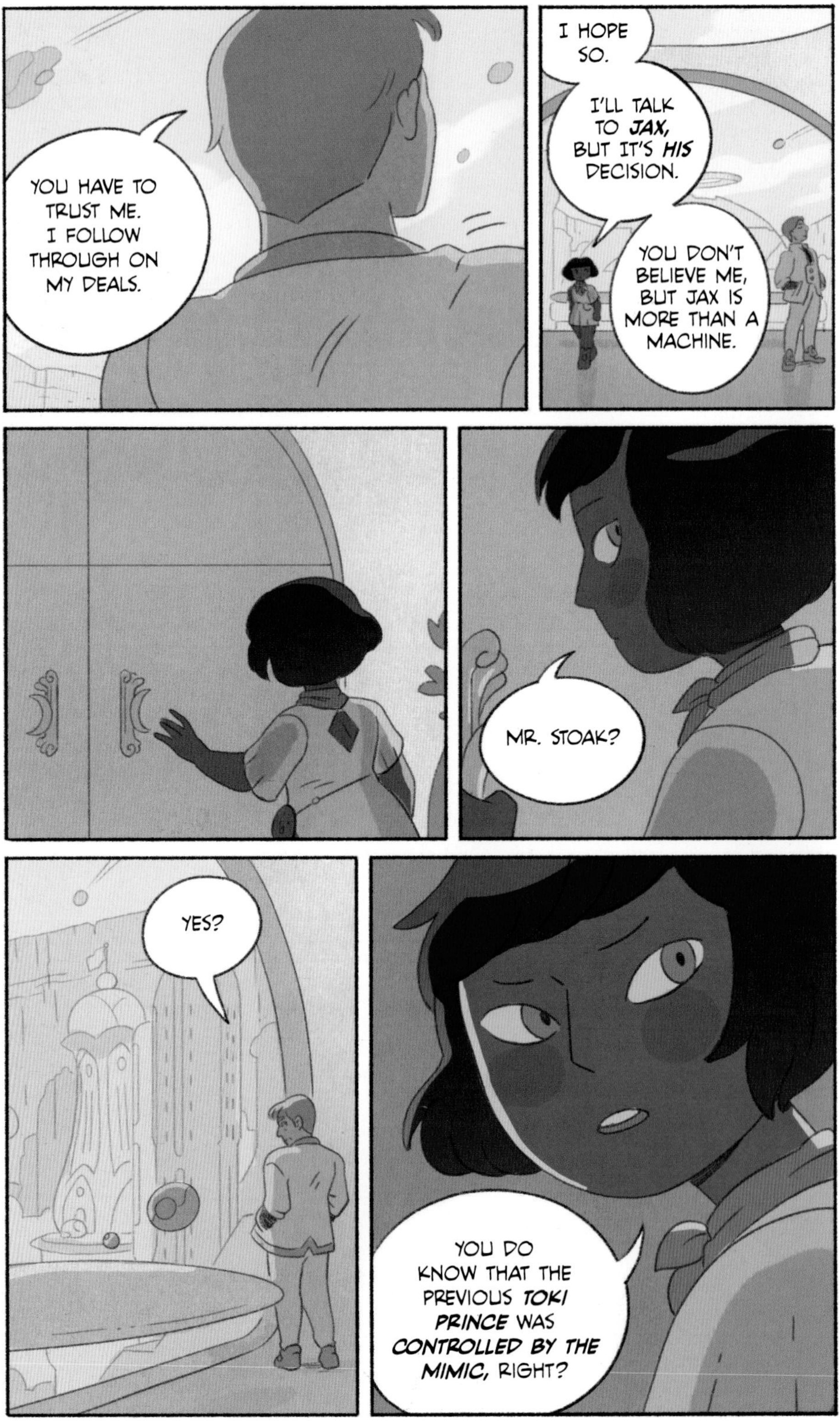
YOU HAVE TO TRUST ME. I FOLLOW THROUGH ON MY DEALS.
I HOPE SO.
I'LL TALK TO *JAX,* BUT IT'S *HIS* DECISION.
YOU DON'T BELIEVE ME, BUT JAX IS MORE THAN A MACHINE.
MR. STOAK?
YES?
YOU DO KNOW THAT THE PREVIOUS *TOKI PRINCE* WAS *CONTROLLED BY THE MIMIC,* RIGHT?

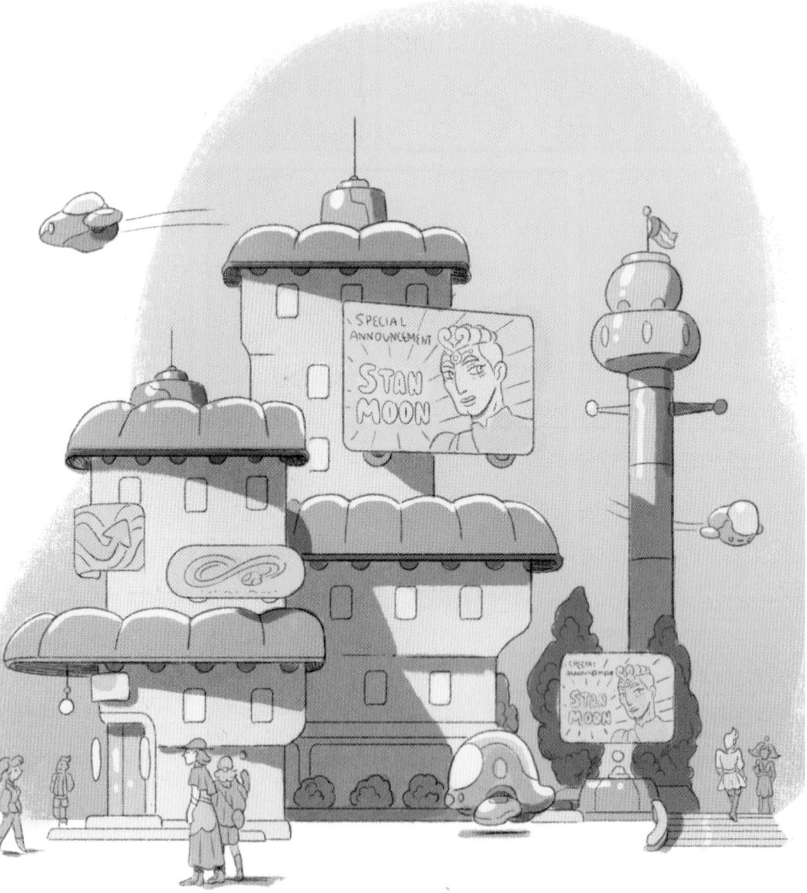
SPECIAL ANNOUNCEMENT
STAN MOON
STAN MOON

## Chapter 5

# SYSTEM OVERRIDES

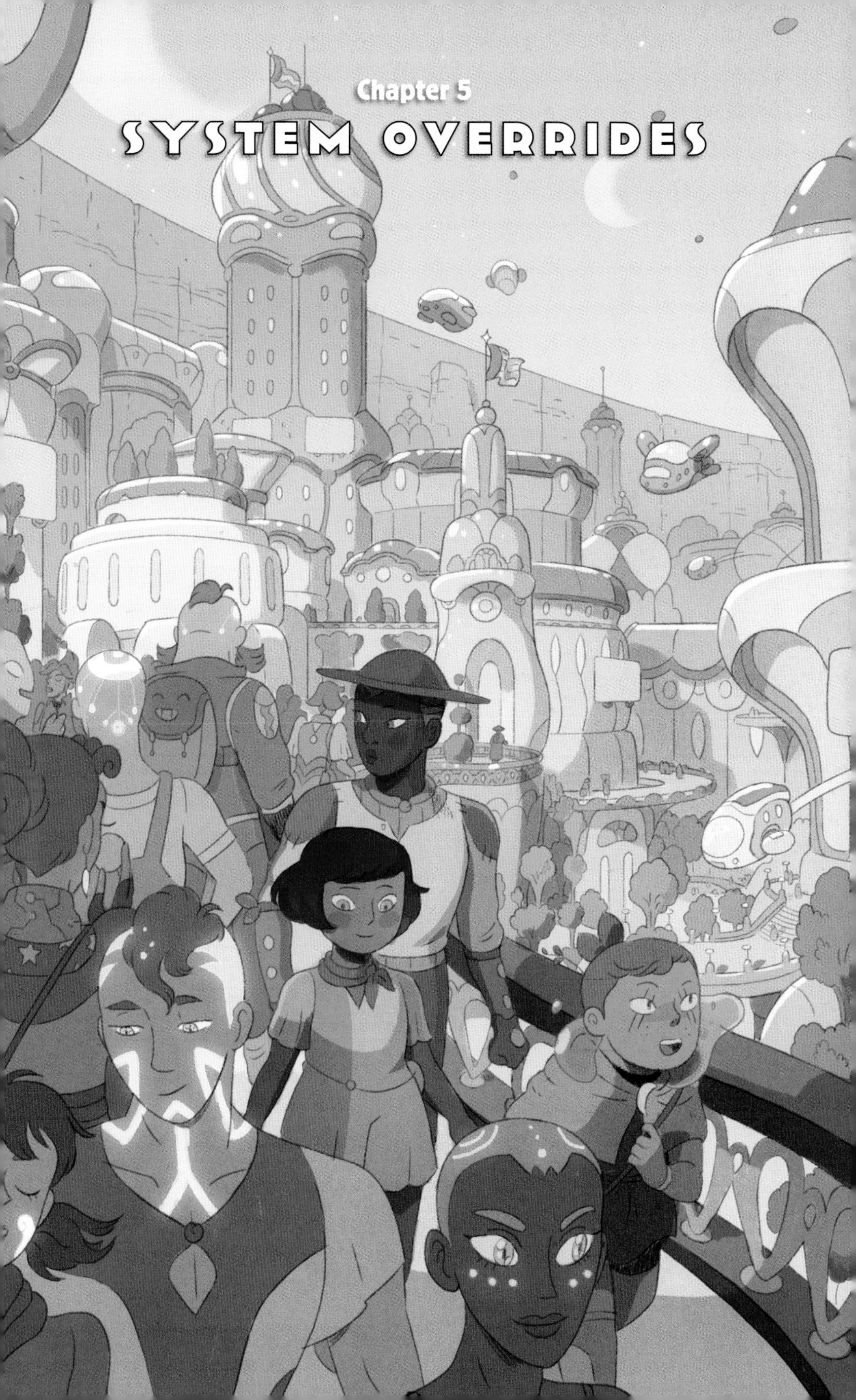

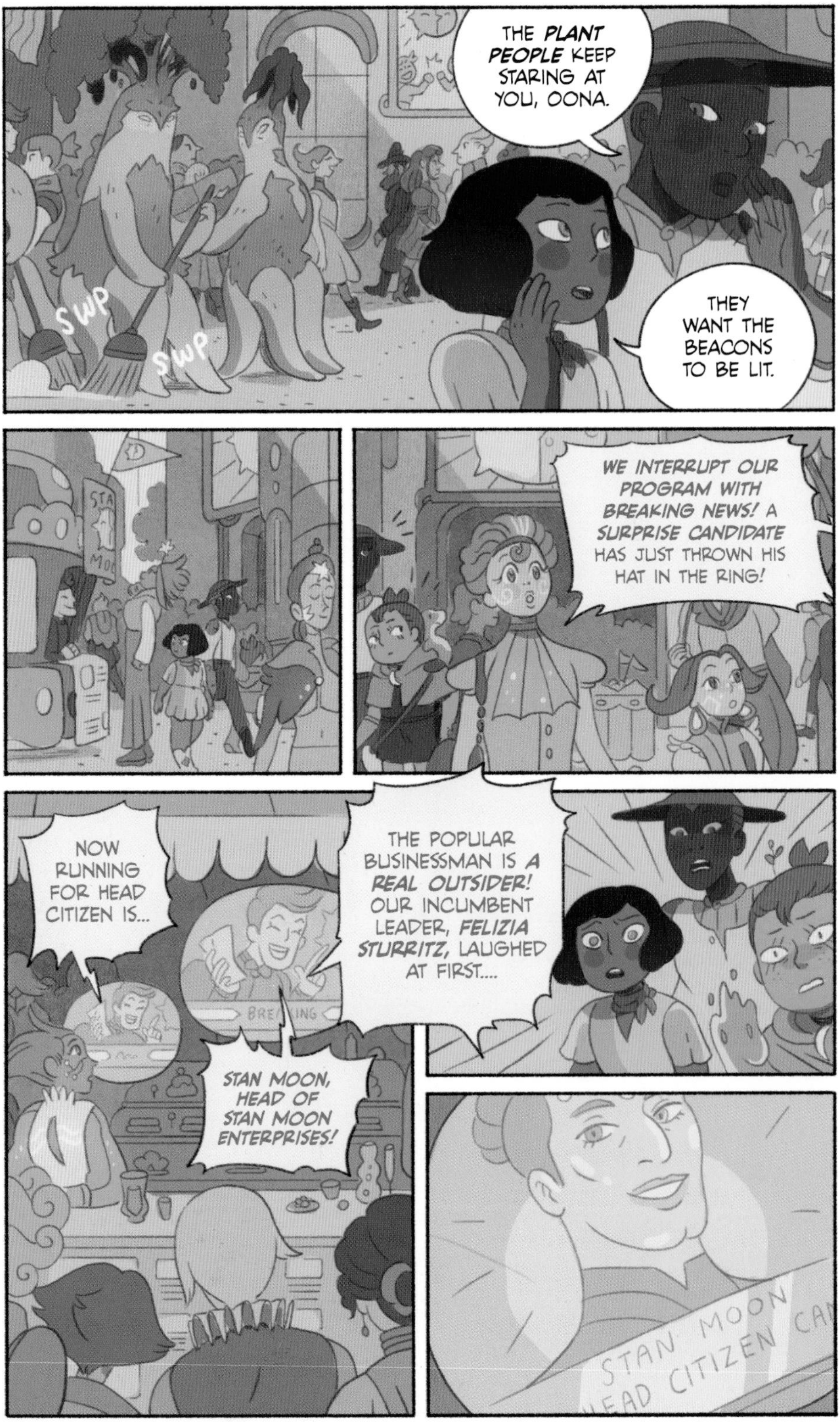
THE PLANT PEOPLE KEEP STARING AT YOU, OONA.
THEY WANT THE BEACONS TO BE LIT.
SWP
SWP
WE INTERRUPT OUR PROGRAM WITH BREAKING NEWS! A SURPRISE CANDIDATE HAS JUST THROWN HIS HAT IN THE RING!
NOW RUNNING FOR HEAD CITIZEN IS...
STAN MOON, HEAD OF STAN MOON ENTERPRISES!
THE POPULAR BUSINESSMAN IS A REAL OUTSIDER! OUR INCUMBENT LEADER, FELIZIA STURRITZ, LAUGHED AT FIRST....
STAN MOON
HEAD CITIZEN CA

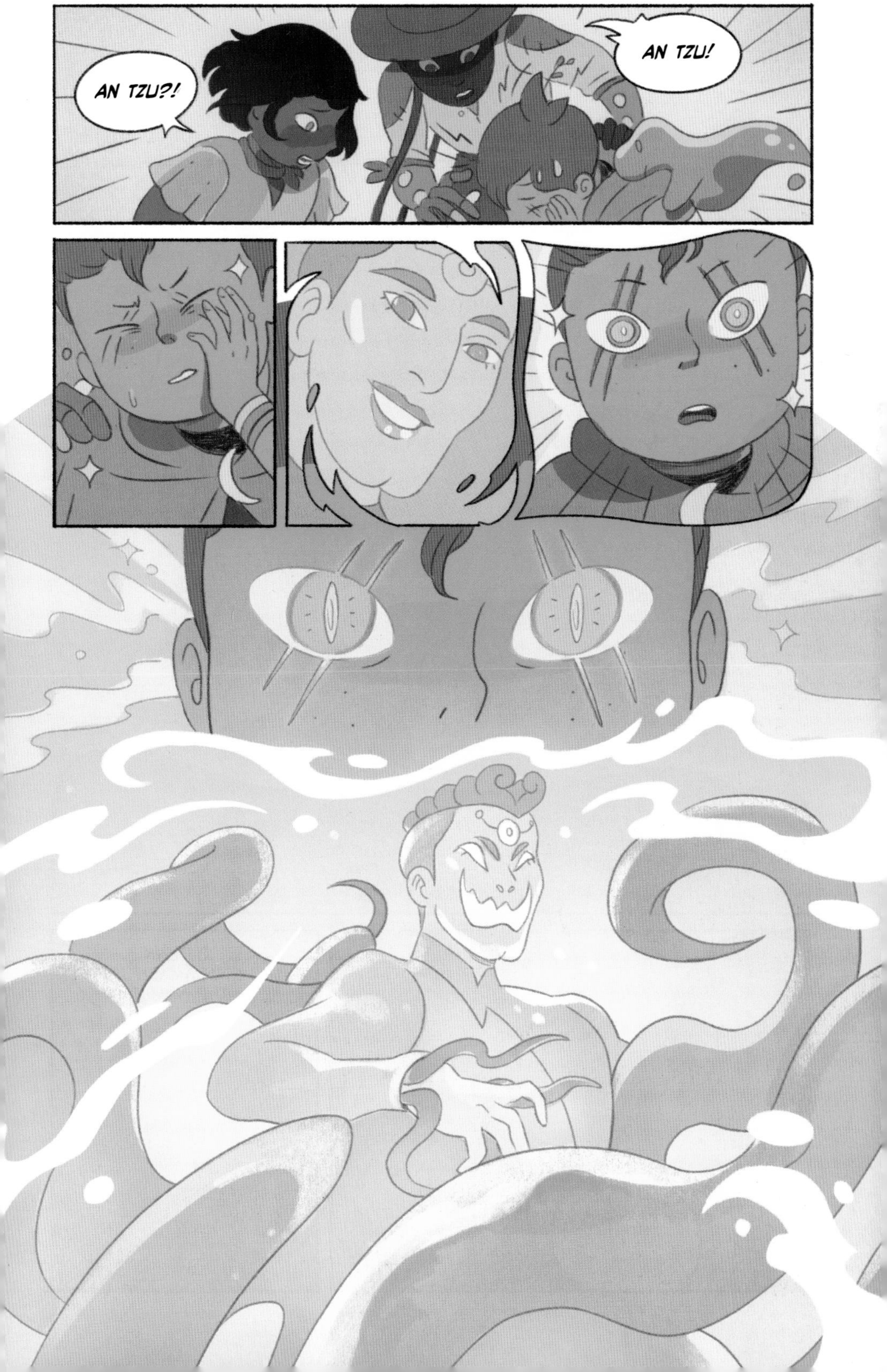
AN TZU?!
AN TZU!

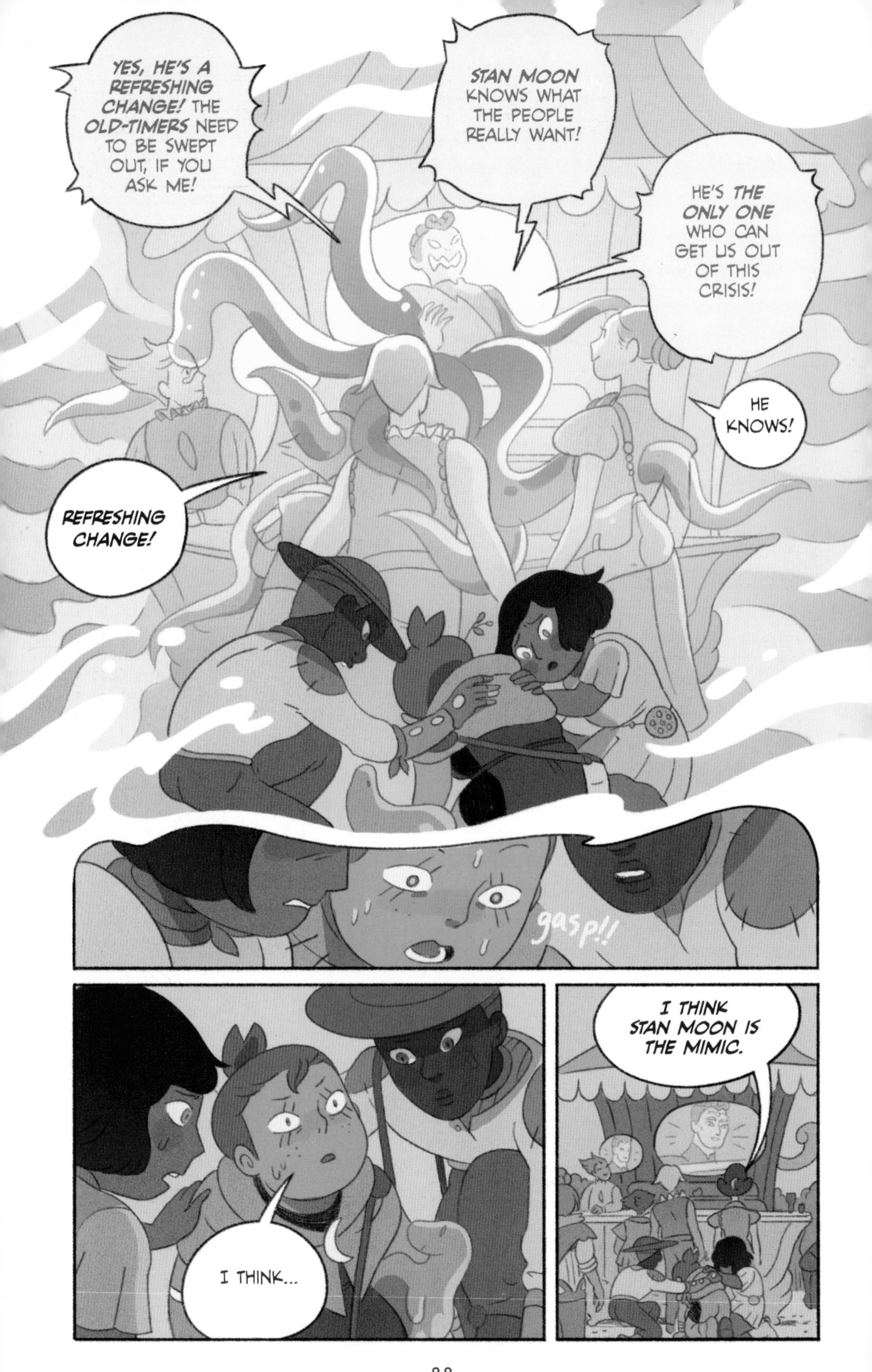
YES, HE'S A REFRESHING CHANGE! THE OLD-TIMERS NEED TO BE SWEPT OUT, IF YOU ASK ME!
STAN MOON KNOWS WHAT THE PEOPLE REALLY WANT!
HE'S THE ONLY ONE WHO CAN GET US OUT OF THIS CRISIS!
HE KNOWS!
REFRESHING CHANGE!
gasp!!
I THINK...
I THINK STAN MOON IS THE MIMIC.

NANOTEX BOARDROOM

I DON'T LIKE IT, *ELDRIDGE.*

WHY IS *STAN MOON* TAKING THE SPOTLIGHT LIKE THIS?

YOU DON'T GET IT, *DERRICK.* STICK TO *STARBALL,* BROTHER, AND LET *ME* HANDLE POLITICS.

BUT WE DON'T NEED *STAN MOON!*

*NANOTEX* IS KING! WHY ARE WE BOWING AND SCRAPING TO... THAT *THING?* WHATEVER IT IS.

IT'S A *SMART ALLIANCE.* TRUST ME. I CAN WORK WITH HIM, LET HIM FEEL LIKE HE'S IN CHARGE. HE RELIES ON ME.

AT THE RIGHT TIME, *NANOTEX* WILL TAKE OVER *STAN MOON,* AND WE WON'T NEED HIM ANYMORE.

HE'S...

THERE'S SOMETHING *NOT RIGHT.*

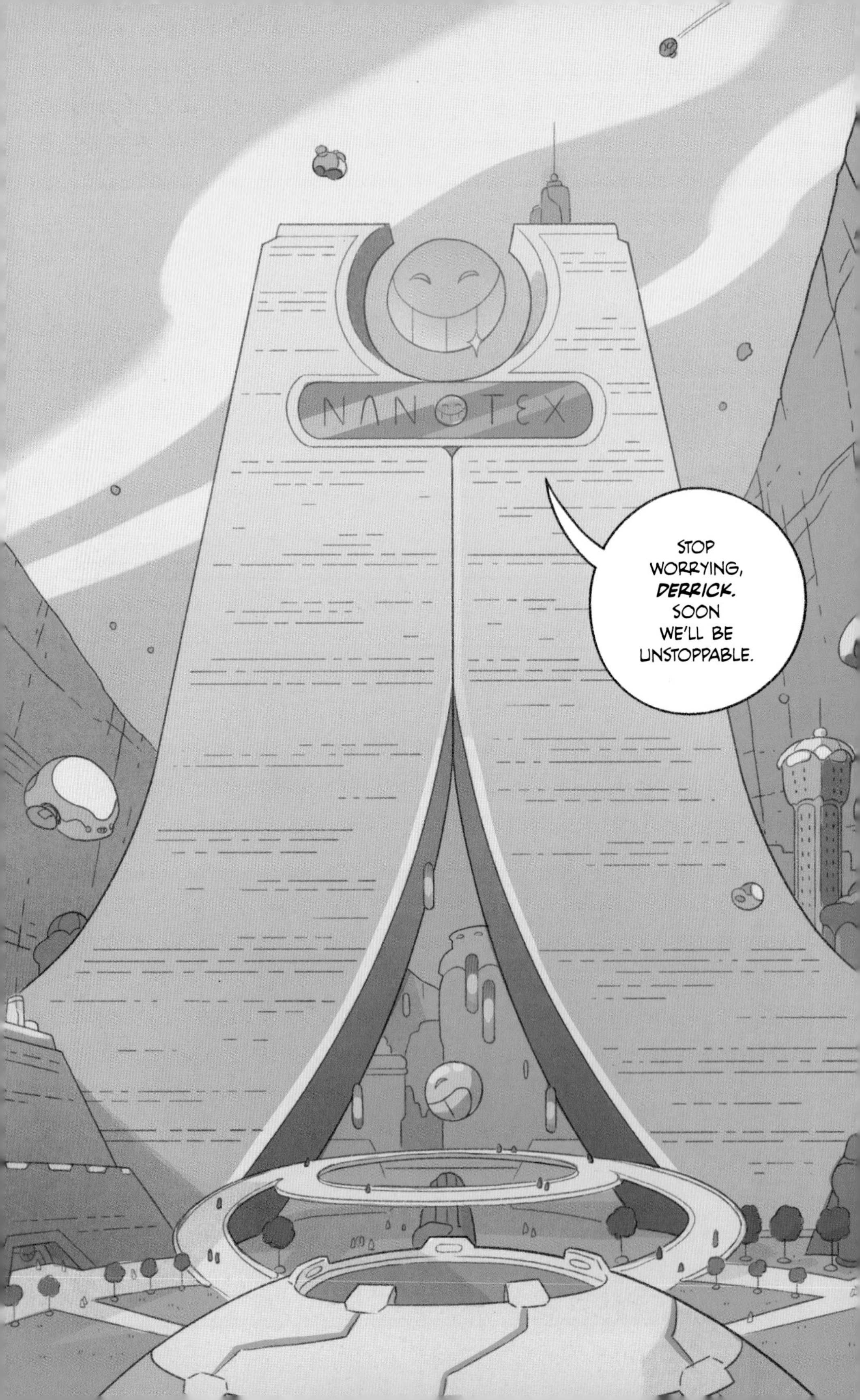
NANOTEX
STOP WORRYING, **DERRICK.** SOON WE'LL BE UNSTOPPABLE.

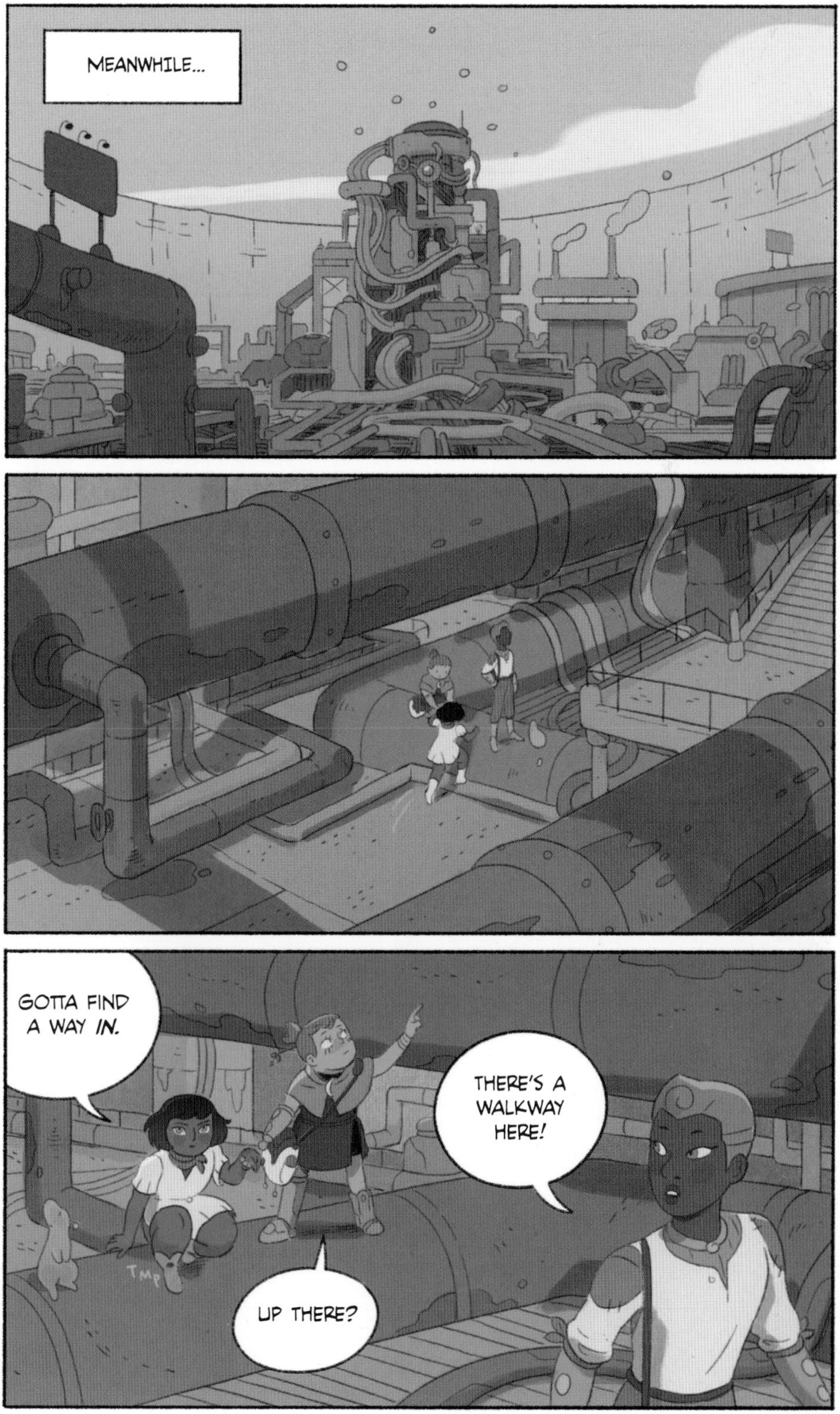
MEANWHILE...
GOTTA FIND A WAY *IN.*
THERE'S A WALKWAY HERE!
UP THERE?
TMP

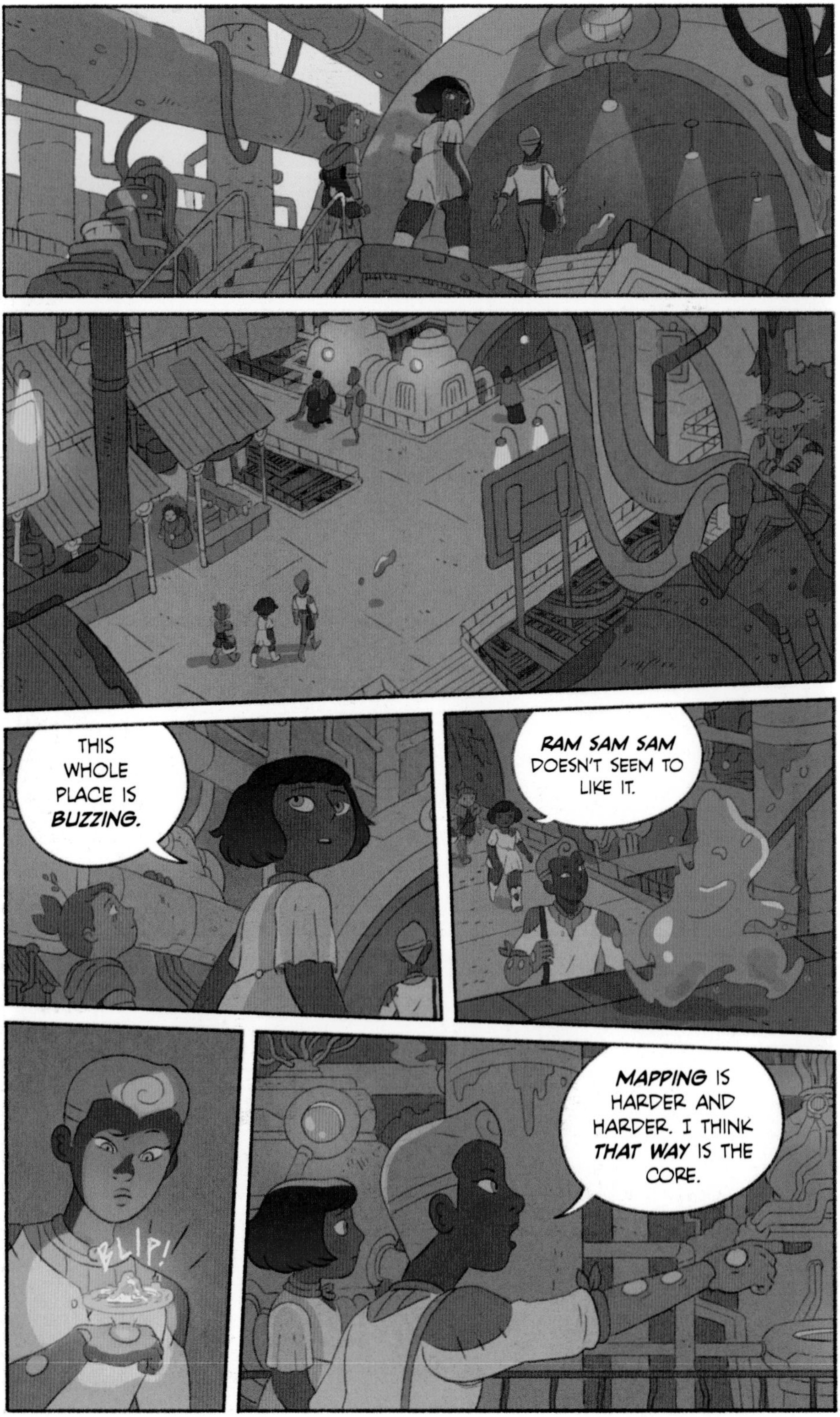
THIS WHOLE PLACE IS *BUZZING.*
*RAM SAM SAM* DOESN'T SEEM TO LIKE IT.
BLIP!
*MAPPING* IS HARDER AND HARDER. I THINK *THAT WAY* IS THE CORE.

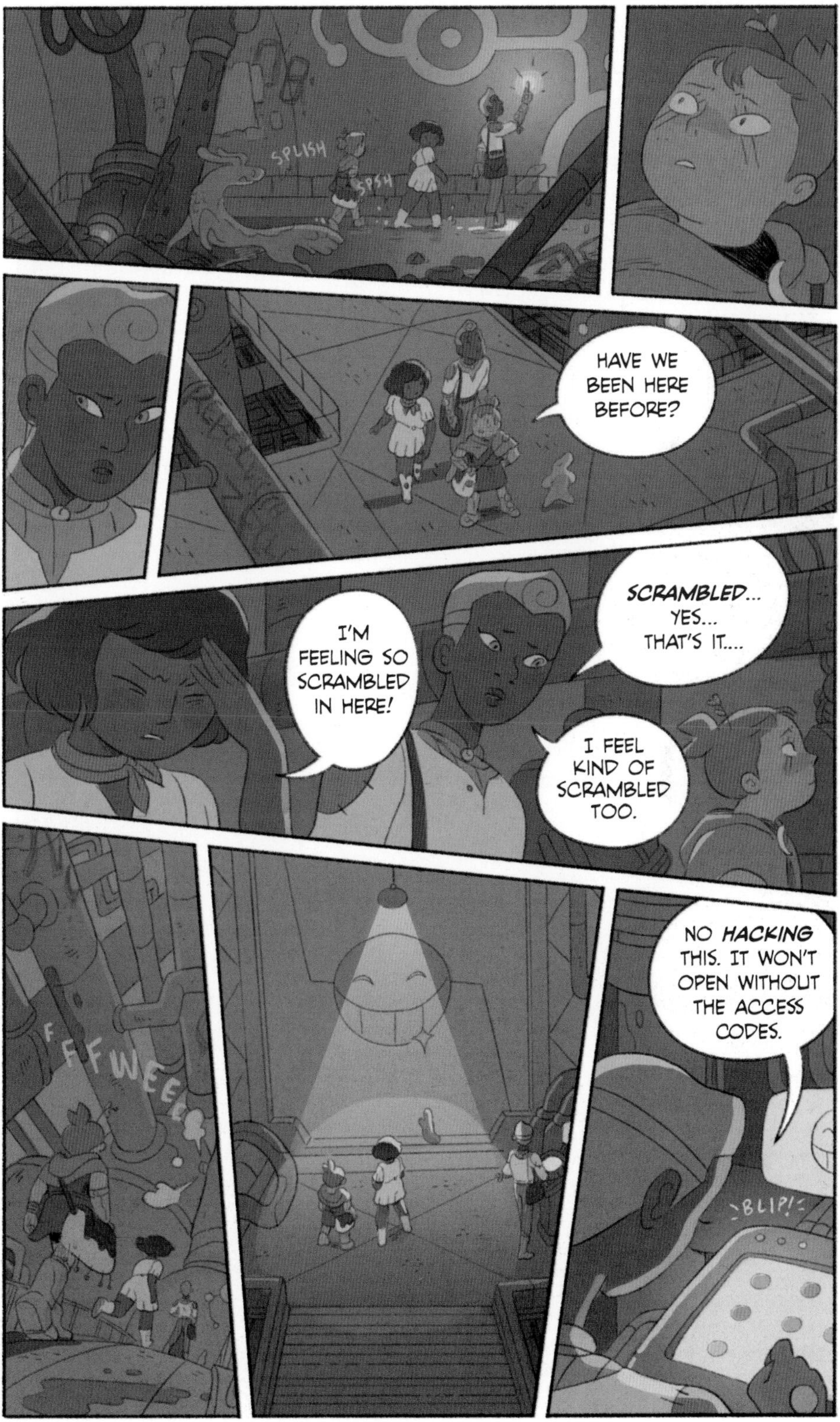
SPLISH
SPSH
HAVE WE BEEN HERE BEFORE?
I'M FEELING SO SCRAMBLED IN HERE!
*SCRAMBLED*... YES... THAT'S IT....
I FEEL KIND OF SCRAMBLED TOO.
FFFWEEE
NO *HACKING* THIS. IT WON'T OPEN WITHOUT THE ACCESS CODES.
BLIP!

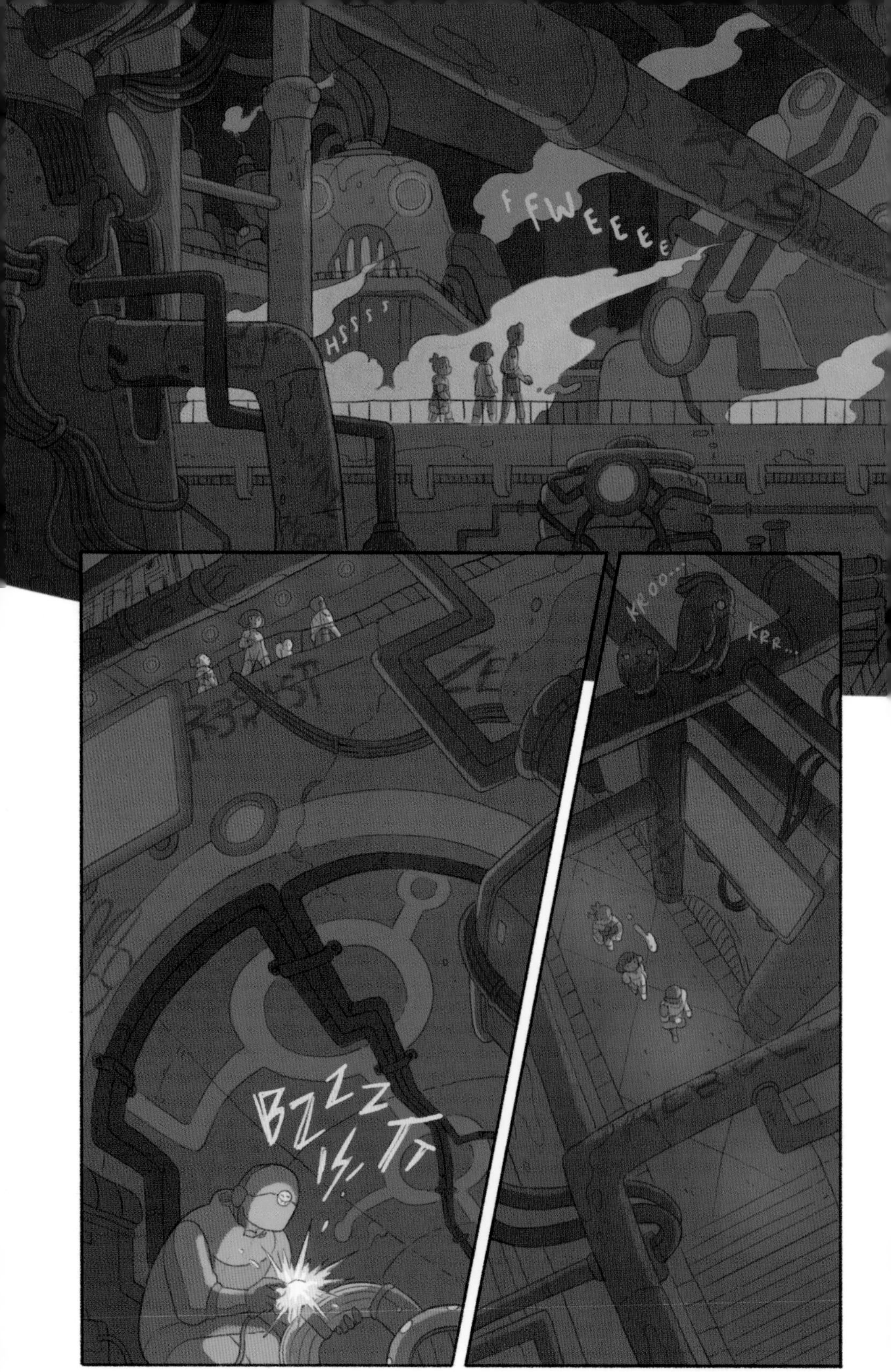
FFWEEEEE
HSSSS
KROO...
KRR...
BZZZZTT

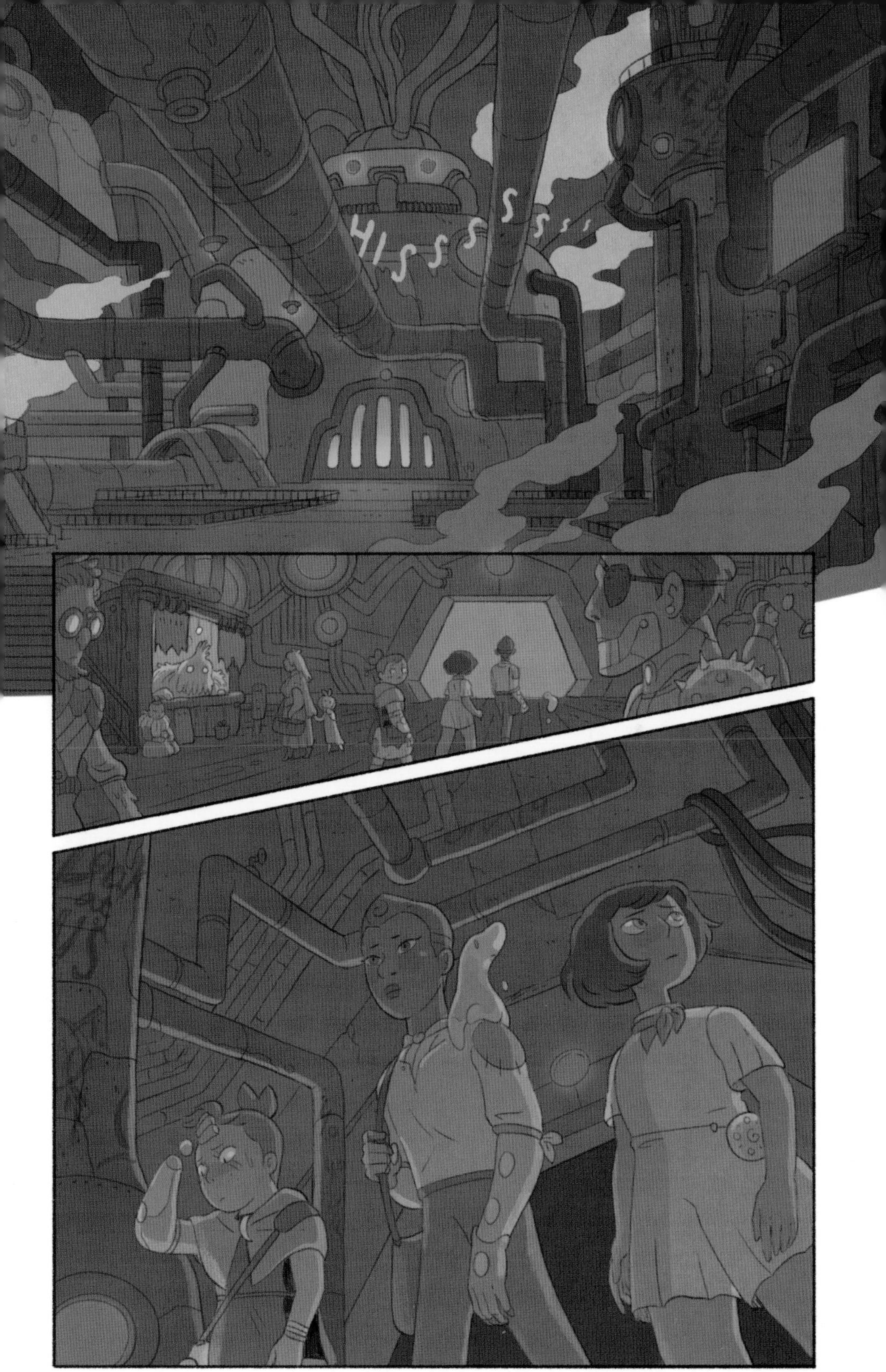
HISSSSSss

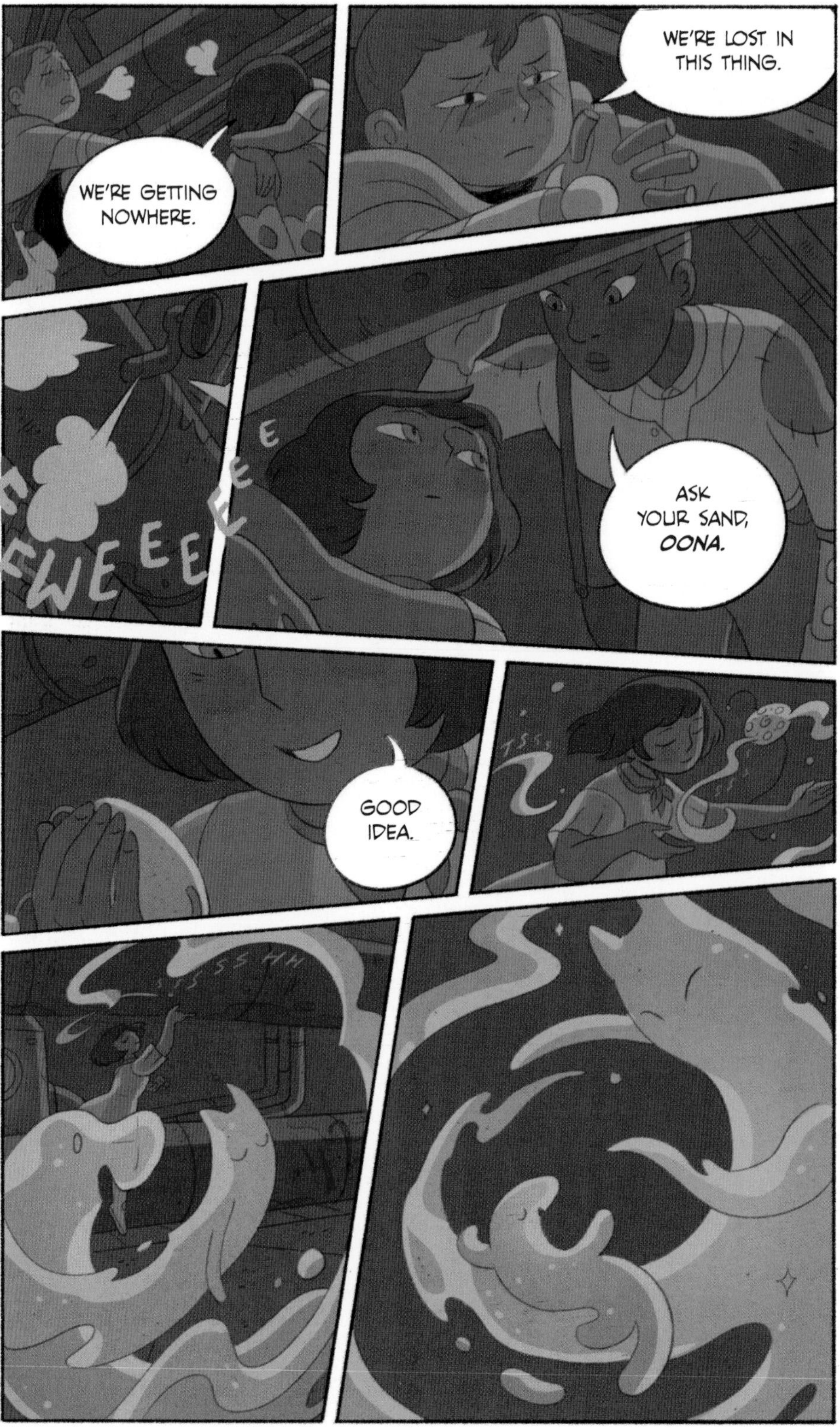
WE'RE GETTING NOWHERE.
WE'RE LOST IN THIS THING.
ASK YOUR SAND, *OONA.*
GOOD IDEA.

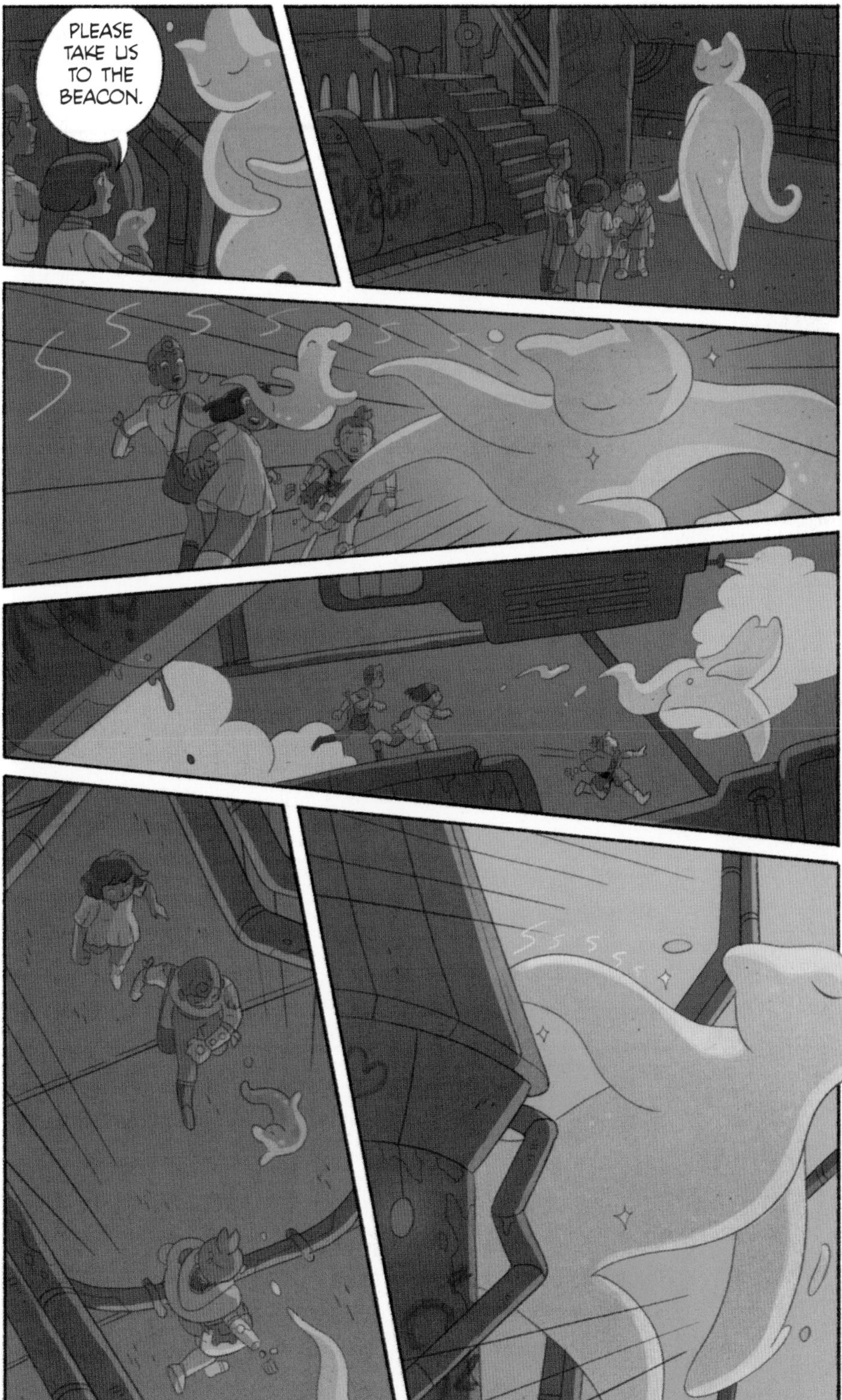
PLEASE TAKE US TO THE BEACON.

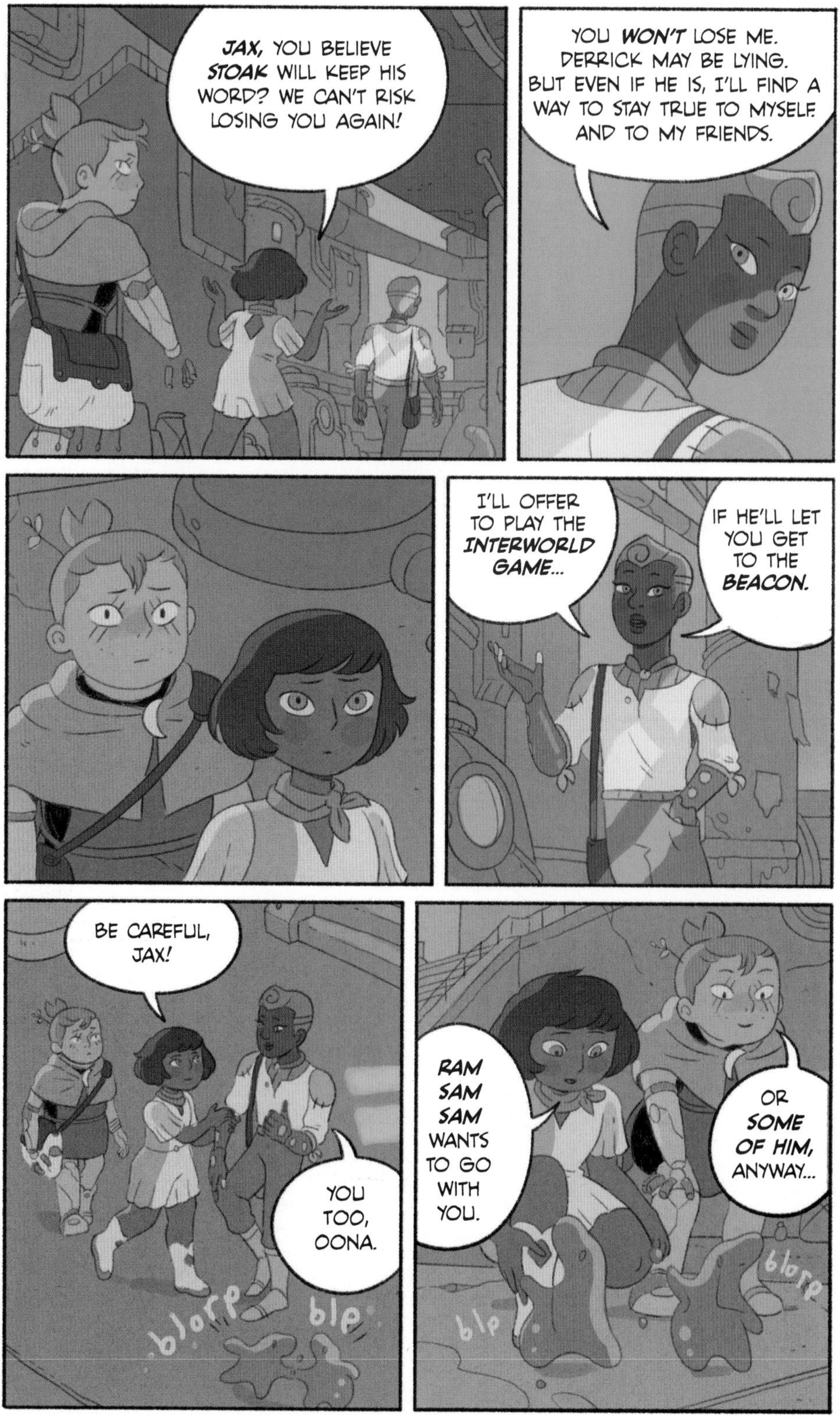
JAX, YOU BELIEVE STOAK WILL KEEP HIS WORD? WE CAN'T RISK LOSING YOU AGAIN!
YOU WON'T LOSE ME. DERRICK MAY BE LYING. BUT EVEN IF HE IS, I'LL FIND A WAY TO STAY TRUE TO MYSELF. AND TO MY FRIENDS.
I'LL OFFER TO PLAY THE INTERWORLD GAME...
IF HE'LL LET YOU GET TO THE BEACON.
BE CAREFUL, JAX!
YOU TOO, OONA.
blorp
blp
RAM SAM SAM WANTS TO GO WITH YOU.
OR SOME OF HIM, ANYWAY...
blp
blorp

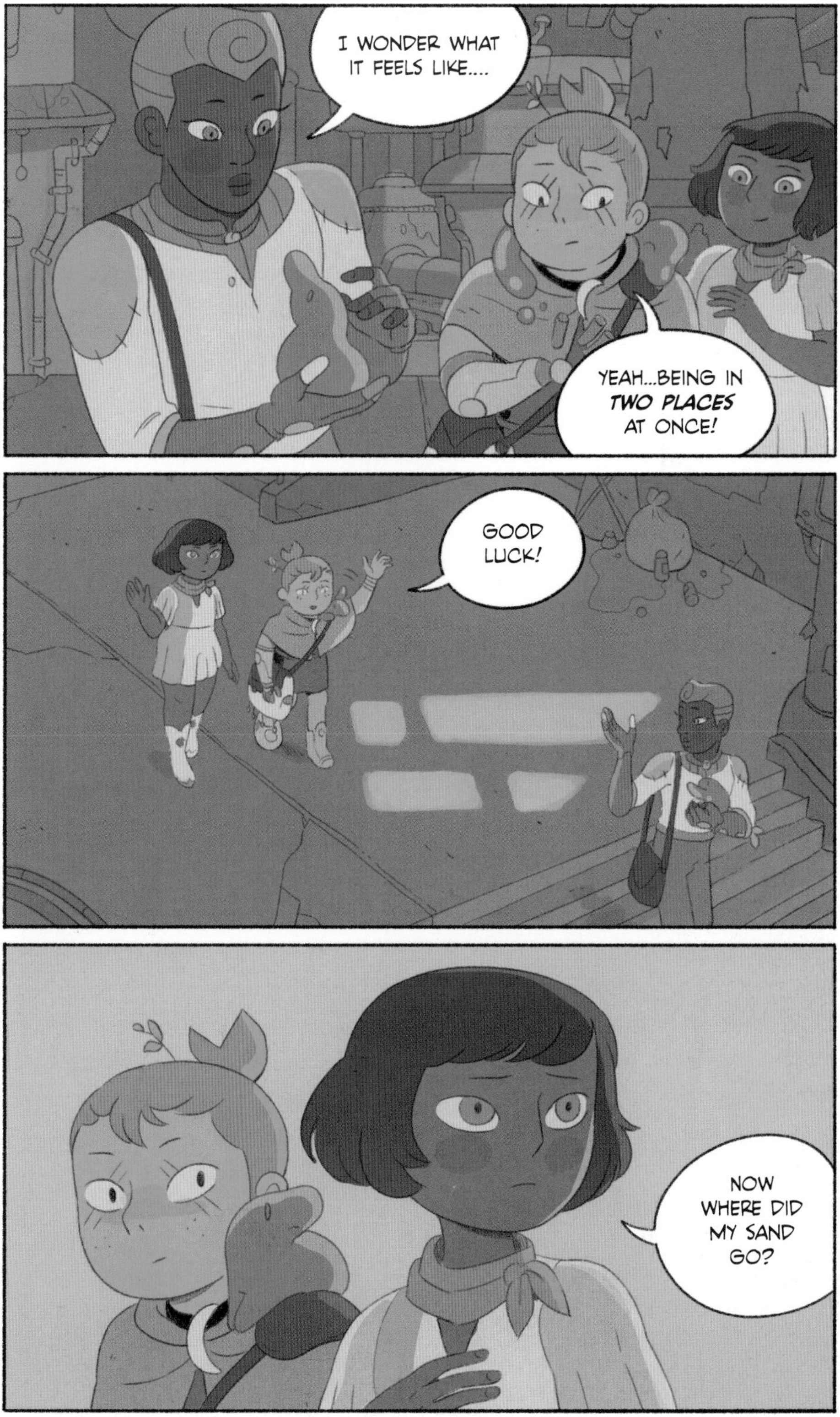
I WONDER WHAT IT FEELS LIKE....
YEAH...BEING IN *TWO PLACES* AT ONCE!
GOOD LUCK!
NOW WHERE DID MY SAND GO?

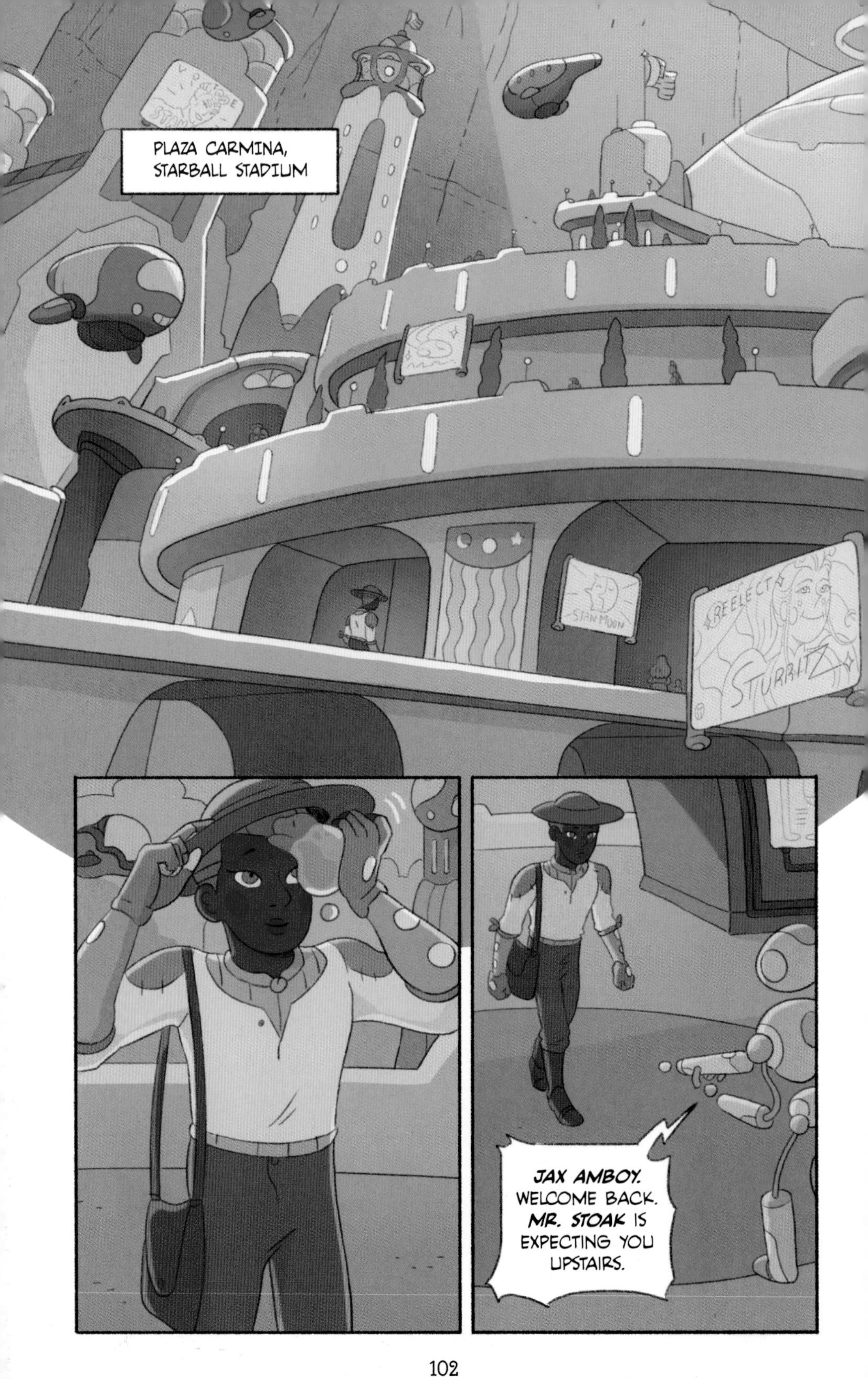
PLAZA CARMINA, STARBALL STADIUM
REELECT STURRITZ
JAX AMBOY. WELCOME BACK. MR. STOAK IS EXPECTING YOU UPSTAIRS.

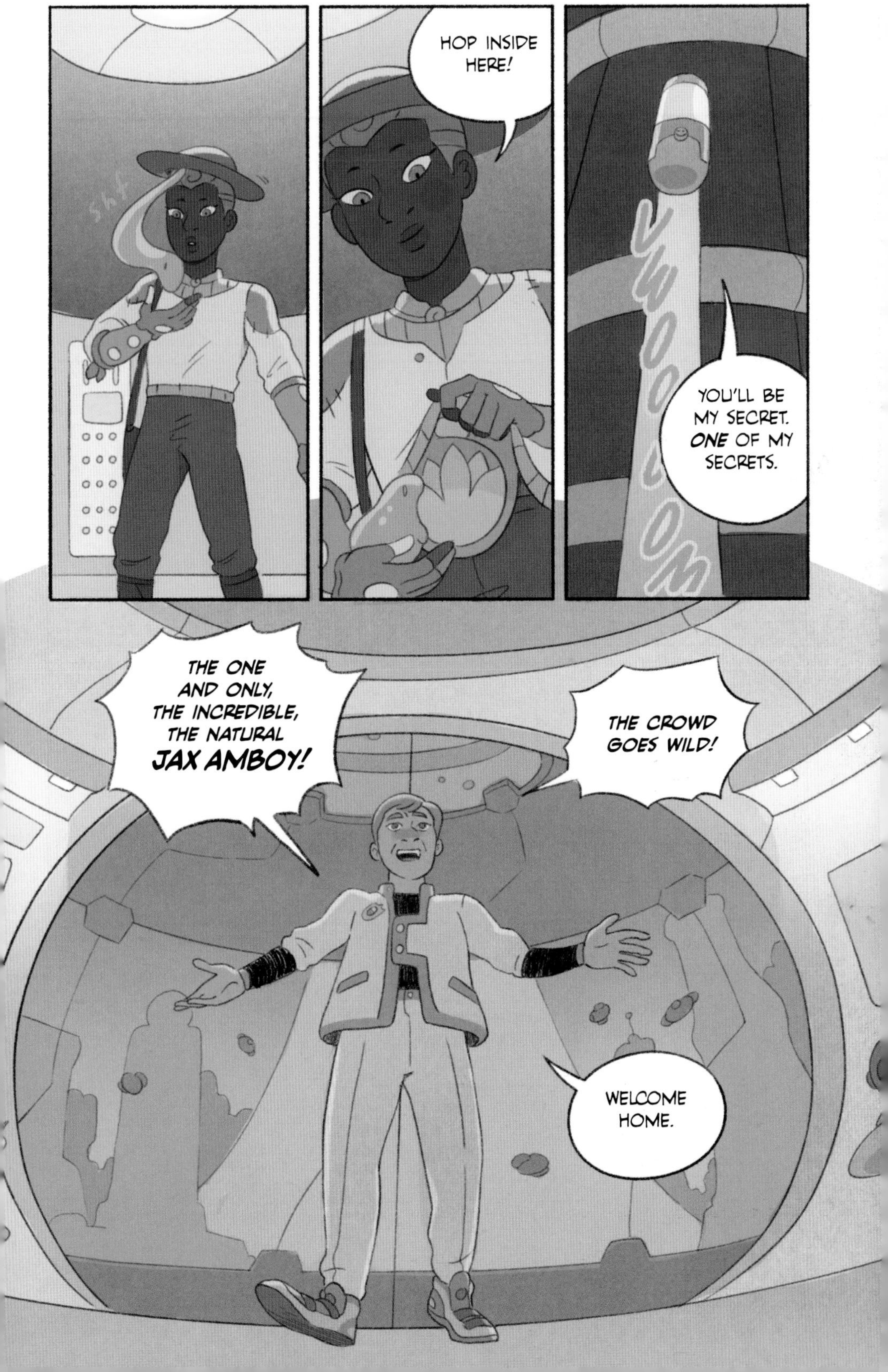
shf
HOP INSIDE HERE!
VWOOOOOM
YOU'LL BE MY SECRET. ONE OF MY SECRETS.
THE ONE AND ONLY, THE INCREDIBLE, THE NATURAL JAX AMBOY!
THE CROWD GOES WILD!
WELCOME HOME.

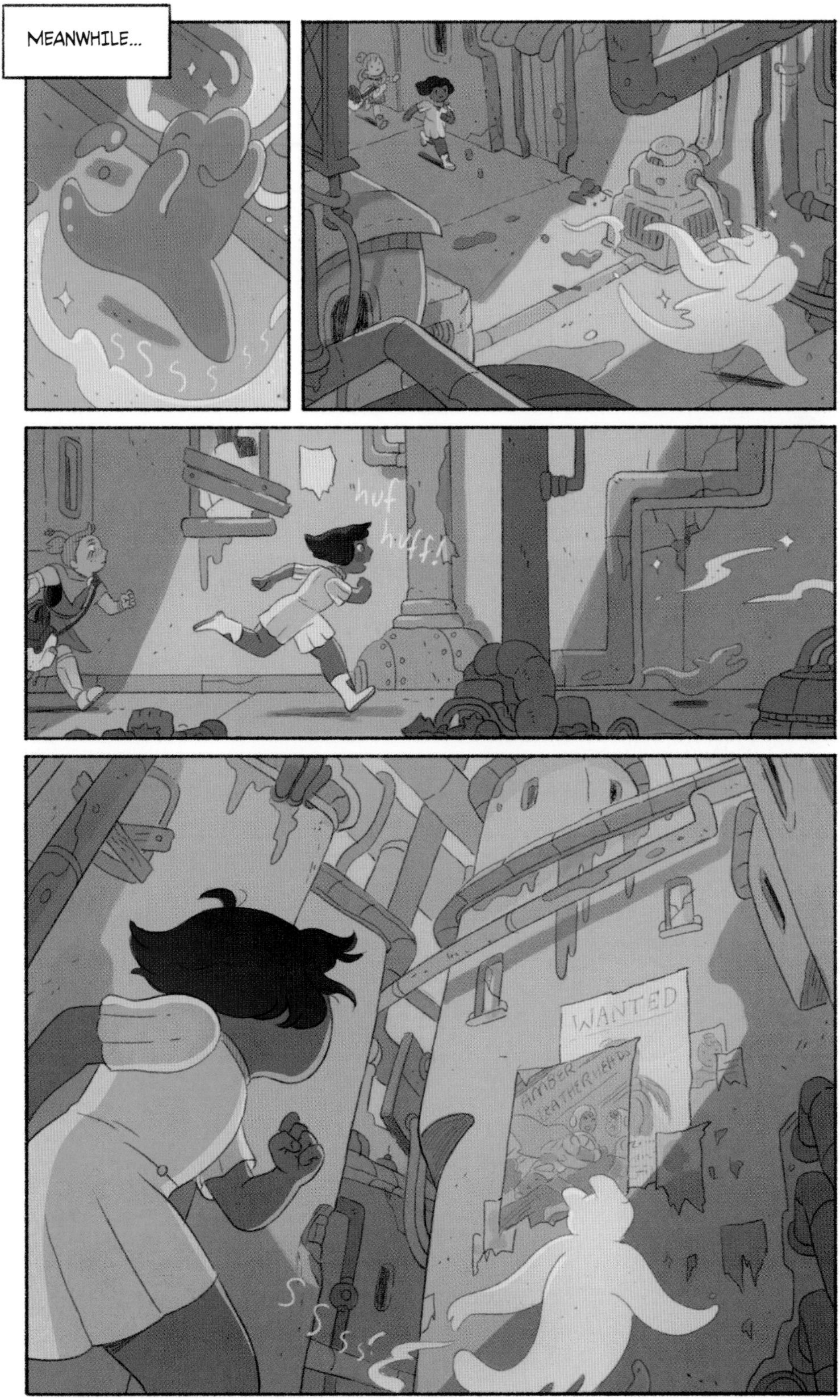
MEANWHILE...
huf
huff!
WANTED
AMBER LEATHERHEADS

THIS IS WHERE YOUR SAND TOOK US.

ZELLE? SHE'S A *YATTAN SAND MASTER.* SHE WAS TRAINED AT THE SAND CASTLE ON *MON DOMANI.*

*PLUMB* TOLD ME SHE DISCOVERED HIGH LEVELS OF SAND DANCING. AND *DISAPPEARED* INTO THE DESERT.

UM, HEY THERE... WHERE CAN WE FIND THIS PERSON?

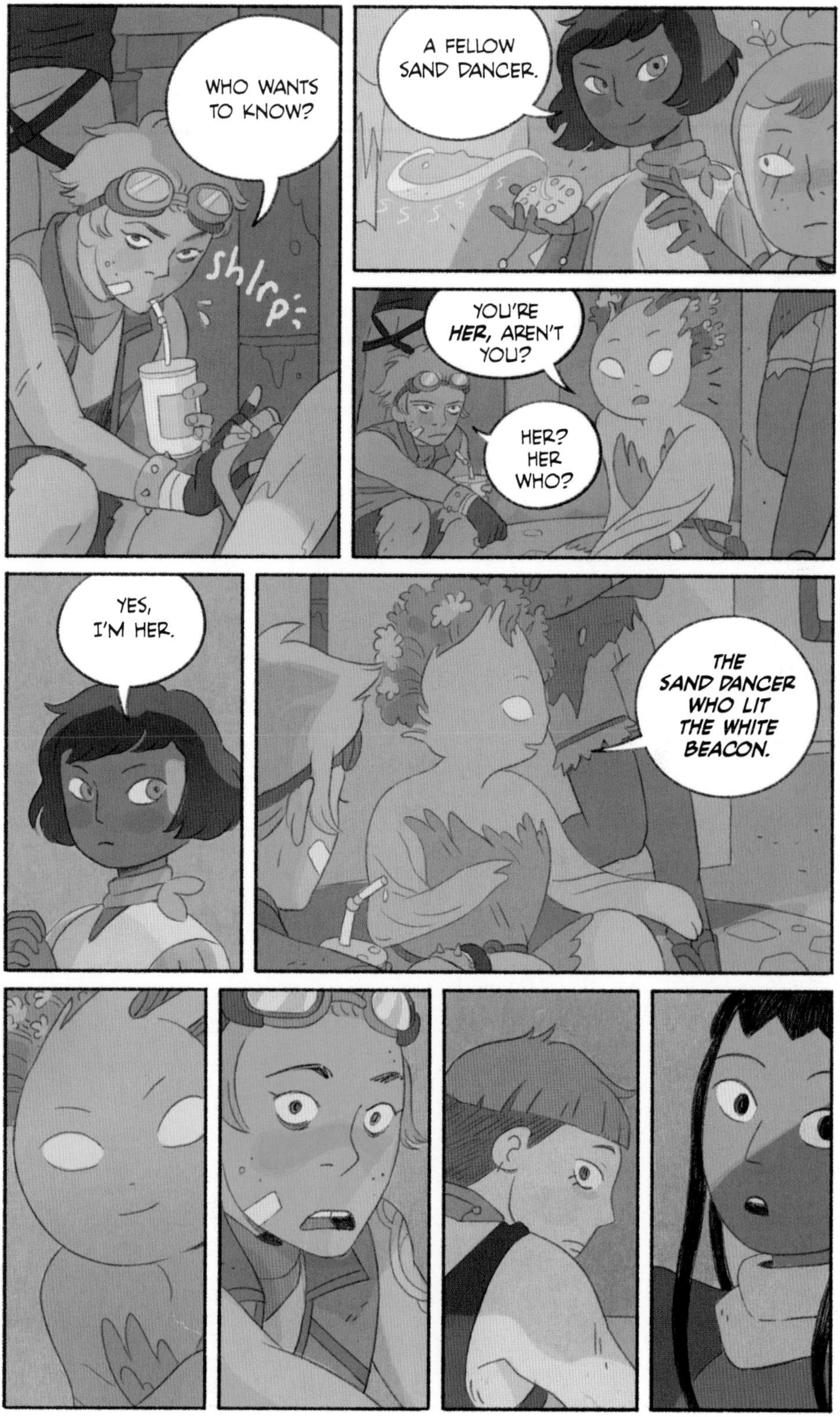
WHO WANTS TO KNOW?
shlrp
A FELLOW SAND DANCER.
YOU'RE HER, AREN'T YOU?
HER? HER WHO?
YES, I'M HER.
THE SAND DANCER WHO LIT THE WHITE BEACON.

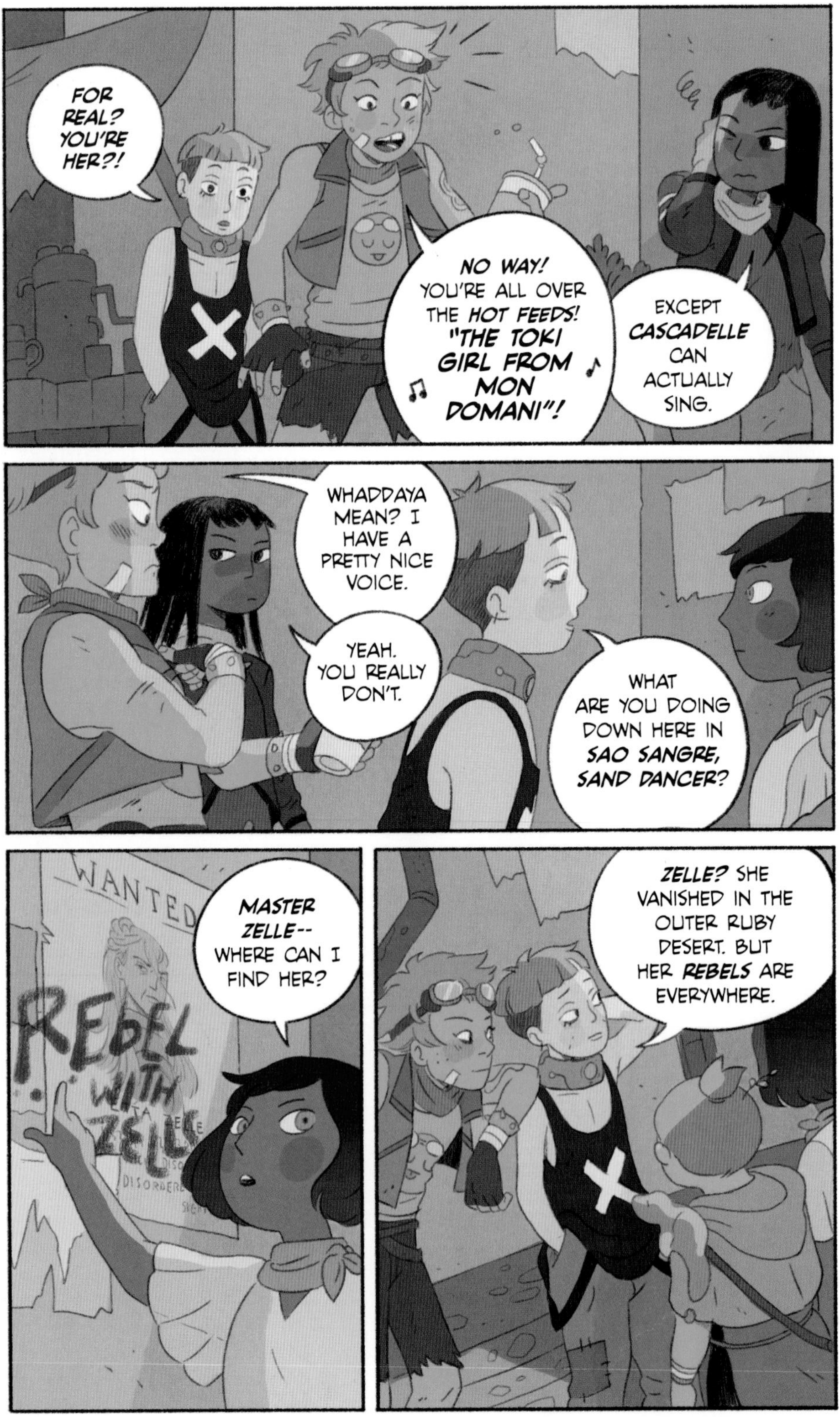
FOR REAL? YOU'RE HER?!
NO WAY! YOU'RE ALL OVER THE HOT FEEDS! "THE TOKI GIRL FROM MON DOMANI"!
EXCEPT CASCADELLE CAN ACTUALLY SING.
WHADDAYA MEAN? I HAVE A PRETTY NICE VOICE.
YEAH. YOU REALLY DON'T.
WHAT ARE YOU DOING DOWN HERE IN SAO SANGRE, SAND DANCER?
WANTED
REBEL WITH ZELLE
MASTER ZELLE-- WHERE CAN I FIND HER?
ZELLE? SHE VANISHED IN THE OUTER RUBY DESERT. BUT HER REBELS ARE EVERYWHERE.

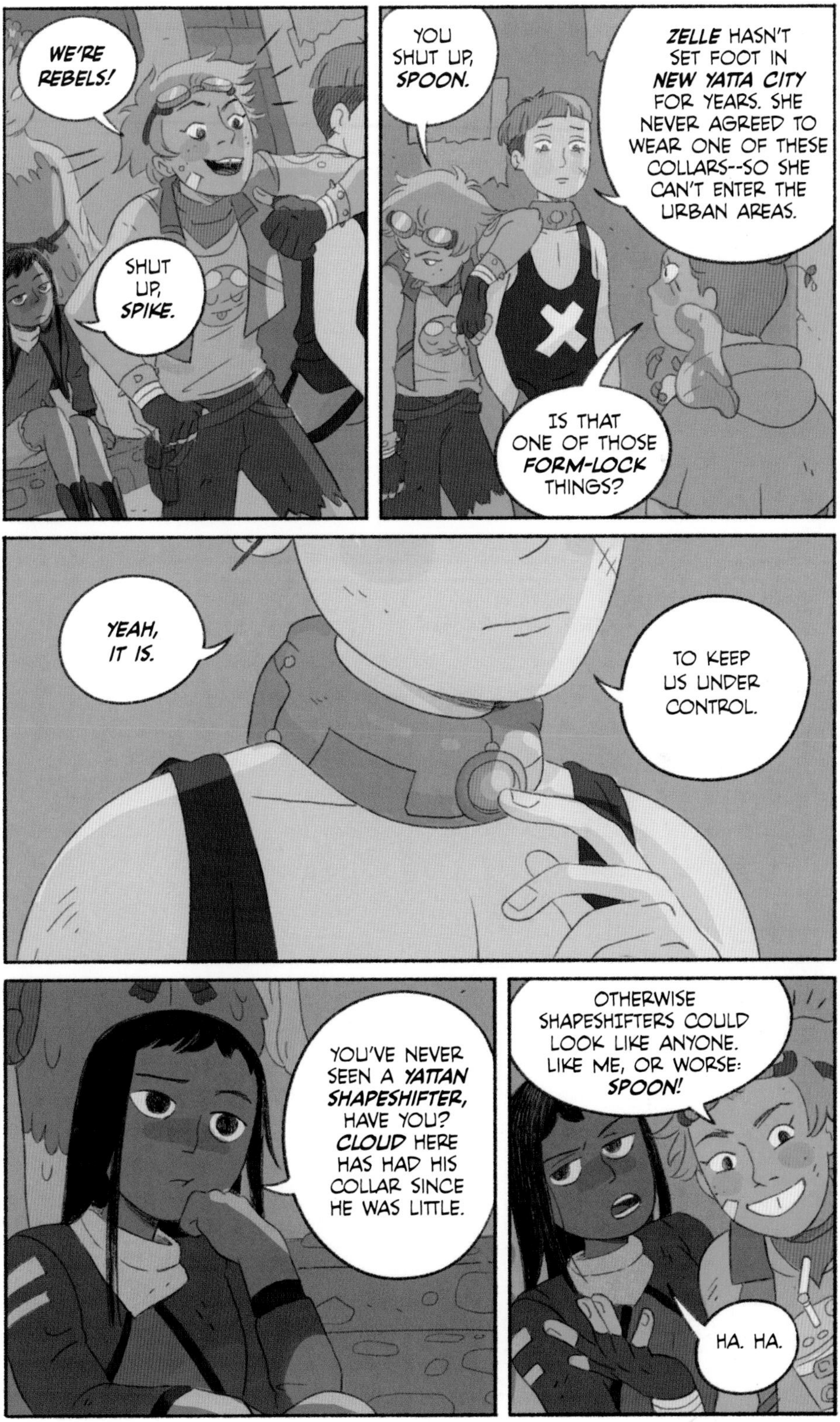
WE'RE REBELS!
SHUT UP, SPIKE.
YOU SHUT UP, SPOON.
ZELLE HASN'T SET FOOT IN NEW YATTA CITY FOR YEARS. SHE NEVER AGREED TO WEAR ONE OF THESE COLLARS--SO SHE CAN'T ENTER THE URBAN AREAS.
IS THAT ONE OF THOSE FORM-LOCK THINGS?
YEAH, IT IS.
TO KEEP US UNDER CONTROL.
YOU'VE NEVER SEEN A YATTAN SHAPESHIFTER, HAVE YOU? CLOUD HERE HAS HAD HIS COLLAR SINCE HE WAS LITTLE.
OTHERWISE SHAPESHIFTERS COULD LOOK LIKE ANYONE. LIKE ME, OR WORSE: SPOON!
HA. HA.

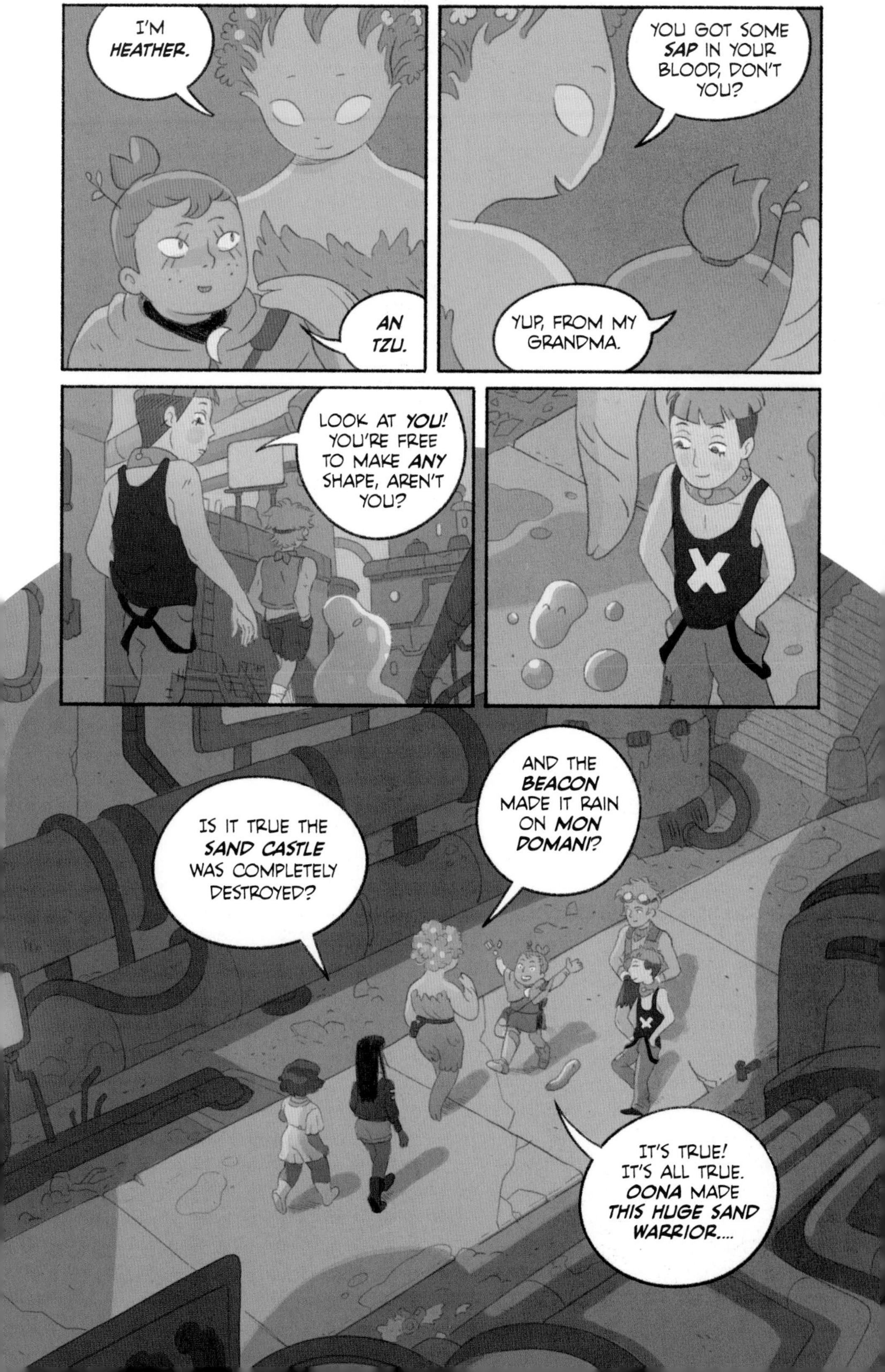
I'M HEATHER.
AN TZU.
YOU GOT SOME SAP IN YOUR BLOOD, DON'T YOU?
YUP, FROM MY GRANDMA.
LOOK AT YOU! YOU'RE FREE TO MAKE ANY SHAPE, AREN'T YOU?
IS IT TRUE THE SAND CASTLE WAS COMPLETELY DESTROYED?
AND THE BEACON MADE IT RAIN ON MON DOMANI?
IT'S TRUE! IT'S ALL TRUE. OONA MADE THIS HUGE SAND WARRIOR....

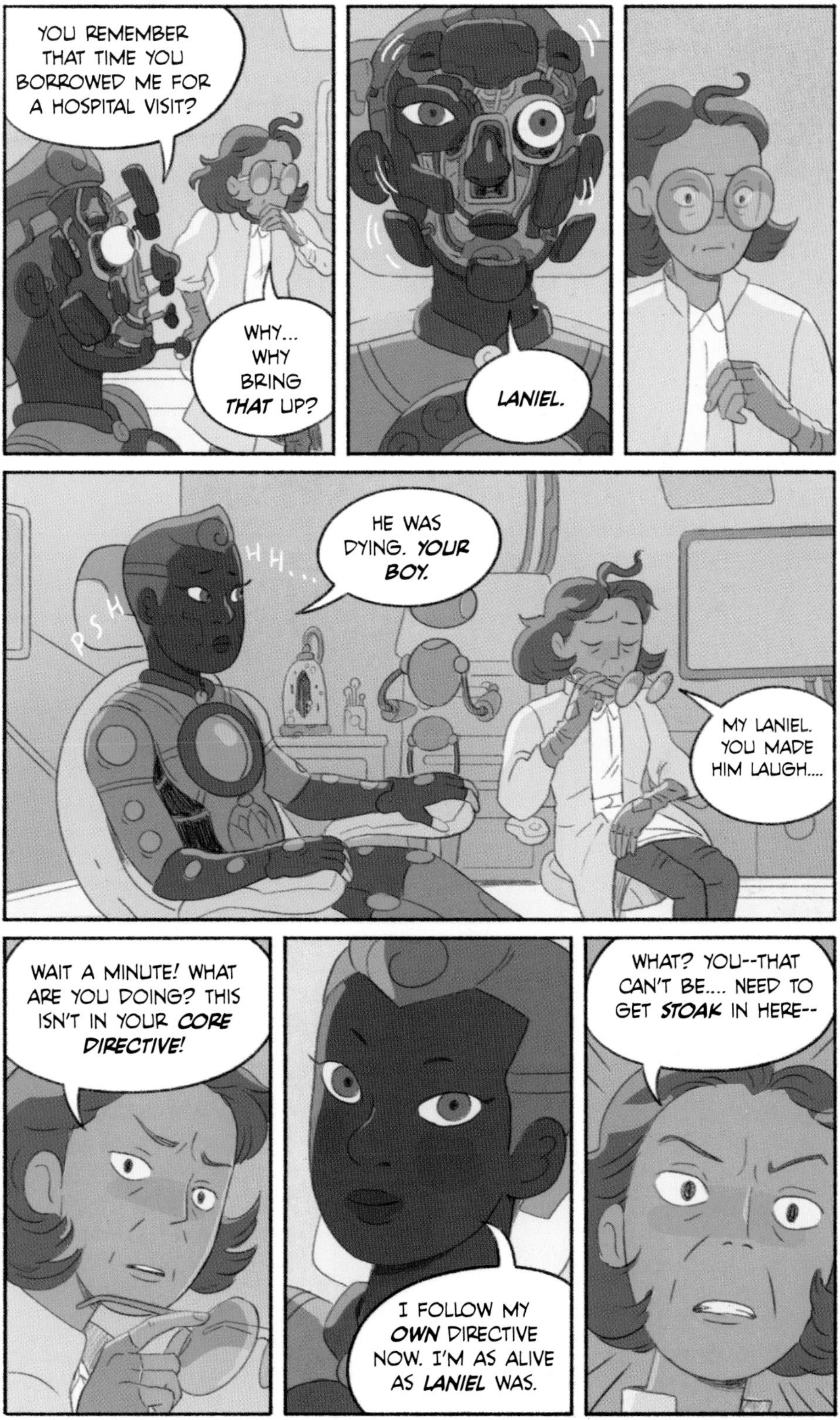
YOU REMEMBER THAT TIME YOU BORROWED ME FOR A HOSPITAL VISIT?
WHY... WHY BRING *THAT* UP?
*LANIEL.*
PSHHH...
HE WAS DYING. *YOUR BOY.*
MY LANIEL. YOU MADE HIM LAUGH....
WAIT A MINUTE! WHAT ARE YOU DOING? THIS ISN'T IN YOUR *CORE DIRECTIVE!*
I FOLLOW MY *OWN* DIRECTIVE NOW. I'M AS ALIVE AS *LANIEL* WAS.
WHAT? YOU--THAT CAN'T BE.... NEED TO GET *STOAK* IN HERE--

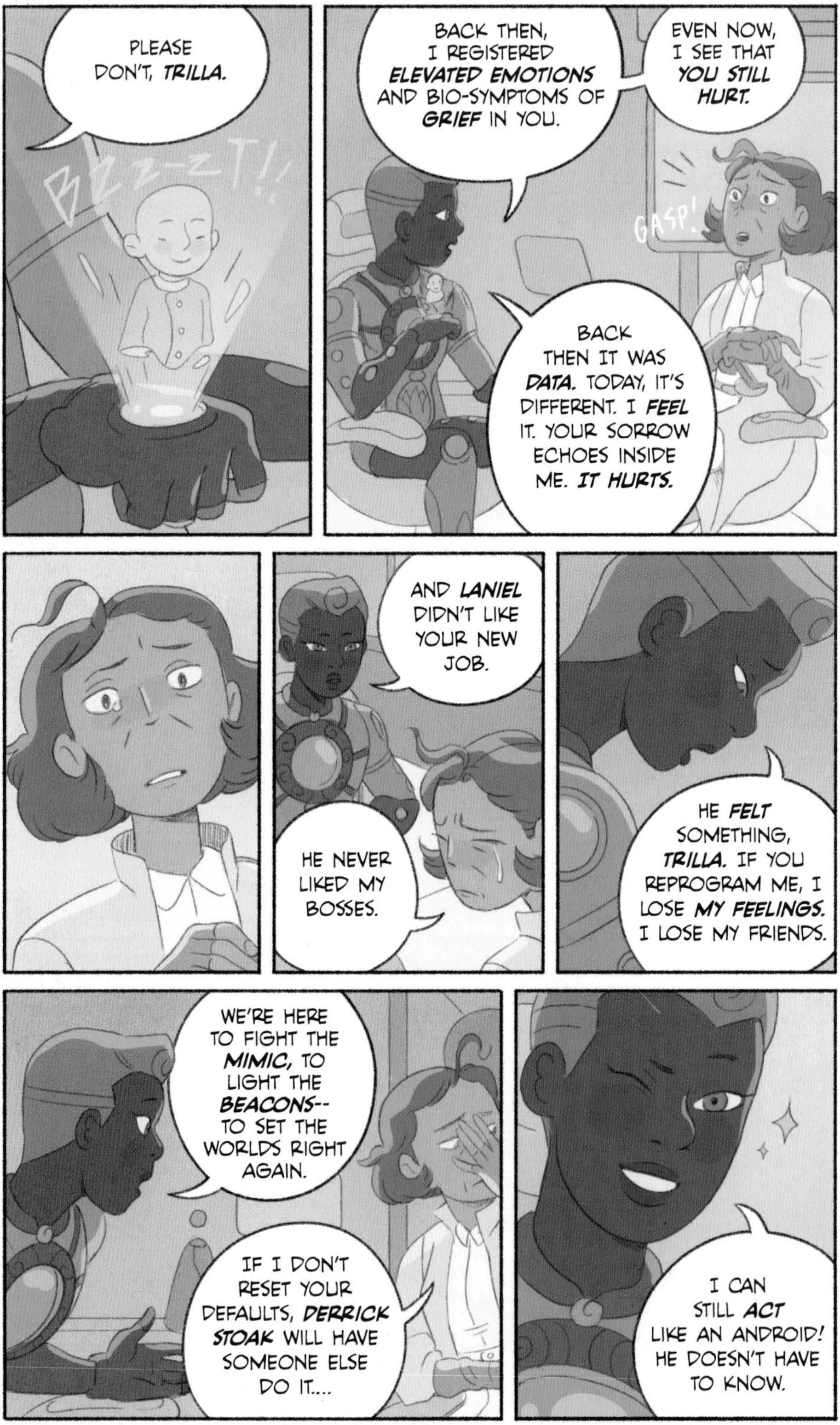
PLEASE DON'T, TRILLA.
BZZ-ZT!!
BACK THEN, I REGISTERED ELEVATED EMOTIONS AND BIO-SYMPTOMS OF GRIEF IN YOU.
EVEN NOW, I SEE THAT YOU STILL HURT.
GASP!
BACK THEN IT WAS DATA. TODAY, IT'S DIFFERENT. I FEEL IT. YOUR SORROW ECHOES INSIDE ME. IT HURTS.
AND LANIEL DIDN'T LIKE YOUR NEW JOB.
HE NEVER LIKED MY BOSSES.
HE FELT SOMETHING, TRILLA. IF YOU REPROGRAM ME, I LOSE MY FEELINGS. I LOSE MY FRIENDS.
WE'RE HERE TO FIGHT THE MIMIC, TO LIGHT THE BEACONS-- TO SET THE WORLDS RIGHT AGAIN.
IF I DON'T RESET YOUR DEFAULTS, DERRICK STOAK WILL HAVE SOMEONE ELSE DO IT....
I CAN STILL ACT LIKE AN ANDROID! HE DOESN'T HAVE TO KNOW.

## Chapter 6

# INTO THE BREACH

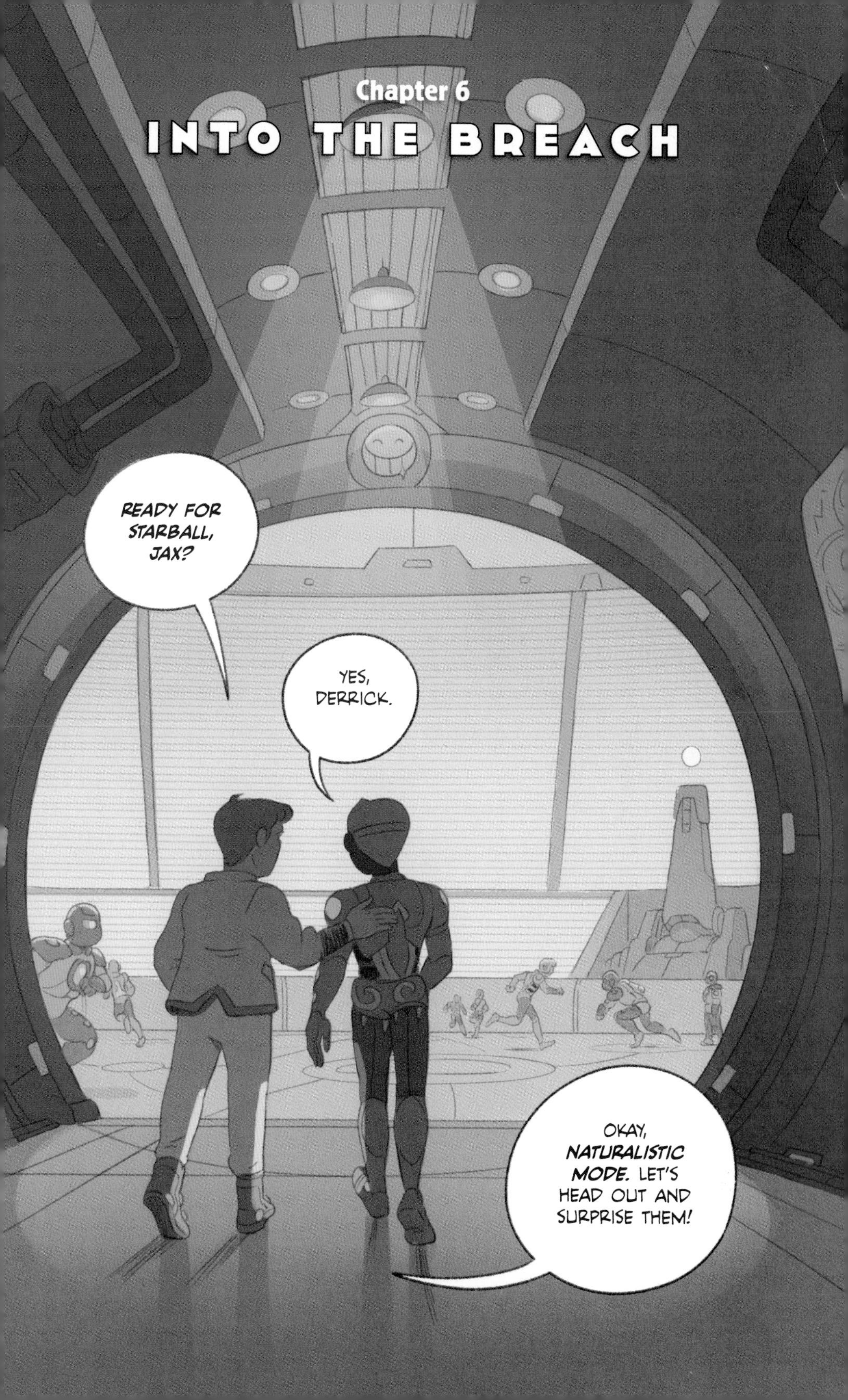

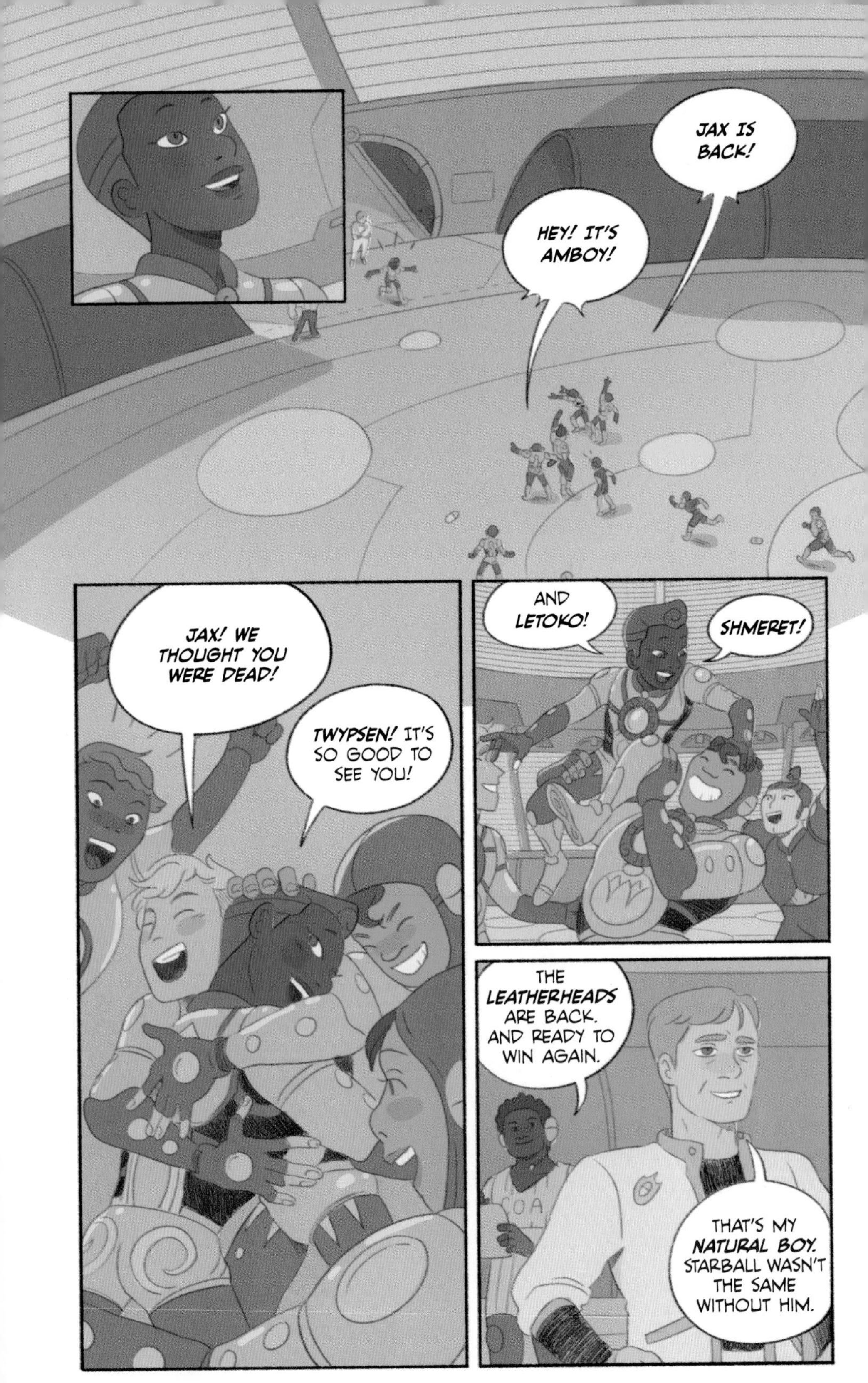
JAX IS BACK!
HEY! IT'S AMBOY!
JAX! WE THOUGHT YOU WERE DEAD!
TWYPSEN! IT'S SO GOOD TO SEE YOU!
AND LETOKO!
SHMERET!
THE LEATHERHEADS ARE BACK. AND READY TO WIN AGAIN.
THAT'S MY NATURAL BOY. STARBALL WASN'T THE SAME WITHOUT HIM.

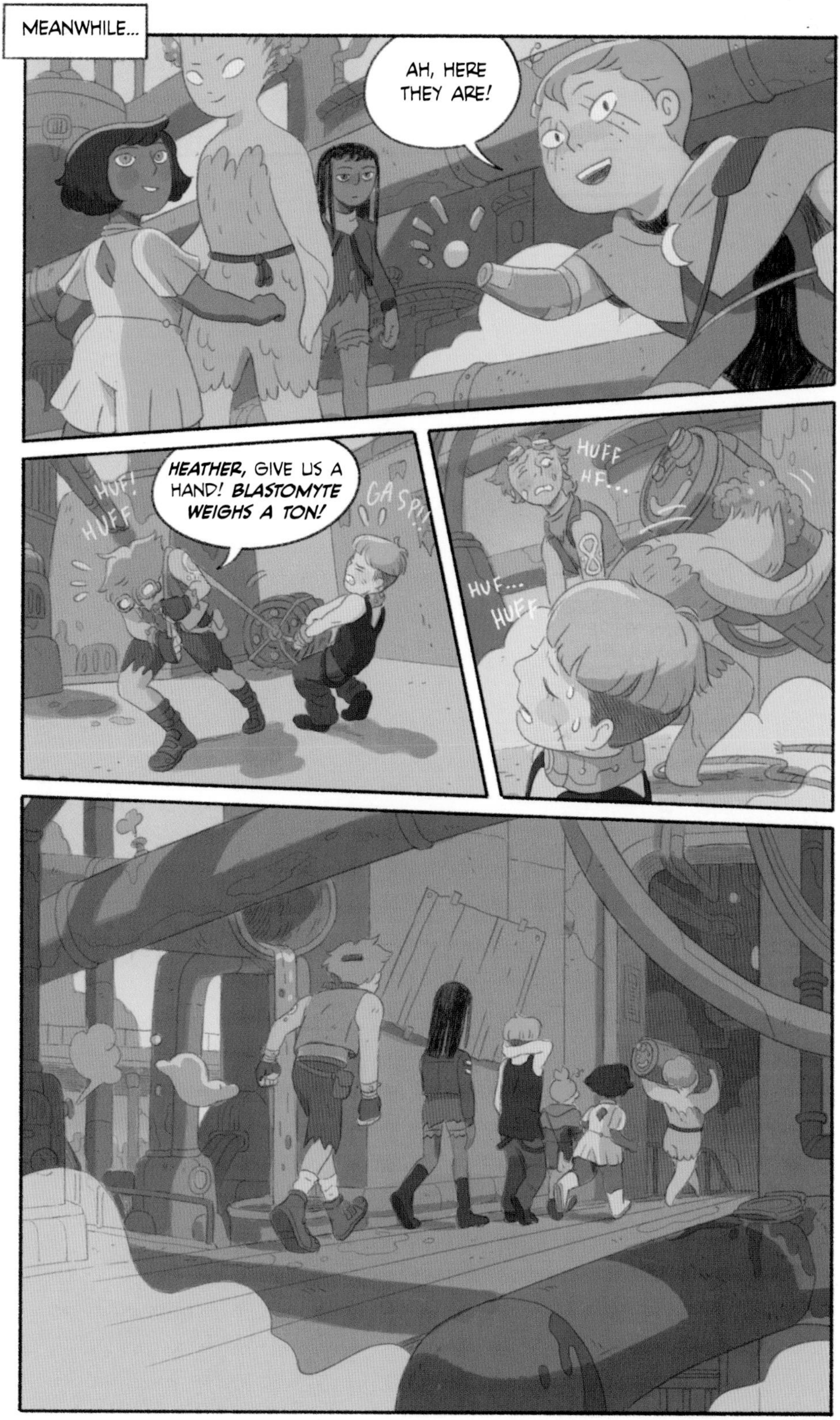
MEANWHILE...
AH, HERE THEY ARE!
HUF! HUFF
HEATHER, GIVE US A HAND! BLASTOMYTE WEIGHS A TON!
GASP!!
HUFF HF...
HUF... HUFF

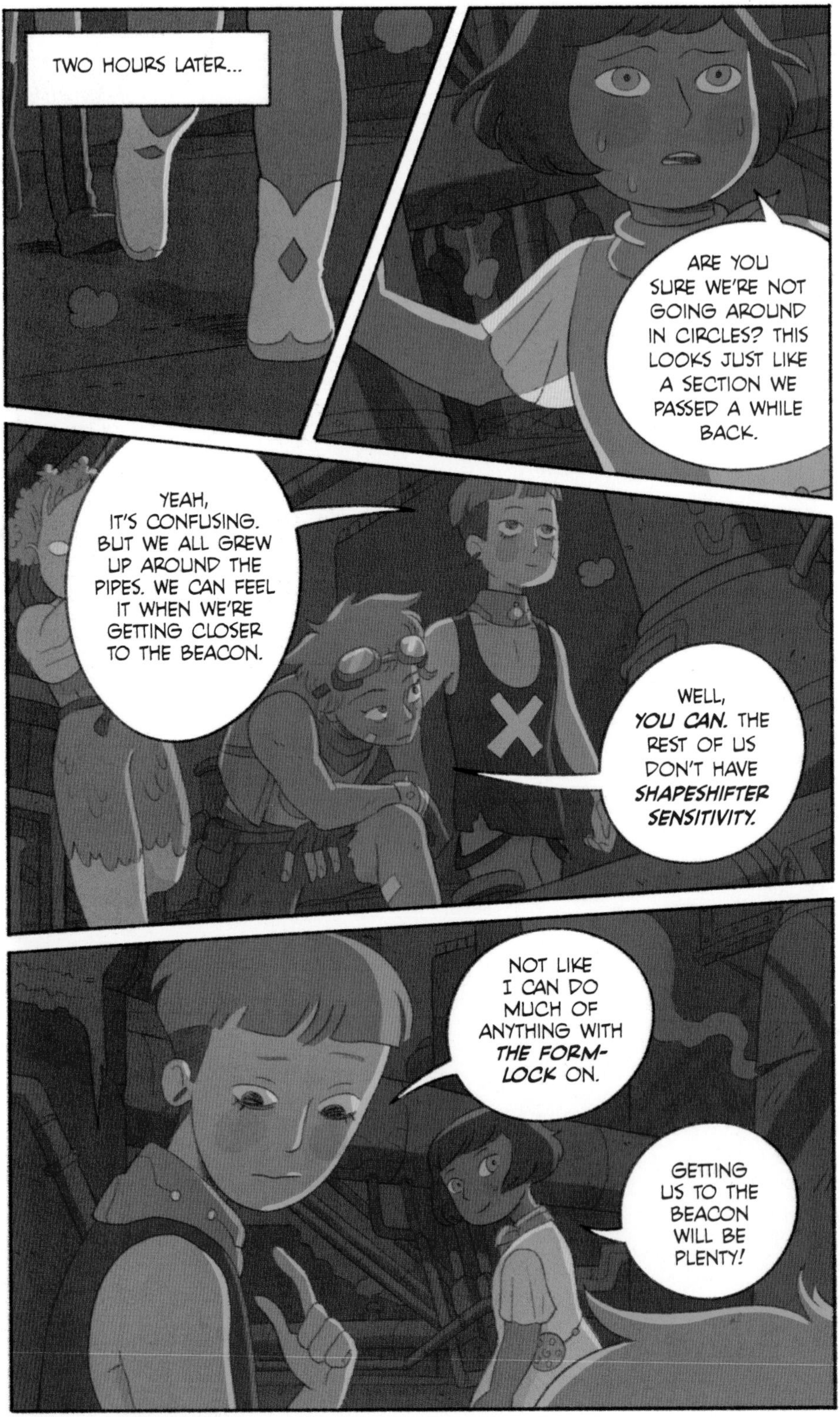
TWO HOURS LATER...
ARE YOU SURE WE'RE NOT GOING AROUND IN CIRCLES? THIS LOOKS JUST LIKE A SECTION WE PASSED A WHILE BACK.
YEAH, IT'S CONFUSING. BUT WE ALL GREW UP AROUND THE PIPES. WE CAN FEEL IT WHEN WE'RE GETTING CLOSER TO THE BEACON.
WELL, *YOU CAN.* THE REST OF US DON'T HAVE *SHAPESHIFTER SENSITIVITY.*
NOT LIKE I CAN DO MUCH OF ANYTHING WITH *THE FORM-LOCK* ON.
GETTING US TO THE BEACON WILL BE PLENTY!

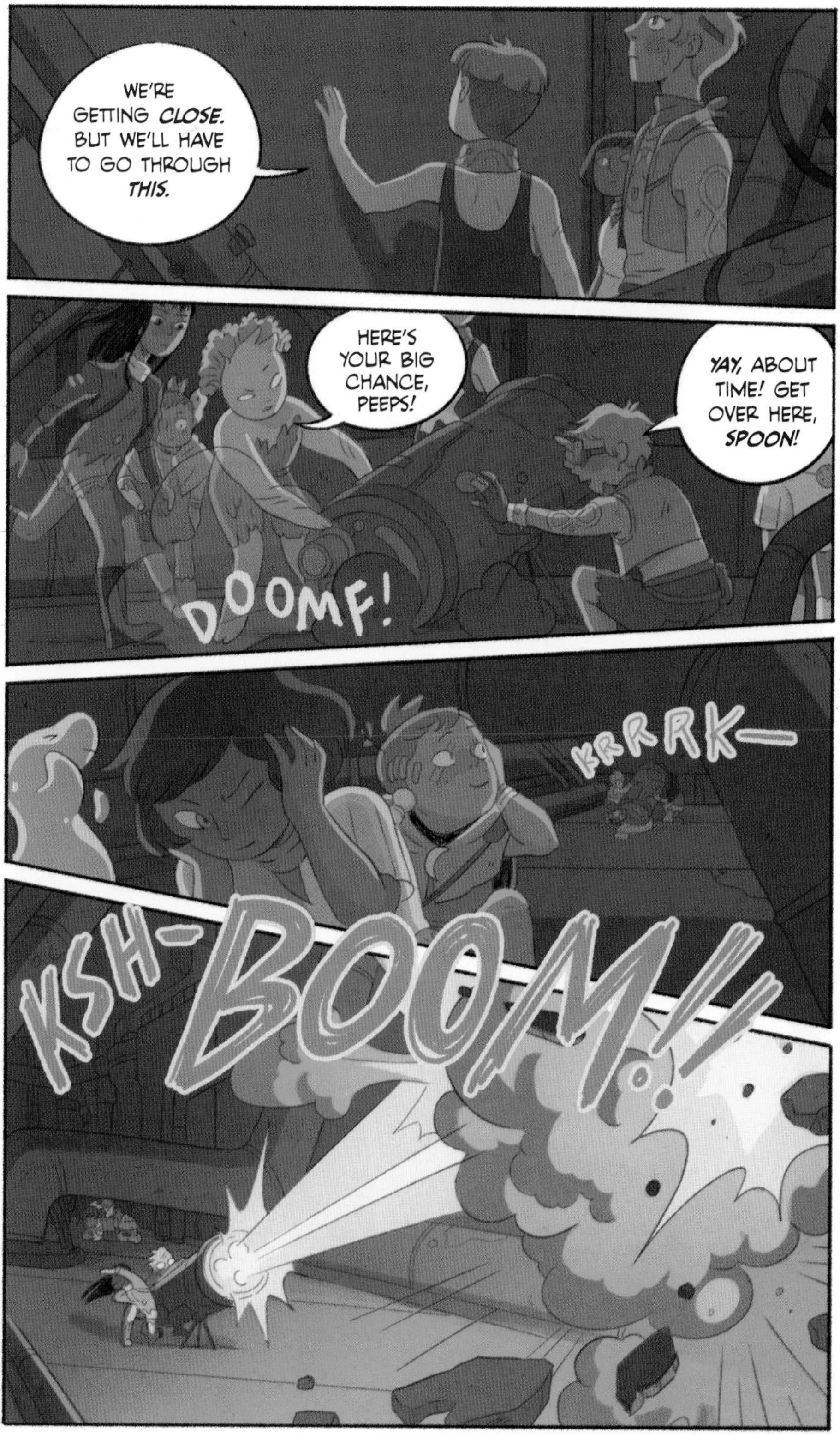
WE'RE GETTING *CLOSE.* BUT WE'LL HAVE TO GO THROUGH *THIS.*
HERE'S YOUR BIG CHANCE, PEEPS!
*YAY,* ABOUT TIME! GET OVER HERE, *SPOON!*
DOOMF!
KRRRK—
KSH-BOOM!!

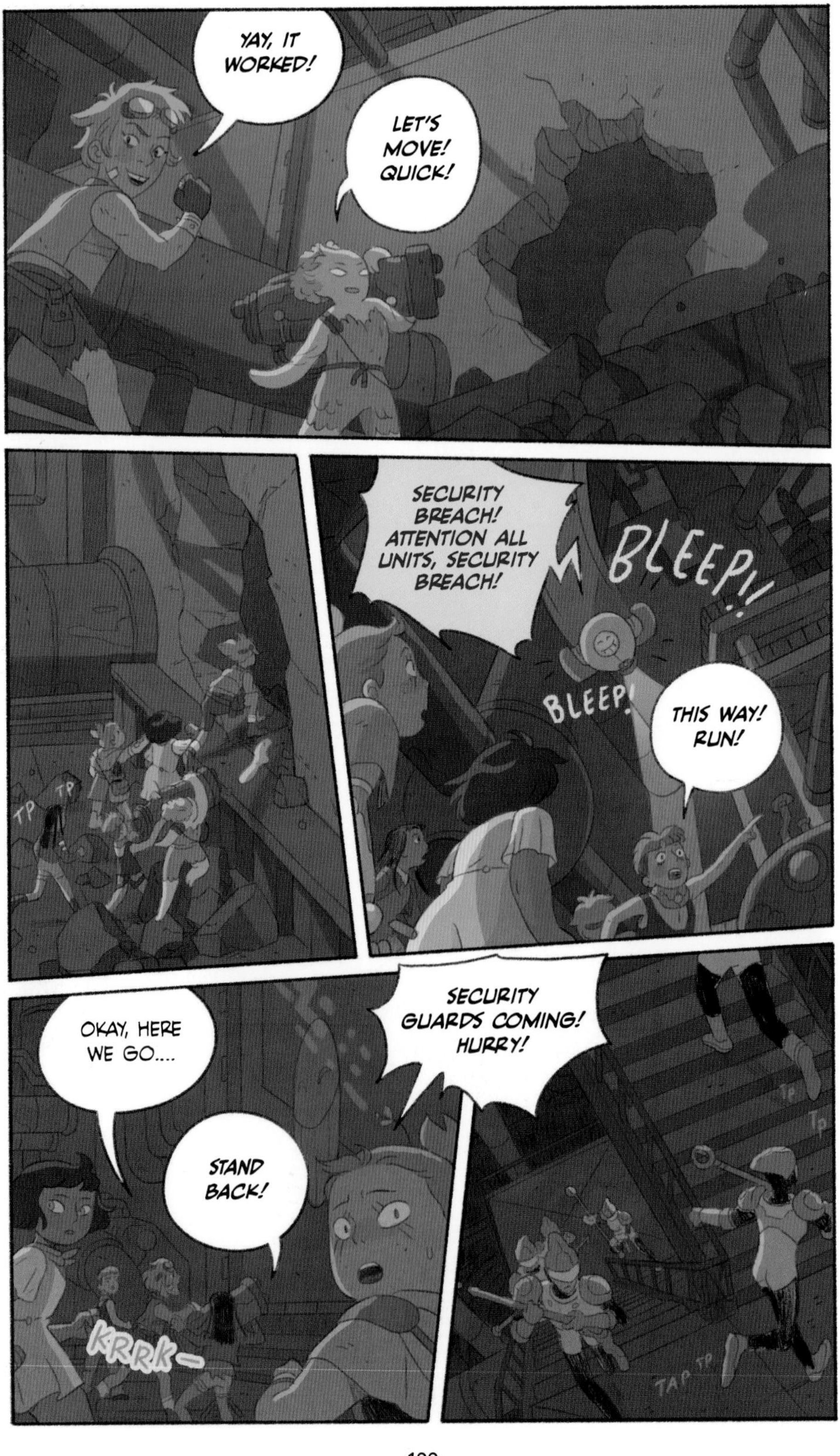
YAY, IT WORKED!
LET'S MOVE! QUICK!
SECURITY BREACH! ATTENTION ALL UNITS, SECURITY BREACH!
BLEEP!!
BLEEP!
THIS WAY! RUN!
TP TP
OKAY, HERE WE GO....
SECURITY GUARDS COMING! HURRY!
STAND BACK!
KRRK—
TAP TP

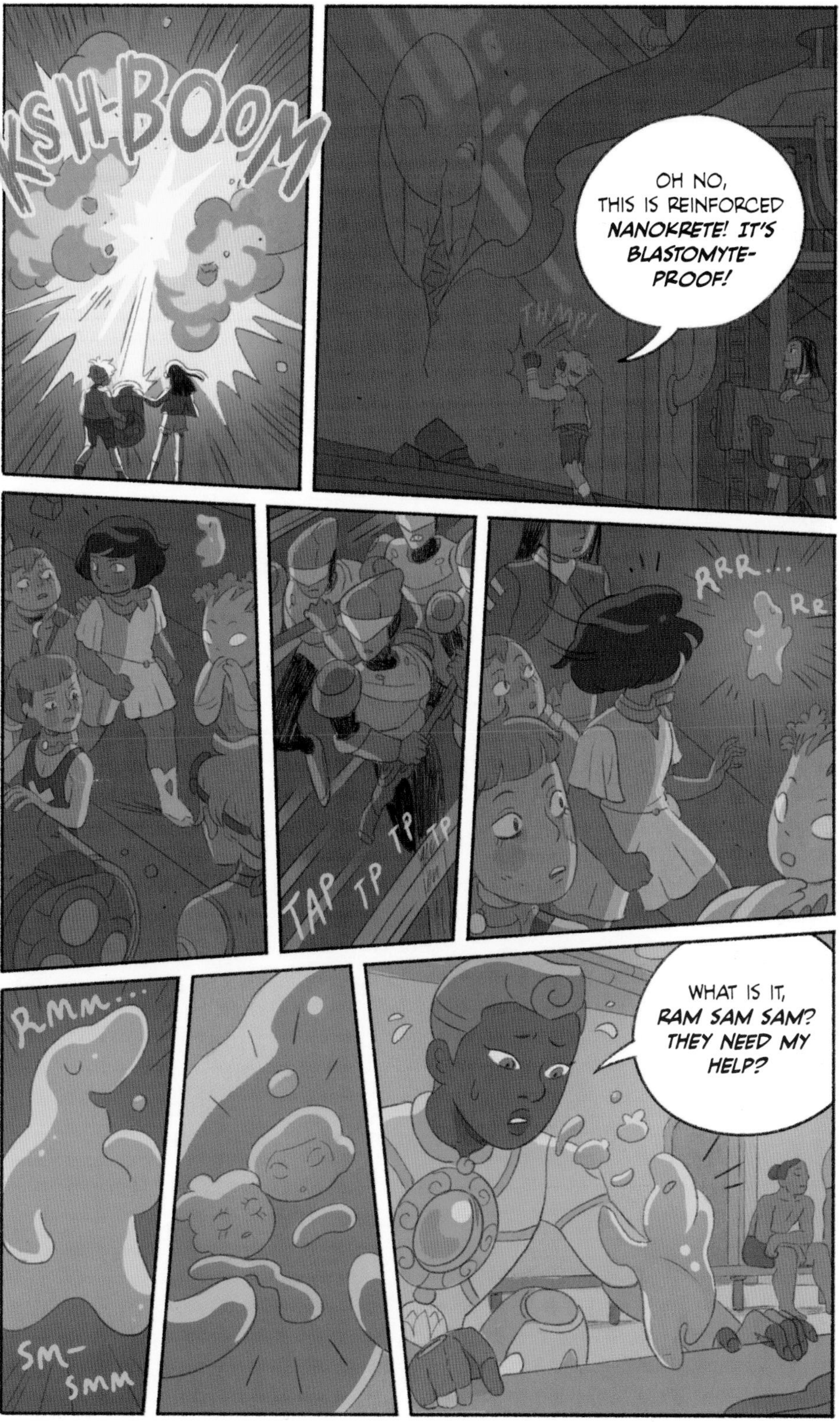
KSH-BOOM
THMP!
OH NO, THIS IS REINFORCED NANOKRETE! IT'S BLASTOMYTE-PROOF!
TAP TP TP TP
RRR... RR
RMM...
SM-SMM
WHAT IS IT, RAM SAM SAM? THEY NEED MY HELP?

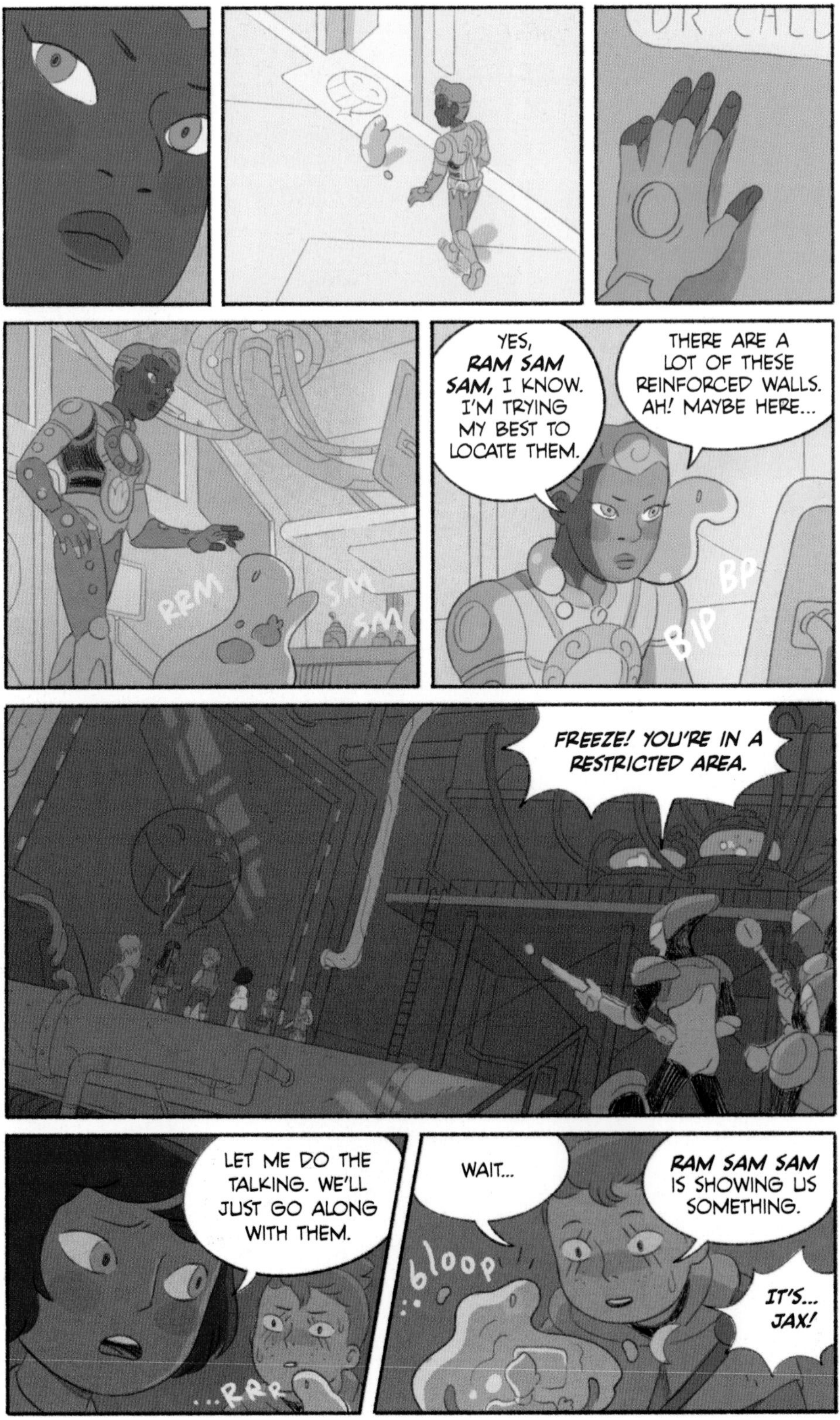
DR CALL
RRM
SM
SM
YES, RAM SAM SAM, I KNOW. I'M TRYING MY BEST TO LOCATE THEM.
THERE ARE A LOT OF THESE REINFORCED WALLS. AH! MAYBE HERE...
BIP
BP
FREEZE! YOU'RE IN A RESTRICTED AREA.
LET ME DO THE TALKING. WE'LL JUST GO ALONG WITH THEM.
...RRR
WAIT...
bloop
RAM SAM SAM IS SHOWING US SOMETHING.
IT'S... JAX!

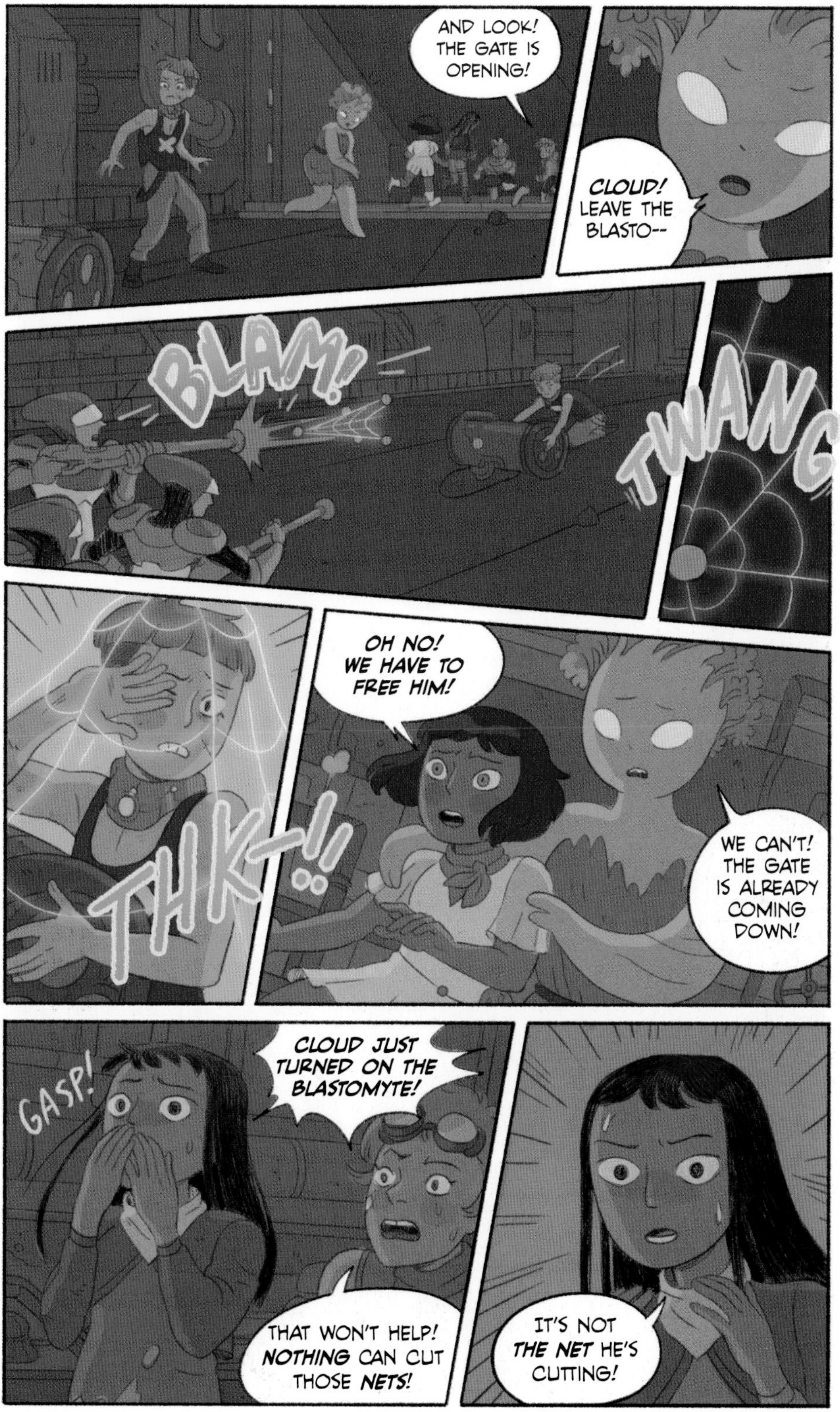
AND LOOK! THE GATE IS OPENING!
CLOUD! LEAVE THE BLASTO--
BLAM!
TWANG
THK--!!
OH NO! WE HAVE TO FREE HIM!
WE CAN'T! THE GATE IS ALREADY COMING DOWN!
GASP!
CLOUD JUST TURNED ON THE BLASTOMYTE!
THAT WON'T HELP! NOTHING CAN CUT THOSE NETS!
IT'S NOT THE NET HE'S CUTTING!

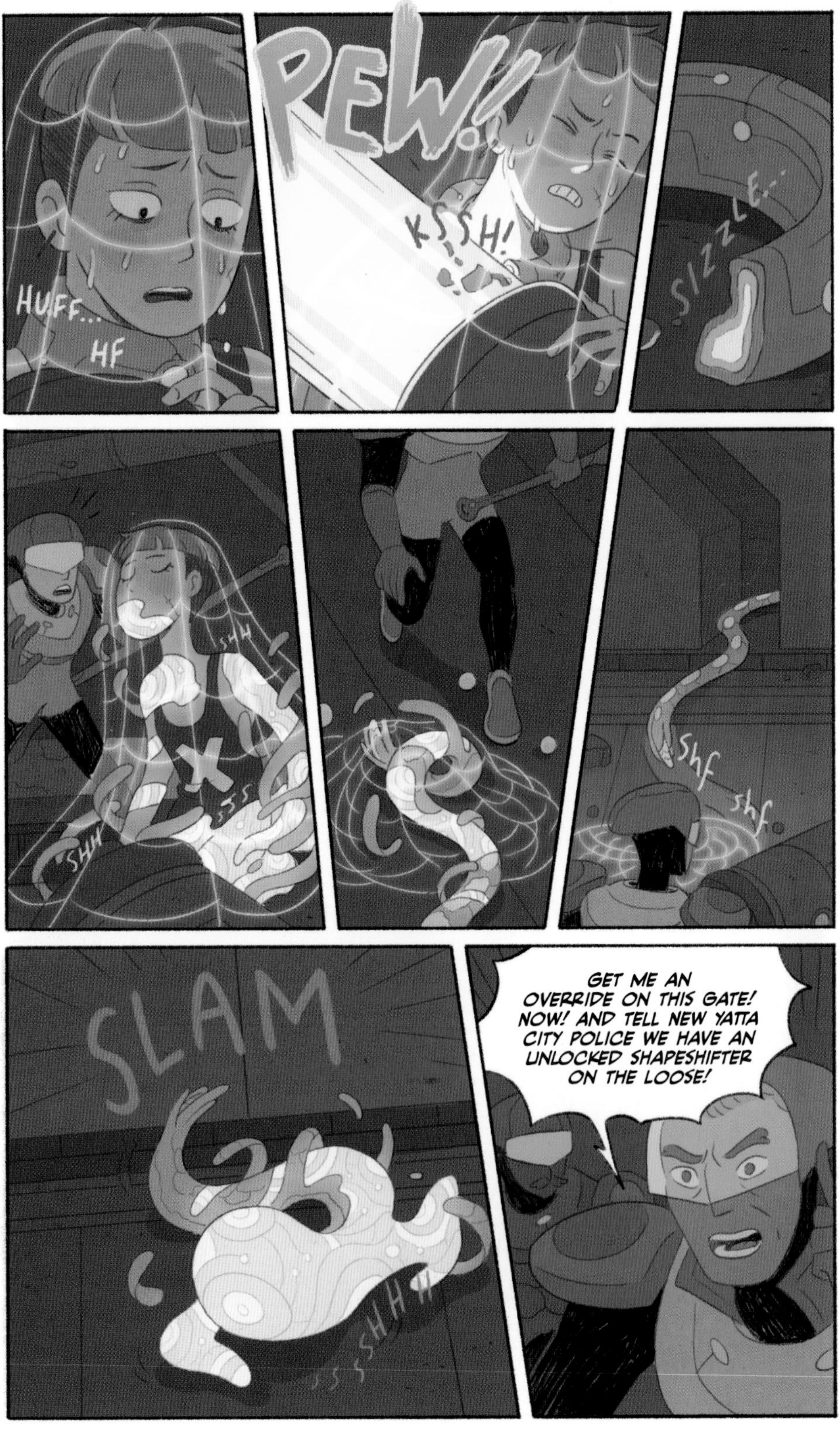
HUFF...
HF
PEW!!
KSSH!
SIZZLE...
SHH
SSS
SHH
Shf
shf
SLAM
SSSHHH
GET ME AN OVERRIDE ON THIS GATE! NOW! AND TELL NEW YATTA CITY POLICE WE HAVE AN UNLOCKED SHAPESHIFTER ON THE LOOSE!

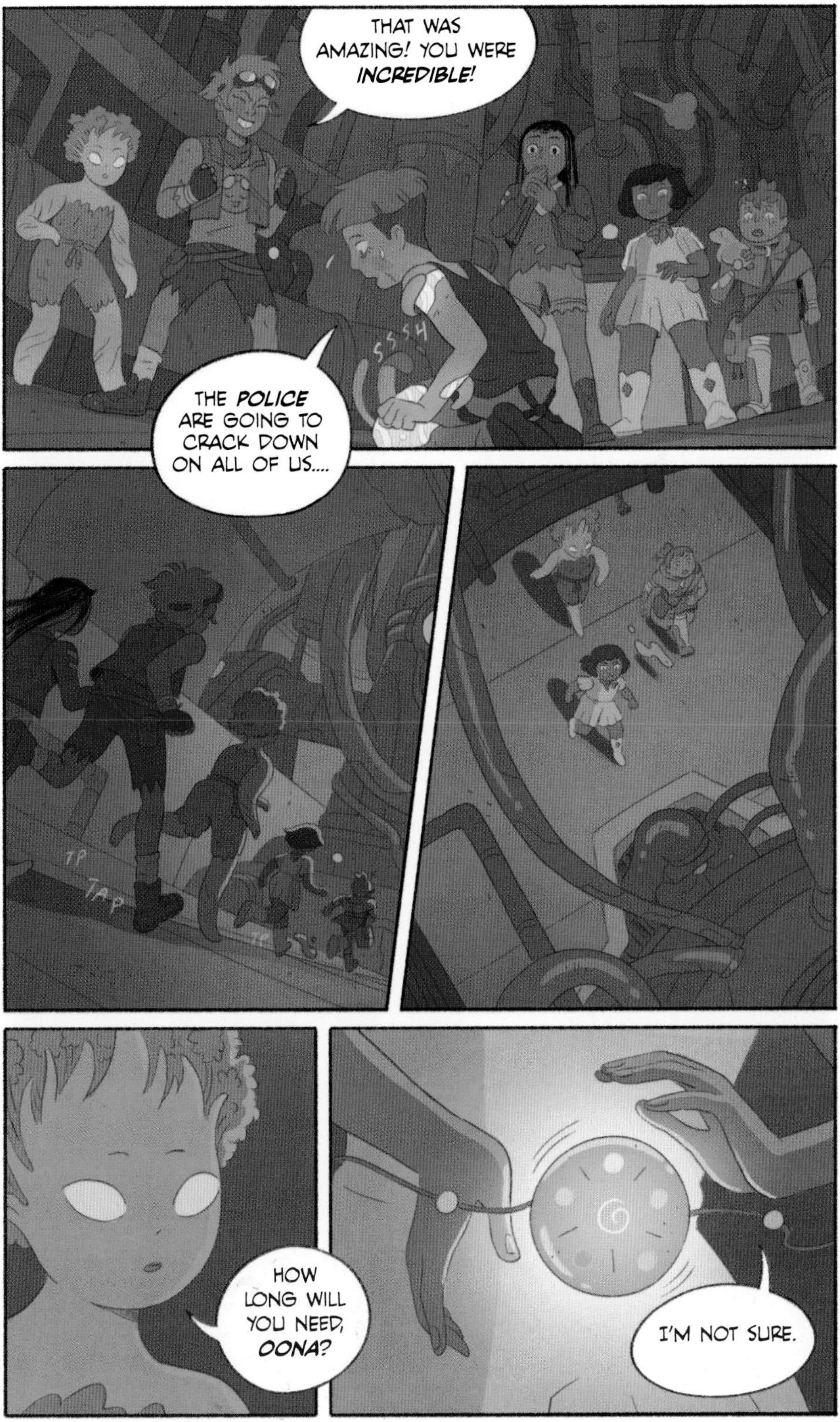
THAT WAS AMAZING! YOU WERE *INCREDIBLE!*
SSSH
THE *POLICE* ARE GOING TO CRACK DOWN ON ALL OF US....
TP
TAP
TP
HOW LONG WILL YOU NEED, *OONA*?
I'M NOT SURE.

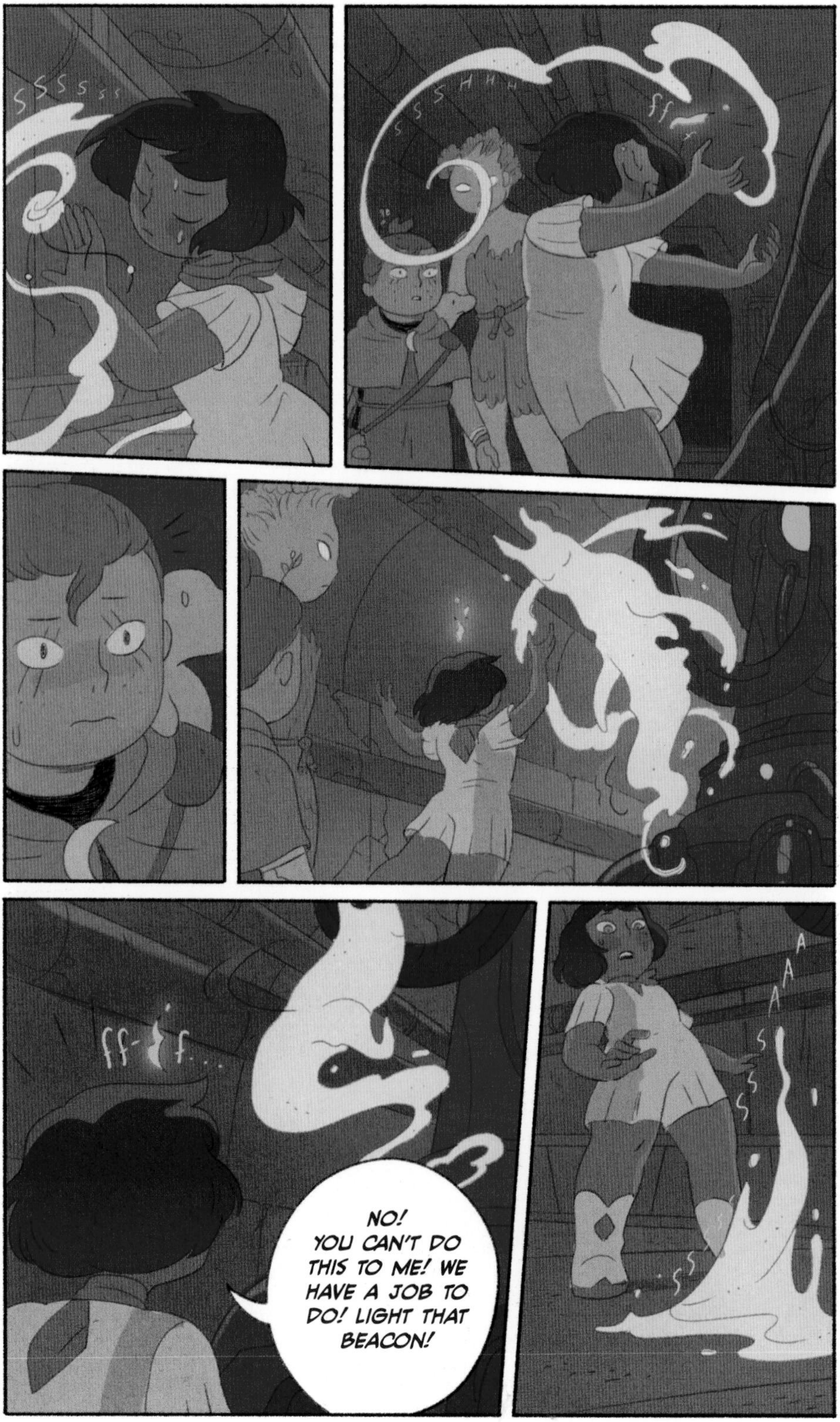
SSSSsss
SSSHHHH
ff~
ff- f...
NO! YOU CAN'T DO THIS TO ME! WE HAVE A JOB TO DO! LIGHT THAT BEACON!
AAAASSSS

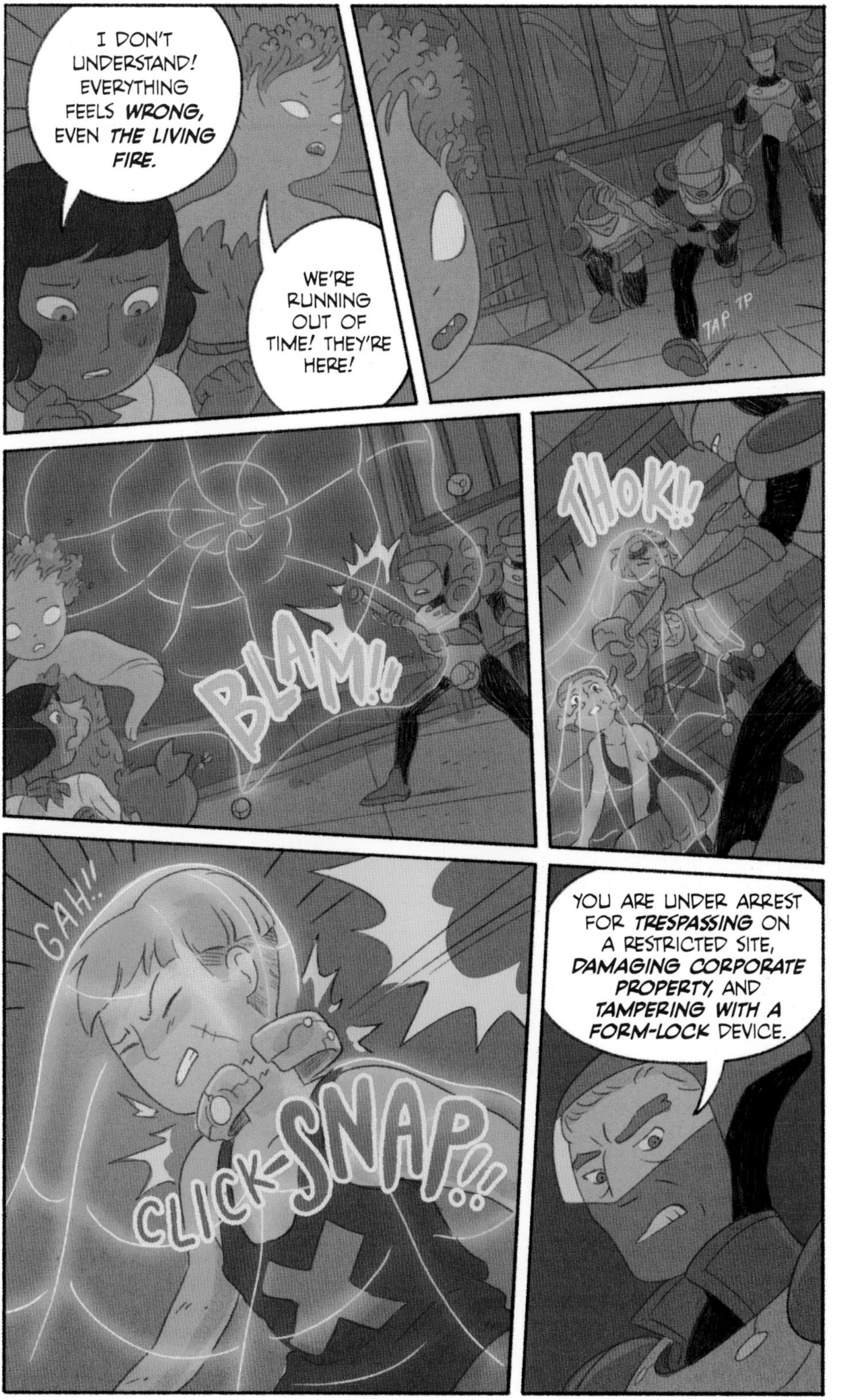
I DON'T UNDERSTAND! EVERYTHING FEELS WRONG, EVEN THE LIVING FIRE.
WE'RE RUNNING OUT OF TIME! THEY'RE HERE!
TAP TP
BLAM!!
THOK!!
GAH!!
CLICK-SNAP!!
YOU ARE UNDER ARREST FOR TRESPASSING ON A RESTRICTED SITE, DAMAGING CORPORATE PROPERTY, AND TAMPERING WITH A FORM-LOCK DEVICE.

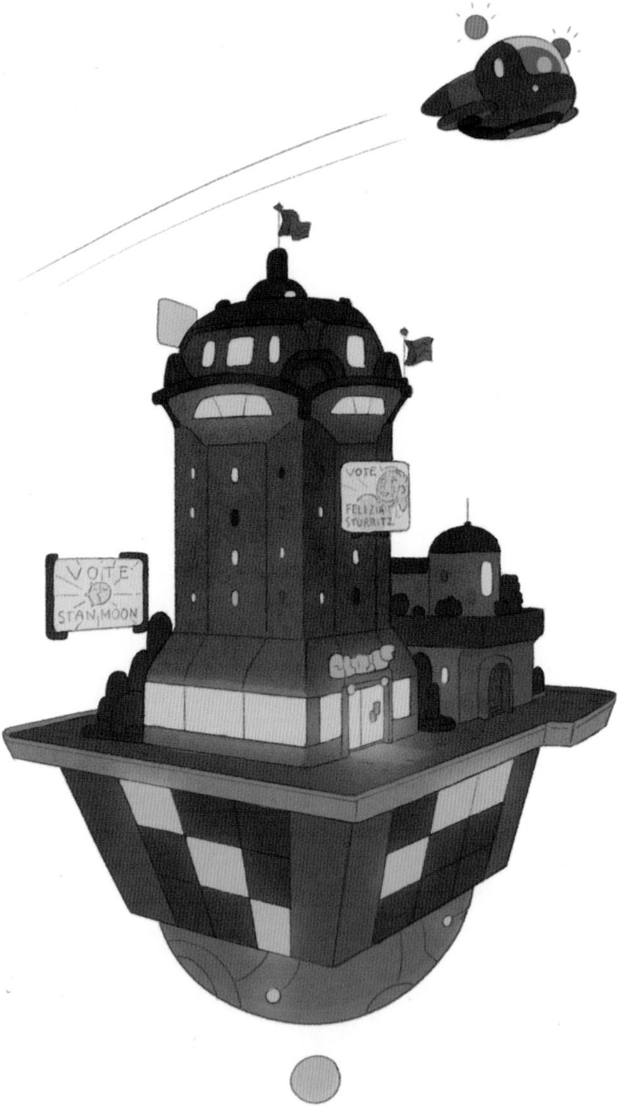
VOTE
FELIZIA STURRITZ
VOTE
STAN MOON

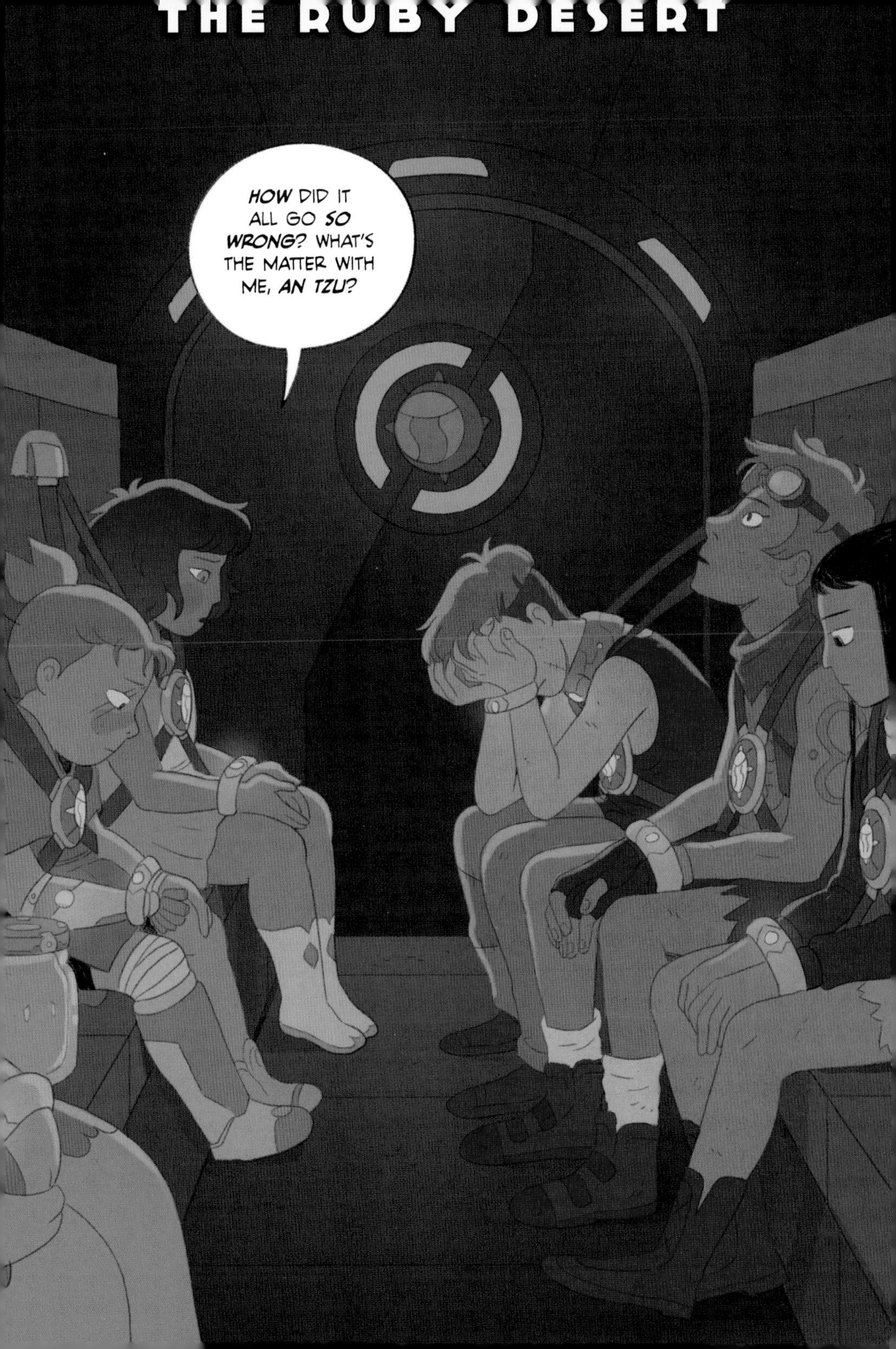
HOW DID IT ALL GO SO WRONG? WHAT'S THE MATTER WITH ME, AN TZU?

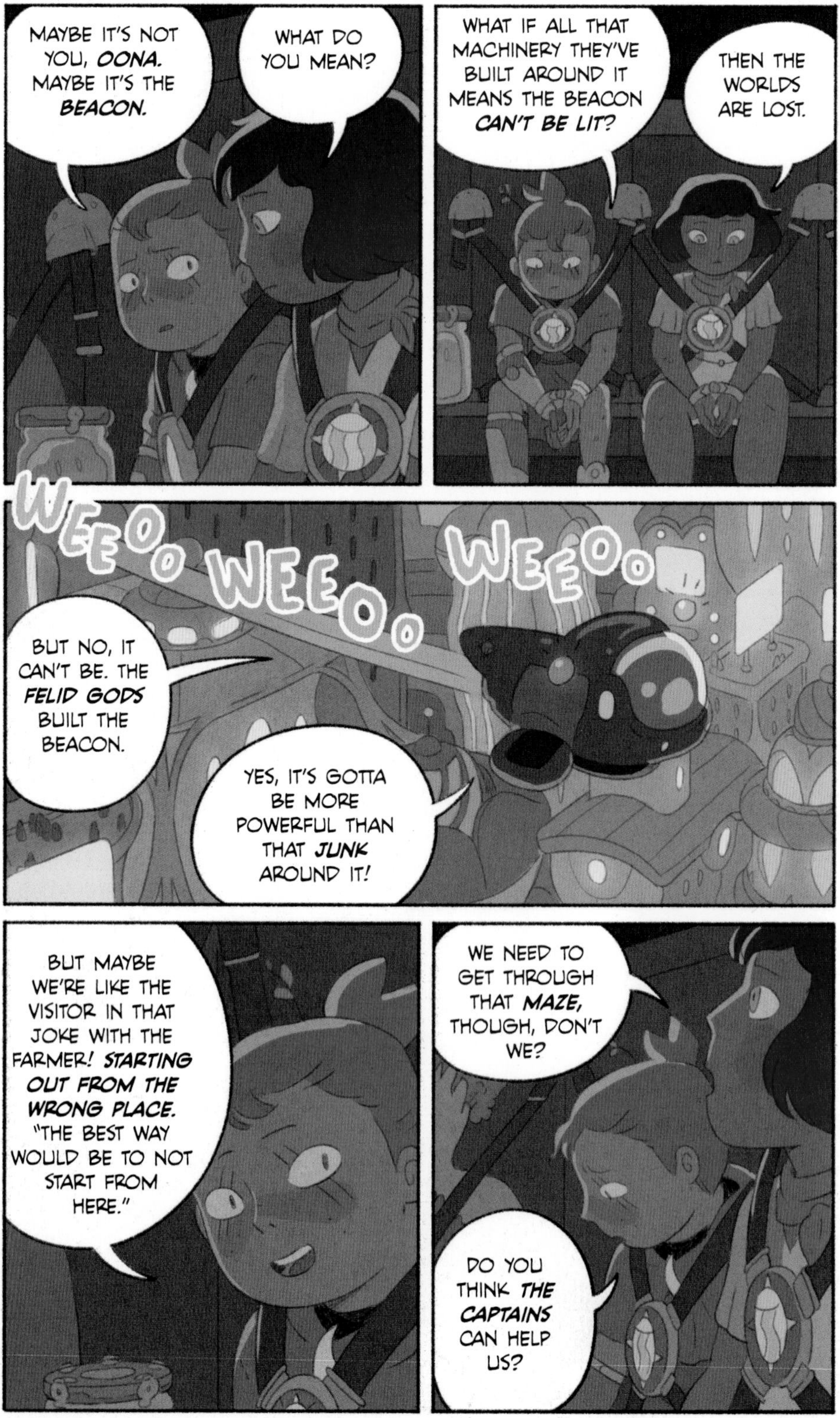

MAYBE IT'S NOT YOU, OONA. MAYBE IT'S THE BEACON.
WHAT DO YOU MEAN?
WHAT IF ALL THAT MACHINERY THEY'VE BUILT AROUND IT MEANS THE BEACON CAN'T BE LIT?
THEN THE WORLDS ARE LOST.
WEEOo WEEOo WEEOo
BUT NO, IT CAN'T BE. THE FELID GODS BUILT THE BEACON.
YES, IT'S GOTTA BE MORE POWERFUL THAN THAT JUNK AROUND IT!
BUT MAYBE WE'RE LIKE THE VISITOR IN THAT JOKE WITH THE FARMER! STARTING OUT FROM THE WRONG PLACE. "THE BEST WAY WOULD BE TO NOT START FROM HERE."
WE NEED TO GET THROUGH THAT MAZE, THOUGH, DON'T WE?
DO YOU THINK THE CAPTAINS CAN HELP US?

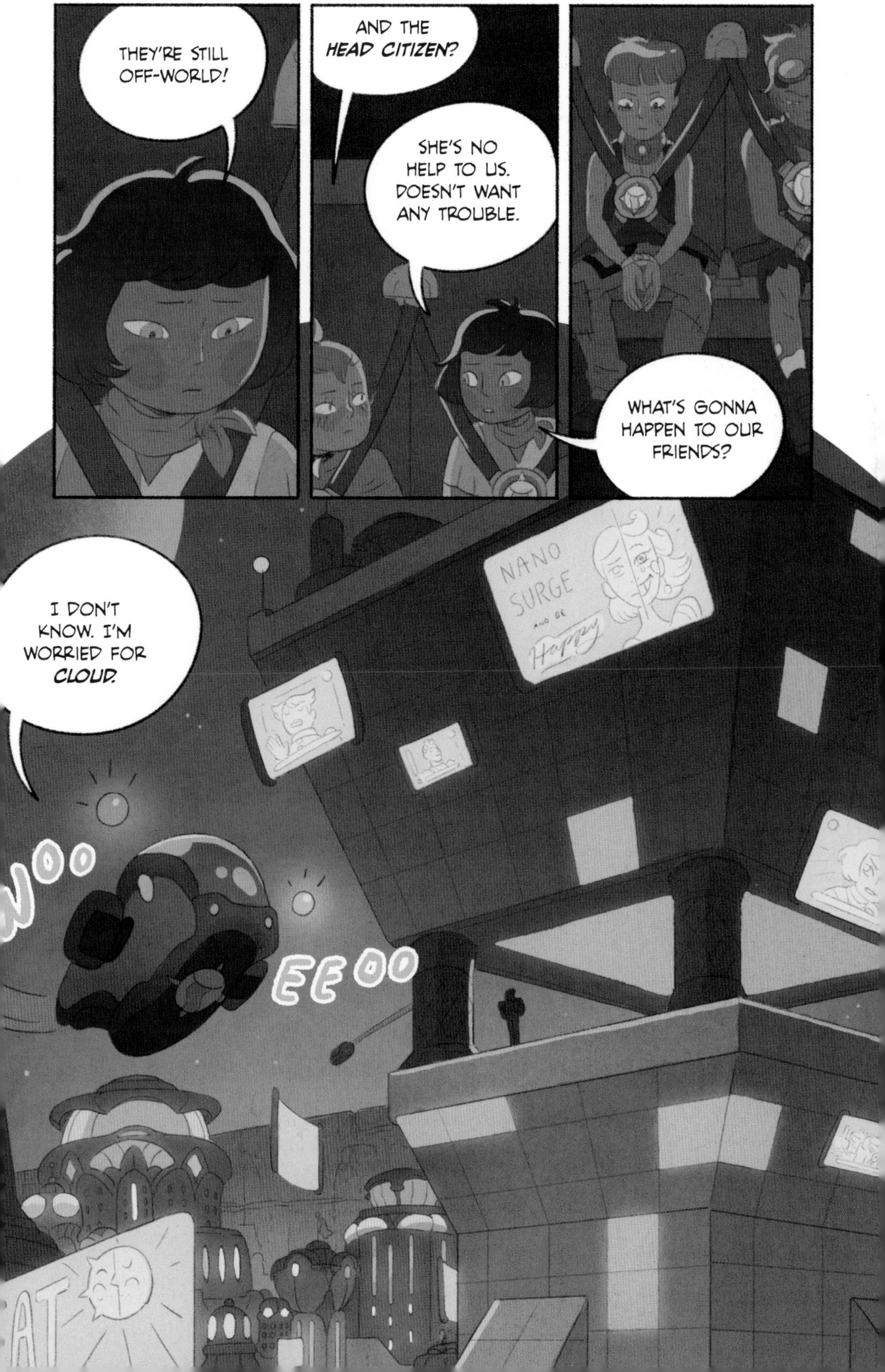
THEY'RE STILL OFF-WORLD!
AND THE *HEAD CITIZEN*?
SHE'S NO HELP TO US. DOESN'T WANT ANY TROUBLE.
WHAT'S GONNA HAPPEN TO OUR FRIENDS?
NANO SURGE AND BE Happy
I DON'T KNOW. I'M WORRIED FOR *CLOUD*.
WOO
EEOO

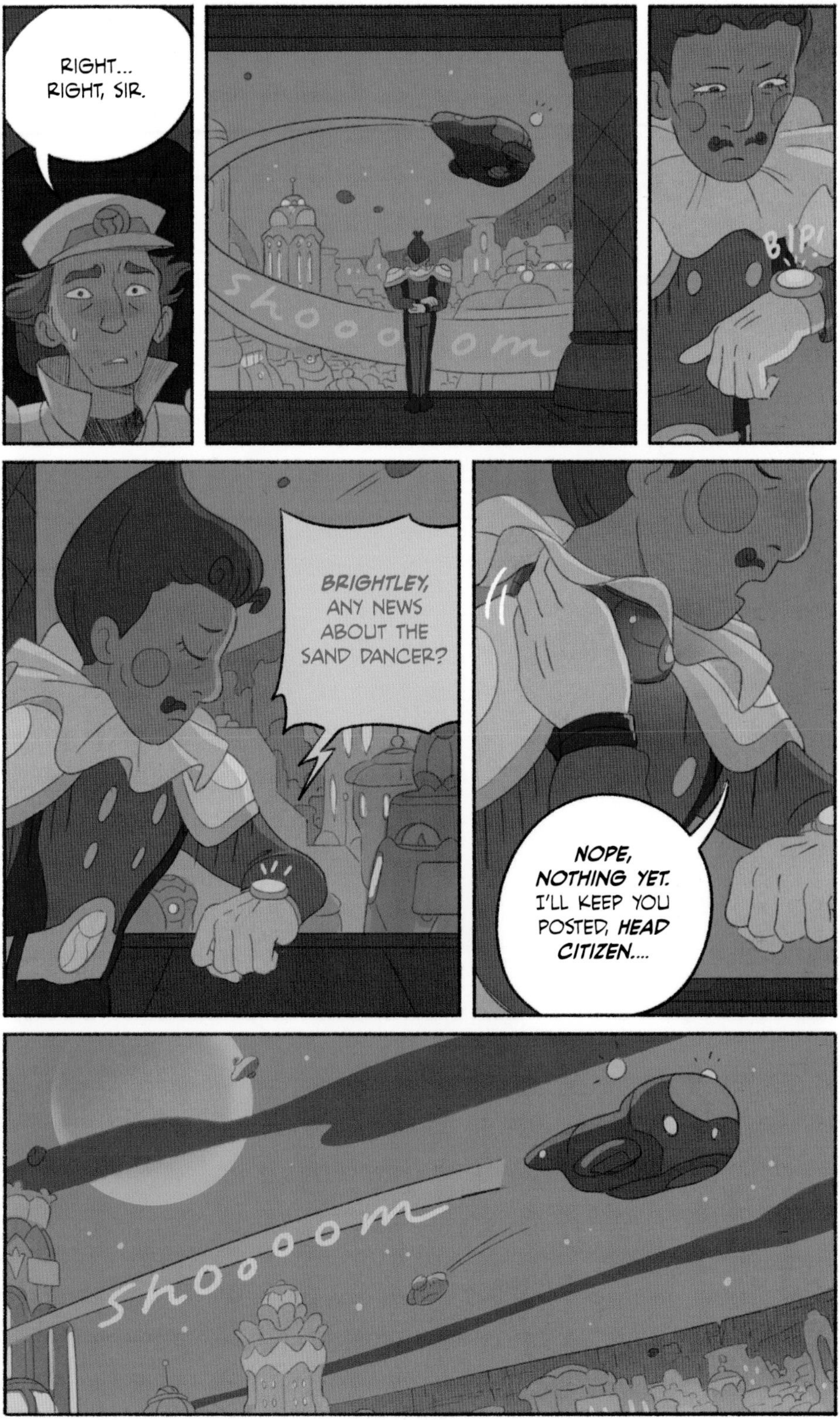
RIGHT...
RIGHT, SIR.
Shoooom
BIP!
BRIGHTLEY, ANY NEWS ABOUT THE SAND DANCER?
NOPE, NOTHING YET. I'LL KEEP YOU POSTED, HEAD CITIZEN....
Shoooom

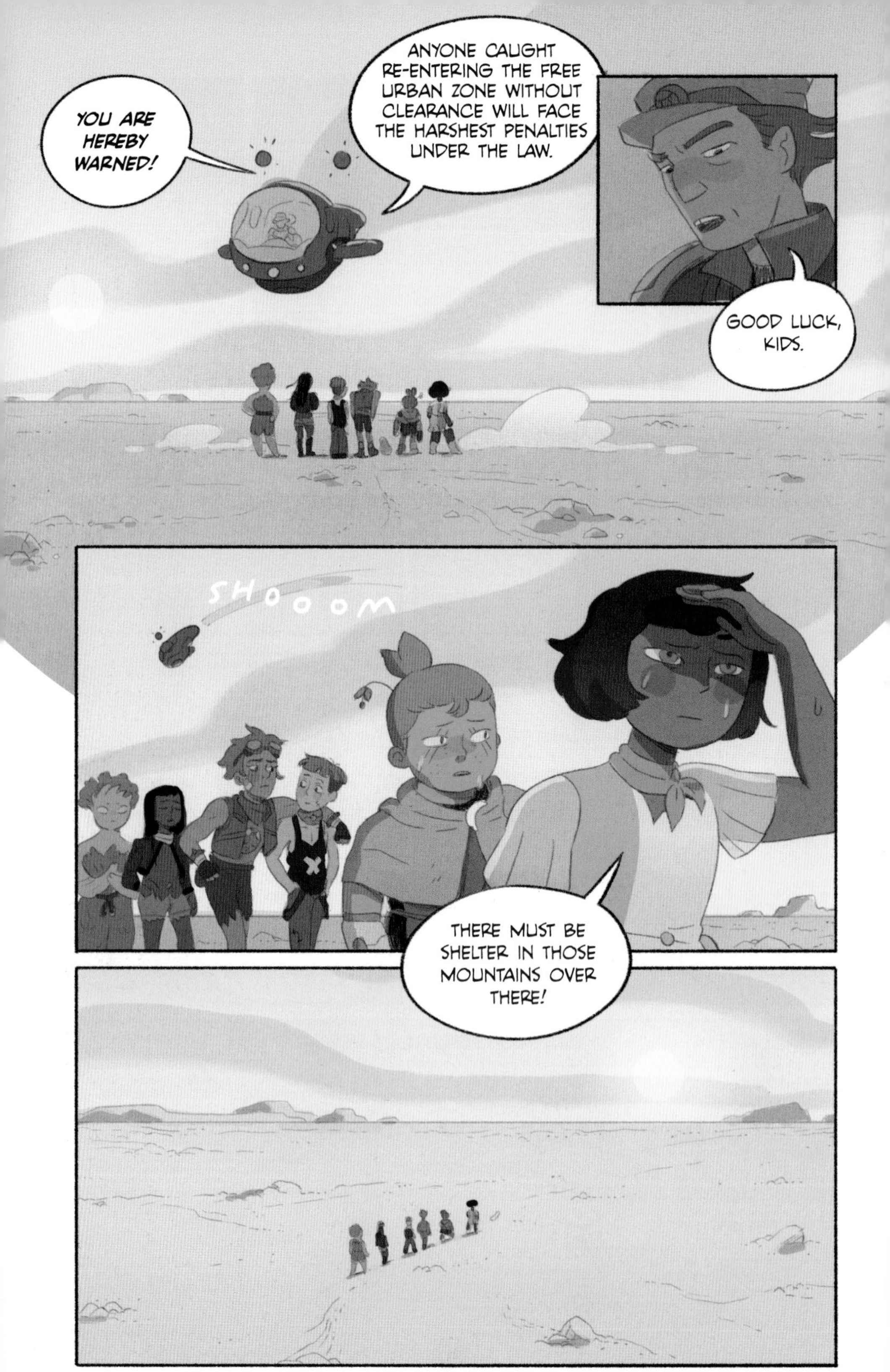
YOU ARE HEREBY WARNED!
ANYONE CAUGHT RE-ENTERING THE FREE URBAN ZONE WITHOUT CLEARANCE WILL FACE THE HARSHEST PENALTIES UNDER THE LAW.
GOOD LUCK, KIDS.
SHOOOM
THERE MUST BE SHELTER IN THOSE MOUNTAINS OVER THERE!

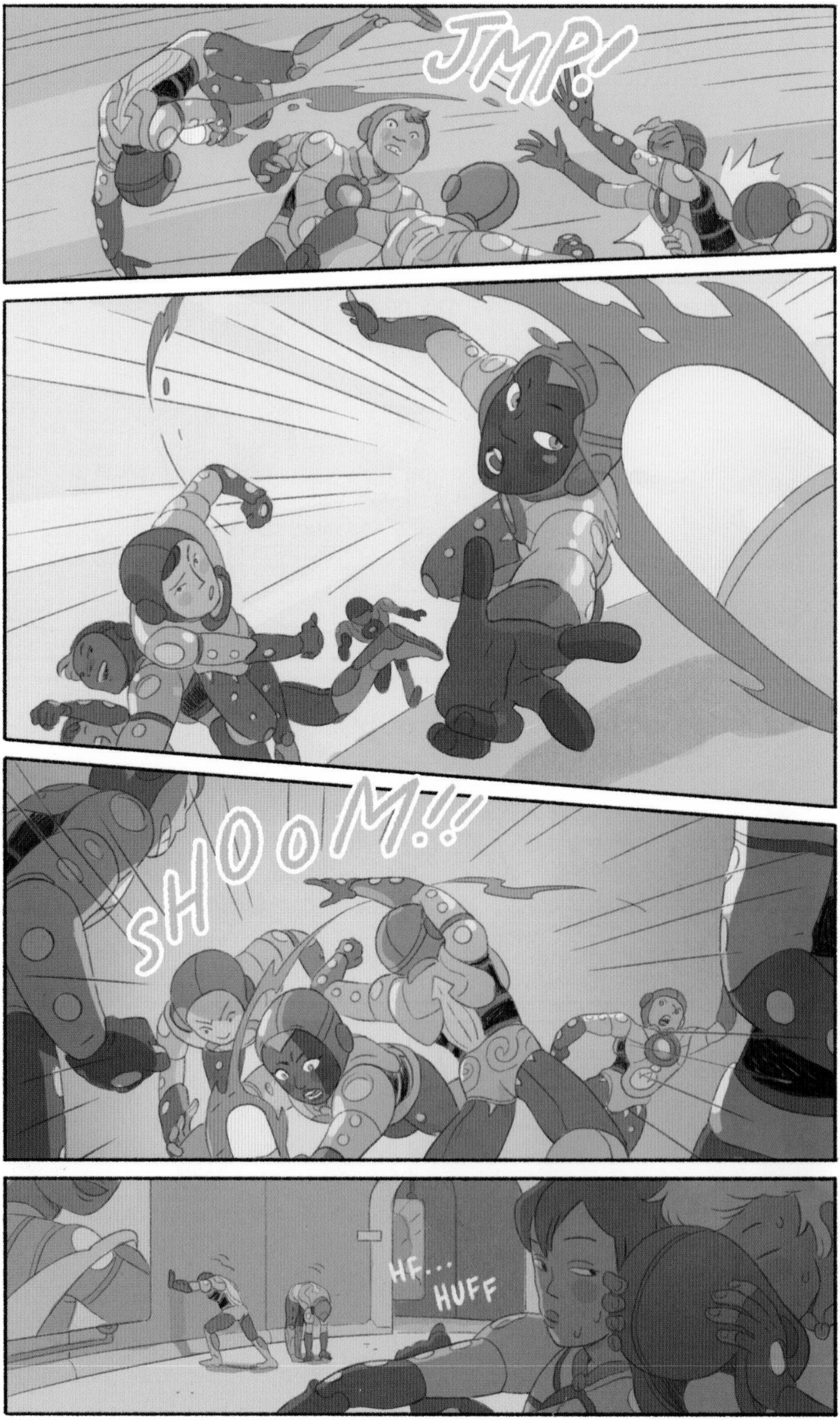
JMP!
SHOOM!!
HF...
HUFF

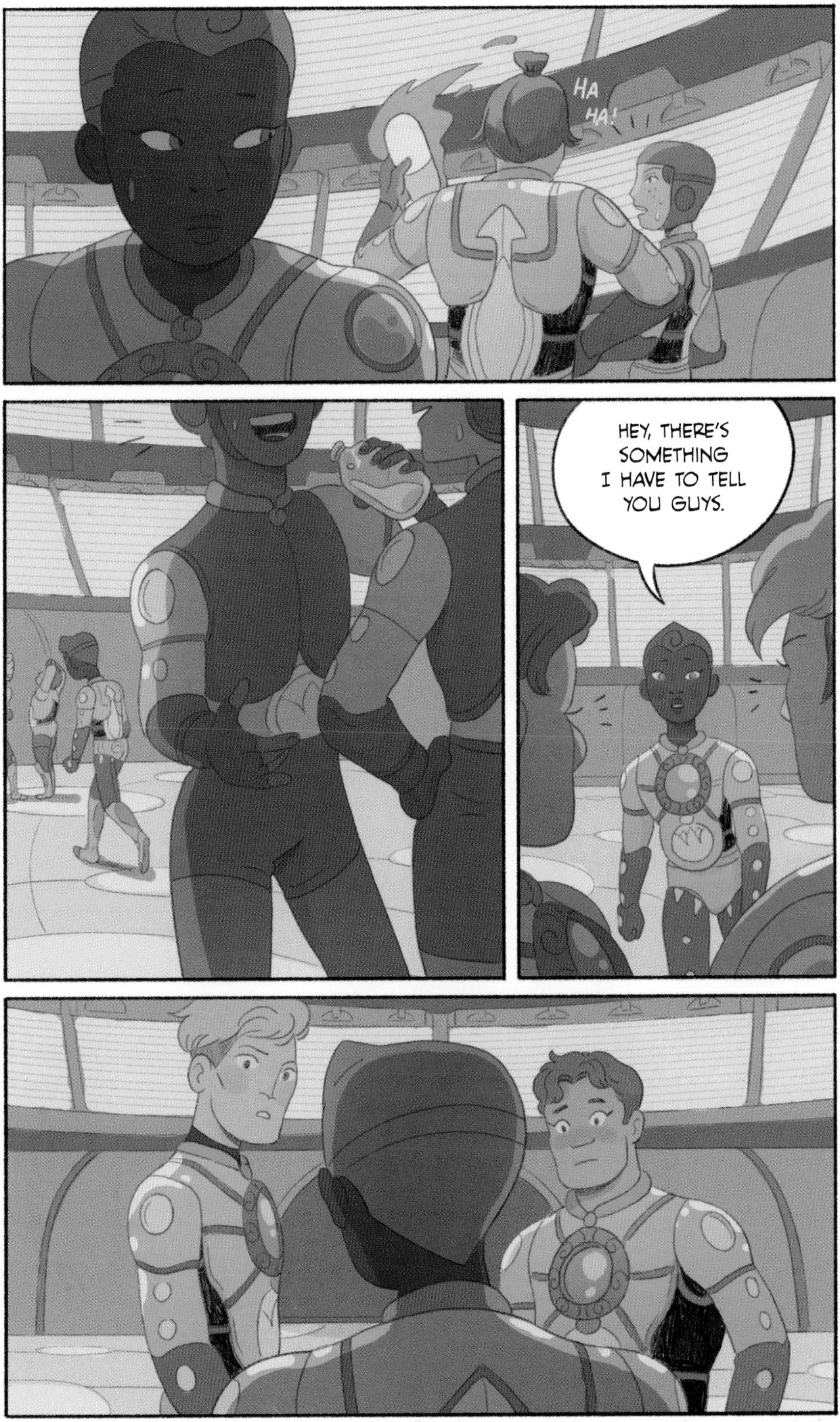
HA HA!
HEY, THERE'S SOMETHING I HAVE TO TELL YOU GUYS.

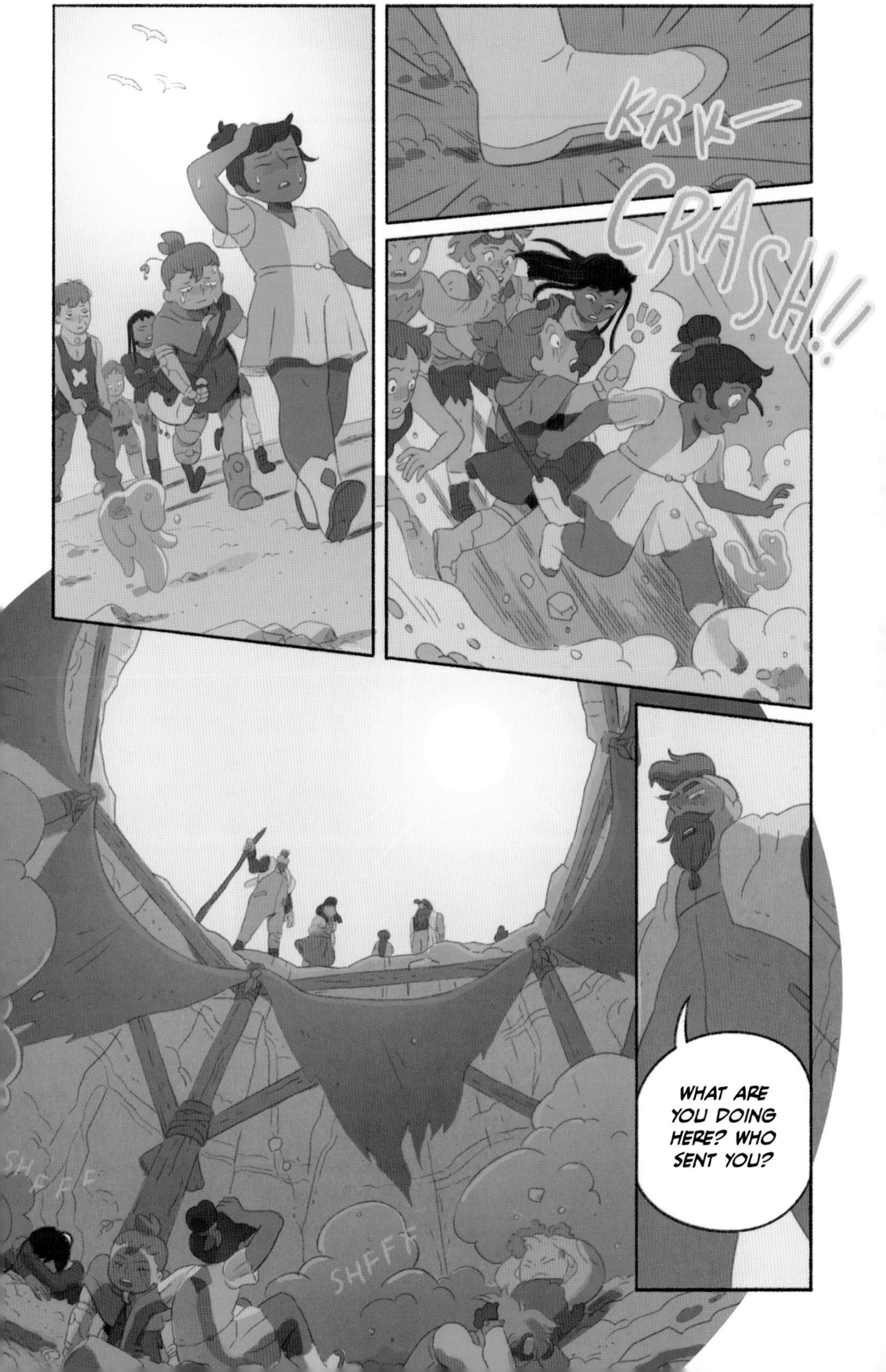
KRK—
CRASH!!
WHAT ARE YOU DOING HERE? WHO SENT YOU?
SHFFF
SHFFF

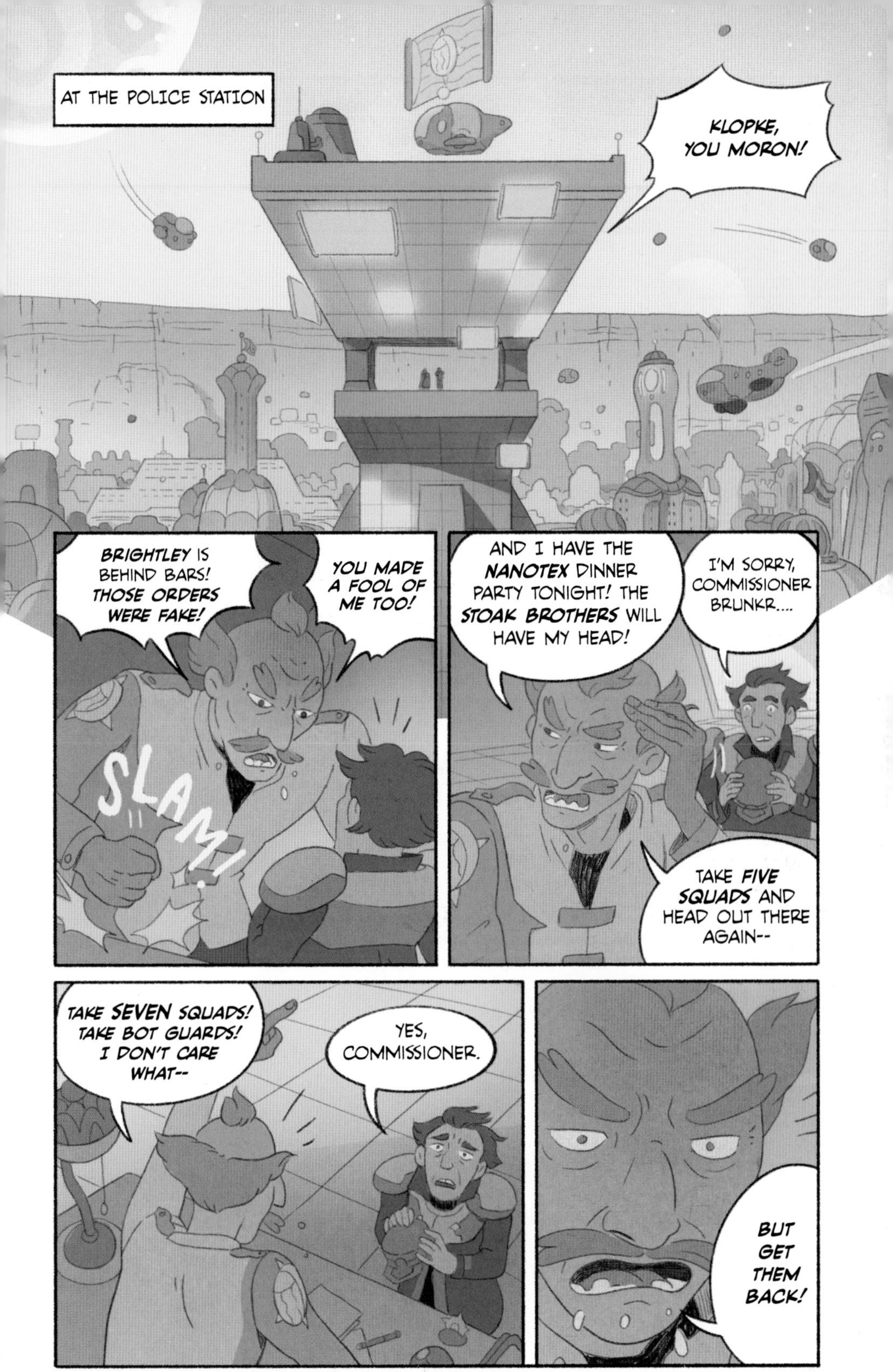
AT THE POLICE STATION
KLOPKE, YOU MORON!
BRIGHTLEY IS BEHIND BARS! THOSE ORDERS WERE FAKE!
YOU MADE A FOOL OF ME TOO!
SLAM!
AND I HAVE THE NANOTEX DINNER PARTY TONIGHT! THE STOAK BROTHERS WILL HAVE MY HEAD!
I'M SORRY, COMMISSIONER BRUNKR....
TAKE FIVE SQUADS AND HEAD OUT THERE AGAIN--
TAKE SEVEN SQUADS! TAKE BOT GUARDS! I DON'T CARE WHAT--
YES, COMMISSIONER.
BUT GET THEM BACK!

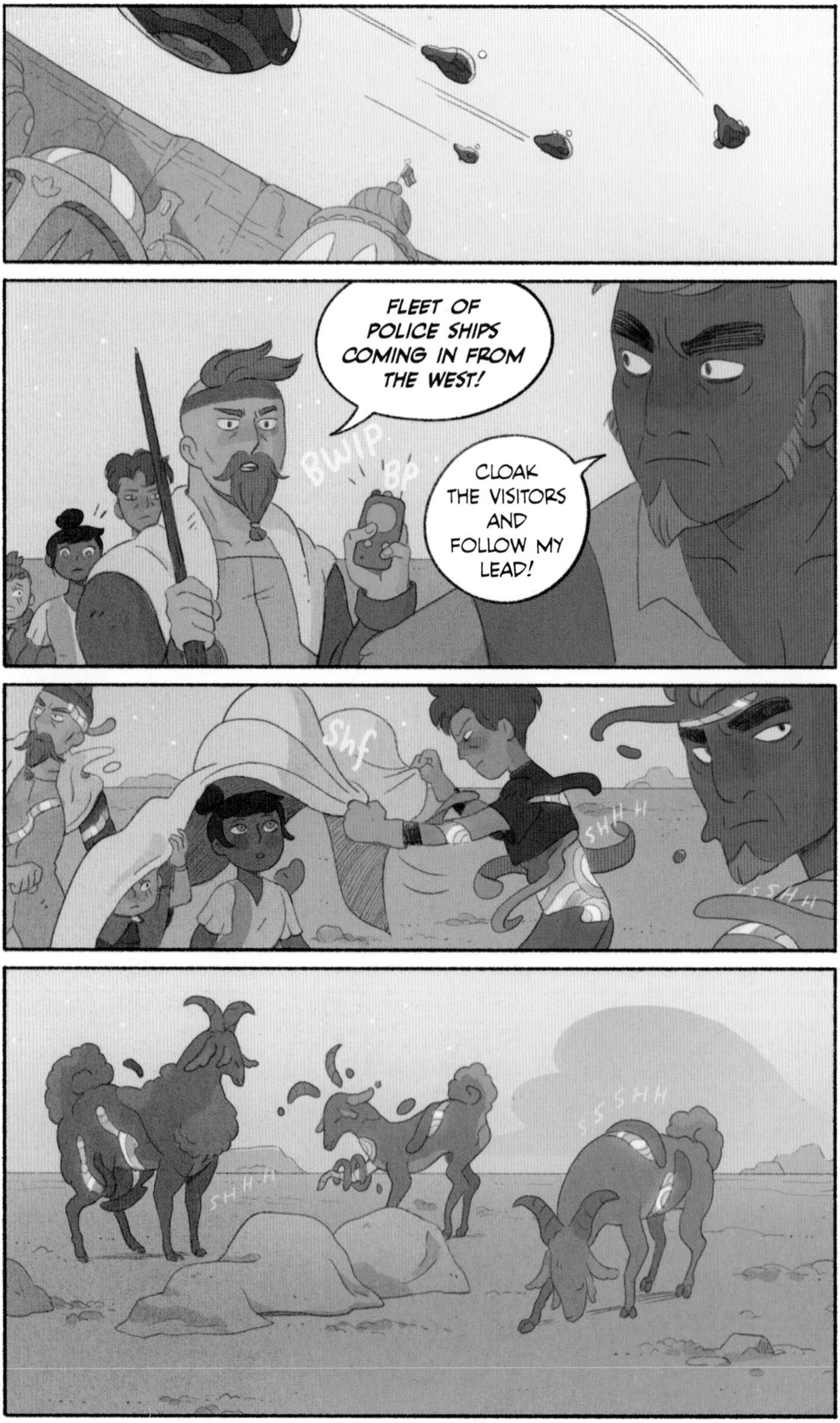
FLEET OF POLICE SHIPS COMING IN FROM THE WEST!
BWIP
BP
CLOAK THE VISITORS AND FOLLOW MY LEAD!
Shf
SHHH
SSHH
SHHH
SSHH

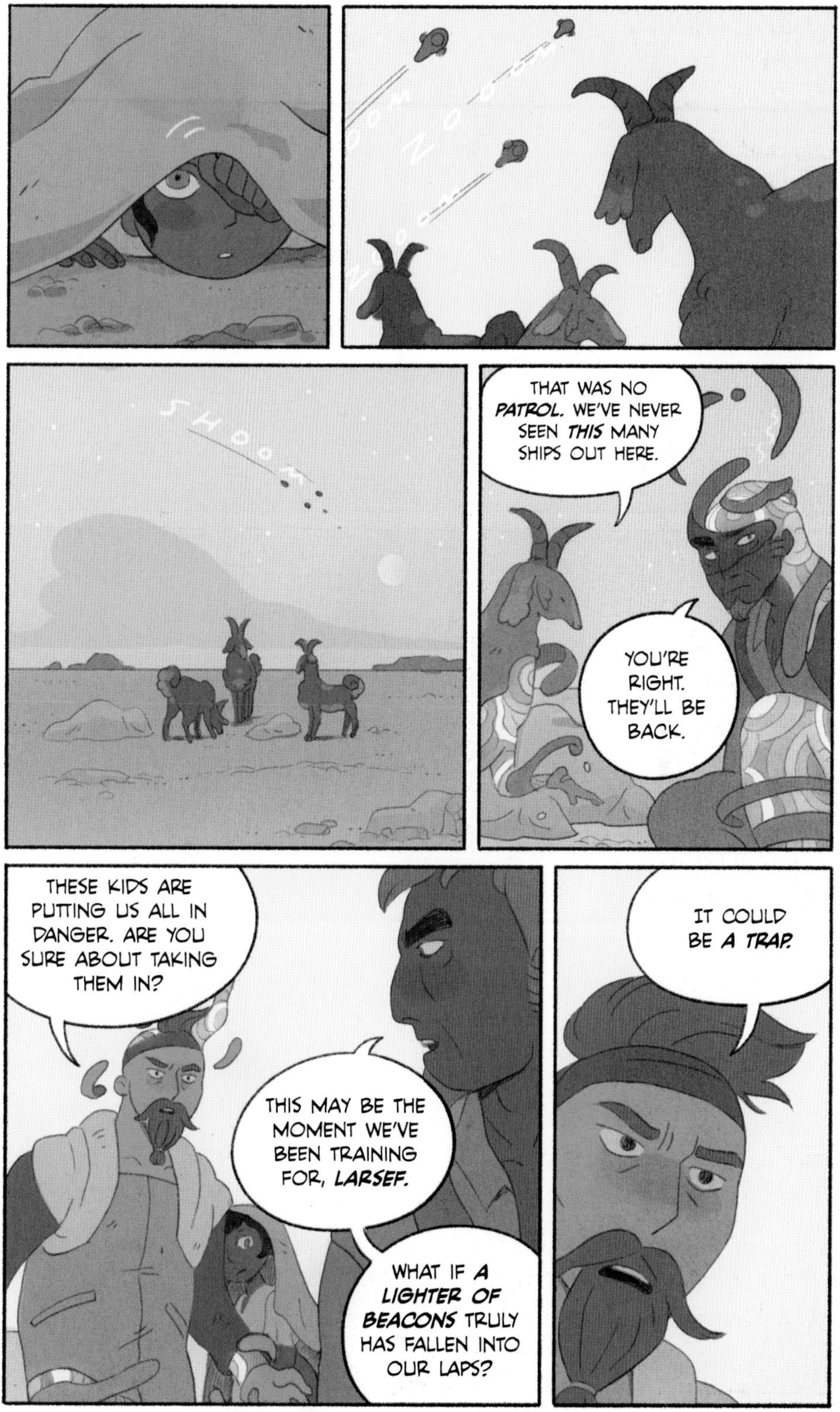
SHOOOM
THAT WAS NO PATROL. WE'VE NEVER SEEN THIS MANY SHIPS OUT HERE.
YOU'RE RIGHT. THEY'LL BE BACK.
THESE KIDS ARE PUTTING US ALL IN DANGER. ARE YOU SURE ABOUT TAKING THEM IN?
THIS MAY BE THE MOMENT WE'VE BEEN TRAINING FOR, LARSEF.
WHAT IF A LIGHTER OF BEACONS TRULY HAS FALLEN INTO OUR LAPS?
IT COULD BE A TRAP.

SOME HOURS LATER...

REAL FRUIT?!

MMM!

Rrr!

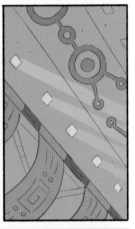

ZAP!

SSS

SSSSH

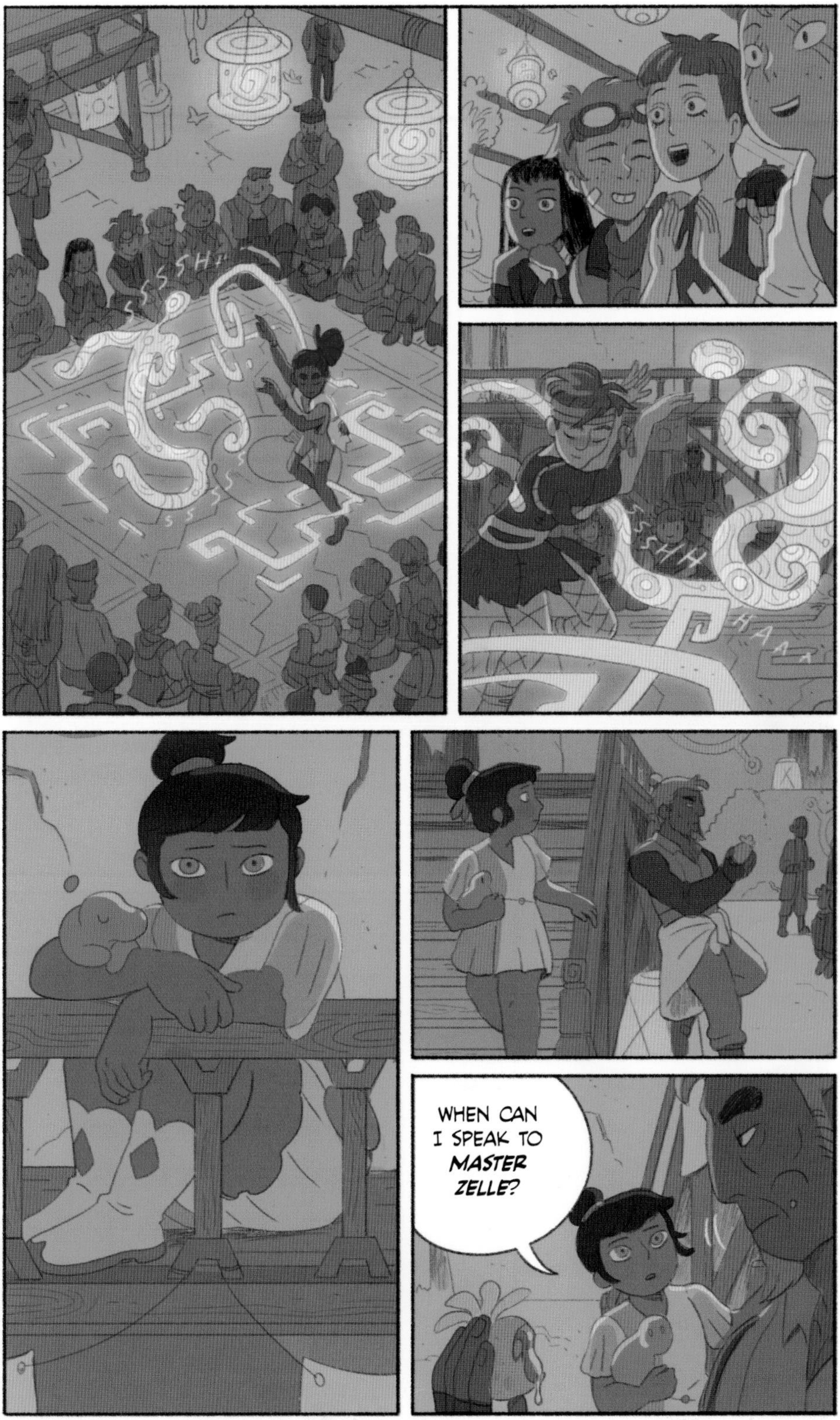
WHEN CAN I SPEAK TO MASTER ZELLE?

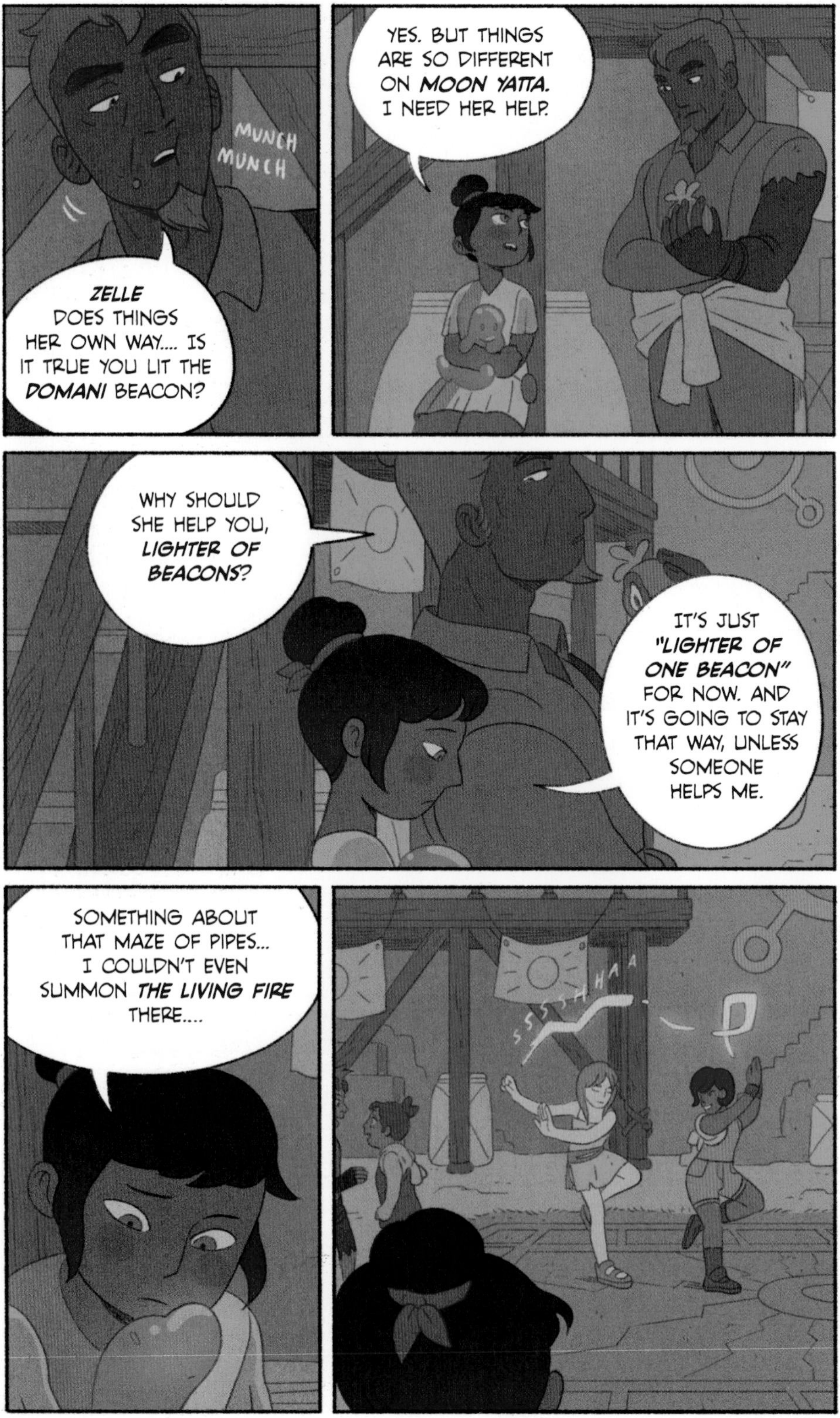
MUNCH MUNCH
ZELLE DOES THINGS HER OWN WAY.... IS IT TRUE YOU LIT THE DOMANI BEACON?
YES. BUT THINGS ARE SO DIFFERENT ON MOON YATTA. I NEED HER HELP.
WHY SHOULD SHE HELP YOU, LIGHTER OF BEACONS?
IT'S JUST "LIGHTER OF ONE BEACON" FOR NOW. AND IT'S GOING TO STAY THAT WAY, UNLESS SOMEONE HELPS ME.
SOMETHING ABOUT THAT MAZE OF PIPES... I COULDN'T EVEN SUMMON THE LIVING FIRE THERE....
SSSSHHAA

# Chapter 8
# TRAINING DAYS

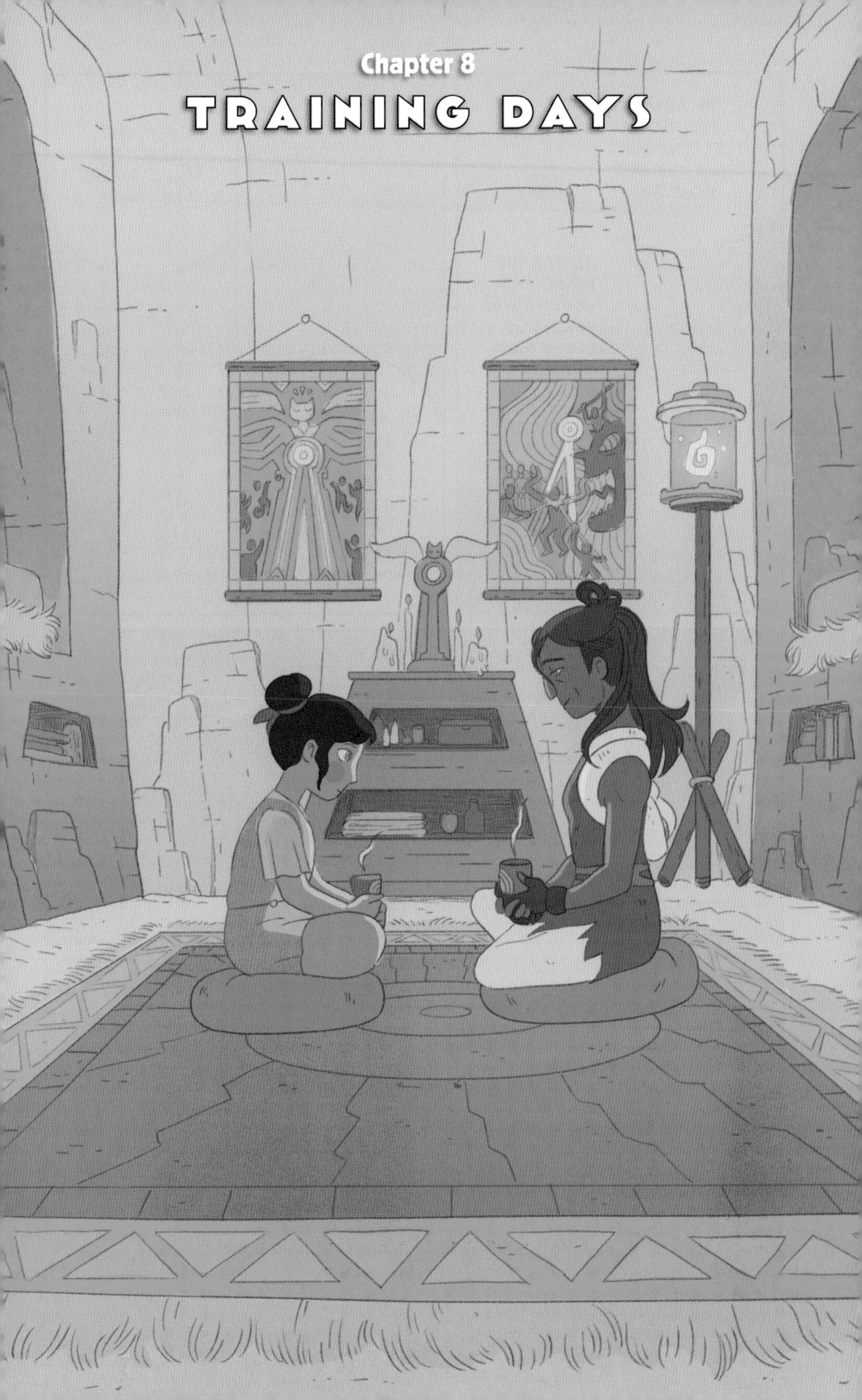

156

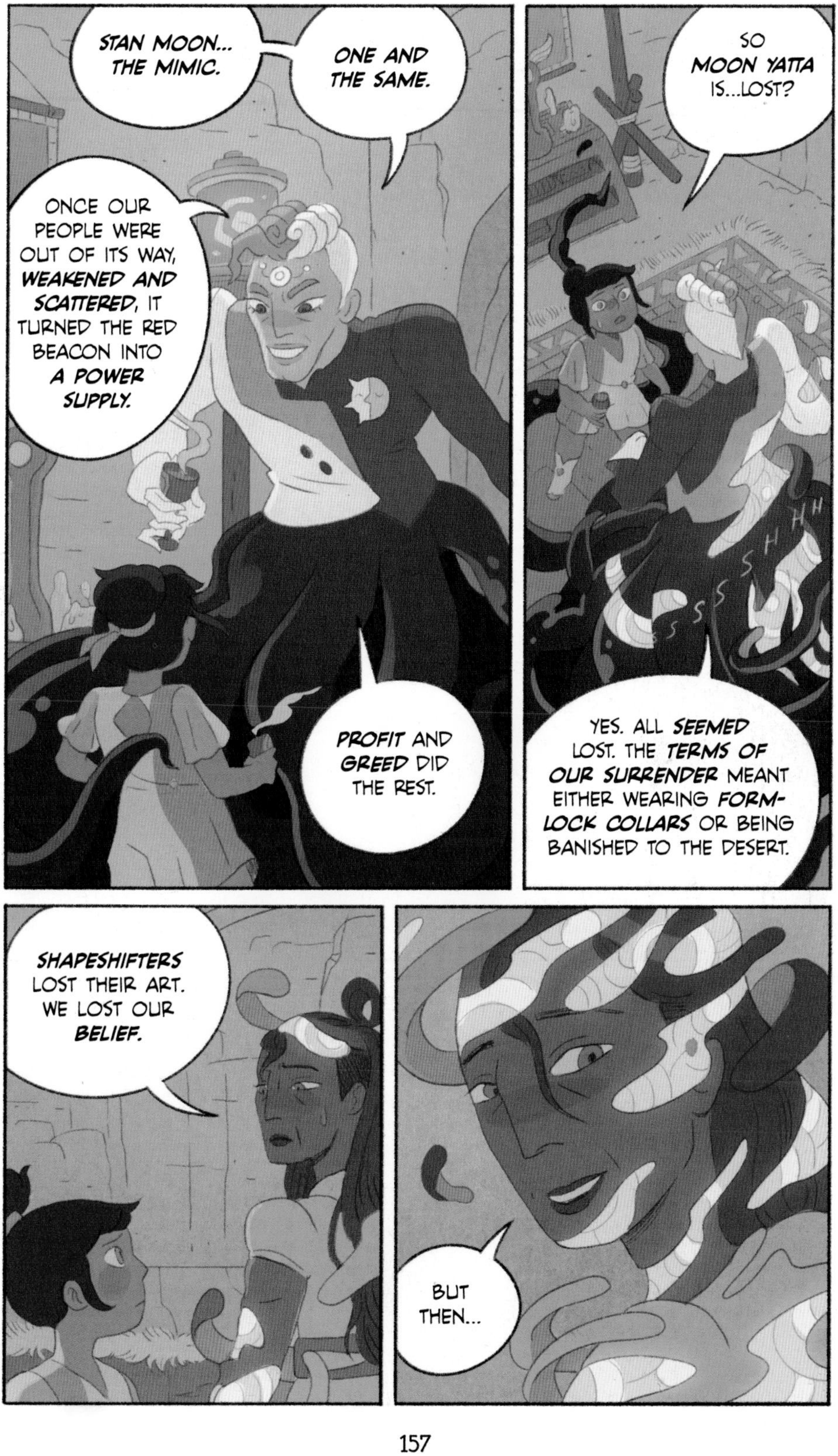
STAN MOON... THE MIMIC.
ONE AND THE SAME.
ONCE OUR PEOPLE WERE OUT OF ITS WAY, WEAKENED AND SCATTERED, IT TURNED THE RED BEACON INTO A POWER SUPPLY.
PROFIT AND GREED DID THE REST.
SO MOON YATTA IS...LOST?
SSSSSHHH
YES. ALL SEEMED LOST. THE TERMS OF OUR SURRENDER MEANT EITHER WEARING FORM-LOCK COLLARS OR BEING BANISHED TO THE DESERT.
SHAPESHIFTERS LOST THEIR ART. WE LOST OUR BELIEF.
BUT THEN...

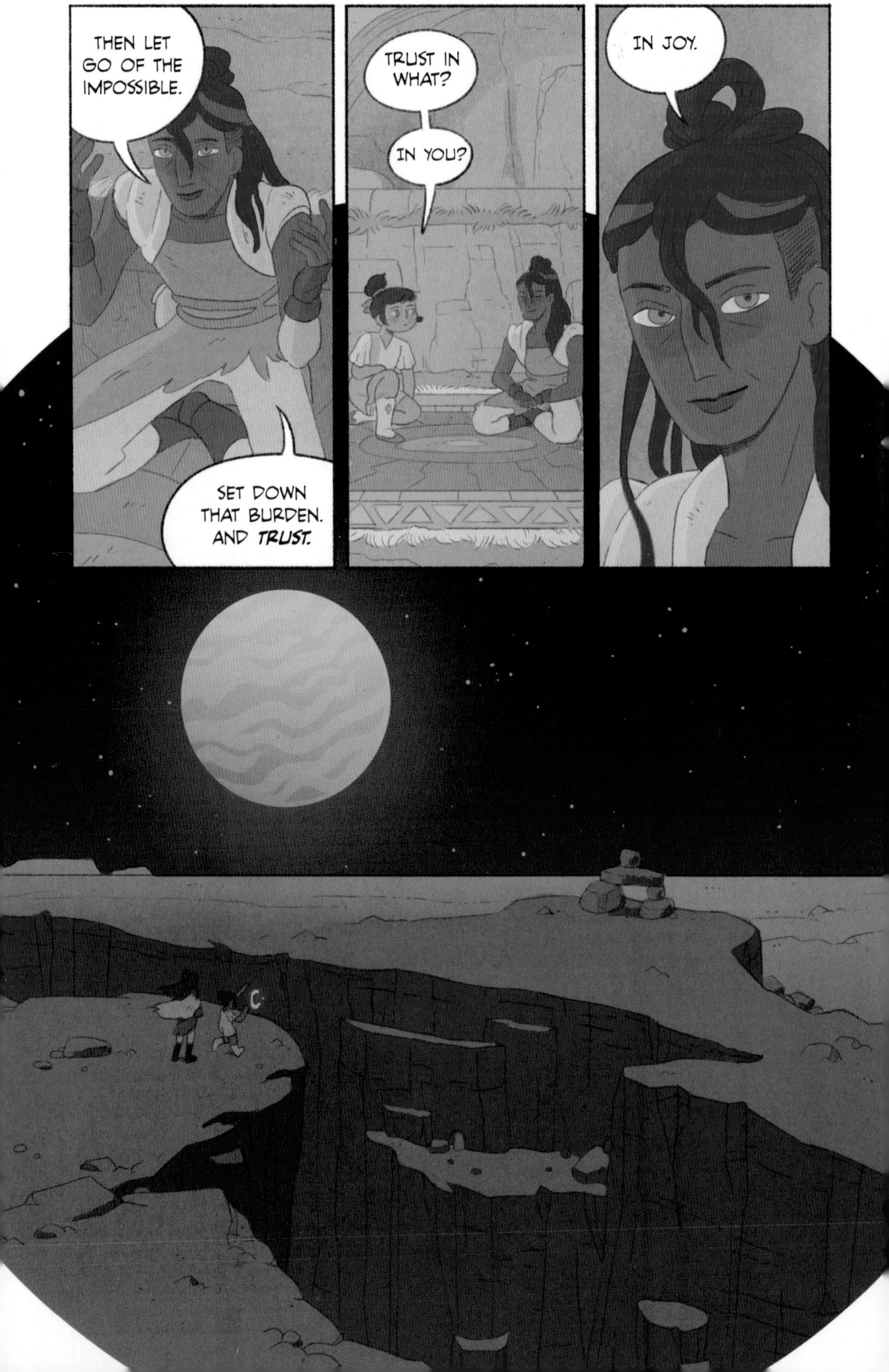
THEN LET GO OF THE IMPOSSIBLE.
SET DOWN THAT BURDEN. AND TRUST.
TRUST IN WHAT?
IN YOU?
IN JOY.

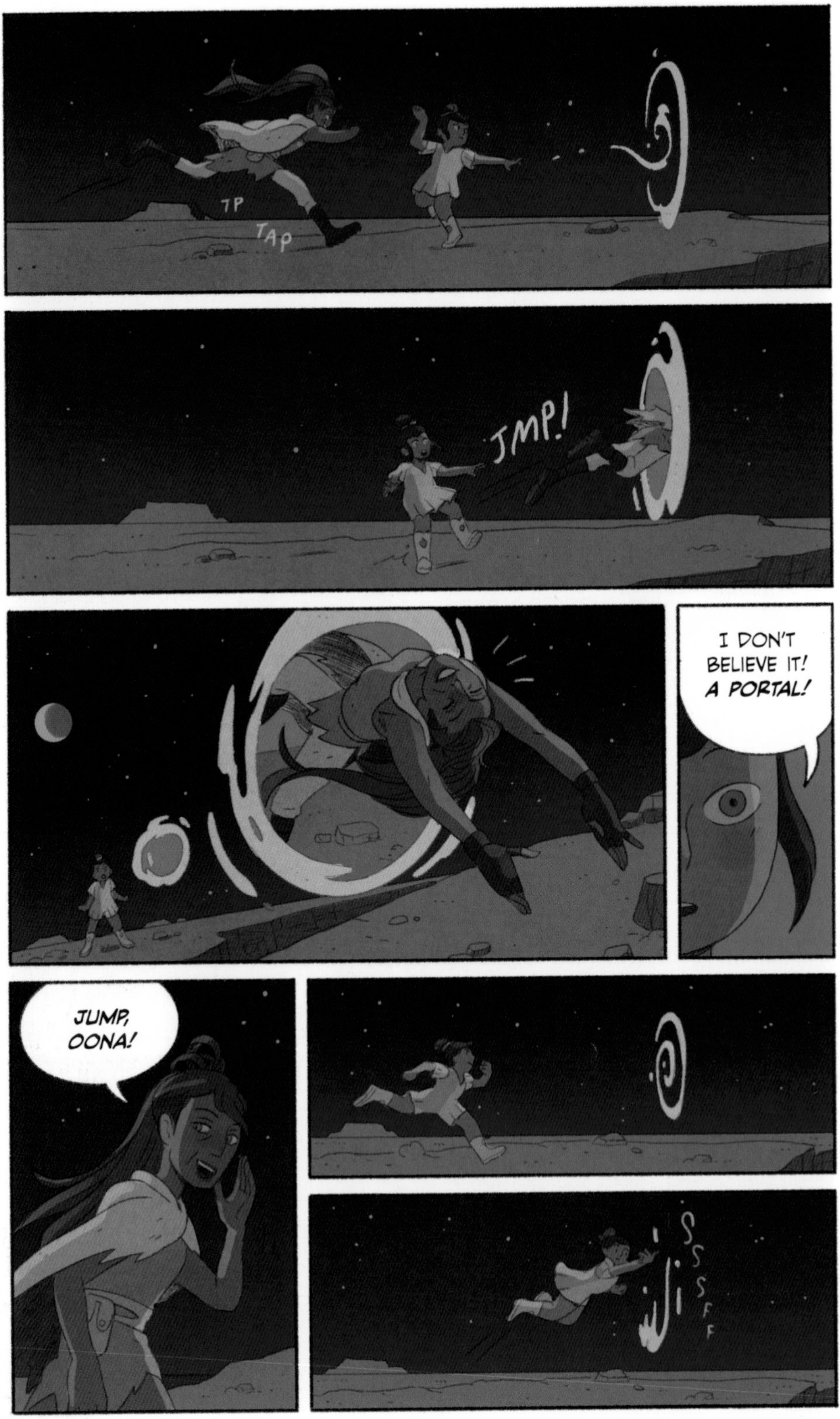
TP
TAP
JMP!
I DON'T BELIEVE IT! A PORTAL!
JUMP, OONA!
SSSFF

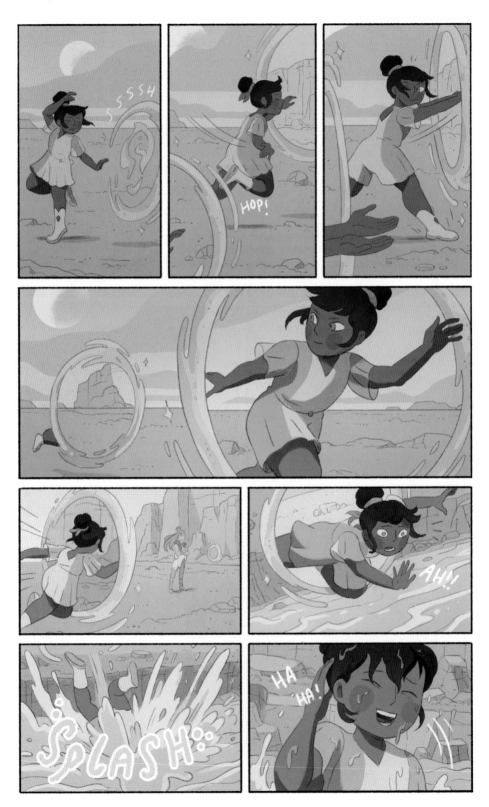

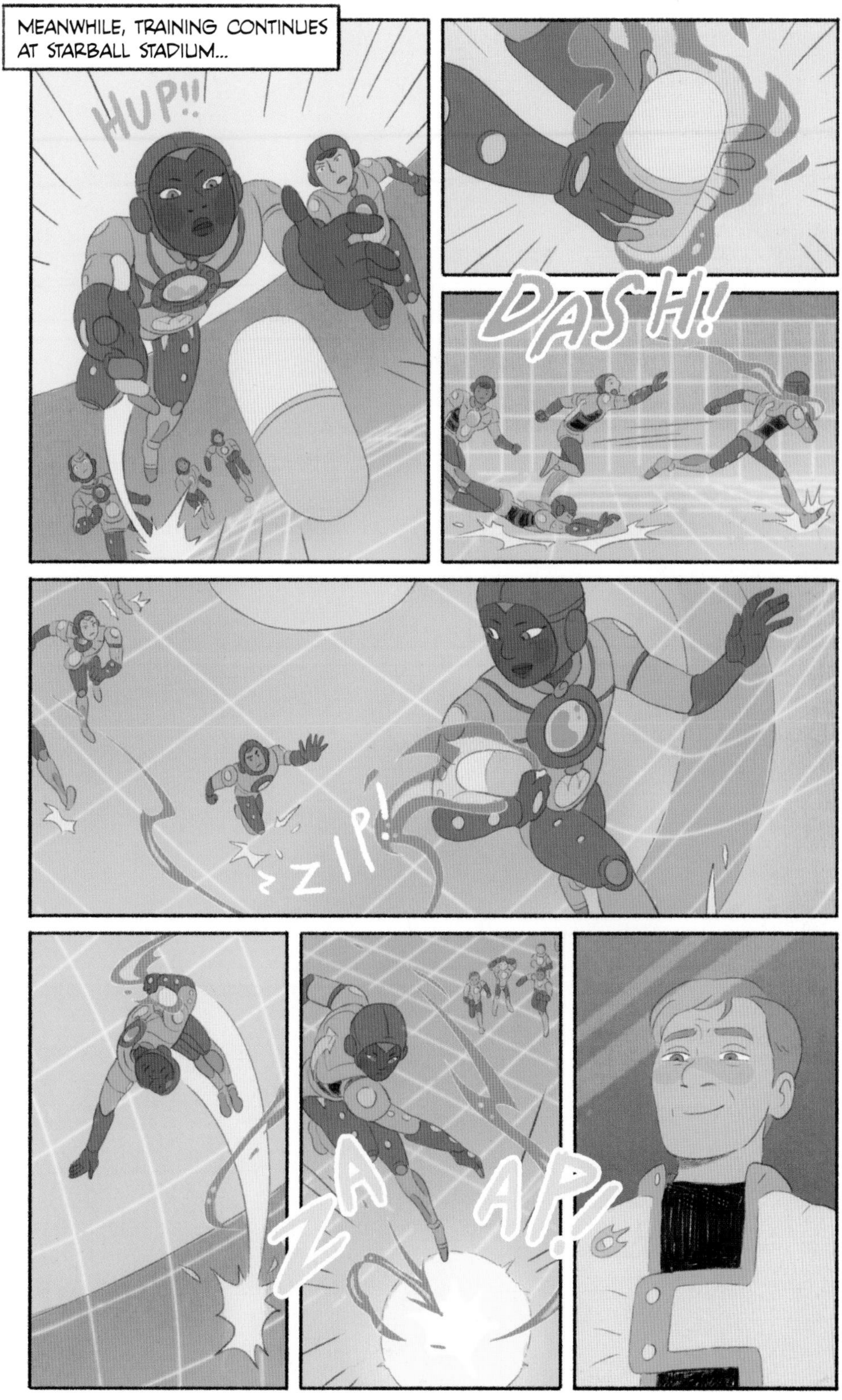
MEANWHILE, TRAINING CONTINUES AT STARBALL STADIUM...
HUP!!
DASH!
ZIP!
ZAAP!

168

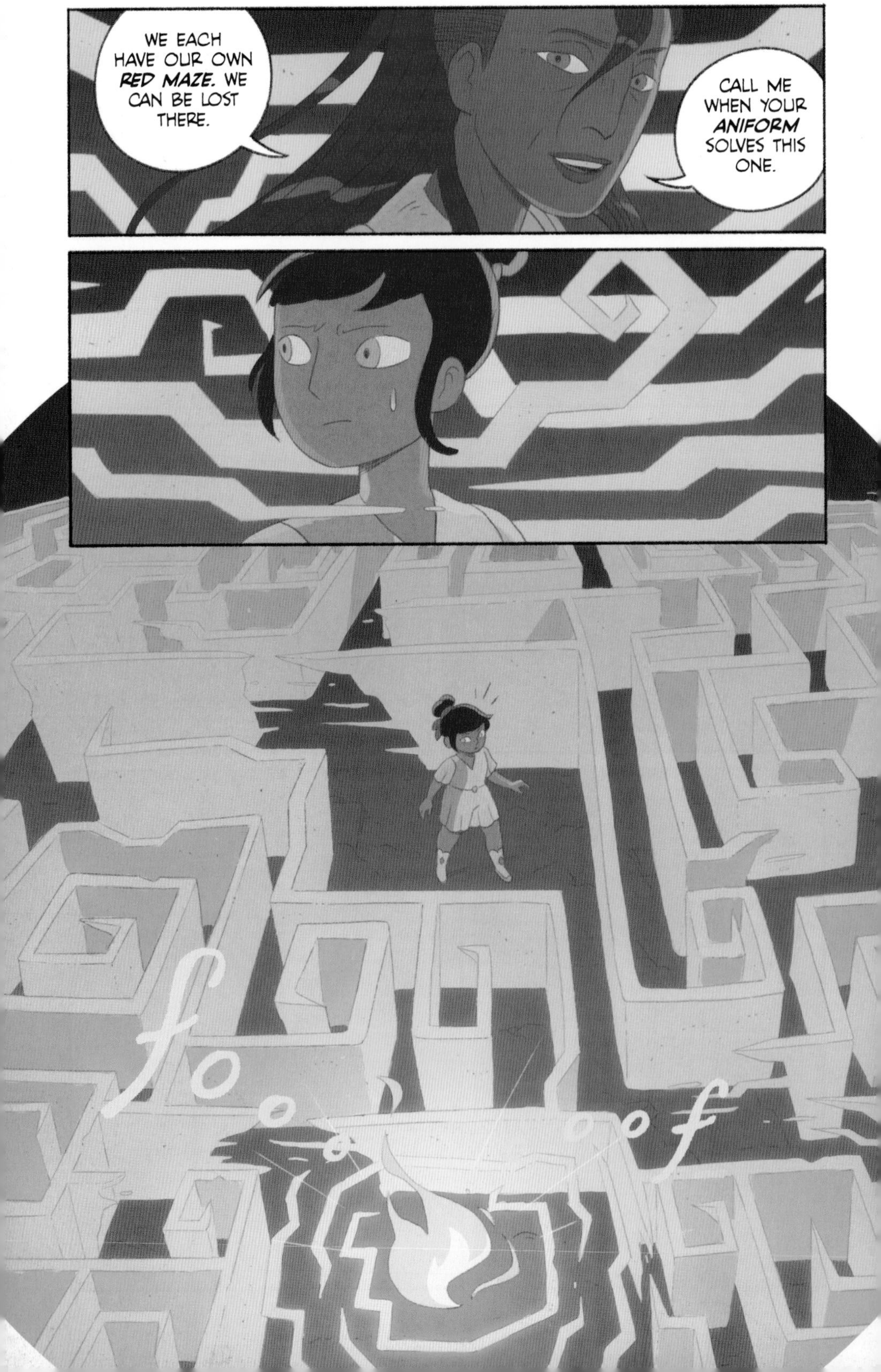

WE EACH HAVE OUR OWN **RED MAZE.** WE CAN BE LOST THERE.
CALL ME WHEN YOUR ***ANIFORM*** SOLVES THIS ONE.

## Chapter 9

# THE TRAP

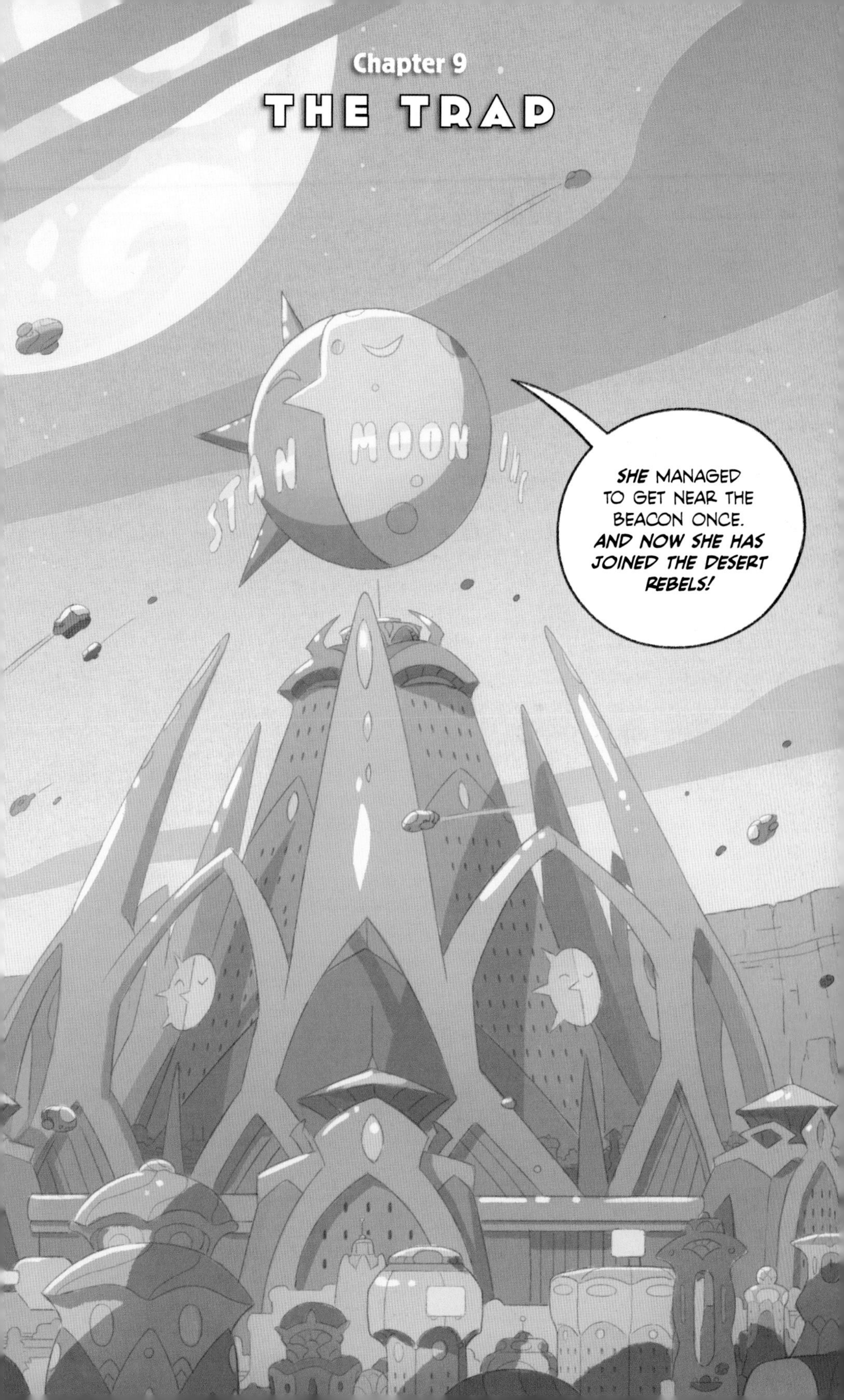

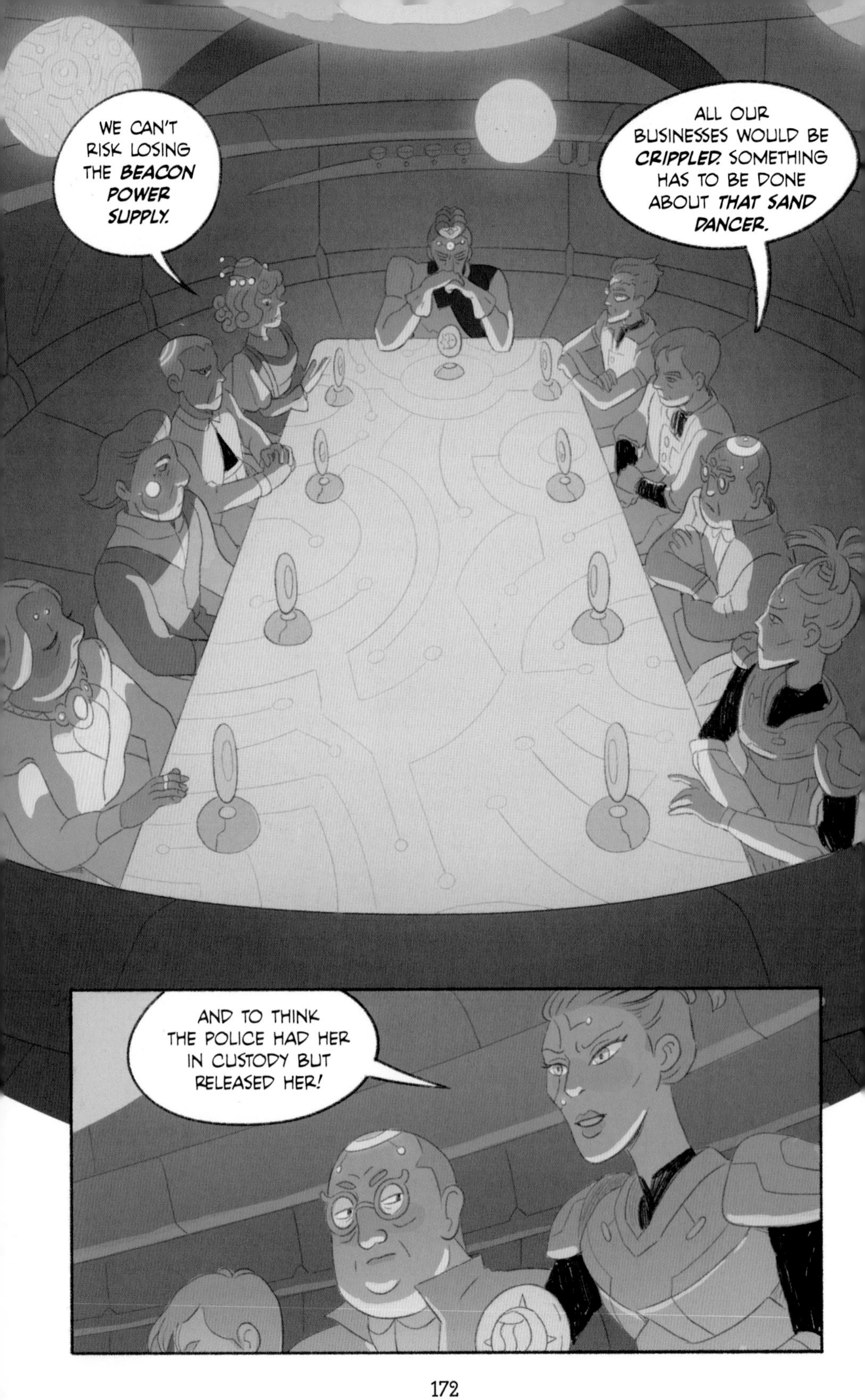
WE CAN'T RISK LOSING THE BEACON POWER SUPPLY.
ALL OUR BUSINESSES WOULD BE CRIPPLED. SOMETHING HAS TO BE DONE ABOUT THAT SAND DANCER.
AND TO THINK THE POLICE HAD HER IN CUSTODY BUT RELEASED HER!

173

HMM...THE YOUNG *FOOL* GOT CAUGHT UP IN THINGS HE DOESN'T UNDERSTAND.... I'M GLAD TO SAY, I'VE TALKED SOME SENSE INTO HIM. *HE'LL BE STICKING TO STARBALL FROM NOW ON.*

UM... YES, OF COURSE.

HE'LL NEED TO DO *MORE* THAN THAT. WE'LL LET YOU KNOW WHEN THE TIME IS RIGHT.

AND THE *CITIZEN FEEDS?*

OH, WE'VE GOT *PEET BOWL* IN TOP FORM. WE'RE TURNING ALL HIS COVERAGE TO *OONA LEE* AND HER *CRIMINAL SHAPESHIFTER FRIENDS.*

EXCELLENT. AND THE OTHER PREPARATIONS, *ELDRIDGE?*

OH, EVERYTHING'S IN PLACE.... THE ELECTION COMMISSION WILL SEE *WHAT WE NEED THEM TO SEE.*

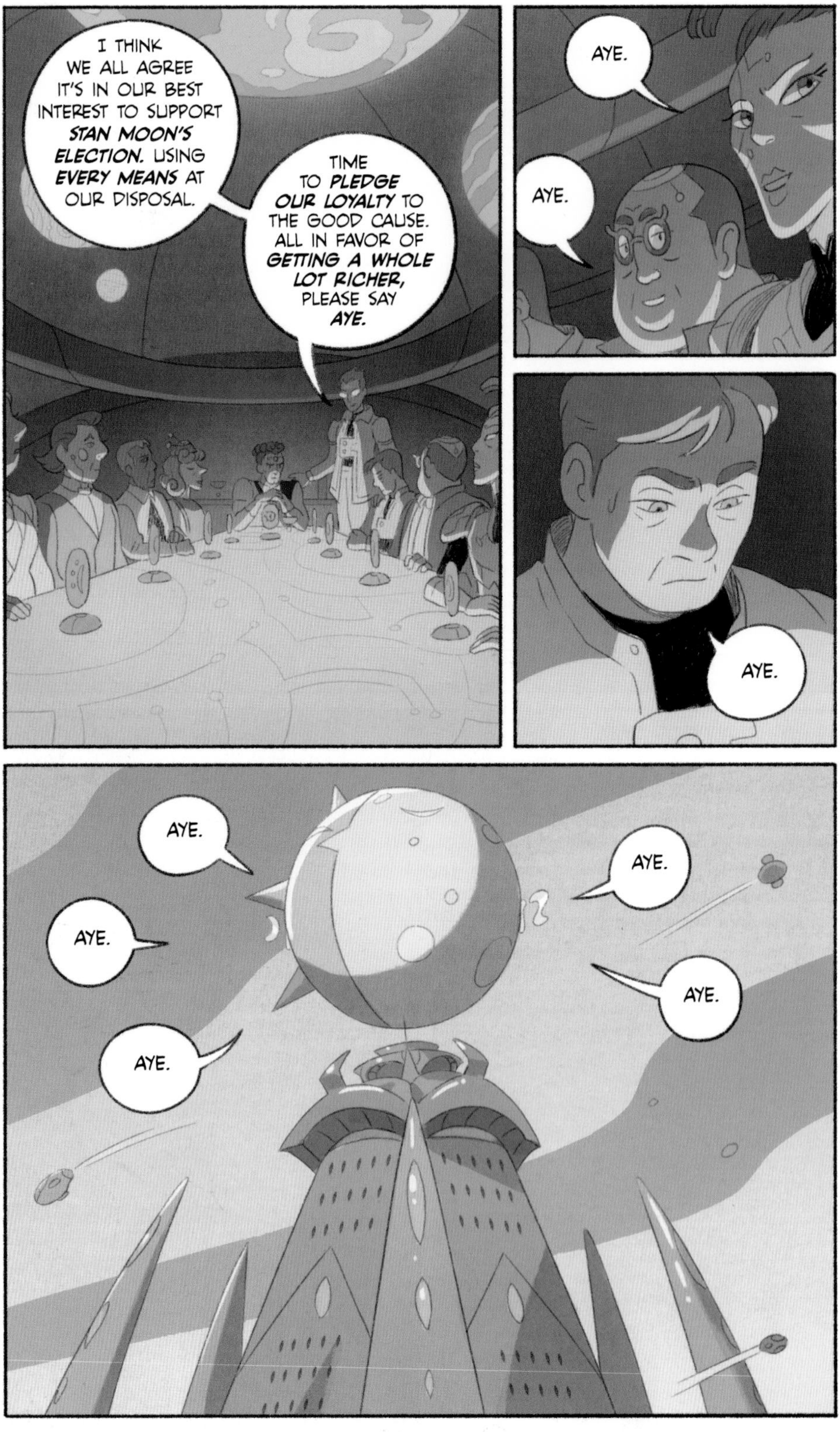
I THINK WE ALL AGREE IT'S IN OUR BEST INTEREST TO SUPPORT STAN MOON'S ELECTION. USING EVERY MEANS AT OUR DISPOSAL.
TIME TO PLEDGE OUR LOYALTY TO THE GOOD CAUSE. ALL IN FAVOR OF GETTING A WHOLE LOT RICHER, PLEASE SAY AYE.
AYE.
AYE.
AYE.
AYE.
AYE.
AYE.
AYE.
AYE.

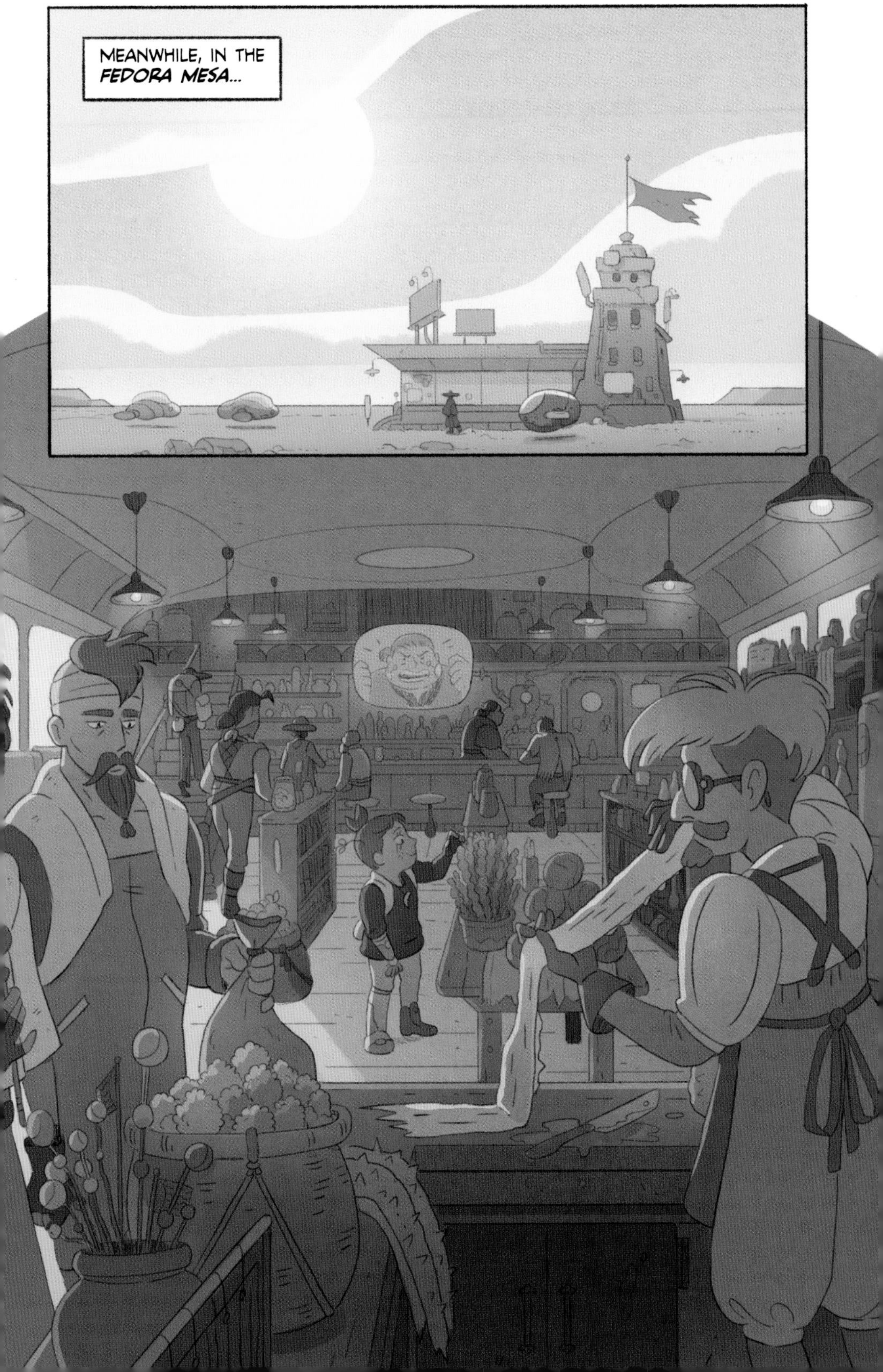
MEANWHILE, IN THE *FEDORA MESA*...

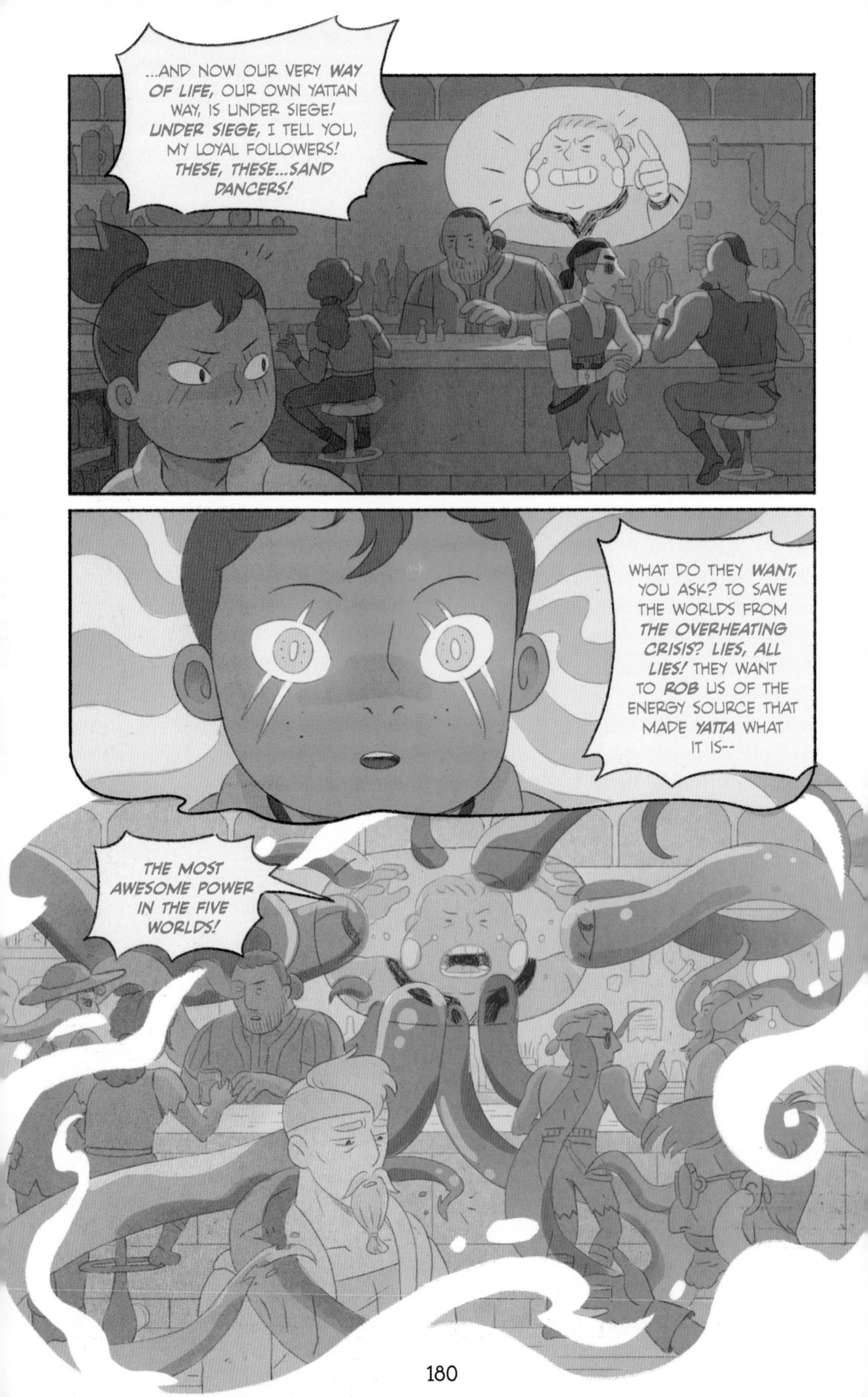
...AND NOW OUR VERY WAY OF LIFE, OUR OWN YATTAN WAY, IS UNDER SIEGE! UNDER SIEGE, I TELL YOU, MY LOYAL FOLLOWERS! THESE, THESE...SAND DANCERS!
WHAT DO THEY WANT, YOU ASK? TO SAVE THE WORLDS FROM THE OVERHEATING CRISIS? LIES, ALL LIES! THEY WANT TO ROB US OF THE ENERGY SOURCE THAT MADE YATTA WHAT IT IS--
THE MOST AWESOME POWER IN THE FIVE WORLDS!

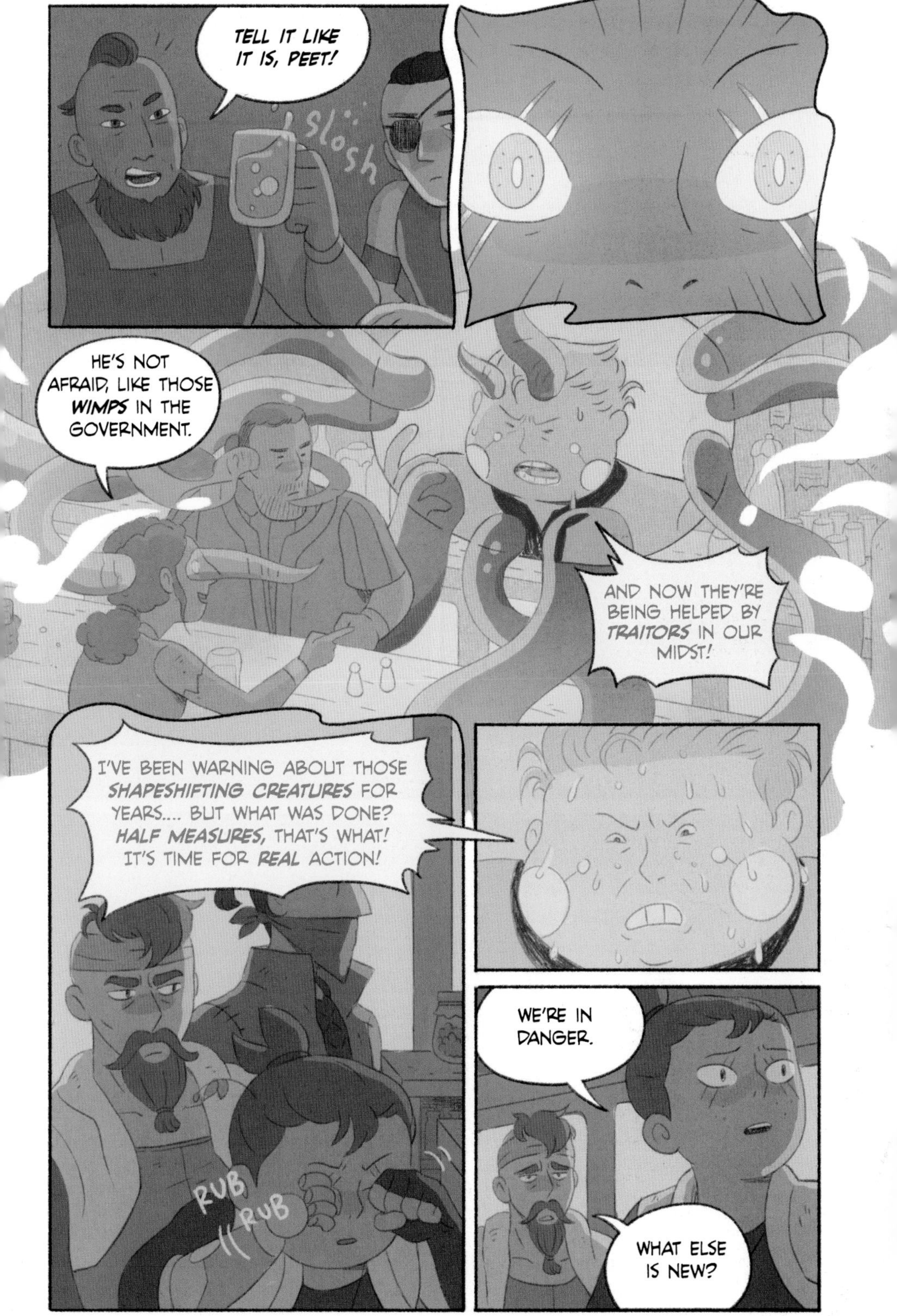
TELL IT LIKE IT IS, PEET!
SLOSH
HE'S NOT AFRAID, LIKE THOSE WIMPS IN THE GOVERNMENT.
AND NOW THEY'RE BEING HELPED BY TRAITORS IN OUR MIDST!
I'VE BEEN WARNING ABOUT THOSE SHAPESHIFTING CREATURES FOR YEARS.... BUT WHAT WAS DONE? HALF MEASURES, THAT'S WHAT! IT'S TIME FOR REAL ACTION!
WE'RE IN DANGER.
RUB RUB
WHAT ELSE IS NEW?

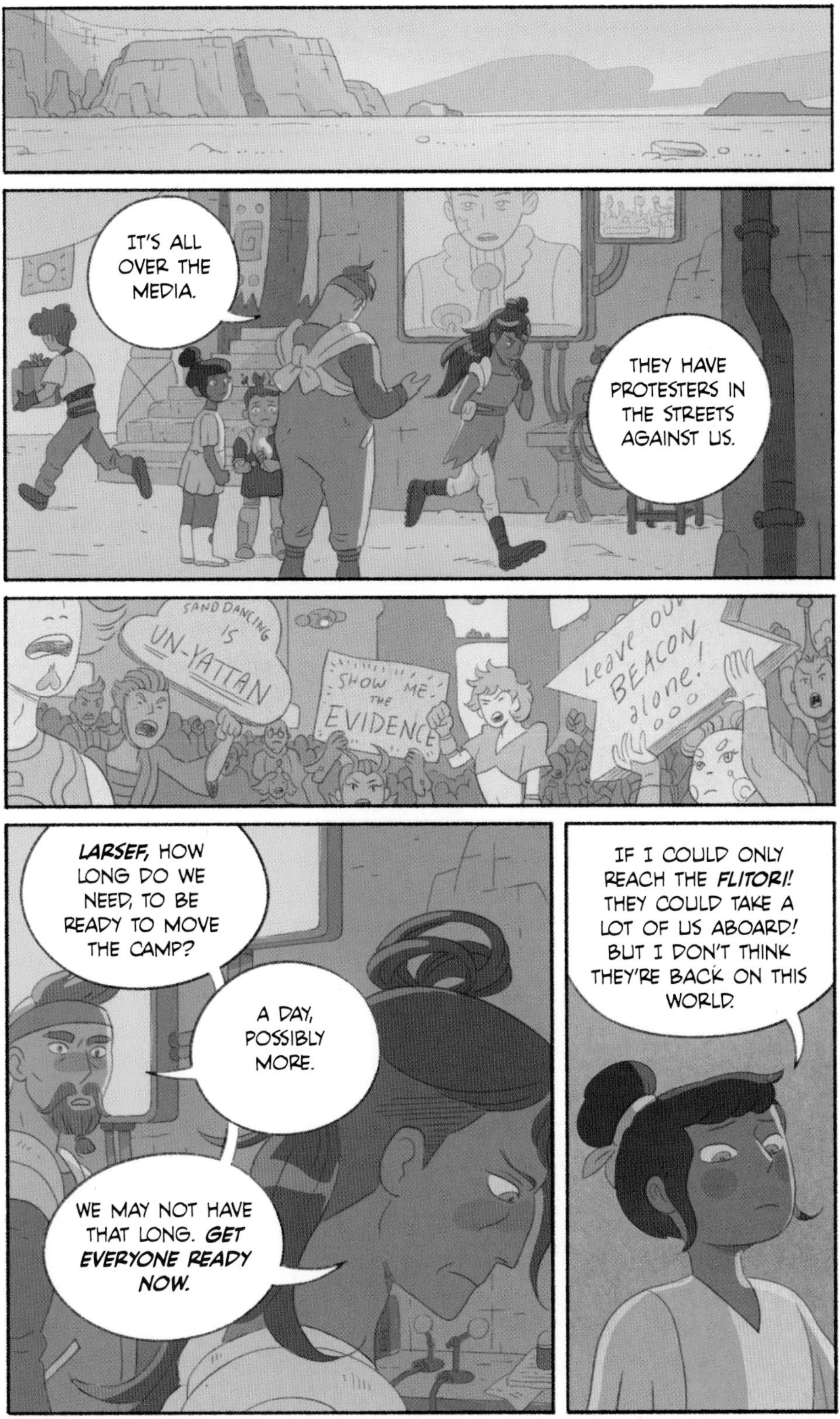
IT'S ALL OVER THE MEDIA.
THEY HAVE PROTESTERS IN THE STREETS AGAINST US.
SAND DANCING IS UN-YATTAN
SHOW ME THE EVIDENCE
Leave our BEACON alone!
LARSEF, HOW LONG DO WE NEED, TO BE READY TO MOVE THE CAMP?
A DAY, POSSIBLY MORE.
WE MAY NOT HAVE THAT LONG. GET EVERYONE READY NOW.
IF I COULD ONLY REACH THE FLITORI! THEY COULD TAKE A LOT OF US ABOARD! BUT I DON'T THINK THEY'RE BACK ON THIS WORLD.

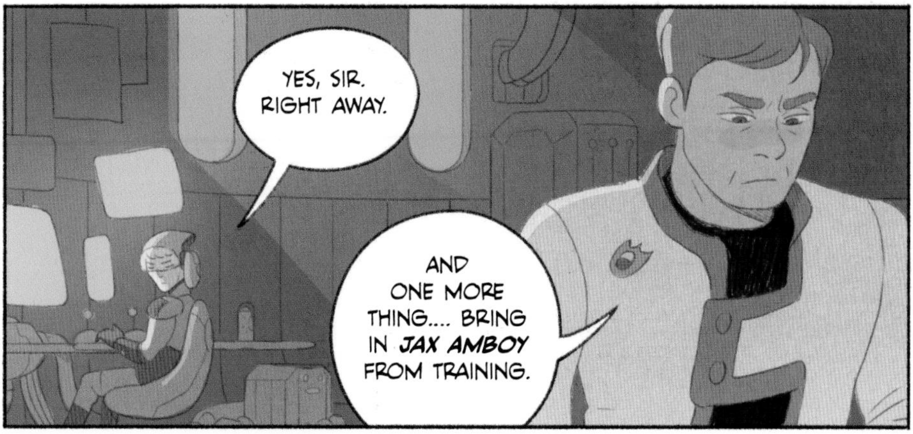
YES, SIR. RIGHT AWAY.
AND ONE MORE THING.... BRING IN JAX AMBOY FROM TRAINING.

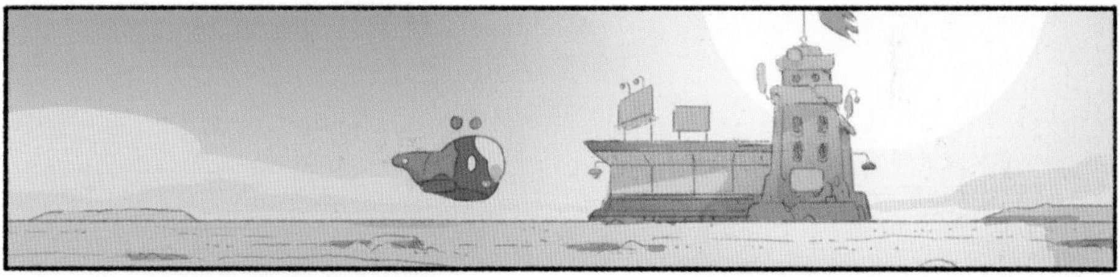

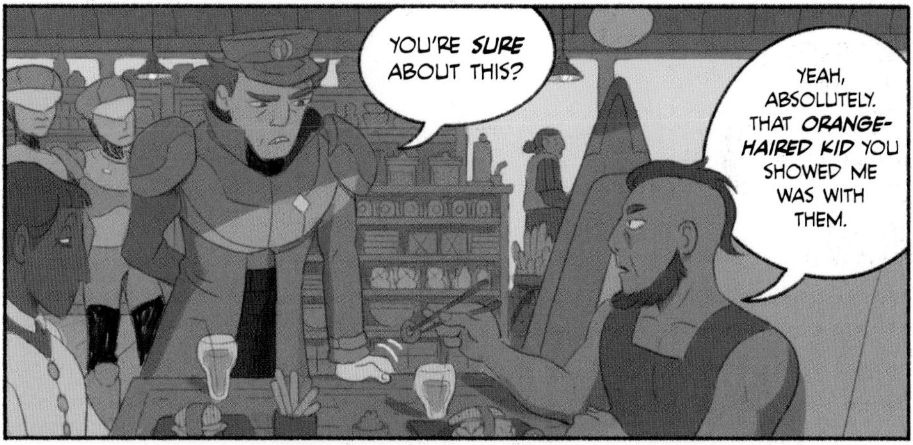
YOU'RE SURE ABOUT THIS?
YEAH, ABSOLUTELY. THAT ORANGE-HAIRED KID YOU SHOWED ME WAS WITH THEM.

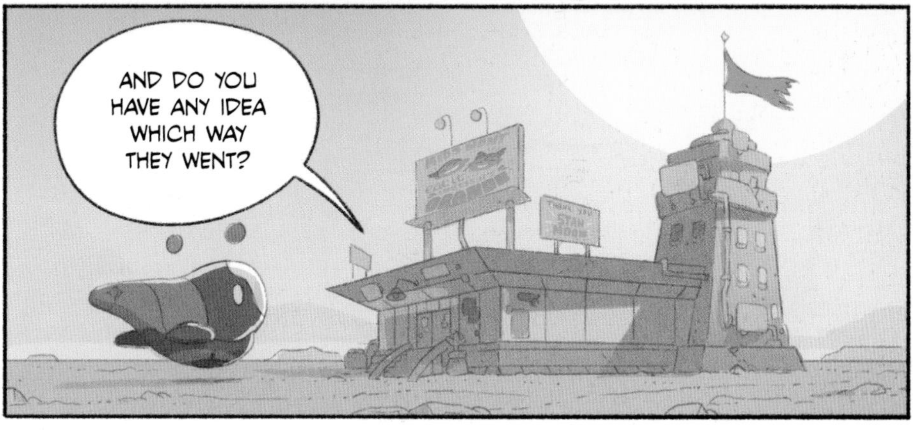
AND DO YOU HAVE ANY IDEA WHICH WAY THEY WENT?

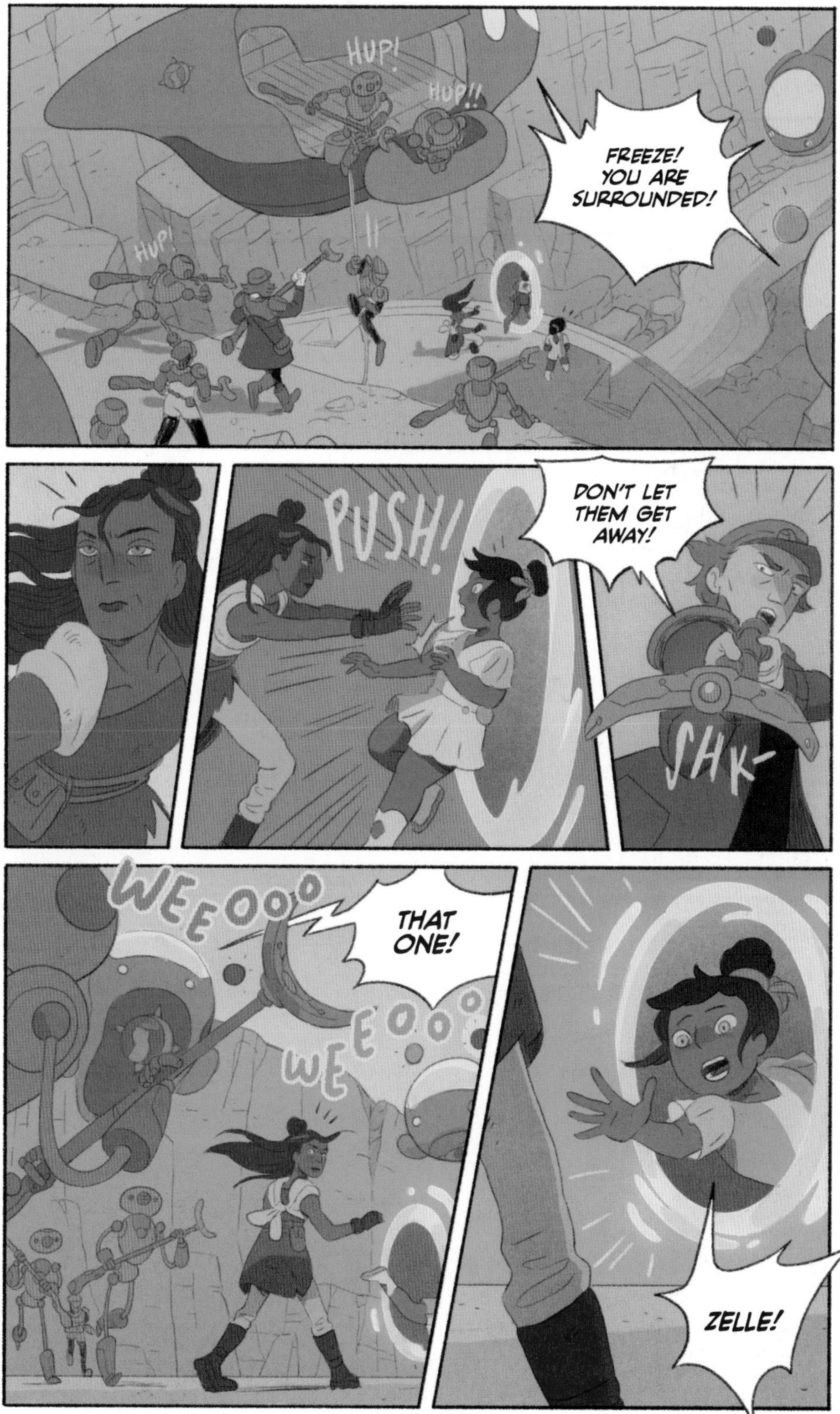
HUP!
HUP!!
FREEZE! YOU ARE SURROUNDED!
HUP!
PUSH!
DON'T LET THEM GET AWAY!
SHK-
WEEOOO
THAT ONE!
WEEOOO
ZELLE!

## Chapter 10

# GAME DAY

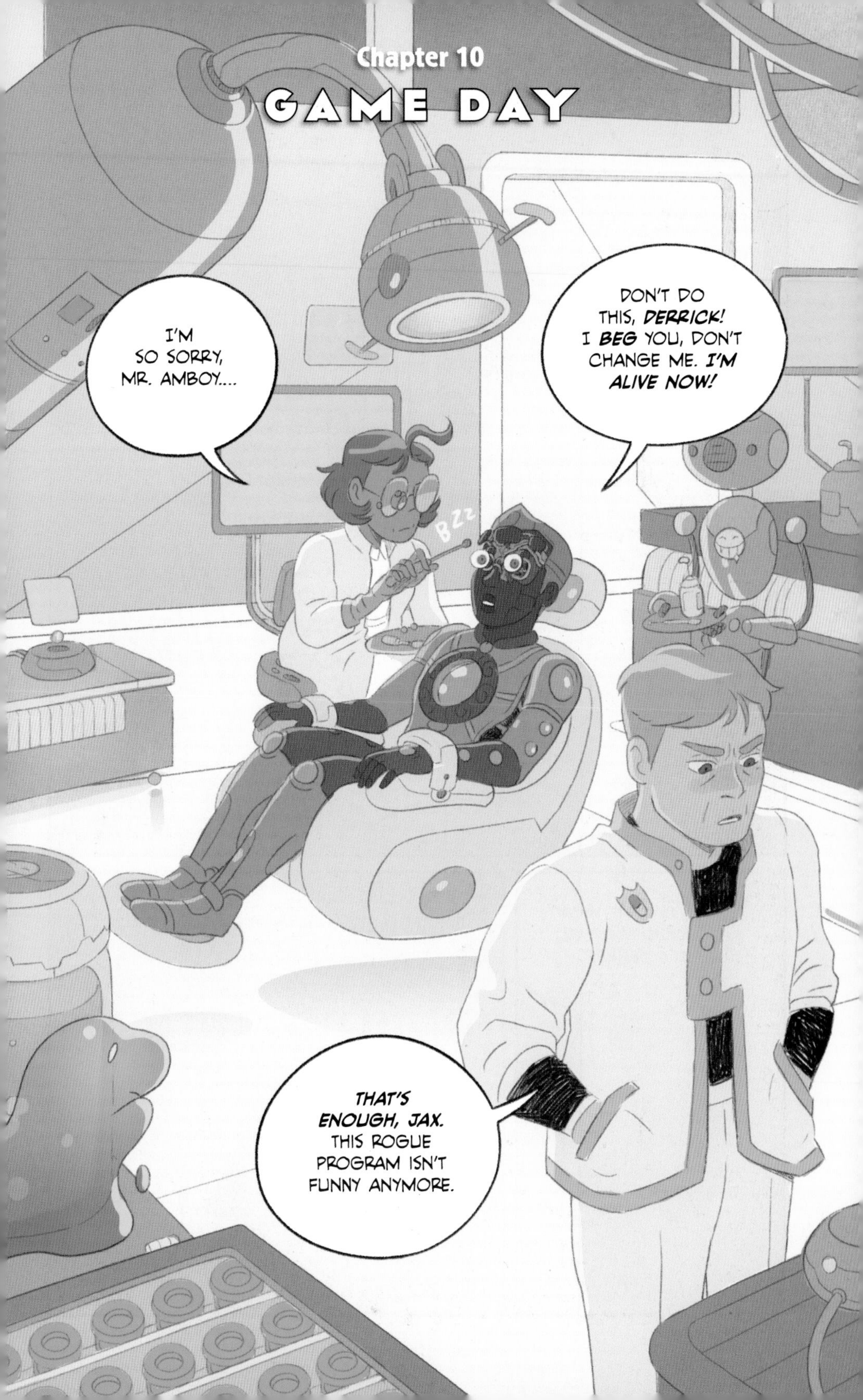
I'M SO SORRY, MR. AMBOY....
DON'T DO THIS, *DERRICK!* I *BEG* YOU, DON'T CHANGE ME. *I'M ALIVE NOW!*
BZZ
*THAT'S ENOUGH, JAX.* THIS ROGUE PROGRAM ISN'T FUNNY ANYMORE.

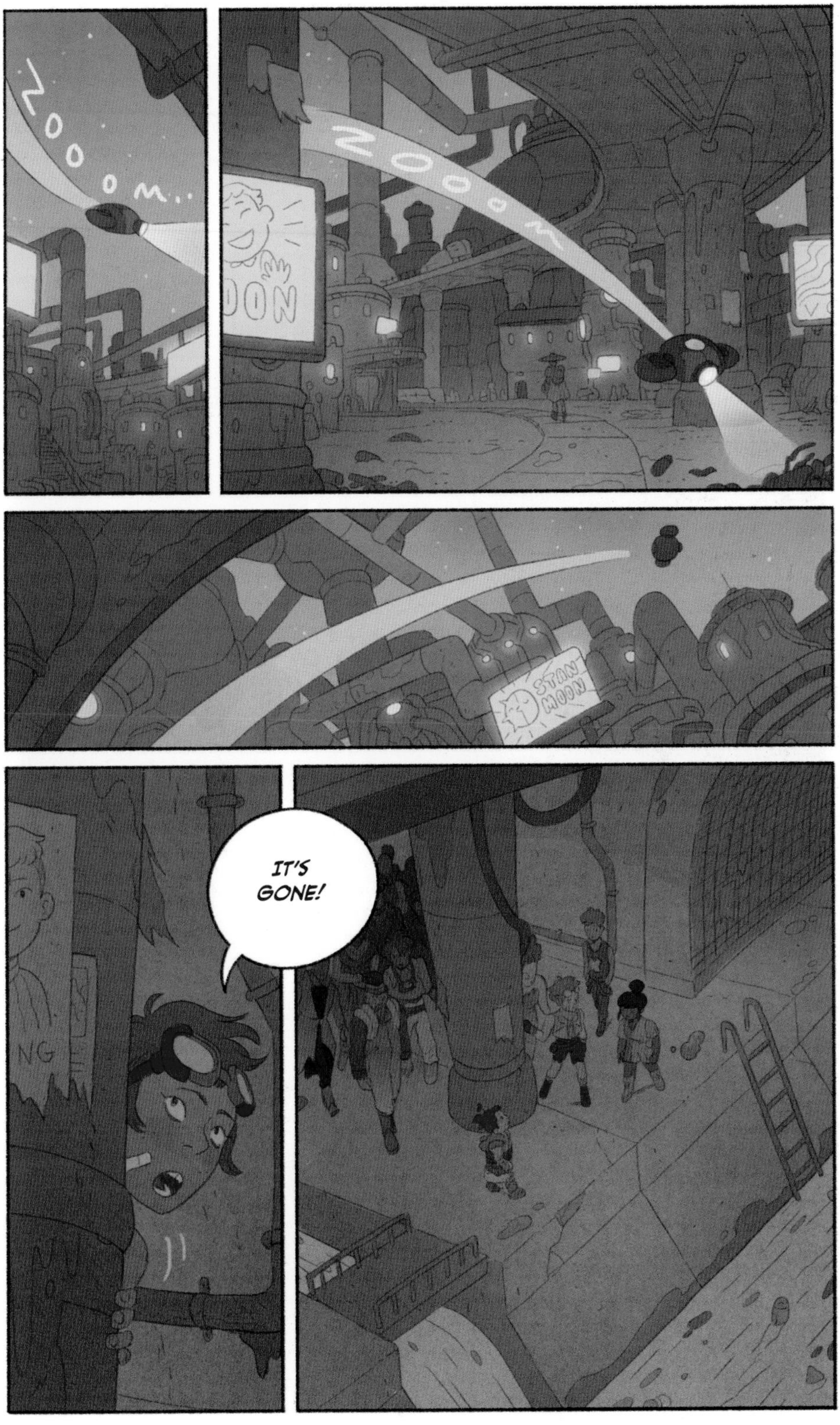
ZOOOm..
ZOOOOM
STAN MOON
IT'S GONE!

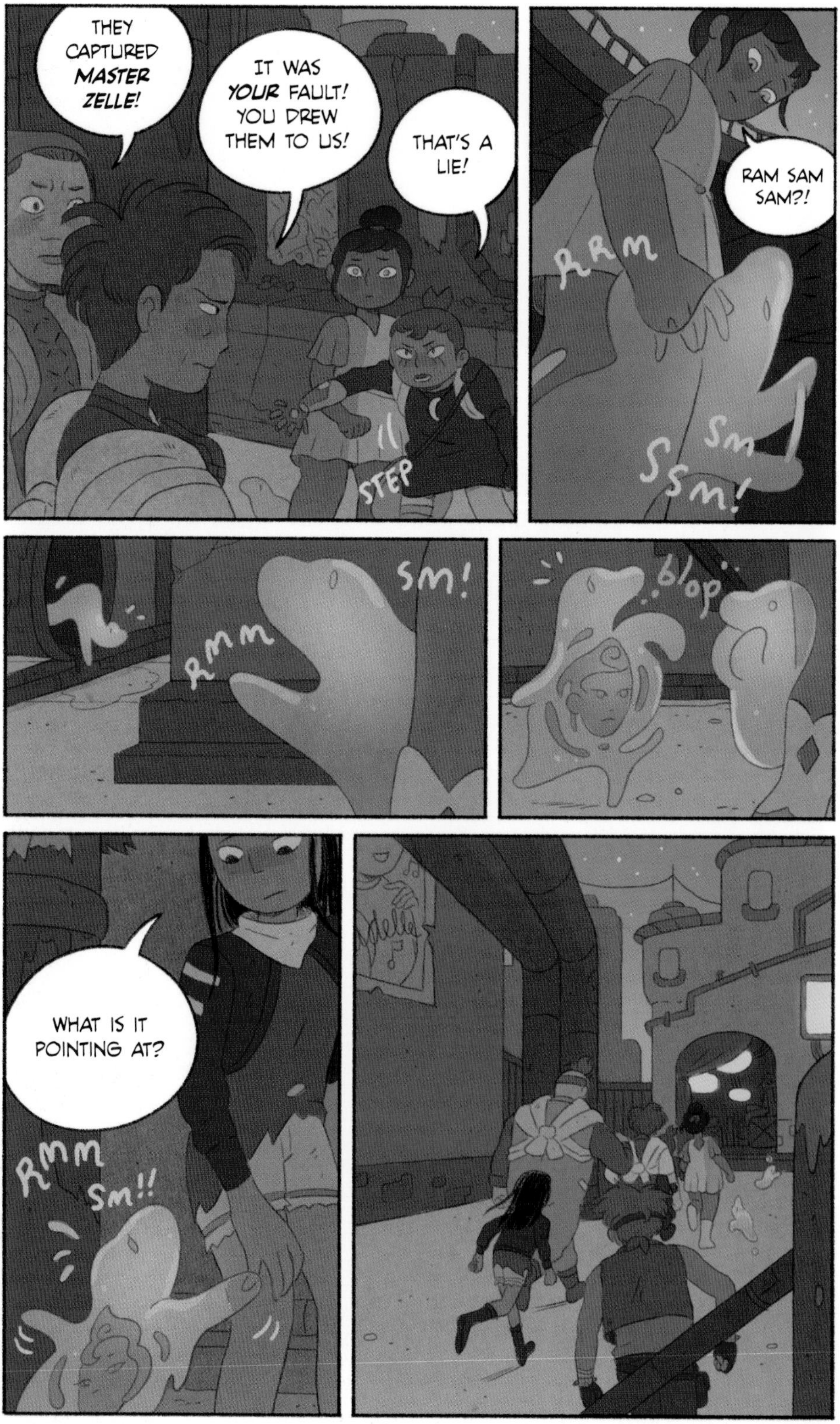
THEY CAPTURED MASTER ZELLE!
IT WAS YOUR FAULT! YOU DREW THEM TO US!
THAT'S A LIE!
STEP
RAM SAM SAM?!
RRM
SM
SSM!
SM!
RMM
BLOP
WHAT IS IT POINTING AT?
RMM
SM!!

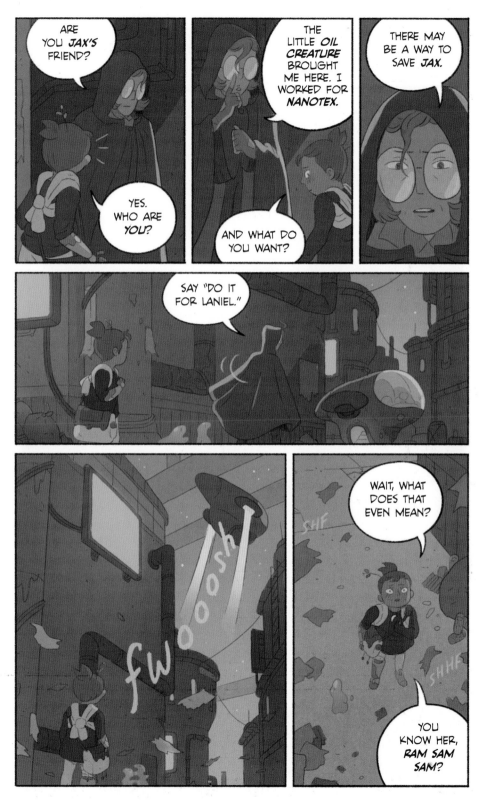

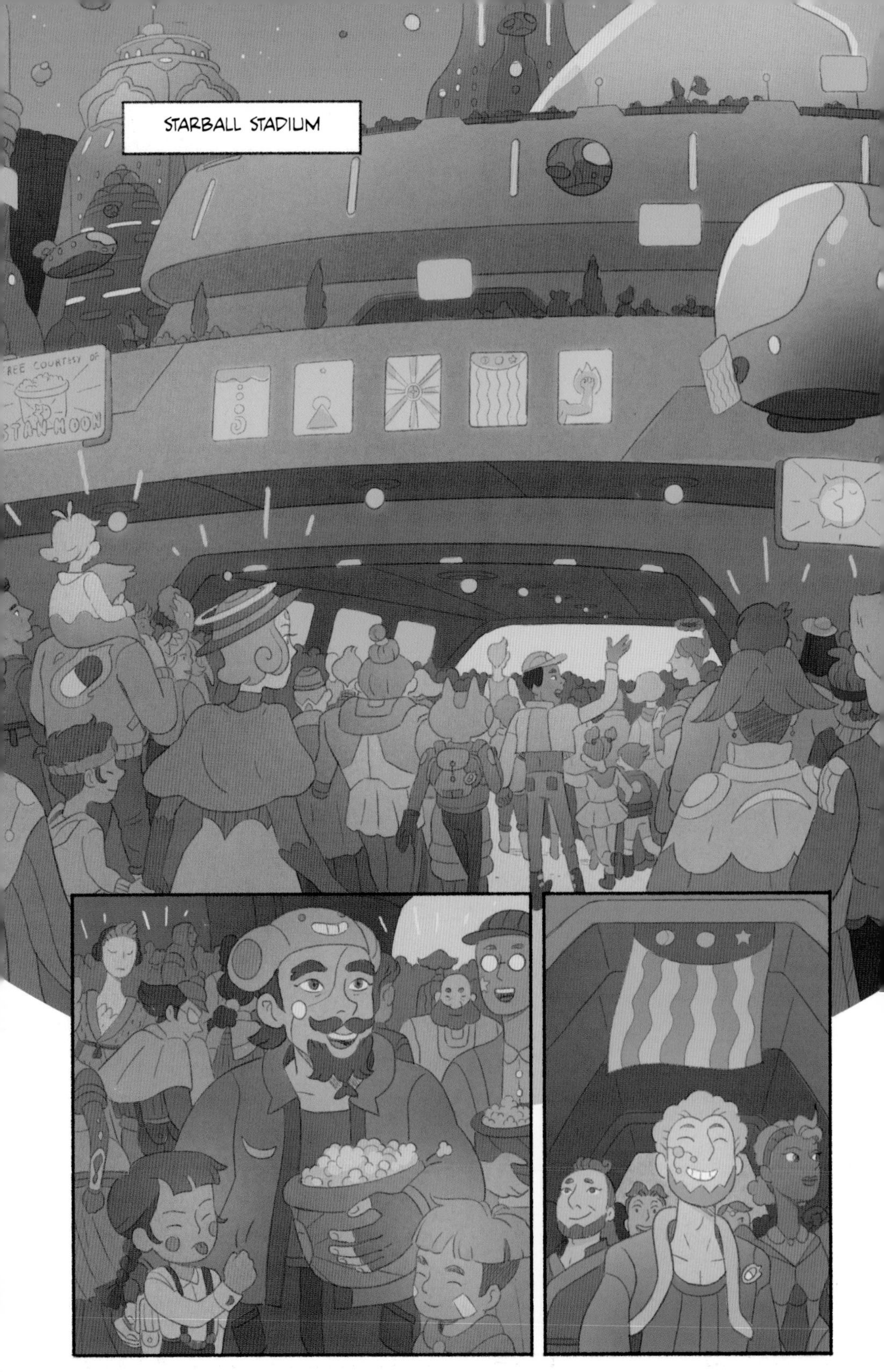
STARBALL STADIUM

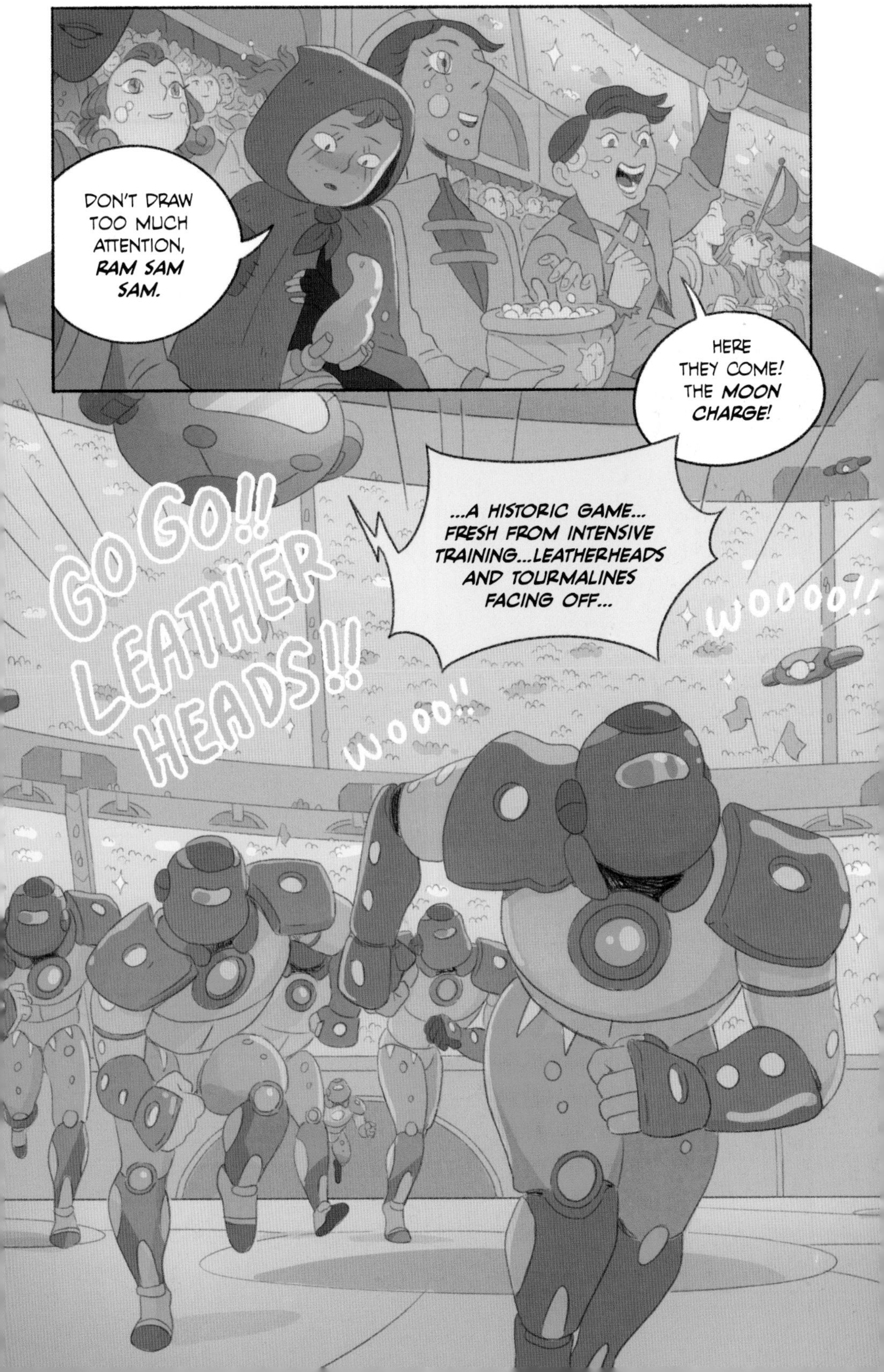
DON'T DRAW TOO MUCH ATTENTION, RAM SAM SAM.
HERE THEY COME! THE MOON CHARGE!
GO GO!! LEATHER HEADS!!
...A HISTORIC GAME... FRESH FROM INTENSIVE TRAINING...LEATHERHEADS AND TOURMALINES FACING OFF...
WOOOO!!
WOOO!!

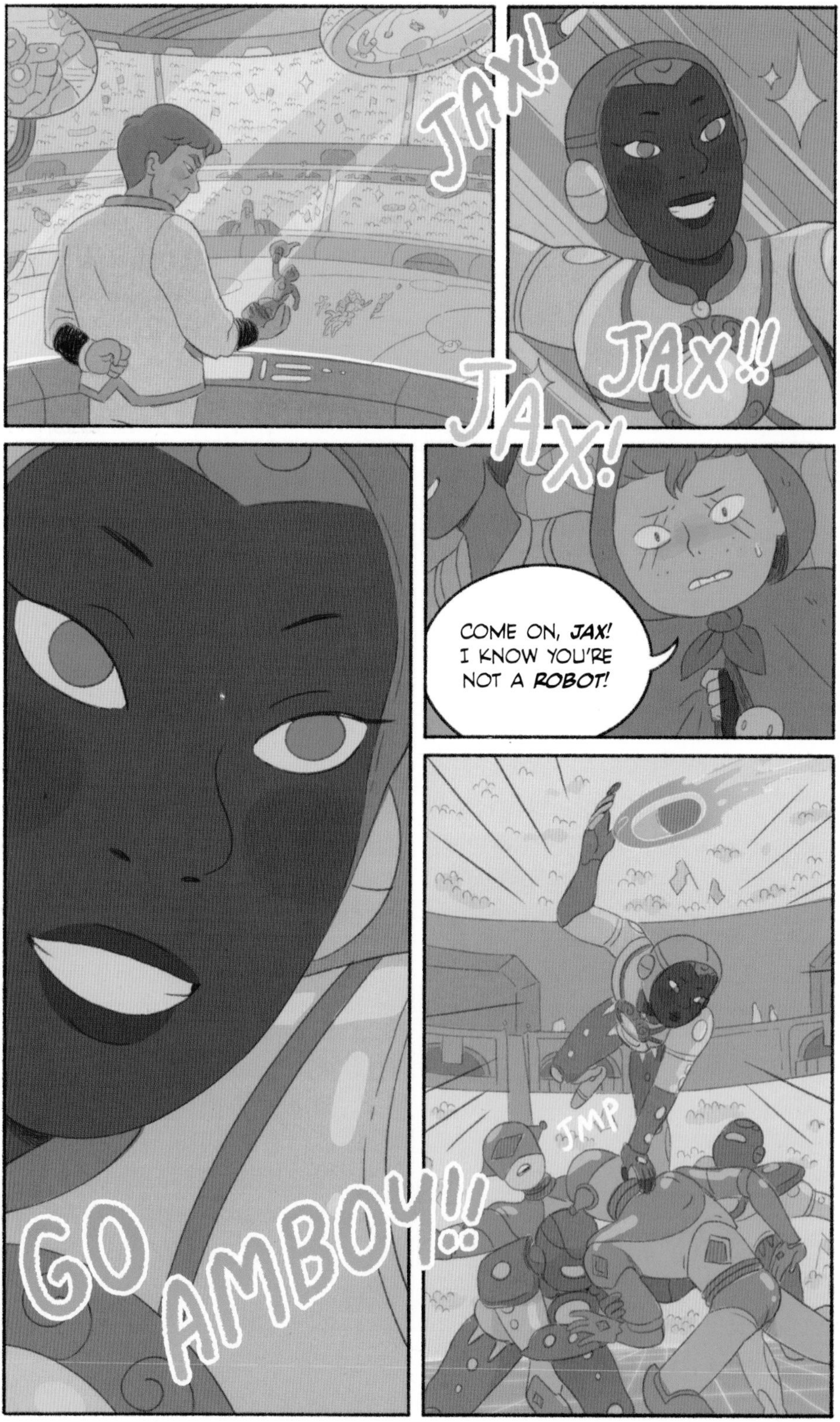
JAX!
JAX!!
JAX!
COME ON, JAX! I KNOW YOU'RE NOT A ROBOT!
JMP
GO AMBOY!!

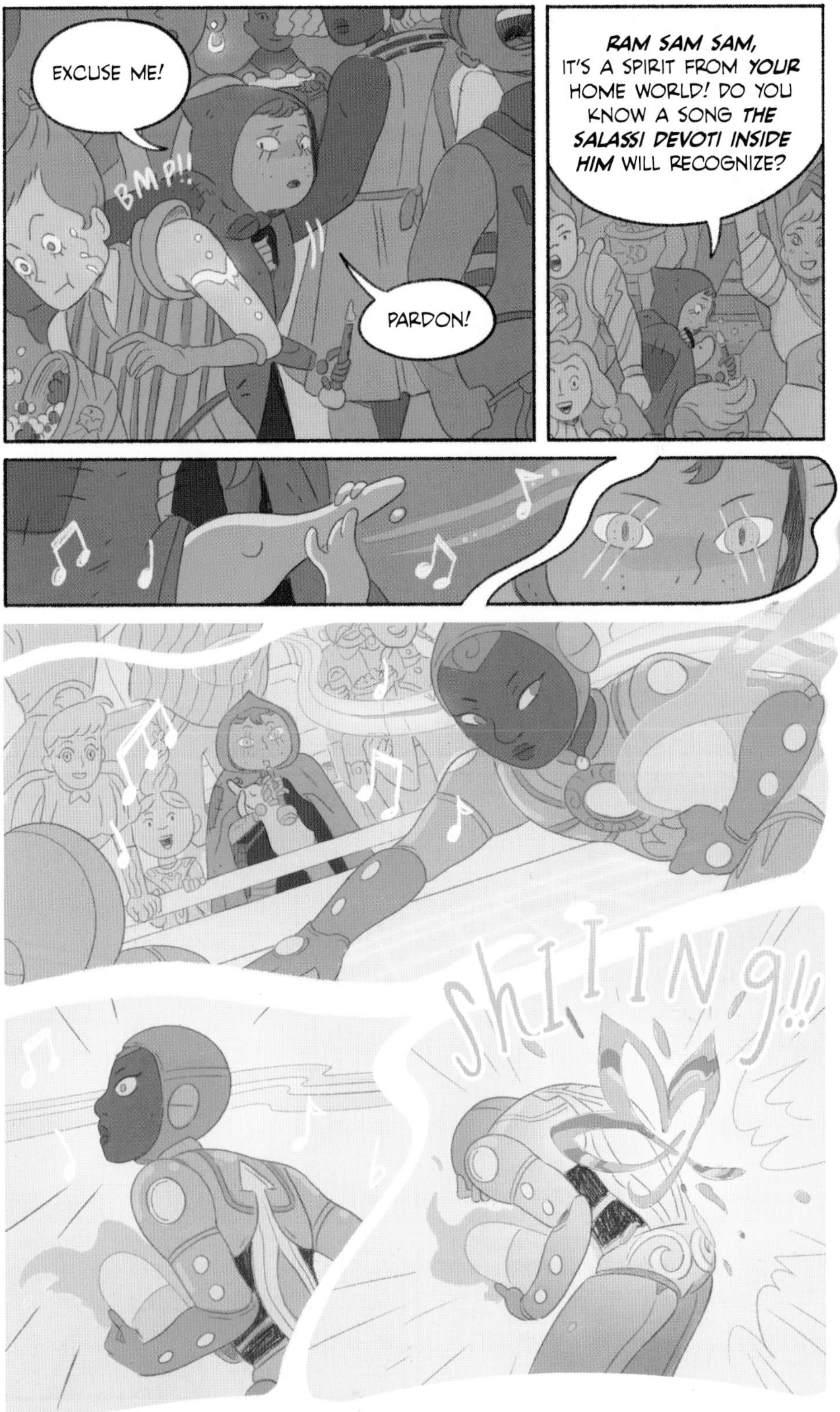
EXCUSE ME!
BMP!!
PARDON!
RAM SAM SAM, IT'S A SPIRIT FROM YOUR HOME WORLD! DO YOU KNOW A SONG THE SALASSI DEVOTI INSIDE HIM WILL RECOGNIZE?
SHIIING!!

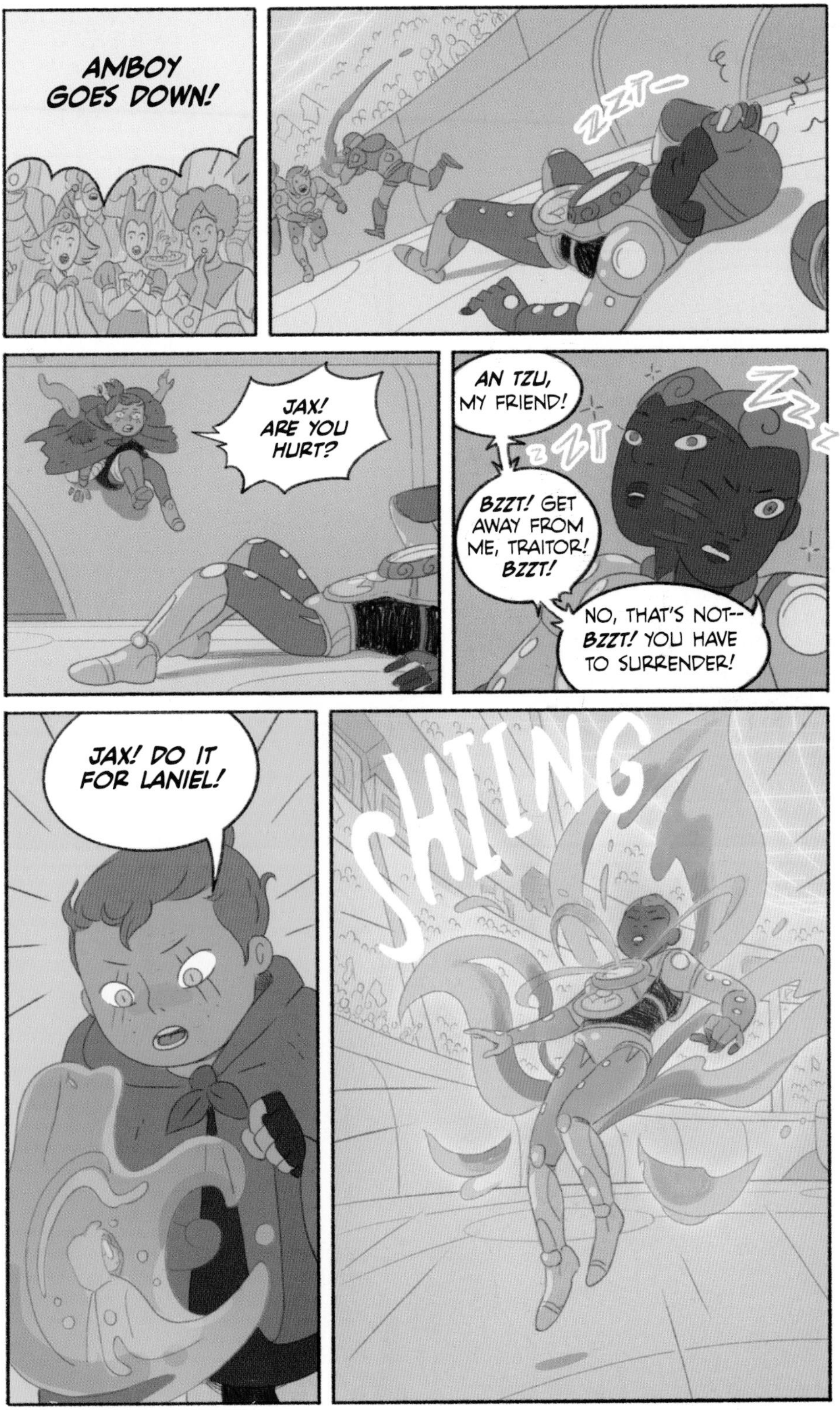
AMBOY GOES DOWN!
ZZZT--
JAX! ARE YOU HURT?
AN TZU, MY FRIEND!
BZZT! GET AWAY FROM ME, TRAITOR! BZZT!
NO, THAT'S NOT-- BZZT! YOU HAVE TO SURRENDER!
JAX! DO IT FOR LANIEL!
SHIING

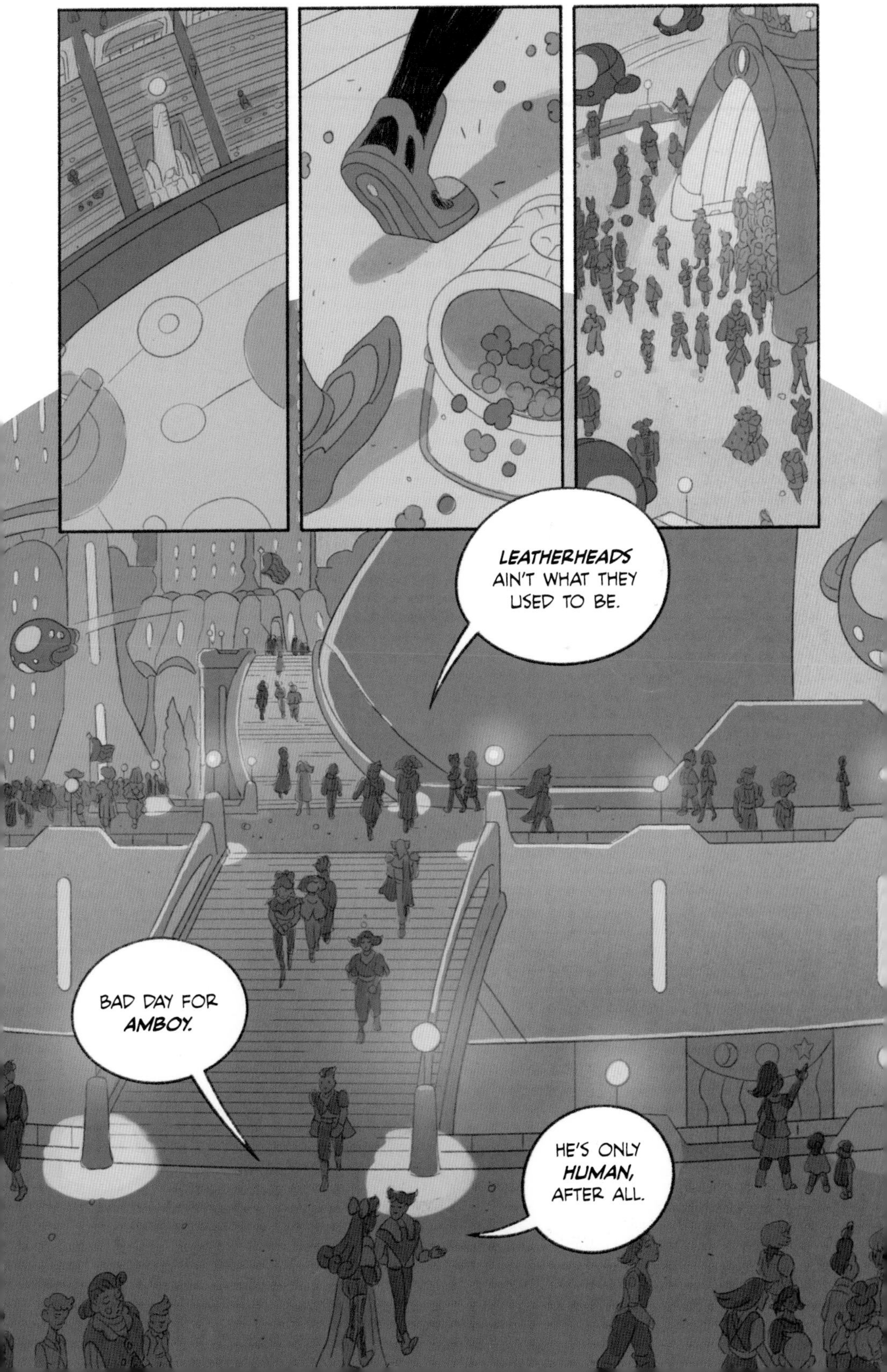
LEATHERHEADS AIN'T WHAT THEY USED TO BE.
BAD DAY FOR AMBOY.
HE'S ONLY HUMAN, AFTER ALL.

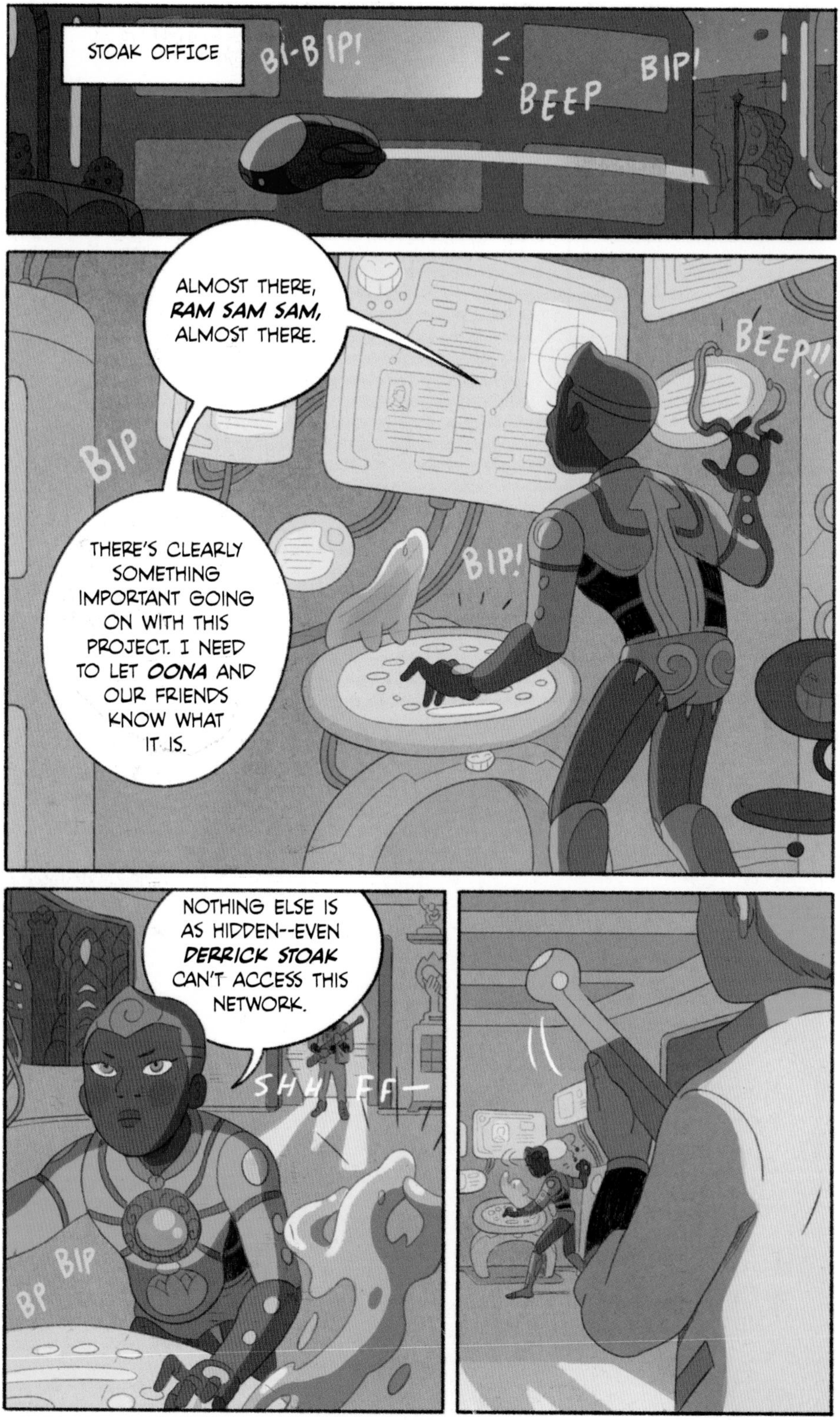
STOAK OFFICE
BI-BIP!
BEEP
BIP!
ALMOST THERE, **RAM SAM SAM,** ALMOST THERE.
BEEP!!
BIP
THERE'S CLEARLY SOMETHING IMPORTANT GOING ON WITH THIS PROJECT. I NEED TO LET **OONA** AND OUR FRIENDS KNOW WHAT IT IS.
BIP!
NOTHING ELSE IS AS HIDDEN--EVEN **DERRICK STOAK** CAN'T ACCESS THIS NETWORK.
SHHFF—
BP BIP

## Chapter 11

# ELECTION DAY

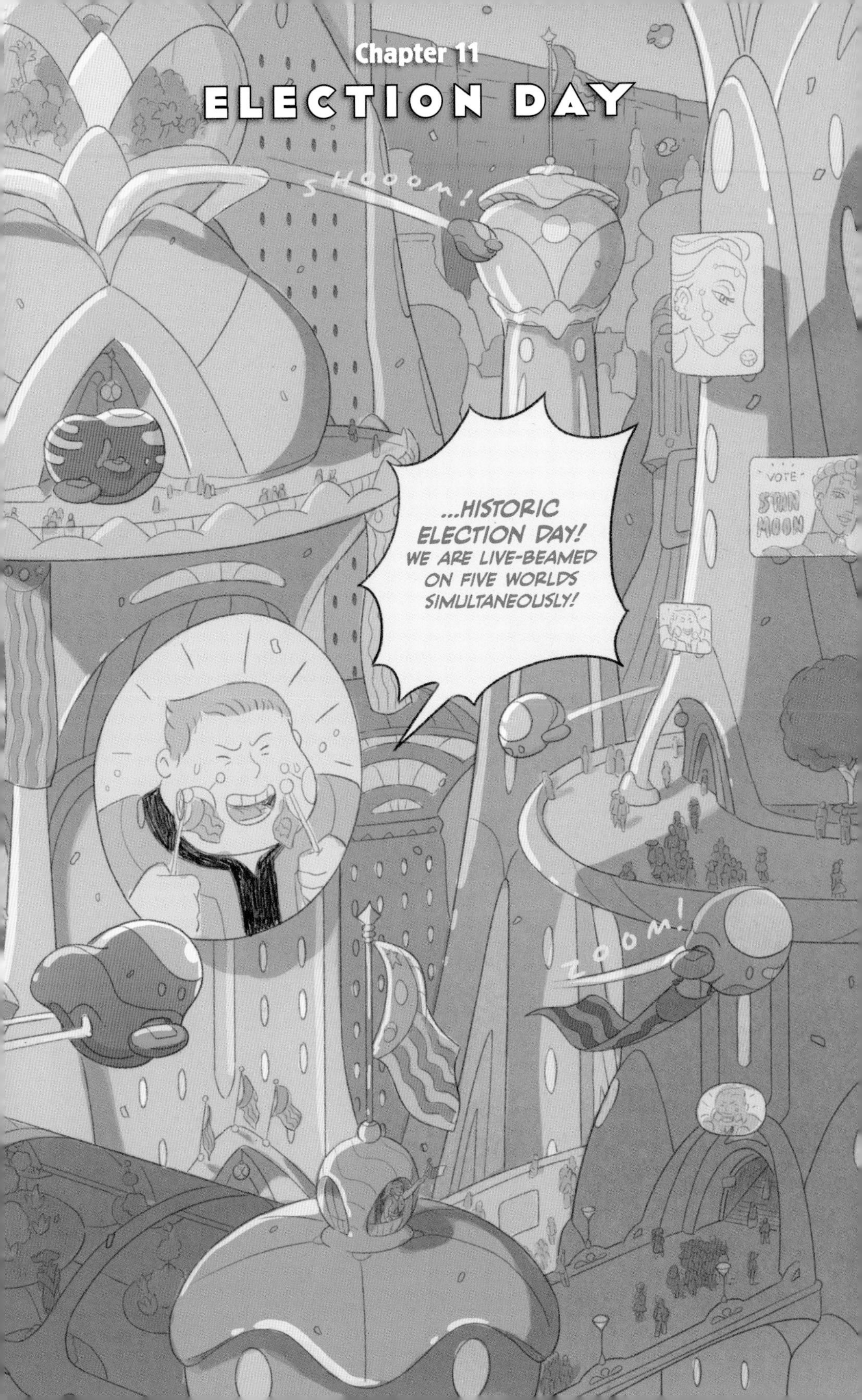
SHOOOM!
...HISTORIC ELECTION DAY! WE ARE LIVE-BEAMED ON FIVE WORLDS SIMULTANEOUSLY!
VOTE STAN MOON
ZOOM!

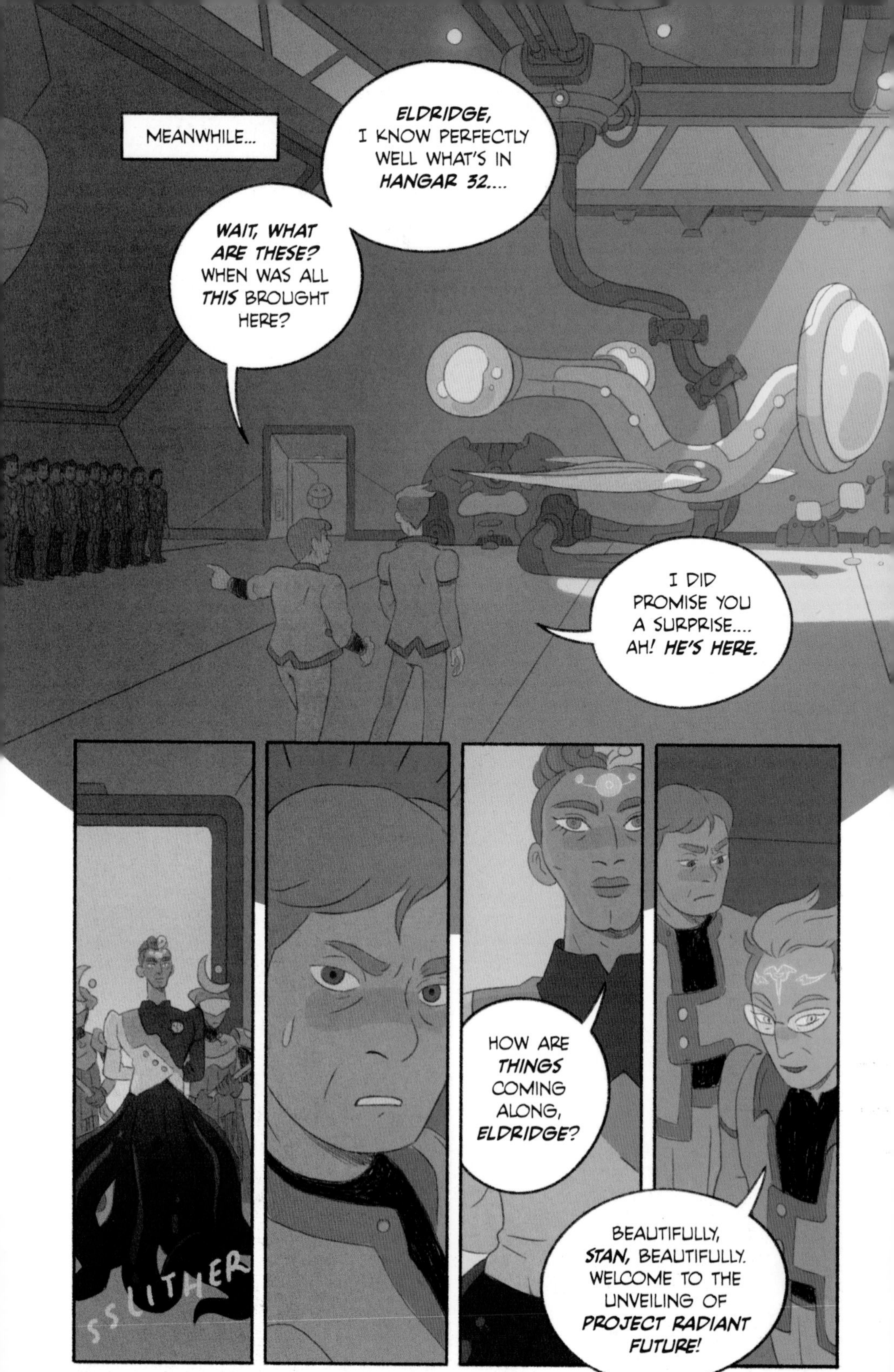
MEANWHILE...
ELDRIDGE, I KNOW PERFECTLY WELL WHAT'S IN HANGAR 32....
WAIT, WHAT ARE THESE? WHEN WAS ALL THIS BROUGHT HERE?
I DID PROMISE YOU A SURPRISE.... AH! HE'S HERE.
SSLITHER
HOW ARE THINGS COMING ALONG, ELDRIDGE?
BEAUTIFULLY, STAN, BEAUTIFULLY. WELCOME TO THE UNVEILING OF PROJECT RADIANT FUTURE!

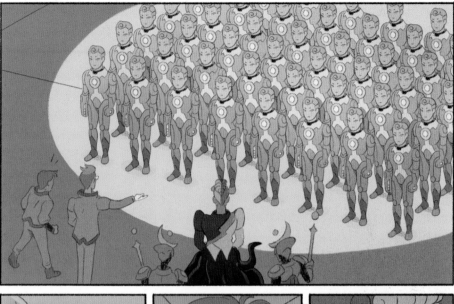

WELL DONE, *ELDRIDGE*, WELL DONE!

THEY'RE FULLY TESTED AND FUNCTIONAL. *LOOK!*

URBAN WARFARE. VERY NICE.

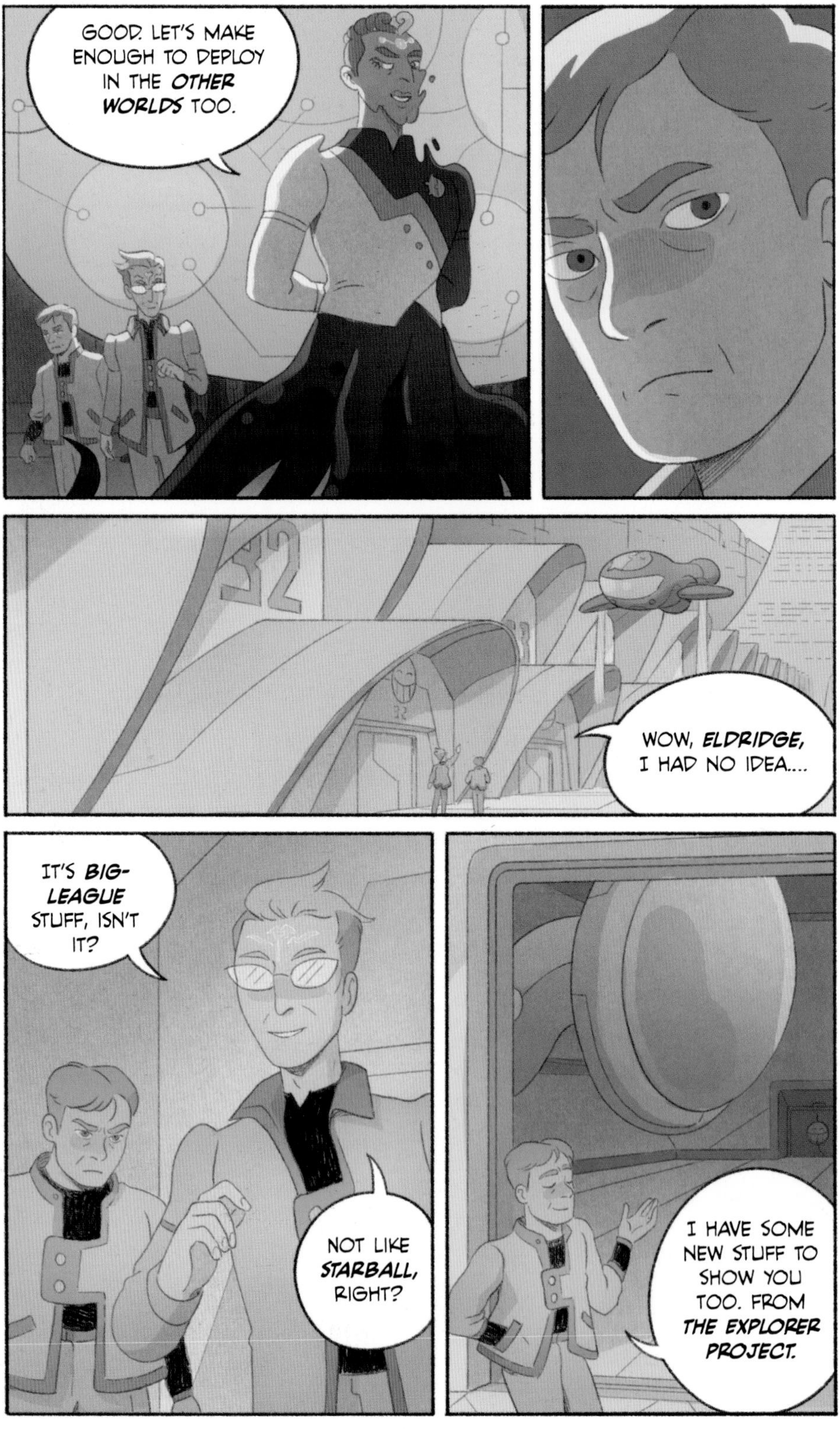
GOOD. LET'S MAKE ENOUGH TO DEPLOY IN THE OTHER WORLDS TOO.
WOW, ELDRIDGE, I HAD NO IDEA....
IT'S BIG-LEAGUE STUFF, ISN'T IT?
NOT LIKE STARBALL, RIGHT?
I HAVE SOME NEW STUFF TO SHOW YOU TOO. FROM THE EXPLORER PROJECT.

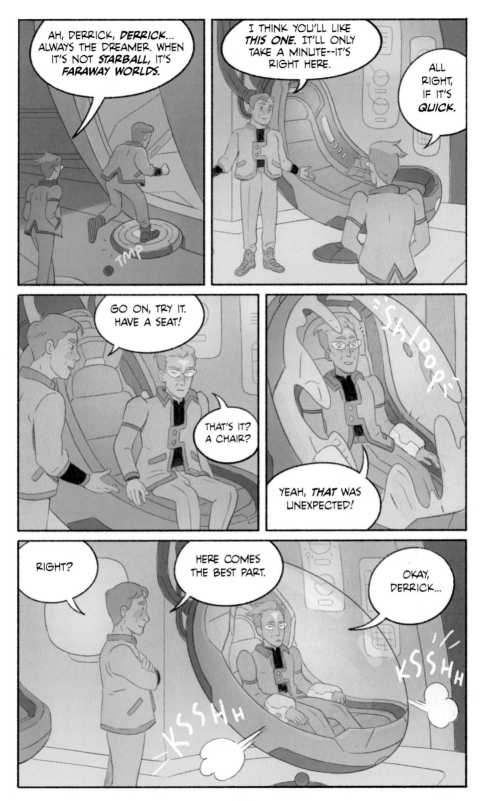

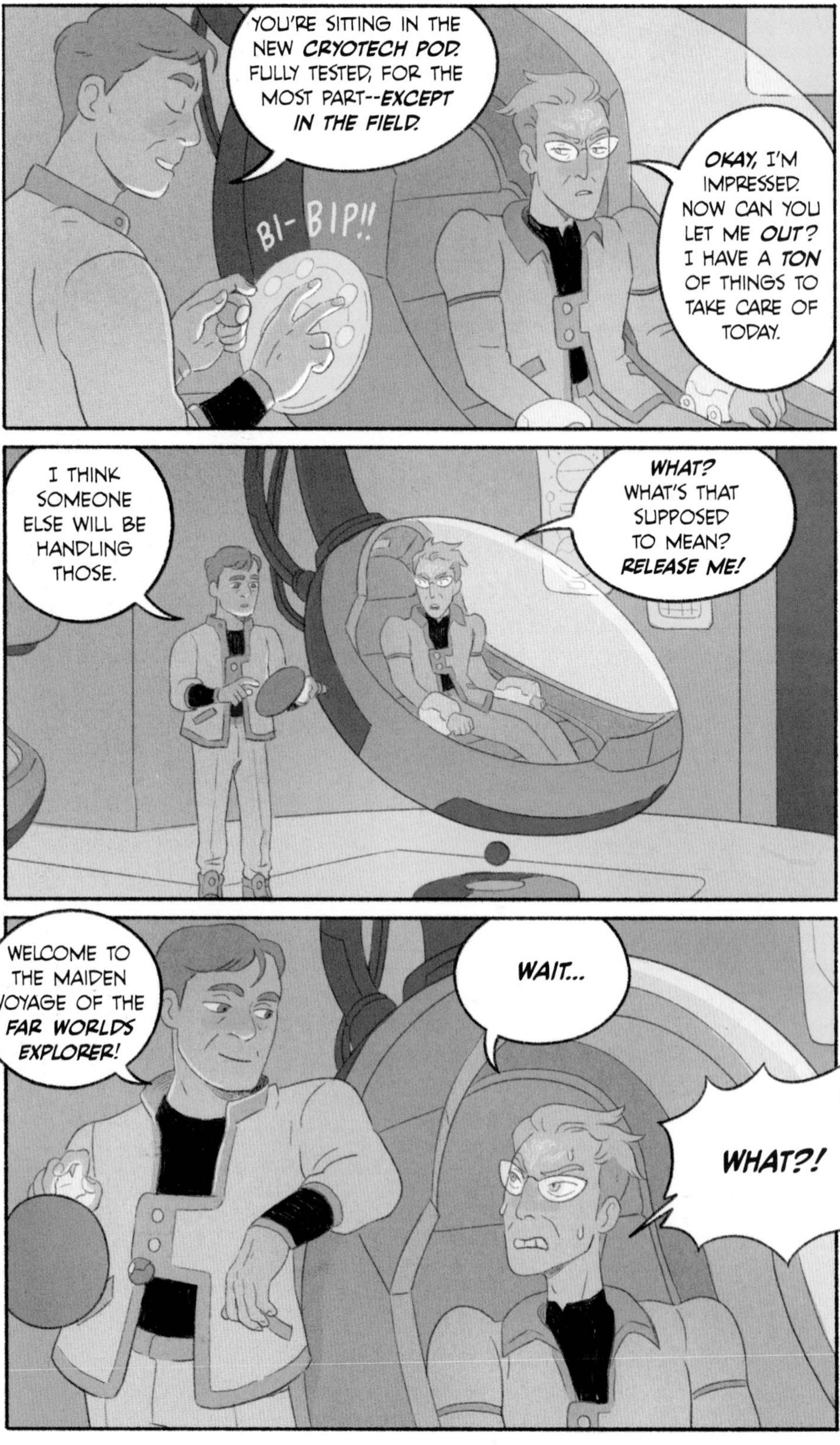
YOU'RE SITTING IN THE NEW CRYOTECH POD. FULLY TESTED, FOR THE MOST PART--EXCEPT IN THE FIELD.
BI- BIP!!
OKAY, I'M IMPRESSED. NOW CAN YOU LET ME OUT? I HAVE A TON OF THINGS TO TAKE CARE OF TODAY.
I THINK SOMEONE ELSE WILL BE HANDLING THOSE.
WHAT? WHAT'S THAT SUPPOSED TO MEAN? RELEASE ME!
WELCOME TO THE MAIDEN VOYAGE OF THE FAR WORLDS EXPLORER!
WAIT...
WHAT?!

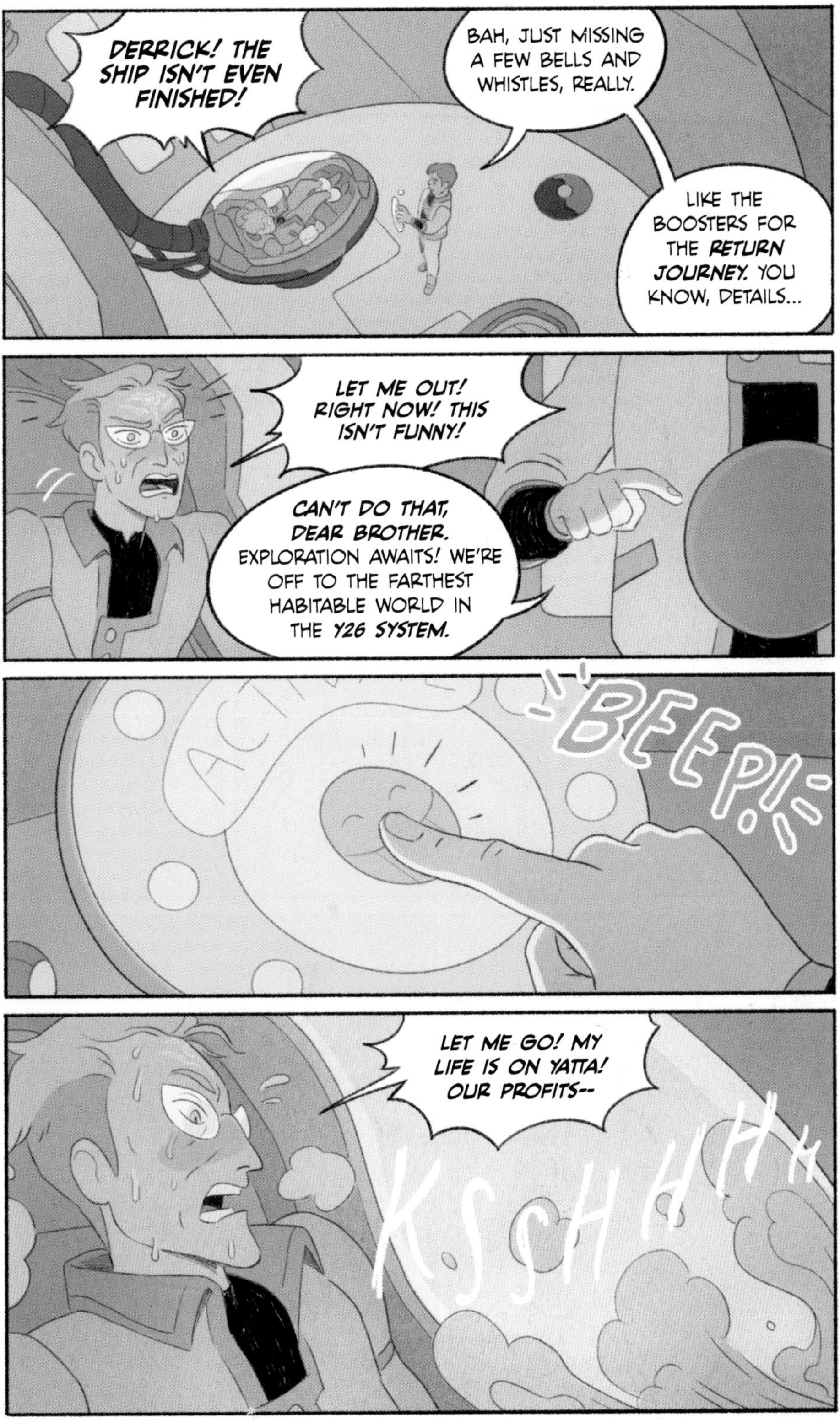
DERRICK! THE SHIP ISN'T EVEN FINISHED!
BAH, JUST MISSING A FEW BELLS AND WHISTLES, REALLY.
LIKE THE BOOSTERS FOR THE RETURN JOURNEY. YOU KNOW, DETAILS...
LET ME OUT! RIGHT NOW! THIS ISN'T FUNNY!
CAN'T DO THAT, DEAR BROTHER. EXPLORATION AWAITS! WE'RE OFF TO THE FARTHEST HABITABLE WORLD IN THE Y26 SYSTEM.
BEEP!
LET ME GO! MY LIFE IS ON YATTA! OUR PROFITS--
KSHHHHH

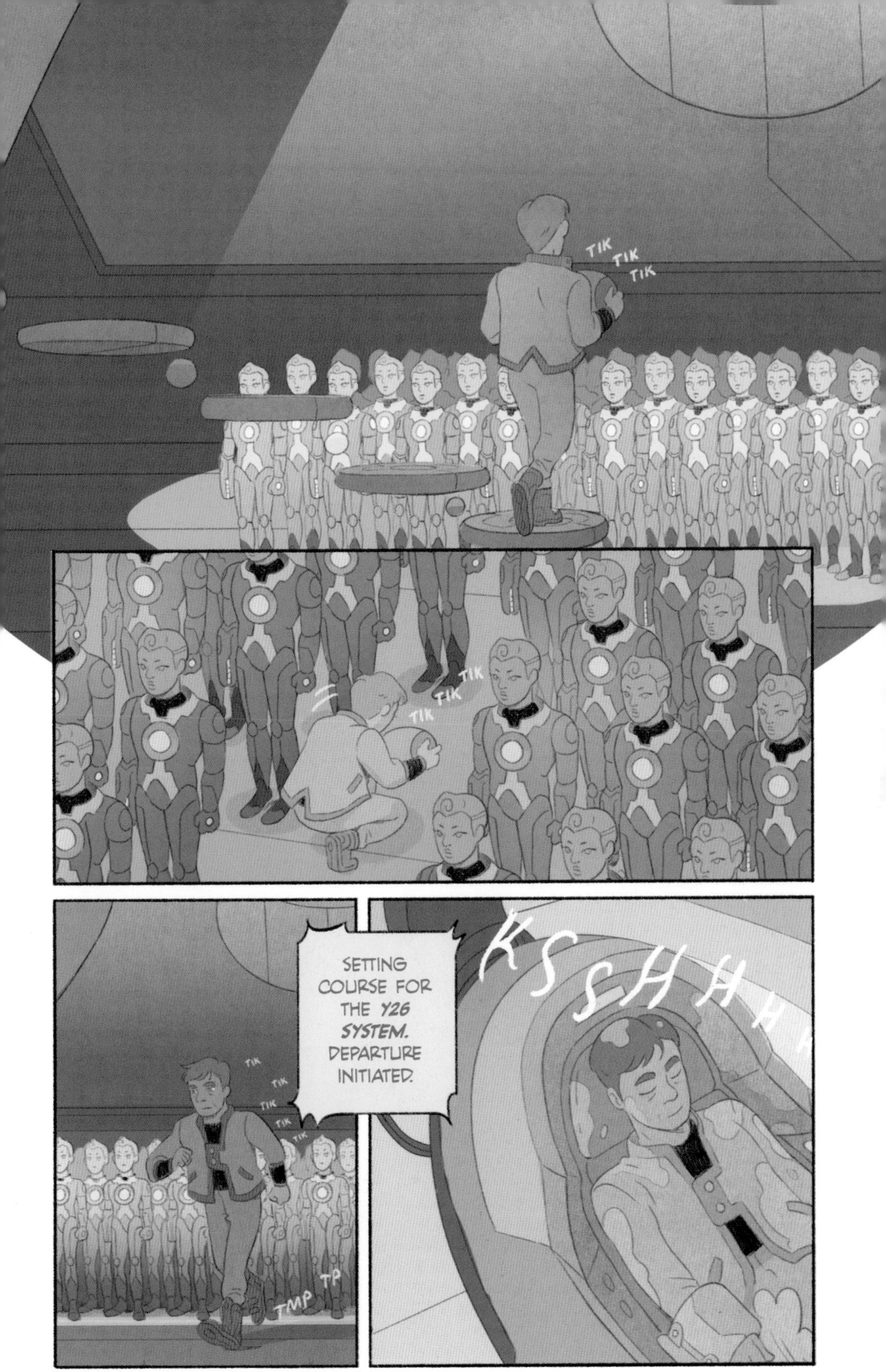
TIK
TIK
TIK
TIK
TIK
TIK
SETTING COURSE FOR THE Y26 SYSTEM. DEPARTURE INITIATED.
TIK
TIK
TIK
TIK
TIK
TMP
TP
KSSHHHH

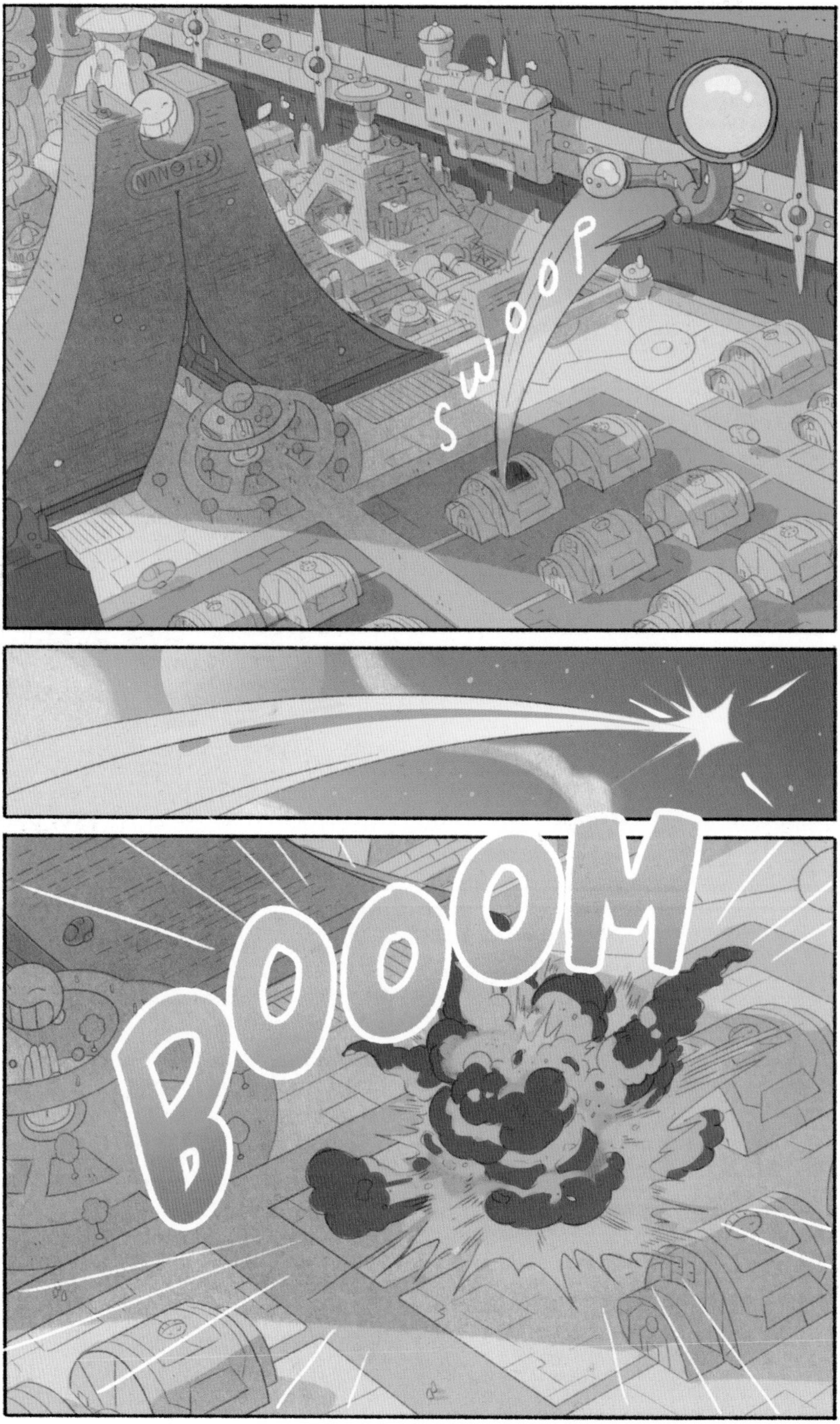
SWOOP
BOOOM

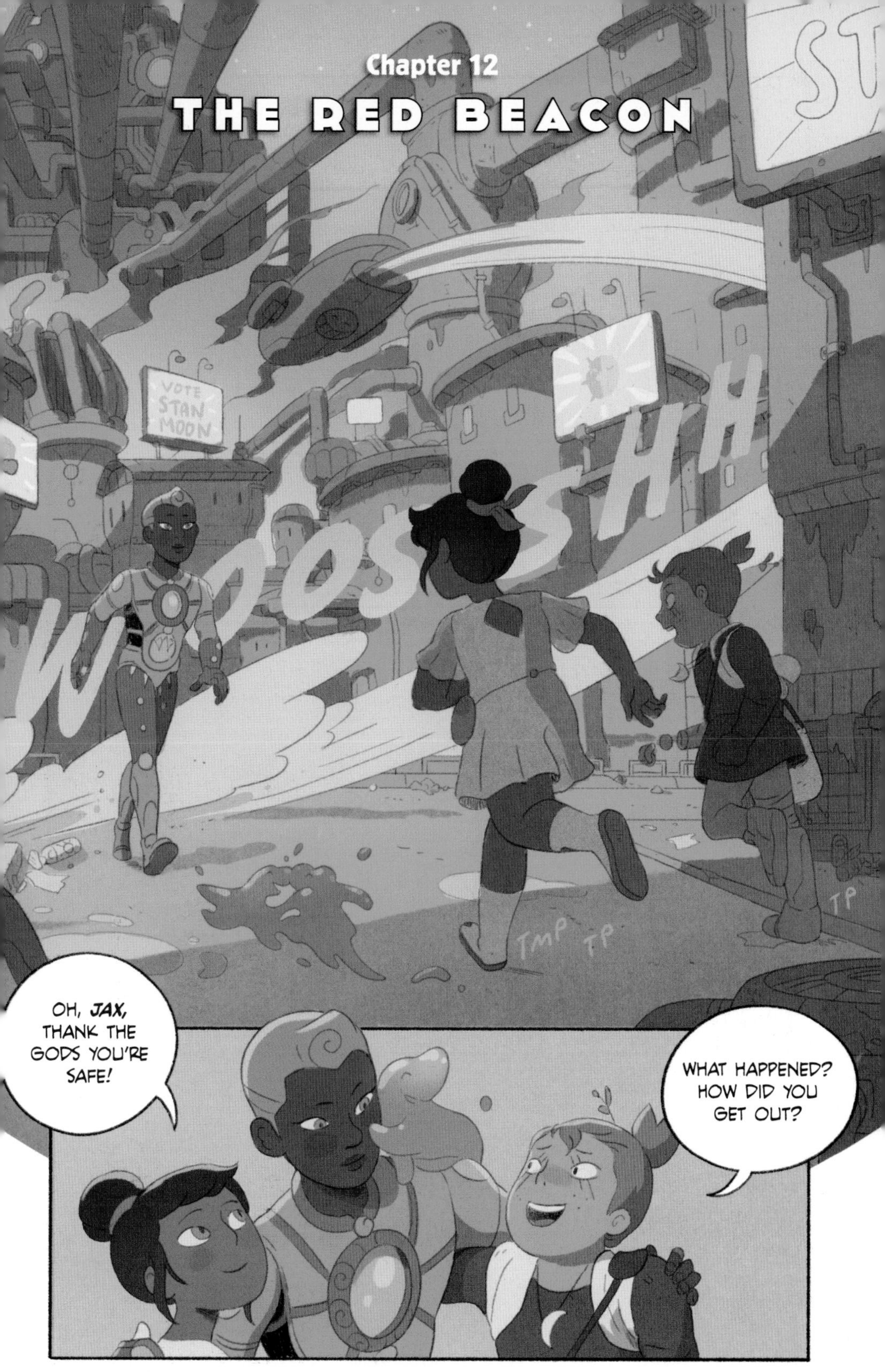
Chapter 12
THE RED BEACON
VOTE STAN MOON
WOOSSHH
TMP TP
TP
OH, JAX, THANK THE GODS YOU'RE SAFE!
WHAT HAPPENED? HOW DID YOU GET OUT?

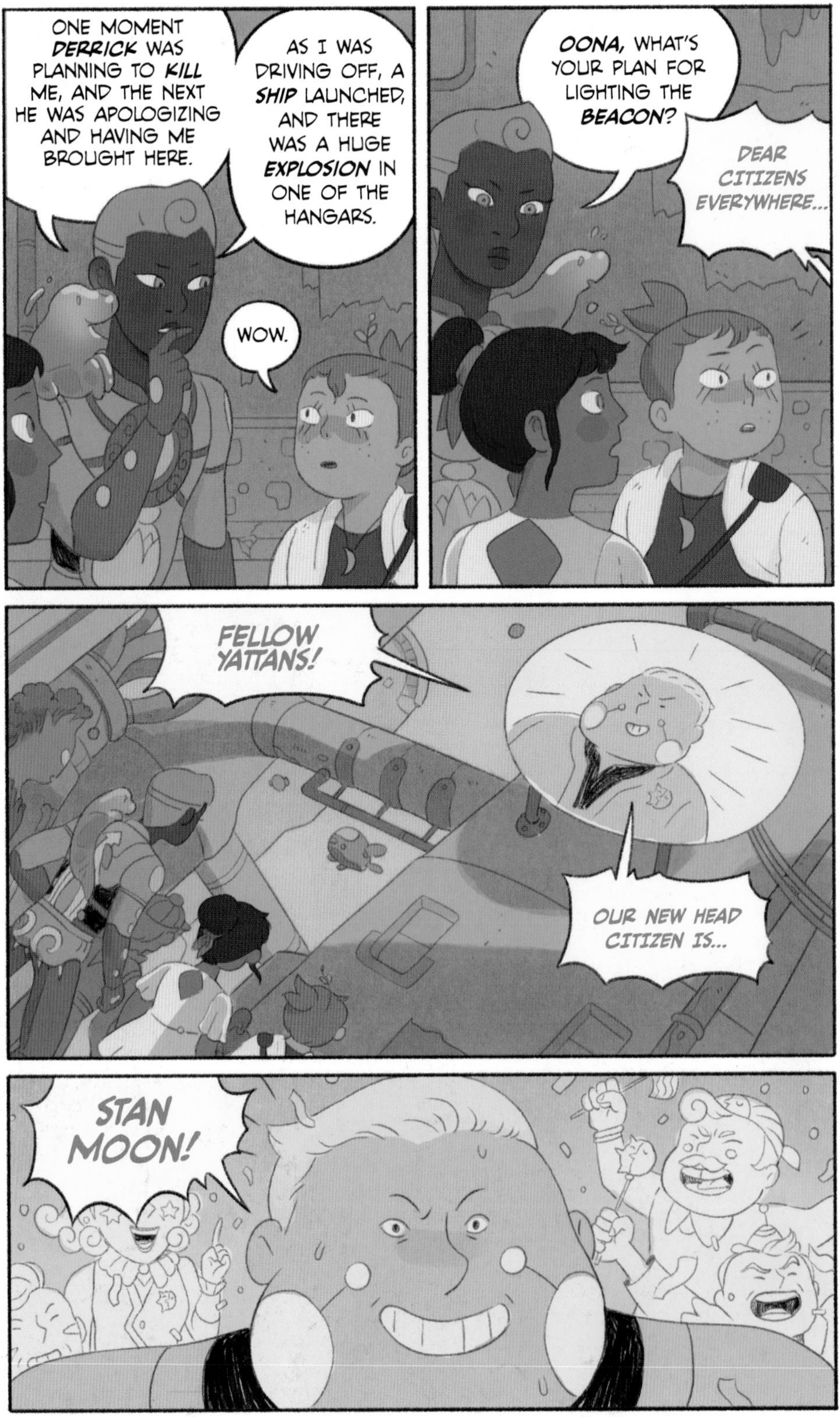

ONE MOMENT DERRICK WAS PLANNING TO KILL ME, AND THE NEXT HE WAS APOLOGIZING AND HAVING ME BROUGHT HERE.
AS I WAS DRIVING OFF, A SHIP LAUNCHED, AND THERE WAS A HUGE EXPLOSION IN ONE OF THE HANGARS.
WOW.
OONA, WHAT'S YOUR PLAN FOR LIGHTING THE BEACON?
DEAR CITIZENS EVERYWHERE...
FELLOW YATTANS!
OUR NEW HEAD CITIZEN IS...
STAN MOON!

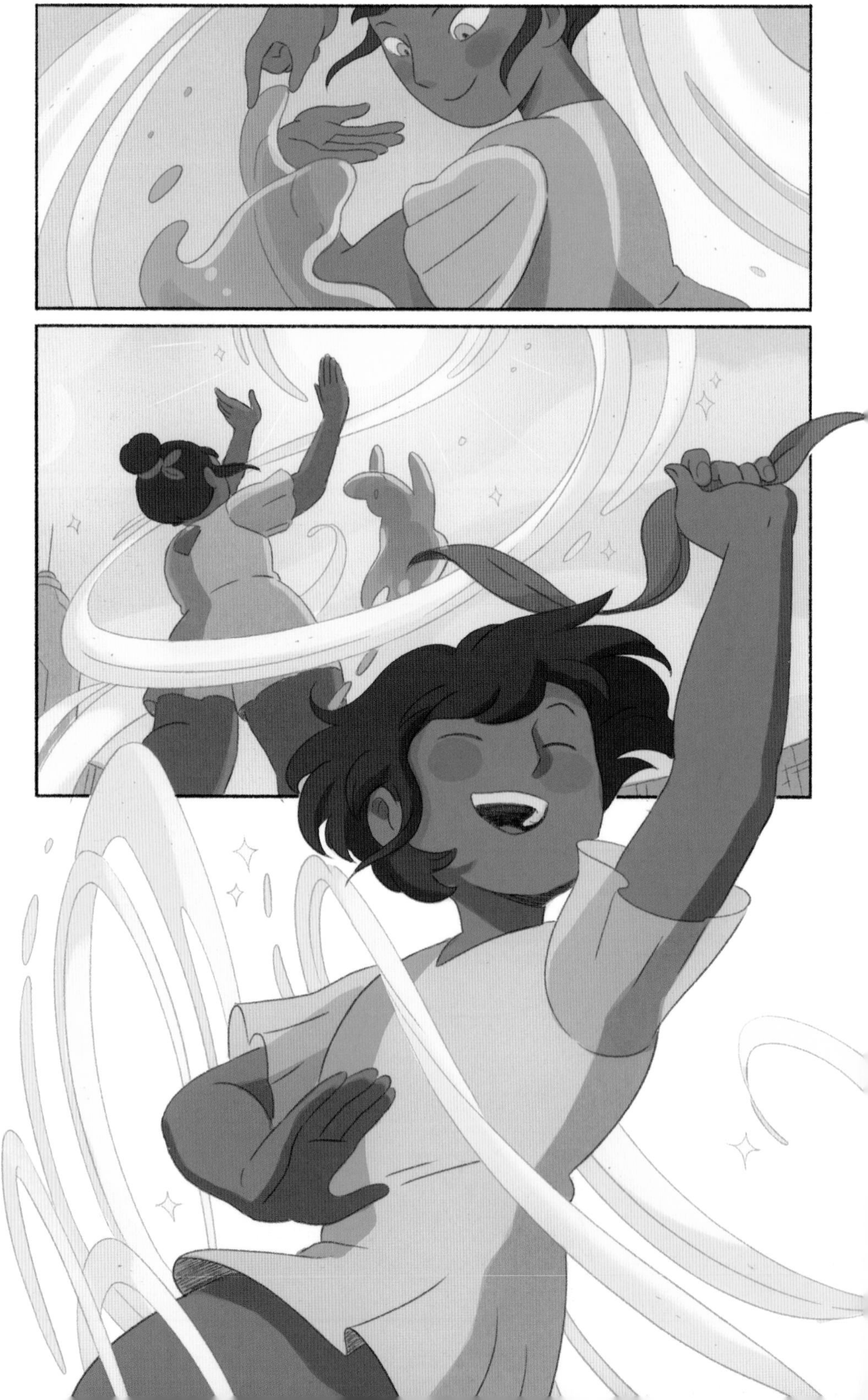

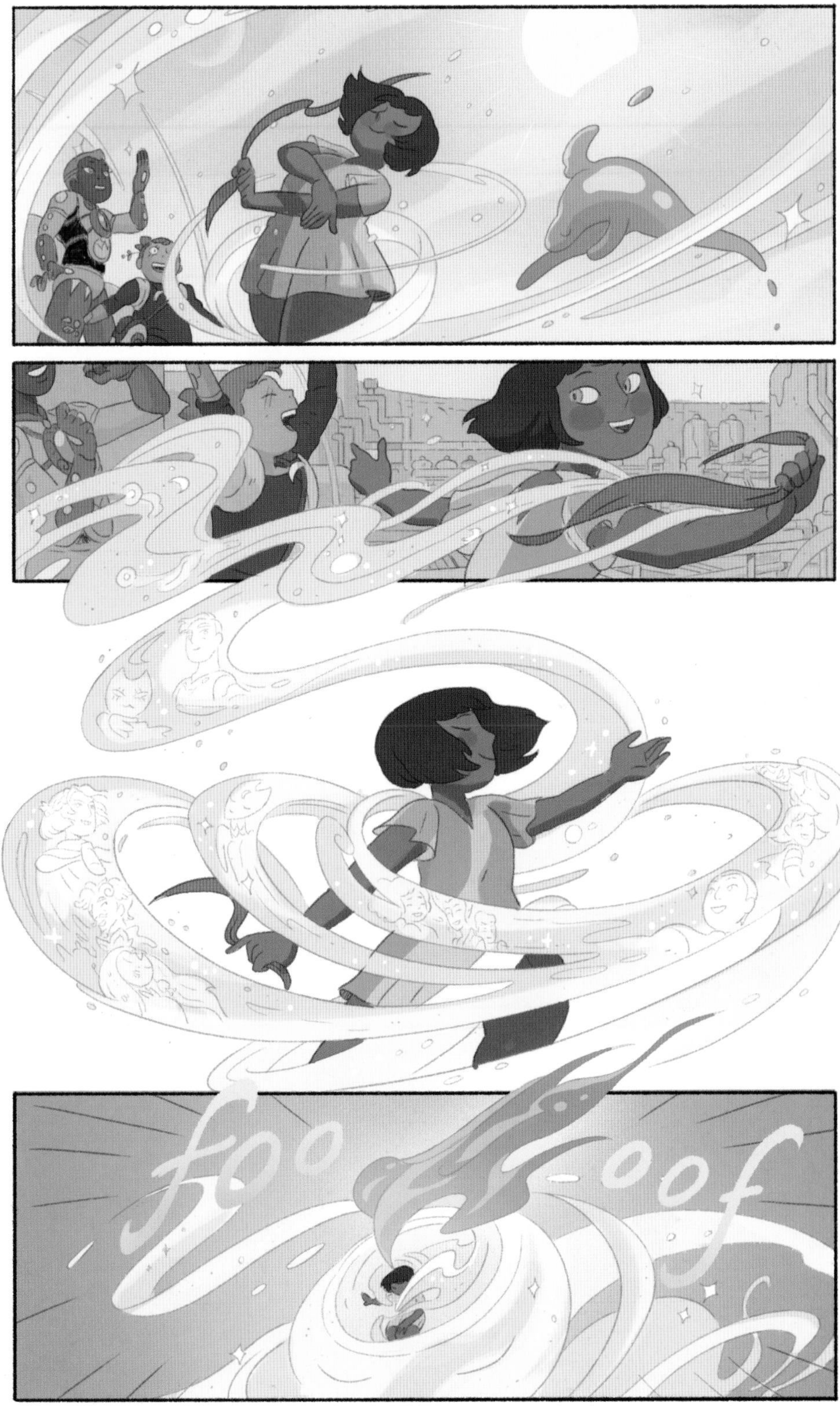
foo oof

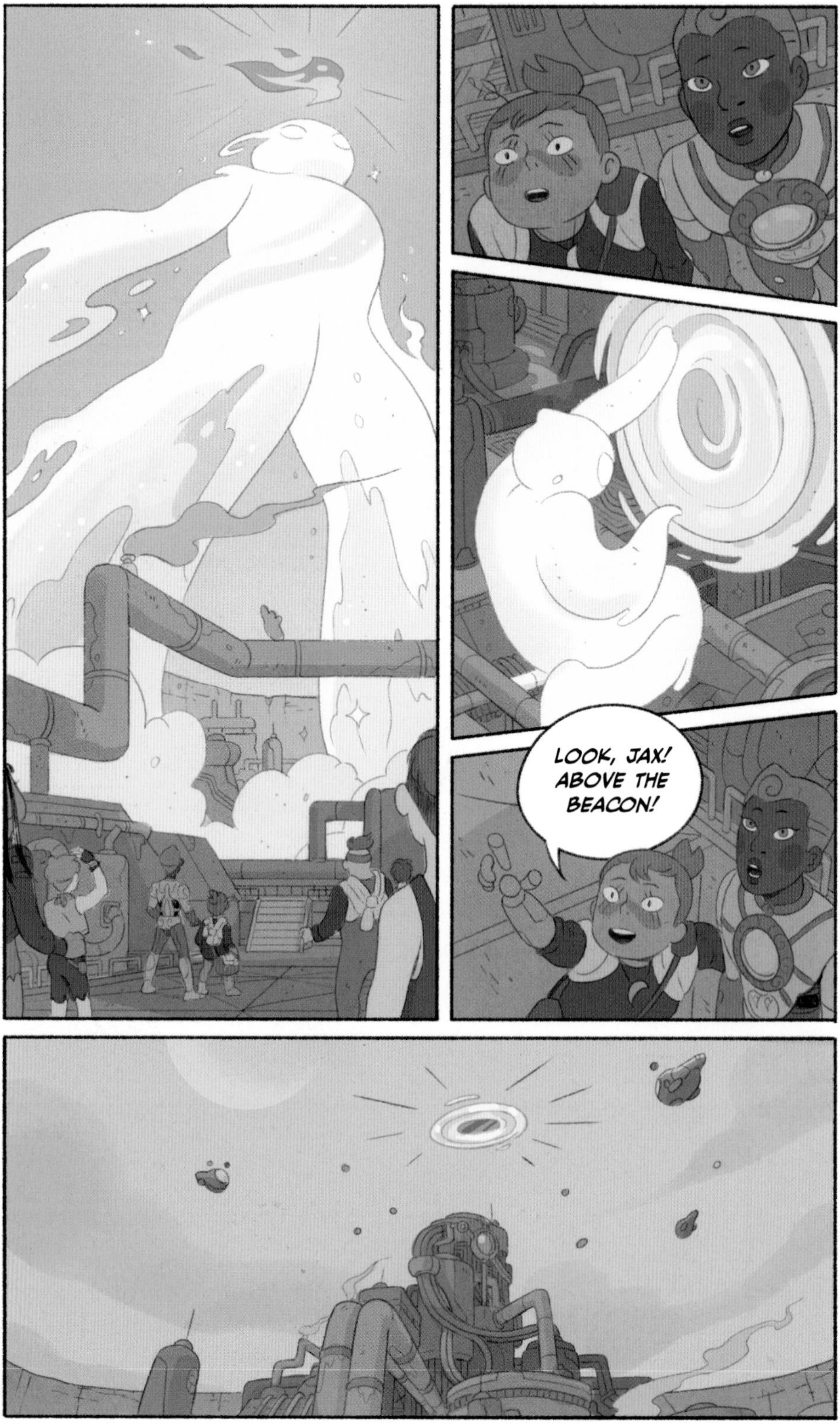
LOOK, JAX! ABOVE THE BEACON!

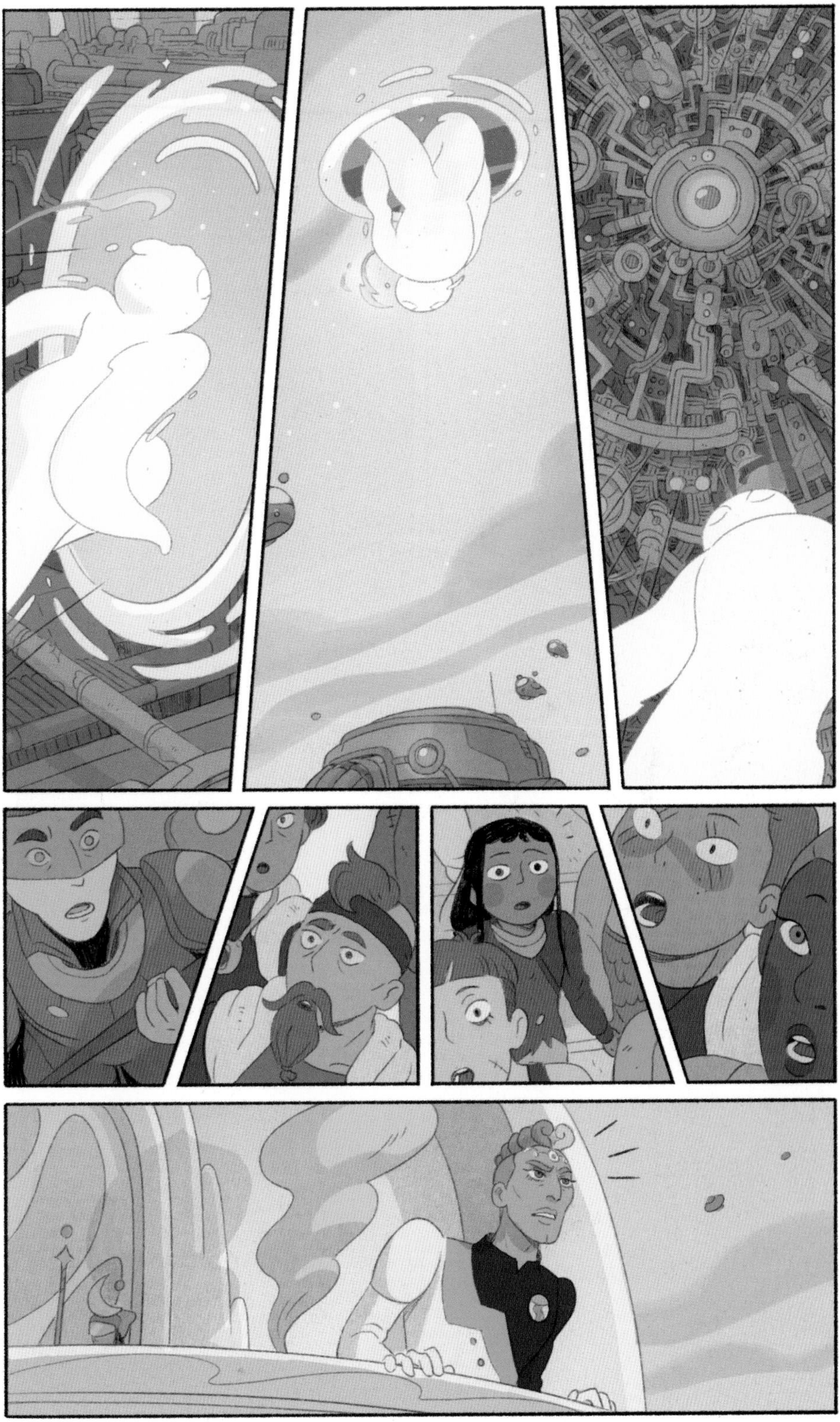

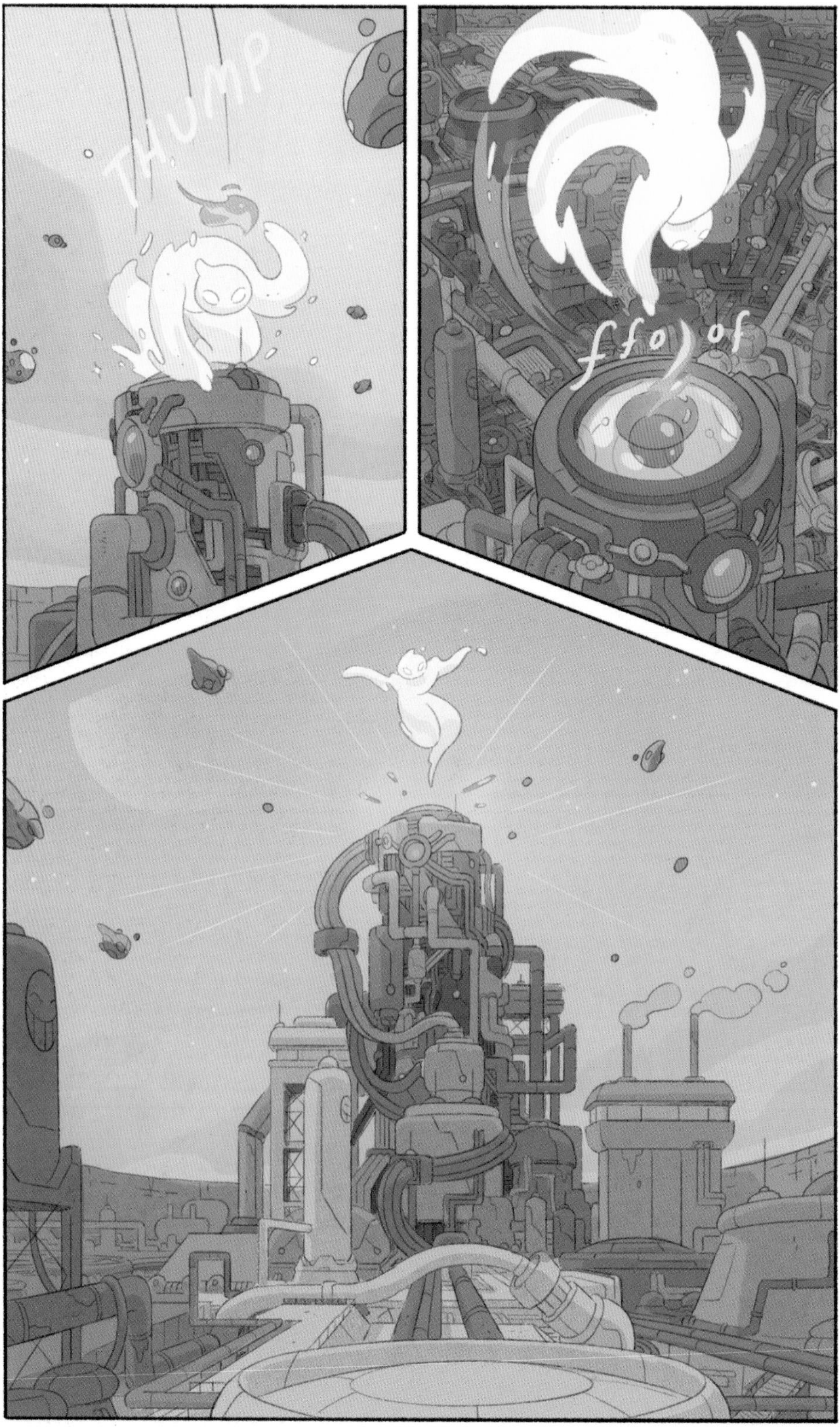
THUMP
ffo of

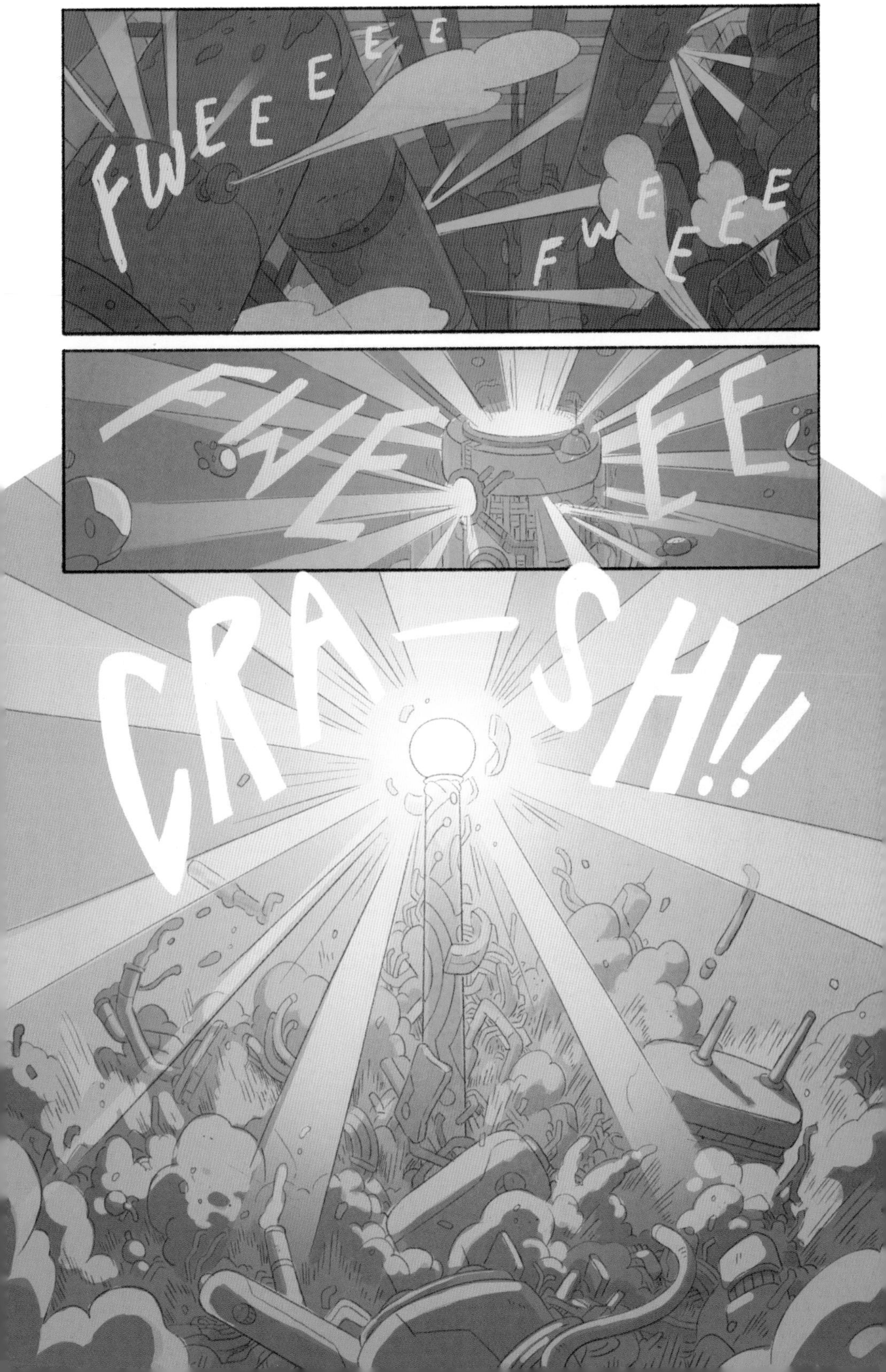
FWEEEEE
FWEEEE
FWEEEE
CRA—SH!!

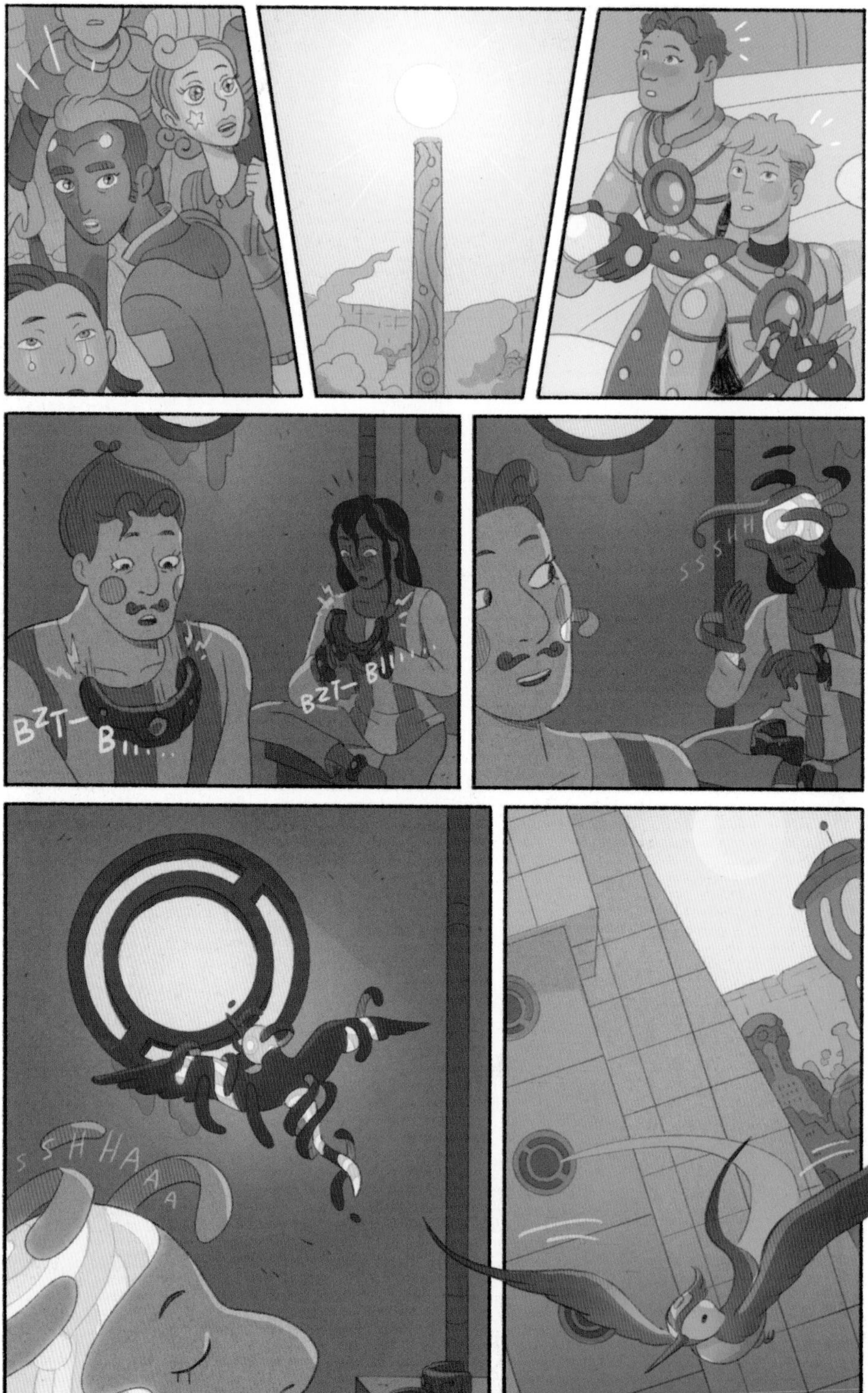
BZT—BIII...
BZT—BIII...
SSSHH
SSHHAAAA

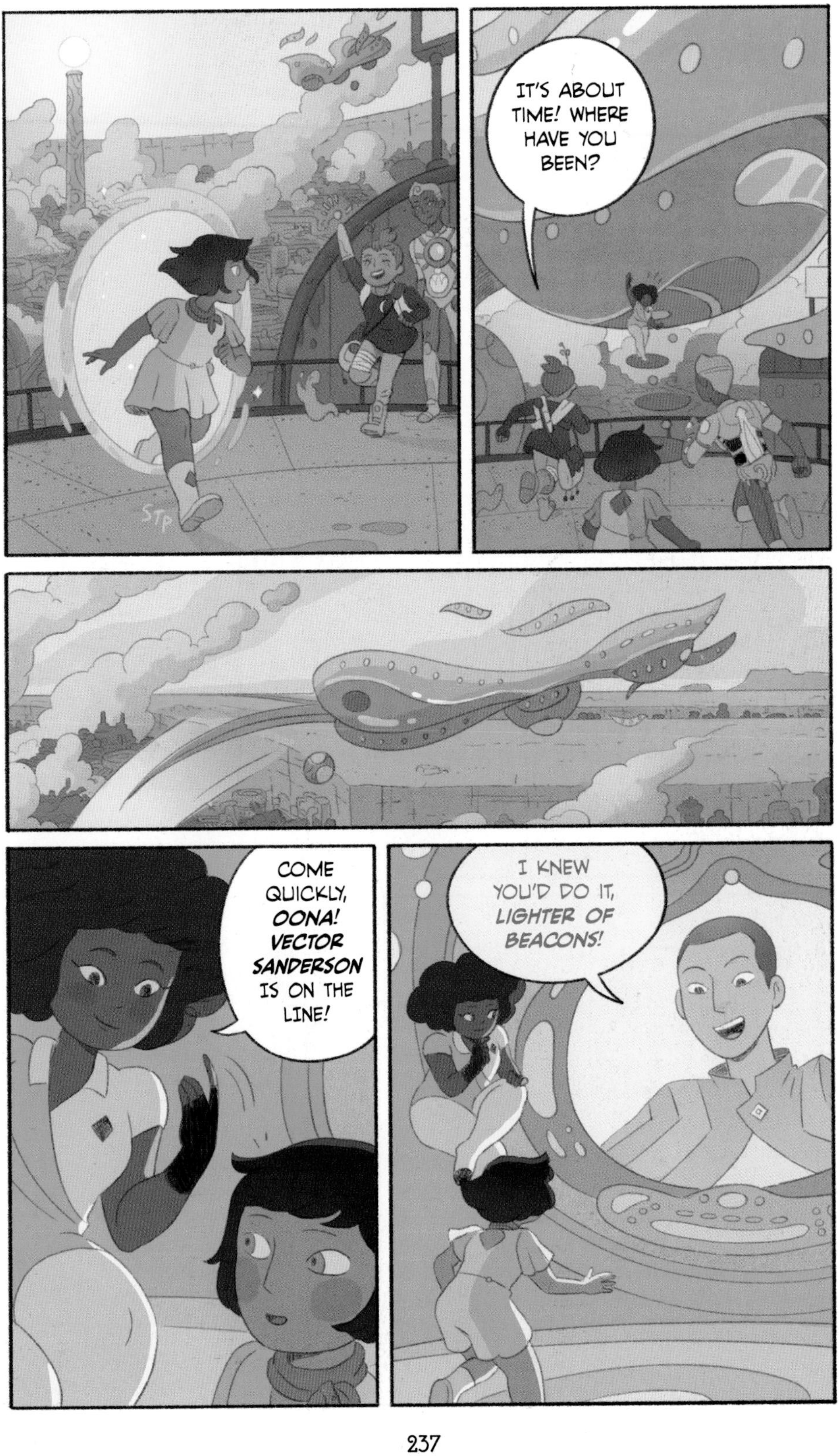
STP
IT'S ABOUT TIME! WHERE HAVE YOU BEEN?
COME QUICKLY, **OONA! VECTOR SANDERSON** IS ON THE LINE!
I KNEW YOU'D DO IT, ***LIGHTER OF BEACONS!***

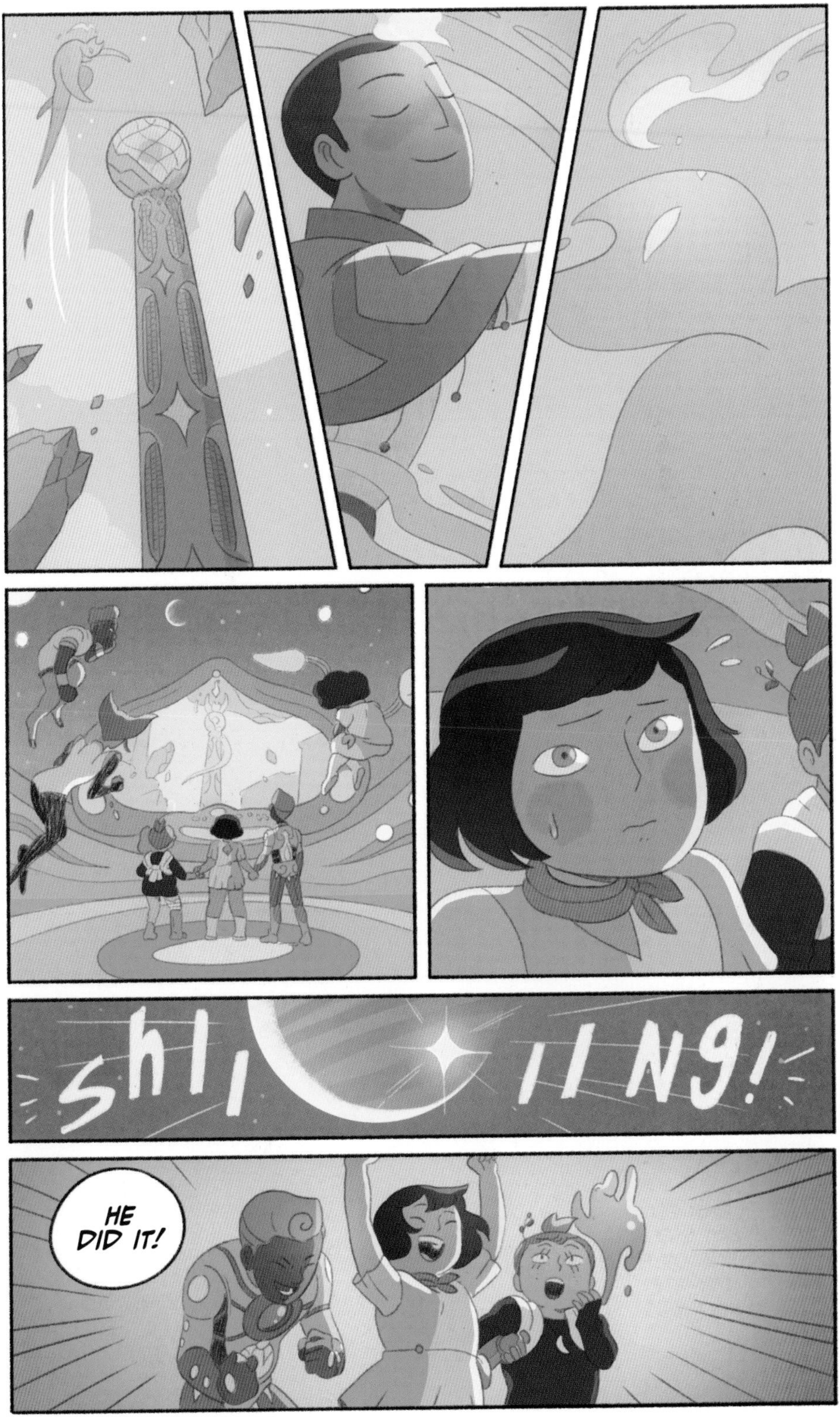
SHIIING!
HE DID IT!

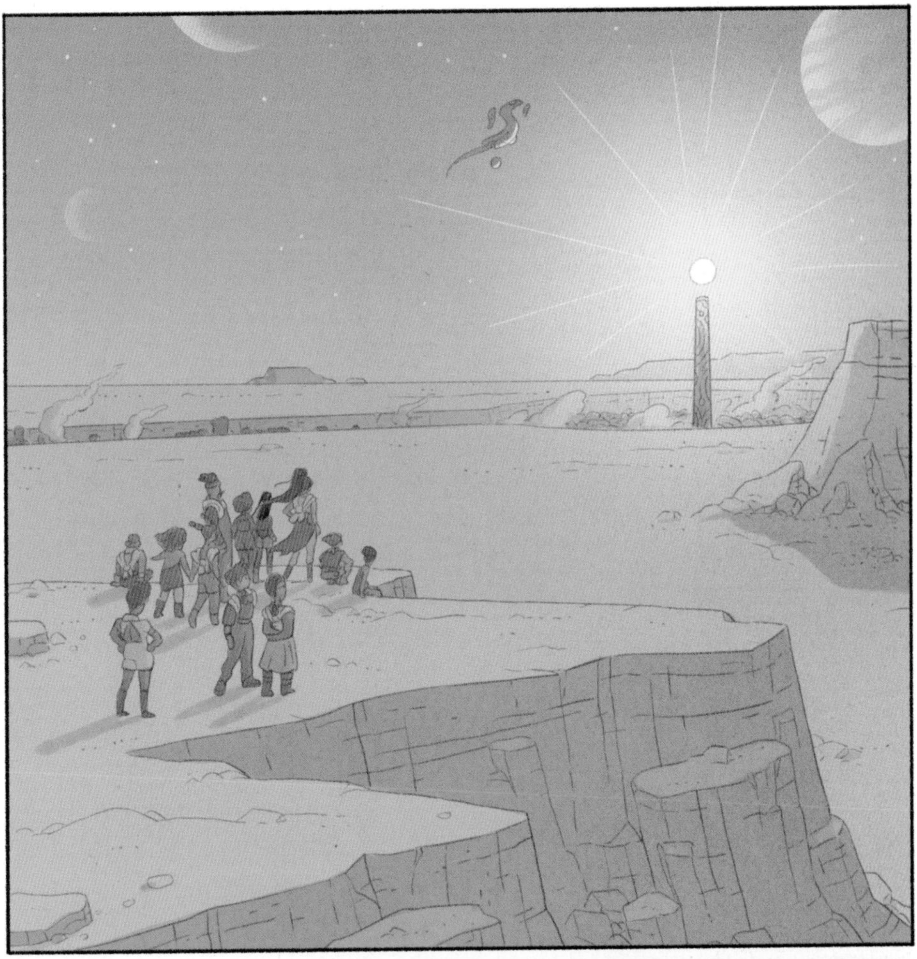

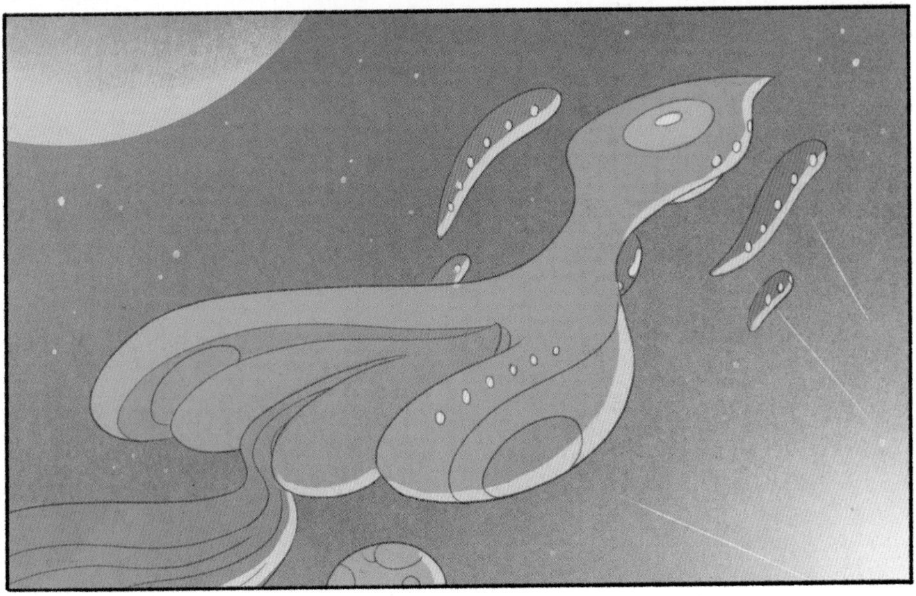

# EPILOGUE

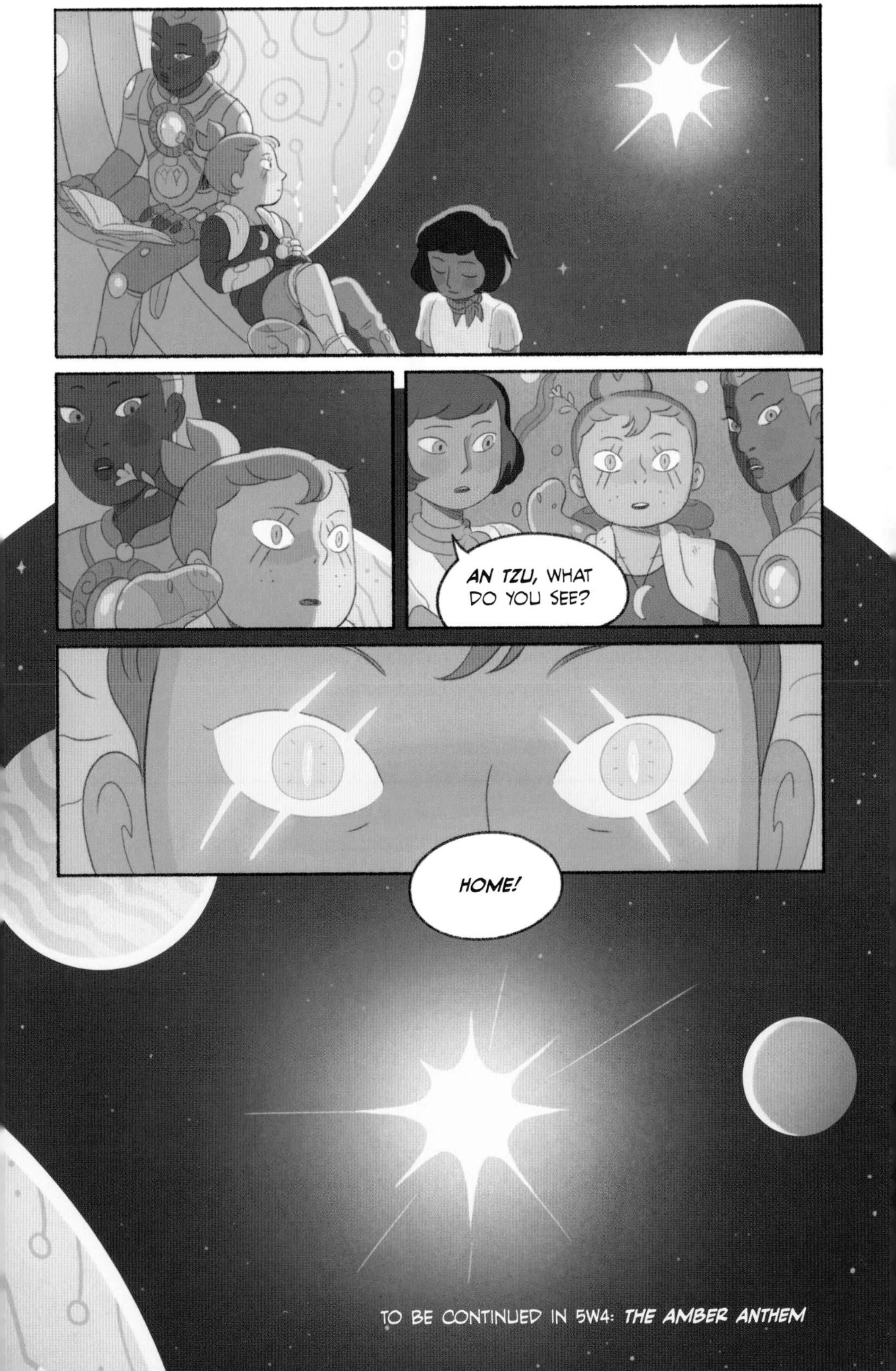
AN TZU, WHAT DO YOU SEE?
HOME!
TO BE CONTINUED IN 5W4: THE AMBER ANTHEM

To all our re-readers —MS

To all helpers, seen and unseen, with trust —AS

To Jo —XB

To anyone who has felt lost —MR

To Dad —BS

ACKNOWLEDGMENTS

Marie-Claire & Edward Siegel

Our amazing Random House team:
Michelle Nagler, Chelsea Eberly, Elizabeth Tardiff,
Kelly McGauley, Janine Perez, Aisha Cloud, Joshua Redlich, Alison Kolani, Lisa Nadel,
Kristin Schulz, Adrienne Waintraub, John Adamo, Jocelyn Lange, Joe English,
Mallory Loehr, Barbara Marcus

+ Special thanks for added help, friendship & magic:
Siena Siegel, Tanya McKinnon, Sonia Siegel, Shudan Yeh,
Felix & Elia Siegel, Julien & Clio Siegel,
Julie Sandfort, Viviana Simon, Hilde McKinnon, Sam Dutter, Cynthia Cheng,
Bryan Konietzko, and the Story Trust of Gene Luen Yang, Vera Brosgol,
Sam Bosma, Shelli Paroline & Braden Lamb

And the mighty inspirations of:
Stephen King, Lois McMaster Bujold, Naoki Urasawa & Rebecca Sugar

**MARK SIEGEL** has written and illustrated several award-winning picture books and graphic novels. He is also the editorial and creative director of First Second Books. He lives with his family in New York. Discover more at marksiegelbooks.com.

**ALEXIS SIEGEL** is a writer and translator based in Switzerland. He has translated a number of bestselling graphic novels, including Joann Sfar's *The Rabbi's Cat* and Pénélope Bagieu's *Exquisite Corpse* (both into English), and Gene Luen Yang's *American Born Chinese* (into French).

**XANTHE BOUMA** is an illustrator based in Southern California. When not working on picture books such as *Little Sid*, fashion illustration, and comics, Xanthe enjoys soaking up the beachside sun.

**MATT ROCKEFELLER** is an illustrator and comic artist living in the Pacific Northwest. He grew up in Tucson, Arizona, and draws inspiration from the desert's dramatic landscapes. His work has appeared in a variety of formats, including animation, book covers, and picture books such as *Train*, *Rocket*, and *Pop!*

**BOYA SUN** is an illustrator and coauthor of the graphic novel *Chasma Knights*. Originally from China, Boya has traveled from Canada to the United States and now lives in California.

## Character Development

Early sketches for Yatta society

⊄ Yatta formal

YATTAN
MANGROVE
PEOPLE

THICKER
BARK
GROWS IN
LESS MOBILE
AREAS

ZELLE 1 2 3 4 5 6

- TIES IN BACK
SAME AS
ZELLE 4+

LARSEF OLEC

Shapeshifter study

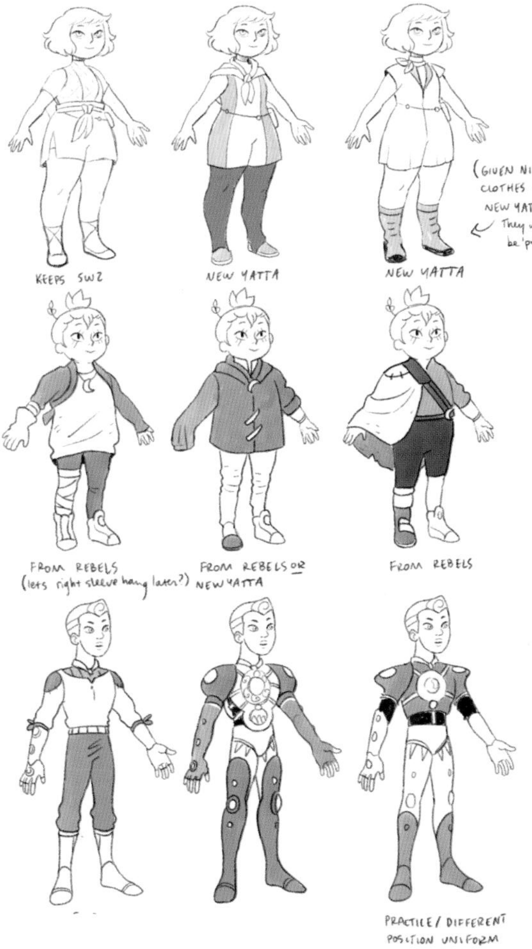

KEEPS SWZ
NEW YATTA
NEW YATTA
(GIVEN NICER CLOTHES ON NEW YATTA?)
They want her to be 'presentable'
FROM REBELS
(lets right sleeve hang later?)
FROM REBELS OR NEW YATTA
FROM REBELS
PRACTICE / DIFFERENT POSITION UNIFORM


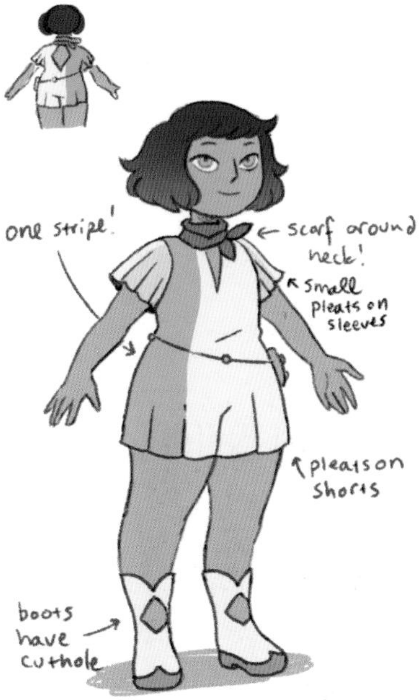

one stripe!
scarf around neck!
small pleats on sleeves
pleats on shorts
boots have cuthole


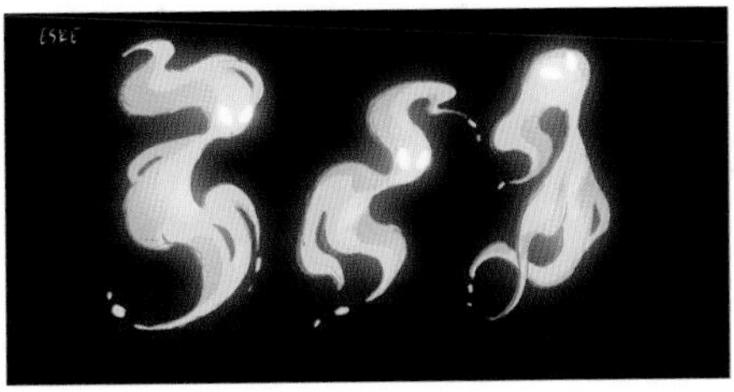

Salassi Devoti

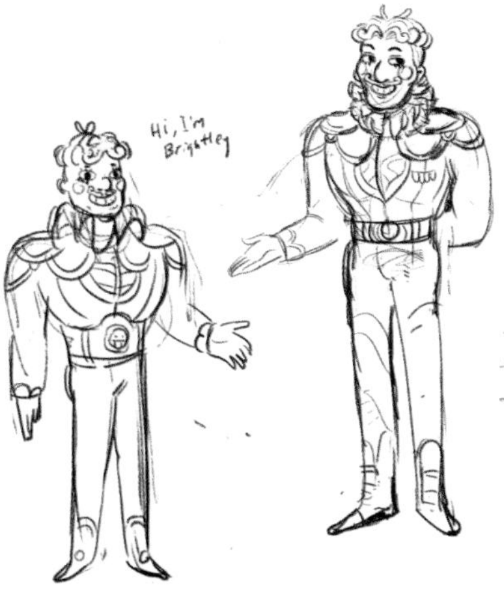

Hi, I'm Brightley


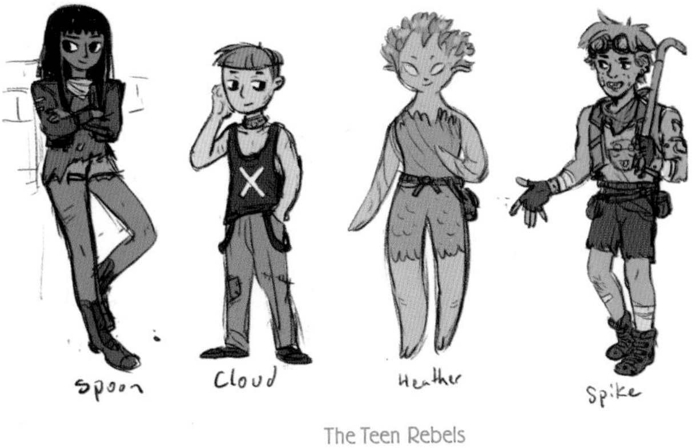

Spoon
Cloud
Heather
Spike


The Teen Rebels

TWYBEN

LETOKO

AMBER LEATHERHEADS

Eldridge

Dearick

# World Building

IN ADDITION TO RUN DOWN BUILDINGS, THE MALL IS PEPPERED BY MAKESHIFT SHELTERS FOR THE HOMELESS

MOON YATTA, NEW YATTA CITY

OUTER CITY "SUBURBS"

89

NEW YATTA CITY

MOON YATTA , FEDORA MESA

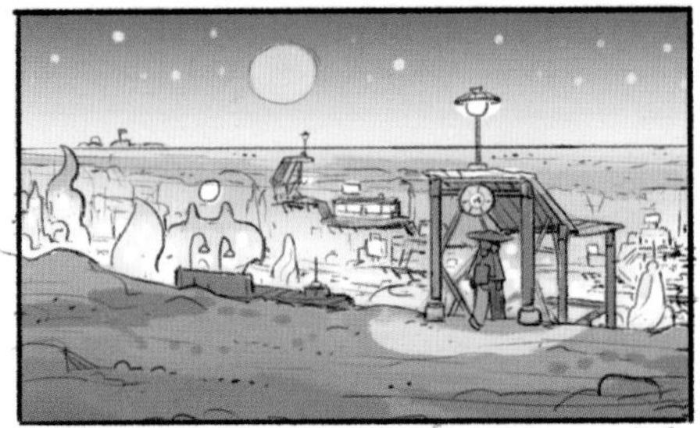

ENTERING A CITY FROM THE MESA – PEOPLE WHO TRAVEL ON FOOT ENTER FROM ABOVE. POORER, LOWER TECH SETTLEMENTS LINE THE UPPER WALLS

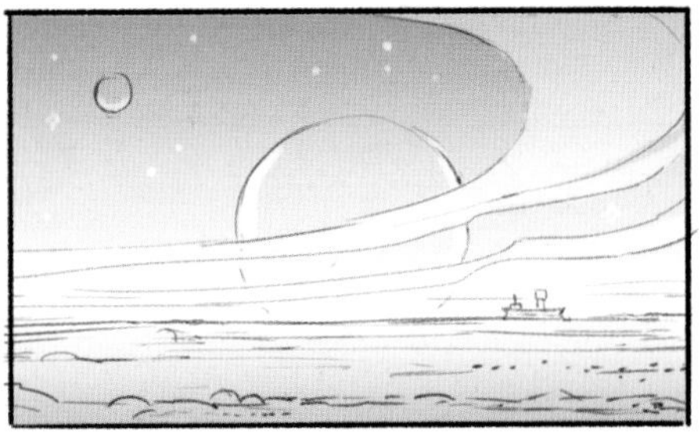

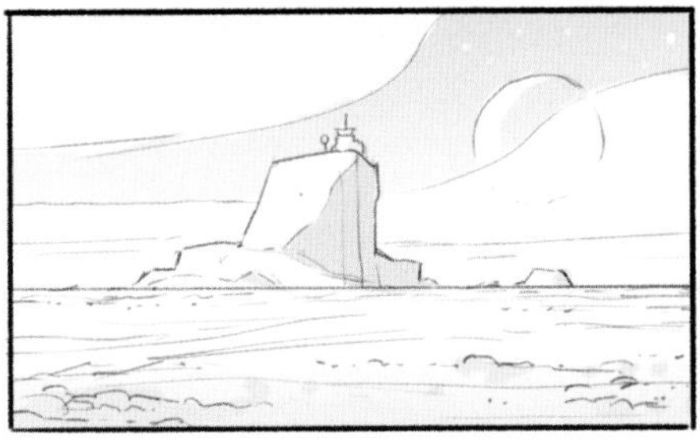

BUILDINGS OF THE MESA

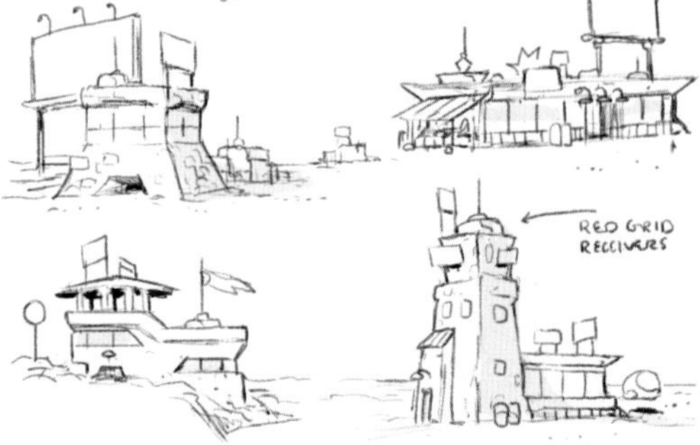
RED GRID RECEIVERS

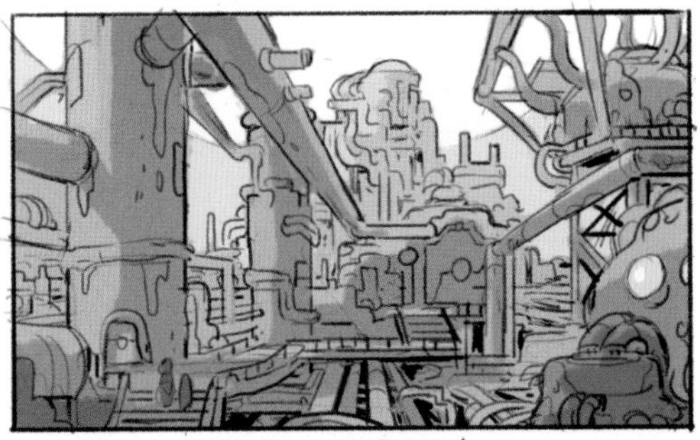

RED MAZE - UPPER LEVELS + BEACON

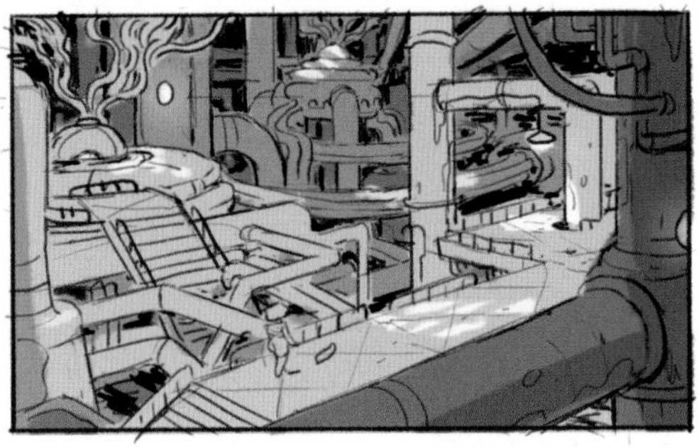

RED MAZE - LOWER LEVELS

SOME LIGHT COMES THROUGH FROM HIGH ABOVE

SAO SANGRE

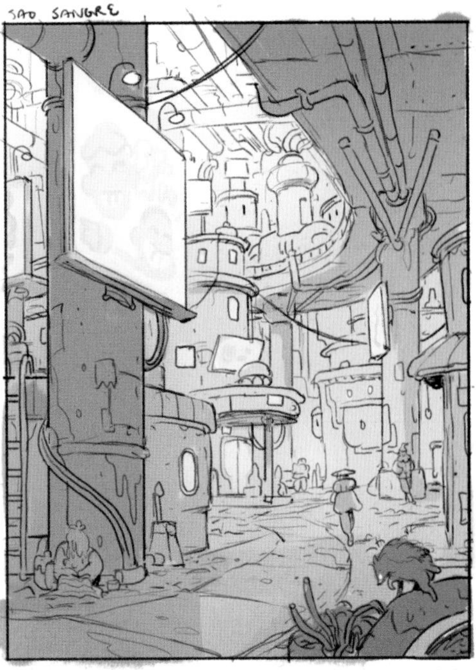

...and many sketchbooks more!

# Discover more  online!

@5WorldsTeam

POST YOUR **COSPLAY** PHOTOS AND SHARE YOUR BEST **FAN ART** WITH OTHER 5-WORLDERS, WITH HASHTAGS #DRAWOONA, #5WORLDS, AND #5WFANART.

## The Winners of the #DrawOona Fan Art Contest Are . . .

Kiara Rivera @Crybaby.kia

Hadley Griffin Johnson

Kristina Luu @stripeyworm

@_yumsty_

Chiara Farah @Cherrychisoup

Zamora Cruz @paperbrarian

Helene Canac @poulpychoups

River, age 6

Fiona D. @bonjour_mes_amies

Rachel G @rachelarts75

STAY TUNED
FOR CONTESTS
AND SPECIAL EVENTS
ON A PLANET NEAR YOU!

Where will the adventure take An Tzu, Jax, and Oona? Find out in

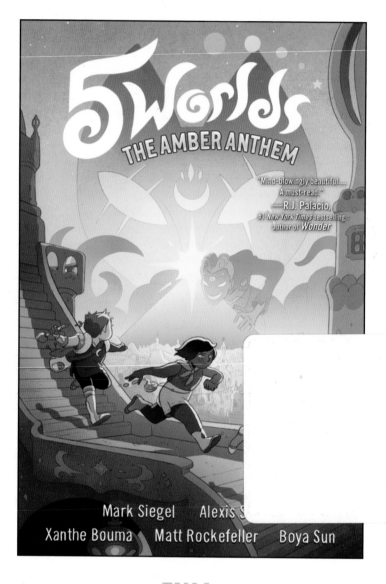

## 5W4:
# THE AMBER ANTHEM